# At the Duke's Wedding

# At the Duke's Wedding

A collection of novellas

Caroline Linden

Katharine Ashe

Miranda Neville

Maya Rodale

This is a work of fiction. Any references to historical events, real people, or real locales are used fictitiously. Other names, characters, places and incidents are the product of the author's imagination, and any resemblance to actual events, locales or persons, living or dead, is entirely coincidental.

ISBN-10:    0-9860539-0-2

ISBN-13: 978-0-9860539-0-0

AT THE DUKE'S WEDDING

*That Rogue Jack* © 2013 Maya Rodale

*P.S. I Love You* © 2013 Miranda Neville

*When I Met My Duchess* © 2013 P. F. Belsley

*How Angela Got Her Rogue Back* © 2013 Katharine Brophy Dubois

Published by The Lady Authors

Printed in the USA

To Gillian and Jon
May you both live happily ever after

# CONTENTS

# THAT ROGUE JACK

Maya Rodale

# CHAPTER ONE

*"I'm off to Dorset for the duke's leg shackling. But first I am to collect the ring from Gold & Son's. Can't believe my cousin the duke trusts me with his wedding ring."*

*—Jack, Lord Willoughby, with laughter, to the crowd at large in White's. Or was it Tattersall's?*

Kingstag Castle

Twelve days before the wedding

The sound of carriage wheels on gravel captured the attention of the ancient Lady Sophronia where she reclined in her apartments on the third floor of the east wing of the Duke of Wessex's vast residence. Miss Henrietta Black, her loyal companion, was with her.

Henrietta was *always* with her.

"That must be another arrival for the duke's wedding," Sophronia said. For his upcoming wedding to the lovely Miss Helen Grey, the Duke of Wessex had invited dozens and dozens of guests to his estate Kingstag, for a celebratory house party. "Go see who it is," Sophronia said. "I am perishing of curiosity."

Lady Sophronia wasn't perishing of anything; she was in remarkably good health. But when she issued a command, Henrietta obliged. No matter how inane or pointless, or how little enthusiasm Henrietta had for the task. When one was a poor orphan utterly dependent upon the goodwill of affluent elder relations, one wished for nothing so much as security.

Security was to be found in being useful, dependable, essential, and never, ever, ever the cause of any trouble.

Thus, ever obliging to Sophronia's curiosity, Henrietta crossed the large sitting room and peered out the windows overlooking the drive. She expected many such journeys across the carpet in the coming days. While the bride had already arrived with her sister, Mrs. Cleopatra Barrows, and their parents, most of the guests were expected to begin arriving today.

Looking out the window, Henrietta spied the high perch phaeton first. It was painted a glossy black, with wheels in a stunning shade of yellow, like a bee in a bonnet or spiked lemonade at a ball. Or so she presumed, having no firsthand knowledge of bees in bonnets or spiked lemonade at a ball.

This phaeton in the first stare of fashion must surely be a London carriage. Surely it was the leading contender for the most impractical conveyance ever created.

It was drawn by a pair of enormous, perfectly matched stallions. Midnight black they were, right from the high tips of their ears down to the hooves pawing impatiently on the gravel drive.

Only one man could be the owner of such a flashy carriage. Henrietta had her suspicions, which were confirmed when he stepped down. Black glossy boots. Fitted breeches. A bottle green jacket that clung to broad shoulders. Tousled hair the color of wheat, streaked with gold. And that infamous smile.

It was none other than Henrietta's least favorite person in Christendom.

Jack, Lord Willoughby.

Wessex had invited his cousin to be his best man. They were an unlikely pair, for the duke was steadfast, responsible, and admirable. And Jack was ...

Jack was the most utterly reckless and reliably unreliable person ever to wake in the morning and sleep at night. If breathing were a task under his command, Jack would probably forget to draw breath. Should he be responsible for the beating of his heart, the thing would skid to a stop. Distractions were aplenty with Jack—there wasn't a woman, wager, or some manner of trouble that didn't catch his fancy.

Every twenty seconds.

Henrietta supposed he could not help his devilish nature. From a young age, he'd caused trouble and wreaked havoc that she could ill afford to indulge in and was obliged to frown upon. Poor, orphaned girl children had to earn their keep with excellent behavior.

What made Jack truly despicable was his smile. Perfectly white and straight teeth. A dimple in his left cheek. So rakish. And then his eyes! When he smiled, they sparkled like sapphires in sunlight. It had been said upon more than one occasion that his smile could free a man from the hangman's noose or seduce a woman in a second.

When an apothecary let it be known that his special formulation of smelling salts was inspired by Willoughby's infamous smile—and the swooning ladies left in his wake—sales of Smythson's Smelling Salts exploded. No lady's reticule was complete without a small bottle.

Jack just smiled. Henrietta scowled just thinking about it.

"Well, girl, quit your fawning!" Lady Sophronia barked. "I can hear your tragically heartfelt sighs from the far side of the room. Before I expire, you might tell me who has arrived, though I daresay I know who is it."

Henrietta turned away from the window to face Lady Sophronia.

"It is Lord Willoughby."

"I like that one," Sophronia said in manner that gave one to understand that she *really* liked him.

"All the ladies do," Henrietta said. Every single one of them. *Except me.*

"He's a tremendous flirt." Sophronia stated the obvious. "If he's ever used his brain for anything other than that, I don't know of it."

"Agreed, my lady," Henrietta said. She fought the urge to take another look out the window at ... that phaeton.

"Well, except for you," Sophronia said pointedly. "He never flirts with you."

*Because I'm the devoted caretaker to a recluse.*

"I appreciate the notice you have bestowed upon me," Henrietta replied demurely.

"I think he can tell you dislike him. You ought to be nicer."

"But I *don't* like him," Henrietta pointed out. As a child, he stayed often at Kingstag and regularly led everyone into troubling escapades, except for her, and he teased her mercilessly for it. "Nevertheless, I am perfectly civil to him. Furthermore, I see no purpose in earning

3

his favor. He is a reckless scoundrel who causes nothing but trouble with his every step."

"I don't think it's his steps that cause trouble," the old lady cackled.

"Sophronia!"

Henrietta fought the urge to take another peek out the window. Was his smile so very captivating from three stories up?

"I think he needs a wife like you. Proper, organized, bossy. You'll keep him on the straight and narrow."

"*Wife? Straight and narrow?*" Henrietta was incredulous. It was either that or be devastated that she'd been described as proper, organized, and bossy. "Are you not acquainted with him?"

"Not *nearly* as much as I would like to be." Her wicked grin elicited another protest from the "proper" Henrietta.

"Lady Sophronia!"

"I'm not dead yet! Neither are you, for that matter."

"I do not know the appropriate response to that," Henrietta mumbled.

"How about an inappropriate one?"

"Definitely not."

Poor, orphaned relations could not afford to be inappropriate. Sophronia might claim not to mind, but surely the duke would, especially if his new duchess took issue with the outspoken old woman and her troublesome companion. No, if they were to keep their place, reliant on the duke and duchess's charity, they would have to be no trouble at all. Whatsoever.

"Oh my dear Henrietta," Sophronia sighed. "I do fear your youth is wasted on you."

"My youth has long since passed."

"Nonsense. You are just four-and-twenty years of age. As a person of five-and-forty years of age, I may say my youth has passed."

"Five-and-forty?" Henrietta echoed. And then, because she couldn't restrain herself *all* the time, she asked, "Do you not mean five-and-seventy?"

"Ha! Whatever gave you that idea?"

"The birthday candles on your cake gave sufficient light to read by."

"I knew you had some spark in you."

4

Henrietta murmured something about fire hazards and ensuring safety first.

"Are you going to avoid him the whole week, then?" Sophronia asked.

"Who?"

"Don't be obtuse."

"Alas, I cannot." Henrietta heaved a sigh. She had *quite* the task before her—but one she hoped would be concluded before nightfall. "At the duke's request, Lord Willoughby brought the wedding ring for Miss Grey down from London after having it reset. The duchess has asked that I fetch it from him *immediately,* for she will be too busy greeting guests. That is, *if* he has even managed to procure it and bring it safely! We all know he is completely irresponsible. After that, I hope to have nothing to do with him."

"Well, you'd better chase after him," Lady Sophronia said. Then with a dismissive wave of her hands she added, "Be off with you. Go get a betrothal ring from that rogue."

Henrietta's plans were immediately thwarted. She took a moment to fix her hair, which she kept secured in a bun atop her head and *not* in the two braids Jack had always delighted in tugging as a child. Then she pinched her cheeks to bring out some color and made her way downstairs.

But Lord Willoughby had already taken his shiny new phaeton around to the stables. Then she was pressed into performing other duties as more and more guests arrived and had to be entertained. At mealtime, she found herself seated far from Willoughby and far too occupied with ensuring that Lady Sophronia didn't insult the other guests too badly with her bluntness.

Hours passed—increasingly anxious, vexing, and maddening hours—before she had a chance to speak with him.

# CHAPTER TWO

*Jack pocketed the ring and whistled a merry tune as he strolled out of Gold & Son's jewelry shop on Bond Street. He glanced around to see if there were any beautiful women requiring his flirtations. But no, just bustling pedestrians and one shiftless wretch wearing a vile purple waistcoat skulking in the doorway of the shop next door. His carriage awaited. As did the duke's wedding.*

The stables

The following day

Eleven days before the wedding

Hippolyta was a beauty. On that, all men agreed. Her curves were so perfectly defined they just begged for a man's possessive caress. She was smooth to the touch—God, so smooth. She was immensely pleasing to the eye—he couldn't wrench his gaze away. Riding her was a pleasure like nothing else. And if he were so inclined, Jack knew Hippolyta wouldn't refuse another man or another woman in addition to him. She was obliging like that. His latest partner in trouble was dangerously tempting and the envy of everyone who laid eyes on her.

Hippolyta was his new phaeton.

The new carriage also provided an excellent excuse to avoid the horrors of the house, which began and ended with a plethora of women hysterical over things he could not care less about. Wedding things. Dresses and ribbons and bonnets, and something or other—Jack was very, very easily distracted when it came to such matters.

A pack of the younger girls mainly comprising Wessex's sisters had formed a terrifying mob—a ghastly, ghostly bunch of white dresses, giggles, and the occasional shriek. The White Muslin Crew, the gents had taken to calling them. They skulked through corridors and lurked around corners. They took to the gardens and drawing rooms. Jack knew for a fact he was not the only man who broke out in a cold sweat when they approached.

On the other end of the spectrum, there was that sharp-tongued old harpy, Lady Sophronia, and her upright companion, Henrietta Black. She was neither old nor sharp tongued, but the two women were never apart.

He'd known her for an age. Even as a child, Henrietta had been far too proper for her own good. He recalled her two braids and how badly he always wanted to pull them. Of course, he gave in to the temptation *constantly*. One day she'd had enough and walloped him with a china breakfast plate, which had shattered after connecting with his thick skull. Damn, had they both gotten in trouble!

Jack's thoughts strayed, as they were wont to do, toward the seduction of a prim miss such as Miss Henrietta Black. Underneath her proper exterior there was surely a passionate minx. He considered the seduction in exquisite detail.

For about twenty seconds.

Then Mr. Blair, a very distant cousin and secretary to the duke, inquired about Hippolyta's speed. Jack obliged him with the information but was interrupted when a footman refilled his glass—and everyone else's—with more ale, which led to a rousing toast.

"To Hippolyta!"

"Hear, hear!" the gents called out.

Even Trent "Crash" Ascot, Viscount Everett, raised his glass slightly in tribute to his beauty of a carriage. After what he'd suffered, a slight acknowledgment to Hippolyta was high praise indeed.

"To Watson!" The footman who had been installed to attend to the gentlemen blushed from the attentions.

The first night they'd sipped whiskey from a flask in the darkened stables. But already, more items had arrived to increase their comfort, such as cards, spirits, and cigars. At this rate, Jack expected they'd all be bunking here by the wedding.

7

"To Wessex! And his bride!" Jack called out.

"Hurrah! Hurrah!" everyone shouted. Everyone except Mr. Blair. And *the groom.* Jack frowned, finding that odd.

"Thank you gentlemen," Wessex said. "Now do shut up. We don't want the ladies to hear."

Quietly the gentlemen raised their glasses in a silent tribute. They definitely did not want the ladies to hear and get wind of this haven they'd created.

Then the gentlemen drank. Admired Hippolyta. Made wagers. Played cards. And drank some more.

Later with the dinner hour approaching, they returned to the house one by one while the ladies were sure to be tightening their corsets, curling and cajoling their hair into intricate arrangements, fussing with stays, shimmying into silk gowns, agonizing over the pearls or the rubies, and generally overthinking everything regarding their appearance.

Except for Miss Black, who must have been watching for his arrival from the house.

"Lord Willoughby."

He stifled a shout. She had surprised him, waiting in the servants' entrance and only making herself known as the door shut behind him. Escape was impossible. He would have to brazen it out.

Because she stood on the steps, Jack had to tilt his head back and peer up at her.

Her complexion was pale—probably because she spent too long indoors with old Sophronia. Her dark hair was in a spinsterish bun atop her head, with not even a tendril for him to tug for old times' sake. Her eyes were dark and intriguing, and he detected sparks of anger in contrast to the set of her lips, which might have been lovely but were currently pressed in a firm line.

He thought about teasing her lips apart with his tongue and kissing her until the corners of her mouth turned up into a smile.

Then he thought, *best not.*

"Good evening, Hen." He gave her the Grin. The one that inspired the formulation of Smythson's Smelling Salts. The one all the ladies loved.

"Miss Black," she corrected.

"Good evening, Miss Black," he said, sweeping into a deep bow.

The lady remained unmoved.

Given the solitude of the servants' stairs and the dim lighting, many women would have thrust their bosom up against him, twined his hair through their fingers, and murmured all sorts of invitations. He was a bit taken aback and more than a bit intrigued when she did no such thing. Speaking of bosoms ...

"I have no wish to bother you, Lord Willoughby. The duchess has charged me with obtaining the wedding ring from you, which I've been trying to do ever since you arrived yesterday."

"Is that so?" Jack supposed he had caught her looking at him as if she wanted to speak to him desperately. But then someone had asked him a question or the footman poured more wine, and he had found his attentions engaged elsewhere.

"If you just hand it over, I shall cease plaguing you about it."

"The ring ..." he echoed.

His damned brainbox hadn't registered a word she'd said because he had noticed that her breasts were exactly at his eye level. Her very fine, full, and pert breasts. Most of his memories of her were from their days as children. There was nothing childish about her now.

"Lord Willoughby!"

"Yes," he said, snapping to attention. He took a step up so he might avoid gazing upon her breasts. For his own good. But then his eyes settled upon her lips, which had parted at his forward step. Nothing childish about her mouth, either.

And it was dark. They were alone. And he was the sort of man who enjoyed a damn good kiss. Especially when the woman was a challenge and her mouth was plump, pink perfection.

She exhaled, impatiently. Women did that around him. Often.

"The precious diamond and sapphire ring that is a priceless Wessex family heirloom that you were asked to collect from Gold & Son's Jewelers in London and safely deliver to the duke?"

"Oh, *that* ring."

He had gotten it. It was ... somewhere. Couldn't think of where exactly at this moment.

Jack took another step up and this one brought him close enough to loom over her. She peered up at him with an expression of peevishness shaded by terror. He noticed the determined rise and fall of her bosom—he tended to have an eye for these things—and noted that she was taking the sort of deliberate calming, deep breaths one took when trying very hard not to panic.

She thought he had forgotten the ring. Well, he hadn't. It was ... God, he was struck with the damnedest desire to slide his hand around her waist and tug her against him. Then he'd taste that mouth of hers in a very improper kiss.

"Lord Willoughby! We must deliver the ring to the duke or else ... we just must!"

She pushed him back with her little palms on his chest. Henrietta did have the right of it. He should find that ring and he should *not* attempt to ravish her in the servants' stairwell. It'd be deuced uncomfortable, for one thing.

"Don't worry, Hen. I have the ring," he said. And then he made a promise as he brushed past her on the stairs: "You shall have it before dinner."

# CHAPTER THREE

*"You're not going to drive that damned carriage all the way to Dorset, are you?" a friend asked skeptically. "A high-flying, delicate vehicle like that won't be able to manage the roads."*

*"Don't say such things about Hippolyta," Jack said, adopting a wounded expression.*

*"You'll be a magnet for trouble in that thing."*

*Jack just grinned. "But Hippolyta goes so fast no one could possibly catch us."*

Two days later

Nine days before the wedding

The decision to knock on Lord Willoughby's bedchamber door had not been an easy one to make. Henrietta had tossed and turned for the better part of the night debating what to do. The other part was spent fretting over whether to seek the opinion of Sophronia. The woman might not be useful, but she would definitely have an opinion as to Henrietta's course of action.

On the one hand, it was beyond the pale for a woman to even be seen on the bachelors' floor, let alone knocking on a gentleman's bedchamber door! That it was Jack wouldn't help matters at all. Then again, no one would believe Henrietta was a player in some debauched exploit. No one.

Above all: the ring. Dear Lord, the ring. Sophronia had informed Henrietta that it had been a gift from the very first Duke of Wessex to his bride. It became a family tradition and one that had been upheld for countless generations. Until now. Possibly.

The Duchess of Wessex—the duke's mother—had been pestering Henrietta for days now. Fearing she'd been too busy greeting guests to track down an infamously distractible gentleman, she'd enlisted Henrietta's help.

*Three days earlier:*

"The longer it is in the hands of Lord Willoughby—who still hasn't returned from the stables, though he arrived hours ago—the more I worry! I never should have consented to having him transport it. But the duke insisted."

"I quite agree, Your Grace. I will do everything I can."

*Two days ago:*

"Really, Henrietta, I must have that ring! As if I didn't have enough to worry about, what with all the plans for the wedding and whatever the gentlemen are doing in the stables."

"Of course, Your Grace."

*Yesterday:*

"Henrietta, where is that ring? Lady Grey is anxiously inquiring about it."

Lady Grey was the bride's mother; she was tremendously impressed by and extremely interested in everything her daughter was about to become mistress of.

"I'll fetch it now, Your Grace!"

She'd been hiding ever since.

Henrietta knocked on the door to Jack's bedchamber. Bright and early.

*Knock, knock, knock.*

No answer.

Every moment she stood waiting outside his bedchamber door increased the odds that she would be caught, which increased the odds that she would find herself in trouble, which increased the odds that she would be deemed an unsuitable companion and relation and would be asked to leave Kingstag. Her life would be over.

*Knock, knock, knock.*

She pressed her ear against the door, hoping to hear the sounds of someone stirring but hearing only silence.

Could one *hear* silence? Henrietta mused. She ought to pose the question to Sophronia. It'd keep the old woman perplexed for days. But really, she had more pressing concerns at the moment.

*Knock, knock, knock.*

What if he were in another woman's bedchamber?

It was eminently possible. Dozens and dozens of guests had arrived, many of them women seeking entertainment. With that grin of his and those sparkling blue eyes ... oh, and his wide shoulders and broad chest ... *yes*, she had noticed, *not* that she would ever let on. Besides, Jack had been flirting shamelessly with other women. It was quite likely he was in a woman's bed at this very moment.

However, Henrietta absolutely could not go knocking on women's bedchamber doors, politely inquiring if one of England's most roguish rogues was with them.

It was bad enough that she was here, risking her reputation and thus her very livelihood.

*Knock, knock, knock. Knock, knock, knock.*

Finally Jack opened the door.

He wore a pair of breeches. Just one pair of fawn-colored breeches.

That was all.

She didn't know where to look! Certainly not at his breeches, which lovingly clad the strong muscles of his thighs, hinting at ... oh, goodness! Henrietta's gaze raked over his absurdly strong and muscled chest. No, she mustn't look there! She lifted her eyes to his wheat-colored hair, which was gorgeously tousled from sleep. That wasn't fair at all! He lifted his hand to stifle a yawn, and she was distracted by the way his muscles rippled in his arms and chest as he did so. And his eyes, heavy-lidded from sleep, still managed a mischievous spark.

Her mouth went dry.

Her wits fled.

This was a mistake. This was why young ladies were not supposed to frequent the bedchambers of rogues.

Jack's hand clasped around her wrist and he tugged her into his room, shutting the door behind them. She glanced around, taking note of the draperies shutting out the morning light and disheveled sheets and blankets on the bed. A fire smoldered in the grate. His bedchamber was oddly warm—what other excuse could there be for her sudden spike in temperature? And his lack of attire?

This was a massive mistake.

"What brings you here, Miss Black?" he said, yawning again.

"The wedding ring, of course. Why else would I be here?"

He gave her *a Look* complete with a slight lift of his brow and a charming quirk of his mouth. Henrietta reddened. Ah yes. Of course. Indeed. *That.*

"I can't believe that didn't occur to you," he remarked.

"Why would it?"

"You're a woman in her prime and illicitly in my bedchamber," Jack remarked. "Truly, seduction should have crossed your mind. But it clearly did not. You really ought to get out more."

"Yes, me and Aunt Sophronia both," Henrietta said dryly. She *hated* that he had just explained the obvious to her and she *hated* that he had needed to. Not for one instant had she ever considered herself in the prime of womanhood and ravishable. However, she would certainly consider it in detail. Later. "Now where is the ring?"

"It's probably in my coat pocket," Jack said with a shrug. He gestured toward a coat flung over a chair. She crossed the room, picked up the garment, tried not to notice how it smelled faintly of him, and searched the pockets—and the lining too, for good measure.

The ring was not in his coat.

"Well, then let's look in my luggage," Jack said, not at all bothered by the absence of a priceless family heirloom that would be needed in just a few days at the wedding. She just couldn't have Wessex stand up there with his perfect bride and *no ring.*

Jack searched his luggage, located in the small closet connected to his room, while Henrietta waited in his bedchamber. It was not in his luggage.

Henrietta took deep breaths and endeavored not to panic.

"I'll ask my valet," Jack offered kindly. He smiled, but that only made her heart beat even faster. He returned to the closet, where his valet was staying.

A nervous moment later, Jack returned from an interview with his valet.

"Nansen has not seen the ring," Jack said. He at least possessed the decency to furrow his brow, indicating the slightest concern for their predicament.

Their terrible, horrible predicament.

Wessex had taken her in when she had nowhere to go. His mother, the duchess, had been exceedingly warm and generous to Henrietta over the years. She could not repay their kindness by losing a priceless family heirloom. Miss Grey did not deserve to be the first duchess to be married without the ring. She and her family would be livid, surely. But would they be angry enough to insist that Henrietta leave Kingstag?

It wasn't a chance she could take. Failure was not an option.

Which meant they would have to find the ring.

Henrietta did the sensible thing—as always—which was to take a deep breath and exhale it slowly. Eyes closed. Deep breaths. *Start at the beginning,* her mother used to say. Then she would ask, *Where was the last place you saw it?*

Henrietta opened her eyes. She asked Jack, "Did you pick it up from the jewelers in London?"

"Yes. I did," Jack said confidently. "Mr. Gold himself handed me the ring."

"And then what did you do?"

"I put it in my coat pocket."

"And then?"

"Hippolyta and I drove to Kingstag."

"Hippolyta?"

Jack winced. Henrietta gasped.

"Did you bring a ...?" Henrietta stumbled over the appropriate term to use. *Woman. Trollop. Ladybird.* "Did you bring an uninvited guest to the wedding?"

"Forget about Hippolyta. I can assure you it's not what you think," he said. "But I cannot explain."

Henrietta closed her eyes and inhaled deeply. One ought not to deal with rogues in the morning. She truly needed some strong black tea to clear her mind and fortify her nerves.

"Did you stop along the way?" Henrietta asked.

"Just for a piss along the road," Jack answered.

"Oh, for Lord's sake! Have you no sense of decency!" Henrietta shouted.

"You asked!" Jack bellowed back at her.

The outburst stunned them both. For a moment they stood there in the dimly lit chamber, just staring at each other. The air was thick with tension. Nerves. Desperation. And something else Henrietta couldn't quite place.

But she was painfully aware that they were alone and facing trouble.

Yet her eyes kept straying to the bed. The sheets and blankets were in utter disarray. Had he been alone? Or had he entertained company and if so, what did it matter to her? She was just Miss Black, dependent poor relation and ever-obliging companion to the impossible Lady Sophronia. For once though, Henrietta found herself wishing she were more.

"I apologize for raising my voice," Jack said kindly.

"I, as well."

"I dined and spent the night at the Red Lion in Dorchester," he offered.

"Is there a chance you were victim to a pickpocket?"

"Doubtful. I'm an intimidating bloke."

"You are obviously wealthy and easily distracted," Henrietta replied. "I'd try to pick your pocket."

"Would you now?" Jack gave her another *Look* that suggested he understood her comment to have nothing to do with thievery and everything to do with her hands in his breeches.

"It's not like that—It's not what I meant! You rogue!"

"Aww, Hen. I'm only teasing," he said with an affectionate smile. That damned smile of his. Made a girl feel dizzy in the head, weak in the knees, and in great need of the restorative powers of Smythson's Smelling Salts.

"The ring," Henrietta said firmly. Again. She would not forget *why* she was in this rogue's bedchamber in the first place.

"The ring," Jack repeated.

"Is lost," Henrietta stated.

"It must be somewhere."

"We have to find it."

His gaze locked with hers. Jack's eyes, she noted, were very blue. The seconds ticked by. His gaze never wavered. She felt a surge of heat from deep within. But it was no match for the sheer crash of panic that seemed to attack them both.

Jack and Henrietta lunged for the bed.

Not for a passionate tumble but in a frantic search for that wayward piece of jewelry. Bed sheets were ripped from the mattress. Pillows were fluffed and punched until they exploded in a burst of feathers. Blankets were shaken out.

There was no ring.

"What of the bedside table?"

Surfaces were swept over, drawers yanked out and discarded on the floor. The armoire was divested of its contents and drawers.

Henrietta dropped to her knees so she might better explore the carpet. Jack stood above her, breeches on but nothing else.

A maid walked in.

Her eyes went wide and round. Henrietta turned a furious shade of red as she imagined what this scene must look like. Jack, unclothed. A woman, on her knees. The bedding in an outrageous state of disorder.

"Nothing to see here," Jack said jovially.

"Excuse me," the maid murmured.

She stepped out and closed the door behind her.

"It's not here," Henrietta said a moment later, her voice rising in panic. "It's not on the carpet or under the carpet. We have searched your room, destroying it in the process. The duchesses will be furious with me. Sophronia and I will have to find somewhere else to live, and she's so *particular*. This is terrible. My life is over."

"Perhaps it is in my phaeton," Jack said softly. Consolingly.

"Let us go there directly," Henrietta urged.

"No, later," Jack said firmly.

"Why not, oh, say, immediately? The sooner we find this ring, the sooner we can relax and enjoy the wedding festivities."

"I cannot explain," Jack replied. "Let us meet there after supper, when the men take port and the ladies take tea. Contrive to get away and *tell no one*."

# CHAPTER FOUR

*Ah, there was nothing more perfect than this: a blue sky, the open road, a bottle of whiskey tucked under the seat. It was a fine day for driving a carriage like Hippolyta through the English countryside. But wait—was that another carriage following him?*

The dining room

Later that night

**M**rs. Cleopatra Barrows was sister to the bride and far too observant.

"Is anything the matter, Lord Willoughby?" she inquired.

Damn. She had caught Jack drumming his fingers on the table and peering anxiously at his pocket watch. Again. And only the second course had been served.

"Everything is just fine. Whyever do you ask?"

But it wasn't fine. He'd lost the blasted wedding ring. But they had a week yet to find it. God willing, he'd never have to tell his cousin how he'd lost the Wessex family heirloom. Jack took a long swallow of wine.

"You seem a bit agitated," Mrs. Barrows remarked.

"What could possibly agitate me?" Jack said grandly, with his infamous grin. "I'm dining on excellent fare, drinking fine wines, the conversation is charming, and I'm surrounded by beautiful women."

His gaze fell on Henrietta, seated with Sophronia further down the table. The candlelight lent a glow to her skin. When she became aware of his attentions, a faint blush stole across her cheeks. His mind, inevitably, wandered to thoughts of her naked skin in candlelight—legs tangled, arms entwined, her belly and, oh, God, her breasts. Would she blush there too?

Candles. He needed candles.

Already, they had an assignation scheduled for later in the evening.

Judging from Henrietta's obvious and frequent glances between him and the large clock on the mantel, she was a nervous wreck about it. Or was she excited? He reckoned she did not have assignations with rogues every day. Or night, rather. Or at all, ever.

She had to be nervous. The ring was missing and Lady Grey, mother of the bride, was requesting to see it with an alarming frequency. She'd even started pestering him about it at every opportunity, which meant he spent an inordinate amount of time taking refuge in the stables. Poor Henrietta was stuck with *him* in her efforts to find it. Jack was under no illusions—he was careless and easily distracted. His heart was good. His attention span was not.

Jack was struck with a ... a ... feeling. If he were to describe it— here he took a long sip of wine—it would be something like the desire for her good opinion of him. Not because he was vain and needed all females to fawn over him.

No, he wished her to think well of him because he'd earned it. Perhaps he'd find the ring and thus rescue her from inordinate amounts of worry. Jack imagined how happy she'd be. "My hero!" she'd exclaim before launching herself into his arms and pressing her lips to his.

Candles. He needed to bring candles to the stable tonight.

He glanced her way once more. But it was Lady Sophronia who caught his eye and *winked* at him! He nearly choked on the sip of wine he'd taken.

But then, of course, he winked back at the old gal.

Shortly before the ladies departed for tea in the drawing room after supper, Jack excused himself. He cajoled a dozen candles from a housemaid. He sent Watson on an impossible errand up at the house and bribed some footmen to pour brandy with a heavy hand. It was imperative that Jack and Henrietta have time alone to thoroughly search Hippolyta.

Taking great care not to be seen, he exited the back of the house and loitered under a large oak tree where he and Henrietta had agreed to meet.

"Hullo, Hen," he murmured when she arrived but a moment later.

"Hello, Lord Willoughby."

"Call me Jack," he said, linking his arm with hers as they set off down the gravel path. "Given that we are embarking on an illicit moonlit assignation, I think Christian names are in order."

They chatted amiably about dinner and the other guests until he was distracted by the sight of another old oak, which had been split right down the middle and was partly cut up for firewood.

"What happened there?" Jack asked. He'd been seeing it for days but never had a chance to inquire.

"Lightning strike. On the day the bride arrived. Quite a sign, isn't?"

He agreed, though he couldn't imagine what it was a sign for. When they reached the entrance to the stables, he had her wait for a moment while he lit the candles.

"Good thinking, Jack," she said kindly. "It wouldn't do to search in the dark and I hadn't thought to bring any."

"Indeed," he said, feeling proud of the recognition but also a bit rakish because the real reason he'd brought them was a desire to see her skin under the glow of candlelight. He decided not to mention that.

"It's a very fine carriage," Henrietta remarked as her hand slid along the smooth curves of the wheel.

"Indeed." His voice was oddly rough.

"I can't quite see what all the fuss is about, though. It is just a carriage. And yet the men at this house party have been entranced with her for days."

"Just a carriage? Don't let Hippolyta hear you say such things."

"Hippolyta? Jack, did you name your carriage?" she asked, laughing.

Jack leaned against the carriage and smiled down at her. "You don't have much experience with men, do you?"

"What part of 'Aunt Sophronia's faithful companion' makes you think that I do?"

"That woman—that old, terrifying woman—is a tremendous flirt. Why, she winked at me at dinner!"

Henrietta groaned and rolled her eyes. "I am upstaged by a woman old enough to be my grandmother."

"Not here. Not tonight. Let me show you how Hippolyta is not just any other carriage."

Jack gave her a tour of all the conveyance's features. He took every opportunity to lean in close to her as he pointed out the finely crafted dashboard, or to slide his hand around her waist to maneuver so they might better see the perfect spokes of the wheels. He wrapped his arm around her, guiding her away from a puddle of spilled whiskey some unruly gent must have left behind.

Hippolyta had many fine features to be pointed out. Jack was eternally grateful. Because he just couldn't get enough of Henrietta. He breathed her in, ached to taste her skin or thread his fingers through her hair. He wanted to know her.

"And now ..." He leapt into the carriage. In one hand he held a lit candle so they might search for the ring along the upholstered seat.

"I suppose you're going to show me how well sprung she is," she retorted.

Jack couldn't help a low chuckle.

"You're incorrigible!"

"C'mon, Hen," Jack said, extending his hand. She hesitated. He gave her that grin. Henrietta placed her small, soft hand in his. Perfect. Fit. His intentions were to gently help pull her onto the seat beside him.

But that didn't happen.

Jack used a little too much of his strength—she was rather light—and Henrietta tumbled against him. Instinctively, he wrapped his arms around her. Unfortunately, he dropped the lit candle to do so. Disastrously, it landed in the puddle of whiskey.

There was a sudden burst of flame, which dissipated as quickly as it had come.

Henrietta screamed. She clutched his shirt with her delicate little hands and buried her face in the crook of his neck and shoulder. He could feel her breasts pressed up against his chest.

*He did not like it he did not like it he did not like it.*

He liked it.

21

Of course he bloody liked it. He was a man. With a pulse. And she was ... she was Miss Henrietta Black, a chronically well-behaved child who had grown into a terminally proper woman.

Or so he had thought.

Facts forced him to reconsider. She had broken at least nineteen different rules when she knocked on his bedchamber door before breakfast. At the moment, she ought to be taking tea and gossiping with the ladies. Instead she was here, warm and luscious, in his arms. Plus, they had embarked upon a high-stakes quest together.

Jack revised his previous opinion. She might be responsible and proper, but she was still up for an adventure. He almost didn't even *want* to find the ring just yet, so this journey could carry on a bit longer.

"It's all right," he said soothingly. Except his voice had that husky quality to it.

"Are you hurt?" She peered up at him. He ached upon seeing the concern in her eyes. Women didn't usually look at him thus and it was ... warm. Nice. He liked it.

"It was just a quick burst of fire. Nothing to worry about."

"You're not even concerned about Hippolyta," Henrietta pointed out.

His beloved carriage's welfare *hadn't even occurred to him.* Another detail he had overlooked: he and Henrietta were still locked in an embrace. That must mean something.

"Hen," Jack said, his voice rough. Desire thrummed through his veins and he had no intention of stopping it. Especially not when Henrietta was still in his arms.

"What is it?" she whispered.

"This," he murmured before claiming her mouth with his.

Hen didn't kiss like a prim spinster. No, she kissed like a lovely young girl. She tasted sweet. The touch of her soft lips on his was light, curious, sweetly unsure. Her innocence was arousing. Or perhaps it was just *her.* It was her first kiss, he reckoned. But he hadn't reckoned on the deep pride and surprising sense of possessiveness this aroused in him.

The unmistakable sound of boots on gravel and the low murmur of men's drunken chatter intruded upon their reverie. It took a moment for Jack's wits to return, and another to reluctantly end the kiss. Yet another for the implications of the looming situation to spur him to action.

"Henrietta, quick." Holding her hand, Jack jumped down from the carriage. Clasping her at the waist, he lifted her down.

"Lift your skirts."

"I beg your pardon!"

The sound of the men grew louder as they grew closer. Her eyes widened in horror. If they were caught ...

"We have to run, and fast, Hen."

With her hand in his, they dashed down the center aisle of the stables, rudely awakening slumbering horses. Taking cover in the shadows, they ran back to the house.

"The ring!" Henrietta whispered, alarmed, as they approached the servants' entrance.

"We'll look again tomorrow," he said. In daylight. Preferably with chaperonage and supervision. Because if he was left alone with her, they would be very distracted indeed.

# CHAPTER FIVE

*Jack urged his horses to go faster. Just to see if that one lone carriage was following him. He glanced over his shoulder, and indeed, the driver had cracked the whip and spurred his horses to pick up the pace.*

On the lawn

The next morning

While the guests were occupied with a cricket match on the lawn, Henrietta left Lady Sophronia in the company of Mrs. Barrows, with whom she got along famously. Then she took the opportunity to sneak off and meet Jack.

She waited by their oak—correction, *the* oak tree—as they had agreed during a furtive conversation at breakfast. Taking advantage of the distance, she indulged in a long, lingering look at him. *Oh, lud. Jack looks so handsome,* she thought as he strolled across the lawn toward her.

His wheat-colored hair seemed nearly golden in the sunlight, and it was slightly ruffled by a caress of wind. Even from a distance, she could see that he smiled and seemed happy. She herself was a bundle of nerves and anticipation. It wasn't just about the ring, either.

Henrietta couldn't help but notice the way his breeches clung to his muscled legs and his green jacket clung to his broad shoulders and wide chest. She couldn't stop herself from imagining what was underneath.

As he approached, she stifled the urge to fuss with her bonnet ribbons. Again. She'd spent a good ten minutes getting them just so. The problem was truly with the bonnet, though. The brim was a touch too large and because of its decorations it resembled nothing so much as a bird's nest. One of the duke's sisters had bought it from the milliner in the village and regretted the purchase once it arrived at the house. It was handed down to Henrietta. Lucky her.

She pulled out a sheet of paper and unfolded it clumsily, all too aware that a very handsome man approached and she was wearing this atrocious bonnet.

"Good morning, Hen."

"Good morning."

It was Jack. Only Jack. There was no reason to be flummoxed. No reason at all. But the paper shook in her gloved hands. Though she'd known him forever, Henrietta felt oddly nervous to be near him. Had he always been this large? Had his blue eyes always fixed upon her thus, and with a mischievous sparkle to boot? No, she couldn't quite recall ...

She didn't try very hard, either. It was a beautiful day, and instead of staying indoors with Sophronia, Henrietta would spend the morning out of doors, in glorious sunshine, with a handsome—if vexing—man for company.

However, this wasn't a frivolous walk about the garden or anything like courtship. They had a purpose.

"I have compiled a list of where the ring might be," Henrietta said. "We shall proceed in order until we find it."

"Very organized of you," Jack said. He leaned against the gnarled tree trunk and gazed down at her.

"There is no point in aimlessly wandering about," she said.

"You might enjoy the view. Or have an unexpected adventure." His mouth slowly turned up into a smile.

"I beg your pardon?" She was distracted by thoughts of kissing him again. They had kissed. Briefly. Fleetingly. He probably kissed all of the girls. Literally, all of them. She should not turn into a ninny about it.

"Wandering aimlessly has its perks," he said. "A beautiful, unexpected view or an unanticipated adventure. Or a kiss ..."

He had to mention the kiss.

"While that was ... nice..." she stammered. She had to stammer, didn't she?

"Nice?" He lifted one brow as only a rogue will do.

"I couldn't sleep for worry while a priceless family heirloom is missing," Henrietta rushed. Between the kiss and the missing ring, her nerves were utterly frayed. Indeed, this morning Sophronia had inquired if she was unwell. Henrietta didn't know what to do about the kiss—would it happen again? Or not? What would it mean? Or not? She should find that cursed ring first. And then worry about kisses. Prioritization, that.

"So you made your list of where it might be," Jack said, trying to peer at the sheet of paper in her hands and casually brushing up against her as he did. She experienced a tingle of anticipation from the touch.

"Yes. Precisely."

"Do tell, my lady."

"I thought we might carefully review the pathway between the stables. Perhaps the ring was in your pocket and it fell out."

"Excellent thinking. Shall we?" Jack offered his arm. Henrietta looked at him warily, curiously.

"If all those people watching the cricket match should see us wandering about arm-in-arm and our heads bowed together, they will think we are having a romantic stroll. If they see us pacing furiously between the stables and the house with our heads down and otherwise ignoring each other, they will be curious. Eventually someone will do the math and determine that we are responsible for the ring, that it is missing, and thus, that we are looking for it."

"You are not so foolish after all," she replied. Her heart twinged at the faint smile he gave her, as if he were sad and tired to always be thought of thusly.

Not knowing what to say, Henrietta slipped her arm in his and strolled alongside him.

Henrietta wasn't the only one to think him a fool. Jack knew the opinion was shared by most who encountered him. He'd never been able to focus on his lessons—Latin, botany, and ancient history just didn't captivate him. Forget about the preacher's sermons. Or most conversations. Even most women couldn't hold his interest with their twittering and harping on this and that. Horses races he liked—they were fast and fascinating and then over. He enjoyed sports. Carriages intrigued him—particularly the design and construction of them.

And Henrietta. She had caught his interest.

And he didn't want her to think him a fool.

"Slow down a bit, Hen," he said to the woman stomping along at a clip beside him. He peered down at her and could see little other than her atrocious bonnet, which seemed to resemble some sort of shrubbery. "Remember, we are lovers indulging in a morning stroll through the gardens."

"You're right," she said, though she kept her gaze firmly fixed upon the grass and gravel underfoot.

"We are *not* two people who are increasingly panicked at the absence of a priceless family heirloom."

"You're right. It must be somewhere," she said firmly. Hen peered up at him expectantly. His heart sank. He had been the damned *fool* to misplace the thing. On the one hand, this mistake was a disaster.

On the other hand, this disaster was allowing for time with Henrietta, which he was finding quite enjoyable. Perhaps it was even more enjoyable than drinking in the stables and accepting compliments on Hippolyta.

But Henrietta thought him a fool for misplacing it. Which he had done, probably while drinking and talking about Hippolyta.

Jack sighed, hopelessly. They *had* to find the ring.

Up and down the gravel path they strolled leisurely once, then twice, then thrice.

"What did the ring look like, anyway?" she asked. "I don't think the duchess has worn it since Wessex's father died years ago."

Jack wracked the recesses of his brain trying to recall what the jeweler had handed him.

"It was a dark stone. Flanked with some shiny white ones. In a gold band," he said finally. "Or was it silver? Also, there may have been rubies."

"You are hopeless."

"I'm a *man*. I'm not supposed to have an eye for jewelry."

"Well, there goes my plan to have someone in the village try to make a forgery in a few days time," Henrietta muttered.

"With all the diamonds, rubies, and sapphires lying around?"

"If you knew the names of the stones," Henrietta said slowly, "why didn't you just say so?"

And then, just to vex her, he said, "It could have been an emerald."

Jack glanced down at her with a grin. Her eyes were flashing and her cheeks were pink—blazing mad, she was.

"You are quite adorable when you make those sounds of strangled frustration."

"I'm so glad you think so," she said witheringly.

"Doesn't old Sophronia feel the same?"

"I don't think she can hear them. Not that she would ever admit it, but her hearing is not quite all it was these days."

In earlier days, it had been—he remembered Lady Sophronia *always* heard when someone muttered something wicked. Now that he thought about it, Sophronia and Henrietta had always been there. Around. They dined with the family but were not quite a part of it. As a child, Jack had never wondered how anyone was related—he merrily played with his cousin, the duke, and the cook's children. In his memories, Hen was always just *there,* off to the side, watching but not participating lest Sophronia need her.

"How did you become her companion anyway?"

"I was an orphan of too high a status to be sent to the workhouse but not high enough to be brought out. Thus, I earn my keep by keeping the crotchety old woman entertained."

"She's not *too* crotchety, is she? I've always found Sophronia fiendishly entertaining. But then again, I haven't had to live at her beck and call."

"She's not bad at all," Henrietta said firmly. "It's just ... nothing." She sighed. Jack thought he understood.

"It's just that a young woman may not want to spend all of her time devoted to an old lady. Not when you could be gallivanting with rogues or taking care of babies of your own."

"Something like that," Henrietta said softly. Then she looked away and obscured his view of her pretty face with that absurdly large bonnet. But it had happened—he knew it. They shared a *moment.*

"Wessex says she came with the house," Jack said, lightening the conversation.

"I'm given to understand that, along with lands and houses, titles also come with an assortment of dependent relations," she remarked.

"I didn't get any," he said. There were some cousins in the Outer Hebrides, but other than Wessex, the rest of Jack's family was long gone. No pesky sisters or brothers. No mad old aunts and their lovely young companions.

"Lucky you," Hen said.

"It's a bit lonely," Jack replied. Not untruthfully.

"Is that why you keep so much company with so many women?"

"Speaking of ..." he murmured as a flash of white caught his eyes. Then another, then another.

"Quick! Hide!"

They'd been having a *moment*. Henrietta was dismayed when it ended abruptly with Jack tugging her under the cover of one of the large, gnarled old oak trees that shadowed the path.

But then she wasn't dismayed at all.

The large branches hung low and created a sort of cocoon where they'd be hidden from whatever they were hiding from. She found her back up against the tree. Jack's body protectively covered hers. He slyly peered around the thick trunk, trying to see if they had escaped.

As he did, his hand strayed from the tree trunk to her hip. Henrietta sucked in her breath. That felt too perfectly wonderful. His hand, casually, possessively on her hip.

"It's the White Muslin Crew," he muttered. "I say, they are a plague among men."

"I beg your pardon?"

"It's the name the gents have given to Wessex's sisters and the other young women who have banded together to stalk the men at this house party."

Henrietta's lips quirked into a smile. She supposed the duke's sisters and other young female guests had been rather forthcoming with their interest in all the young, handsome male guests in attendance. The ladies were too occupied with wedding matters to reign in the flighty girls.

"Oh, they can't be so bad. They are just excited for the wedding."

"They are uncivilized harpies with an unquenchable taste for male flesh. I haven't had a moment's peace since they set eyes upon me."

"Vanity, thy name is Jack ..." she murmured. But it was true. They divided their attentions between Jack and Lord Bruton, an aloof aristocrat whose wicked scar inspired all manner of outlandish speculation.

"I truly fear for my life," he said, gazing down at her.

"Your bachelor life, you mean," she replied flippantly.

"Of course. Exactly."

"Have not the wedding activities and all the romance softened your heart? Do you not wish to wed?"

"Thus far I have been chased to and fro by a terrifying pack of marriage-minded young women, all the while searching for the blasted wedding ring for the bride. I've noticed that Wessex seems awfully morose about the whole affair. My conclusion is that marriage and women are a tremendous amount of bother. It should go without saying that I'd rather not endure a tremendous amount of bother."

"None of that sounds very romantic," Henrietta murmured.

"Not very romantic at all," he murmured.

For a moment she wondered if he might kiss her.

"It's not very sunny under the shade of this tree," he remarked, and she tried not to cry. Was he truly initiating a conversation about the weather when they were in a secluded place, having a moment? "Since we are shaded, perhaps you want to remove your bonnet."

"It's dreadfully inconvenient to arrange just so and—"

"It's just easier to do this when you don't have a massive bonnet in the way."

*This* was his mouth claiming hers. A kiss. He hadn't been talking about the weather at all. Who was the foolish one now? Certainly her. Especially since he was right. This bonnet got in the way of things.

Henrietta fumbled with the strings. The hat tumbled unceremoniously to the ground, where it was promptly forgotten.

Henrietta peered up at him, a little bit dazed after a long moment of a deep kiss. Tugged at his heart, that.

"What was that for?" she asked breathlessly.

Jack couldn't explain—to her, or himself—that he just had to kiss her. Once the idea had occurred to him, he didn't pause to consider an alternative course of action. He just needed to kiss her. That was all.

"Just because," he said.

"Just because," she repeated.

"I wanted to," he said.

Her brow furrowed adorably. She tilted her head and peered up at him curiously. Her lips parted, then closed, then *curses* she decided not to say whatever words were on her tongue.

"What else is on your list? Where shall we look next?" he asked.

"We didn't finish searching the pathway," she answered.

"We have walked to the stables and back at least four times, Hen. It's probably not there."

"We never did properly search your carriage. Next we ought to look in the stables."

Jack winced. Not the stables. He could not take a woman into that haven of masculinity without serious questions he was not prepared to answer. As more guests arrived—and as more men sought a refuge—the stables had increased the comforts offered. On the first day they had lounged on hay bales; today footmen had brought in upholstered furniture from the house.

"Why not the stables?" Hen asked, which was a question he could not answer. He didn't know which Wessex would be more angry about—losing the ring or revealing the secret club they had established.

"I have a better idea," Jack said. "Why don't I search Hippolyta and the stables while you search something else on your list. What else is on your list?"

"The entire road between Kingstag and London," she answered, and he groaned.

"What else?"

Henrietta smiled and it did things to his insides.

"Your bedroom," she replied. "Again."

"Perhaps you could look around the house instead," he said, because if she was going to be in his bedchamber, he would be there too. "I'll take care of the stables."

"What are you hiding in there? I demand to know!"

"I can't say, Hen," he said forlornly. "Truly, I cannot."

31

# CHAPTER SIX

*Why the Devil would someone be following him? He had nothing of value—save for Hippolyta. And the duke's wedding ring.*

The stables

**A**fter kissing Henrietta under the tree, Jack went to the stables as promised. Alone. In truth, her kiss had left him a little bit dazed. This wasn't something that usually happened after he kissed a woman. At least not that he could recall. But this warm, pleasant daze was the kind of feeling a man never wanted to let go of.

Which was terrifying.

Which required a drink and a distraction.

Thus, the stables.

And in a predictable fashion, he immediately forgot his purpose and instead found himself occupied by a game of dice with Frank Newnham, Trent Ascot, and a few others. Jack didn't manage to find a moment alone with Henrietta for the rest of the day, which was for the best since he had nothing to report. Or was it tragic, because all he really wanted to do was kiss her again?

Immediately following breakfast the next morning, Jack set off once again for the stables, intent on a thorough search of Hippolyta. He'd assumed everyone would be off hunting, or playing bowls, or something. But no, they'd all found their way to the stables.

Hippolyta, shiny and new, stood proudly in the center of the carriage house. In an adjoining tack room whose open door afforded a good view of the phaeton, gentlemen lounged on chairs—

upholstered chairs in the bloody stables!—and against bales of hay. In one corner, Watson stood attendance over the ale and whiskey. In another corner, a table had been set up and a few gents were in the midst of a card game. In another corner, a game of dice was in progress. Aside from the supple leather saddles and shiny bits and bridles hung along the walls, it was as if White's had been transported from London's St. James's Street to the Duke of Wessex's stables.

"There he is!" Newnham called out. Heads turned.

"We were afraid the women had wrangled you into opining on seating arrangements for the wedding breakfast," Wessex remarked.

"How much longer until the wedding, anyway?" Jack asked.

"Seven days," Wessex and his secretary, Mr. Blair, both said flatly. Jack looked from one bloke to the other, not able to tell who was less enthused about the wedding. Shouldn't a man be more enthusiastic about his upcoming nuptials? Not that the duke could match his mother's excitement for the event, but still ... Why did the secretary have to be so morose about it?

"Until then, we have the perfect haven here. Ale, spirits, card games, food, the company of the lovely Hippolyta. Most importantly, there is no wedding talk whatsoever," Jack said.

No plaguing women, either.

Jack imagined Henrietta surveying this scene of idle debauchery and he started to grin at the image of her pursed lips. She'd cross her arms over her chest, like a vexed governess, but that would push her breasts together and up. She'd narrow her eyes in disapproval. But perhaps, deep down, she would wish to join in.

His wicked brain then set about imagining the things he would do to soften her. To tempt her. He got hard just thinking about it.

Even though it was *Henrietta*.

Whom he had kissed. Twice.

*He had kissed Henrietta.*

He recollected a solemn child, watching the world with large brown eyes. She had become a solemn young lady. Never missing a "Yes, Your Grace," or "Thank you, Your Grace," or "Of course, Your Grace." While he, Wessex, and the others had run wild, she'd taken care to keep her voice at a reasonable level and her dresses clean and unwrinkled.

In short, she was a very well-behaved young woman who frowned upon the reckless exploits of others. Had it not been for this lost ring, their paths would not have crossed. He'd have spent every waking moment in the stables and she would have languished in the drawing room, endeavoring to keep Lady Sophronia from offending the other women present.

*Thank goodness he'd lost the ring.*

The thought—the mad, crazy, odd thought—came unbidden.

She'd never see it this way. He could never explain it. But he was glad that she was having an adventure and humbled to be a part of it. If only he could *find* the damned thing so their quest would end happily.

Such were his thoughts until someone handed him a mug of ale and Crash Ascot invited him to a game of dice. Time passed pleasantly in the company of gents happy to while away the hours playing cards, throwing darts, drinking, and conversations of little of importance.

It was only when the underbutler came down to announce that nuncheon would soon be served in the gardens that Jack realized he had not found the ring. Worse: he had not even looked. Again! In his defense, it was impossible to do so without arousing the suspicion of others, particularly the bridegroom himself.

Henrietta would be horribly disappointed in him, the knowledge of which made his gut ache. He wanted her to think better of him. But he could easily imagine her wary frown as she struggled between satisfaction that her low expectations had been met and the wish that he would, just once, focus, succeed, and be her hero and find the damned ring.

He suddenly was stricken with the intense and absurd desire to be her hero.

Flowers. He should bring her flowers.

It wasn't until the following day that he was able to sneak off to the garden—where he spied Miss Lacy and Lord Bruton walking together, which was odd, because he thought Frank Newnham was courting her. For once, Jack refused to be distracted. Not by the romantic assignations of other guests. Not by bees, or birds, or worry that he was picking weeds or poisonous plants instead of flowers. He needed a bouquet of flowers for Henrietta. By God, he was going to get them.

*The corridor*
*Later, with flowers*

**W**hen Jack presented her with a bouquet of freshly picked flowers outside of the dining room after luncheon, Henrietta fought the urge to turn around in search of the woman he really meant to give them to. Perhaps one of the Misses Lacy? Or even Miss Cowdrey, a young woman who had arrived mysteriously the other day. But there was no one else.

Just her. And Jack. And flowers. From Jack. For her.

The flowers were extraordinary. And extraordinarily large—proving to be quite the armful as he handed them to her. The bouquet was a massive riot of plump red roses, soft pink peonies, and some deep purple irises. There were also some branches, possibly a bit of shrubbery, and an assortment of unidentifiable greenery. A fat little bumblebee floated out from being stuck inside a blossom and lazily buzzed off down the corridor.

"Did you pick these yourself, Jack?" She couldn't imagine that Johnson, the head gardener, would have presented something quite like this.

"Yes, and I almost died in the effort," he said grimly.

"Whatever you suffered, it was worth it. These are beautiful, Jack. Thank you."

A smile tugged at her lips. It wasn't every day a handsome man brought her flowers. In fact, the lovely gesture had never occurred before. Oh, she suspected it had nothing to do with romance and everything to do with a failure to find the ring, but for one glorious moment, Henrietta allowed herself to pretend that Jack brought her flowers because he fancied her, wished to woo her, and would (she hoped) kiss her for a third time, if not more.

It was a glorious moment, in which her heart was aflutter and her nerves tingled in anticipation of *more*. She buried her face in the blossoms, inhaling the sweet fragrance deeply and thinking *if only*.

But she suspected the flowers were presented because the ring was still at large. He'd not found it in the stables. Or on the ground. Or in his bedchamber. Or anywhere.

Worried as she was about that, she really just wanted to enjoy the flowers. Was that wrong?

"You're right," Jack said softly.

"Am I? About what?"

"I can read your thoughts. You're right. No, I don't have the ring and yes, you should just enjoy the flowers."

"How did you do that?" Henrietta asked with wonderment and a dash of nervous apprehension. Had he read her other thoughts about his legs and his fitted breeches? Or how she'd nearly fainted from the pleasure of his kisses? Or how she wished to kiss him this very moment?

"Is it because you are so expressive? Or am I so observant?" Jack mused. Then he gave her That Grin of his.

"I'm sure I couldn't say," Henrietta murmured. And she couldn't stay either. Not when she was on the verge of throwing herself at him or falling for him. "I ought to go put these in water."

"Wait." Jack reached out and clasped her wrist, spinning her around to face him.

"Where shall we search next?" Jack asked. Their eyes locked. More. He was asking about more.

"We should try the stables again," Henrietta replied. Not because it was the most likely place or because it hadn't been thoroughly searched. She suggested it because it was dim and secluded. He'd kissed her once there before and Lord, she hoped he'd do it again.

"Very good. Let's meet after dinner," Jack said. "Until then, Hen ..."

Henrietta just smiled and inhaled the lovely fragrance of the flowers again as she skipped up the stairs. She'd need a housemaid's help with the vase and water, then she'd place them in her own bedchamber—not Sophronia's.

Sophronia!

Henrietta had been so distracted by that rogue she'd forgotten her one purpose in life: to keep that crotchety old lady happy and entertained.

Henrietta quickly made her way to Sophronia's chambers. It was wrong of her to spend so much time away. After all, Henrietta's sole purpose in the world was to be the old lady's companion, and she'd hardly done that while off with Jack, searching for the ring. Or daydreaming about Jack.

And kissing Jack.

Henrietta couldn't completely regret that she'd been remiss in her duties. His kiss had made her feel young, lovely, and alive for the first time in her life. His kiss made her feel tingly and magical. She just couldn't be too negligent and risk losing her employment. But then she *had* to find that ring *or else*, and it certainly wasn't lost in Sophronia's chambers.

"Well, look who has deigned to remember a poor, neglected, old woman," Sophronia remarked from her favorite upholstered chair as Henrietta slipped into the room.

"You are hardly poor," Henrietta pointed out, "or neglected. You have dozens of housemaids and footmen at your disposal."

"I'm not old either," Sophronia said witheringly.

Henrietta murmured "hmm," while fluffing pillows and arranging the blanket on Sophronia's lap just so.

"I suppose I can guess where you have been all this time," Sophronia said.

"Wedding plans," Henrietta replied.

"Hmmph. You've been cavorting with that rogue, Jack."

"You mean Lord Willoughby," Henrietta replied. She was oddly delighted to have been thought cavorting with a rogue.

"He's a handsome one," Sophronia said with a very wicked gleam in her eye.

"I suppose," Henrietta replied lightly. She turned away to hide the blush on her cheeks that revealed just how handsome she really found him.

"You ought to see a doctor about that," Sophronia said. "Must be something wrong with your vision or ... well, never mind that. Suffice it to say, he's a handsome rogue, no doubt about it."

Of that, Henrietta was well aware. Achingly aware. Constantly aware.

But to confess to that was to confess to not being completely committed to being Sophronia's companion. What if she were let go? She didn't think Jack was the marrying kind.

A subject change was in order.

"How have you been, Sophronia? I'm sorry I haven't been so attentive as I have been helping the duchess with plans for the big day."

"Oh, I've been just fine. Enjoying all the hysteria around the wedding," Sophronia said. "I've also made the acquaintance of a charming young woman. The American girl, Miss Cowdrey. Have you met her?"

"I'm not sure that I have," Henrietta replied. Not when she had spent half her time with Jack.

"Well, she's a delight. Much less fussy than English girls."

"Is that so?"

"She's got spirit, that Miss Cowdrey," Sophronia said, smiling fondly, and Henrietta felt her insides tie up in knots. Was she too proper, organized, and bossy for Lady Sophronia? Would she lose her position to a girl with much more spirit? Dear Lord above, was Henrietta *boring?* And why was she more afraid that Jack would find her so? Sophronia carried on, "I have decided to invite Miss Cowdrey to stay with us here."

"How generous of you," Henrietta murmured, finding her insides even more knotted up.

"We shall rename these rooms Lady Sophronia's Refuge for Young Ladies Pining for Rogues."

"I don't know what you are talking about," Henrietta replied. "I have been busy with wedding things."

Technically, it wasn't a lie.

"Do those wedding plans include flowers from a handsome rogue?"

"How did you know about that?" Henrietta asked, shocked. "I only just received them!"

"One of the maids told me. Someone has to keep me apprised of all the gossip. Tell me, is he a good kisser?"

"Sophronia!"

"That's a *yes*. Or perhaps 'I don't know but desperately wish to.' Which is it?"

"This is not an appropriate topic of conversation," Henrietta reprimanded. Wanton companions to esteemed elderly women were not wanted. *Or were they?* Henrietta mentally begged the pardon of this Miss Cowdrey for assuming her wanton. It's just that ... she had "spirit." Apparently more than Henrietta.

"Exactly. Which is why I wish to have it," Sophronia said resolutely.

But Henrietta ... just ... couldn't. She touched her lips, thinking of the kiss and wanting the memory to be hers alone.

"Shall I read to you?" she offered.

"No. I want to hear about kissing rogues," Sophronia said, pouting.

Henrietta picked up a book and began to read.

"Oh look! *Lady Stewart-Wortly's Guide to Good Behavior.* Why, this sounds like a lovely book for me to read to you this afternoon."

"Oh, not that one," Sophronia said with a dramatic roll of her eyes. "Duller stuff I can't imagine."

"Chapter One: Minding One's Own Business," Henrietta read firmly.

"You're making this up!" Sophronia shouted. Henrietta just smiled. She wanted spirit, did she?

"In matters of a personal nature, one must endeavor to exercise restraint and delicacy. One must at all times be respectful of others' personal matters."

Sophronia muttered something incomprehensible. It was probably a string of extremely unladylike words.

Henrietta kept reading: "Gossip is the Devil's own language. Do endeavor not to be a mouthpiece of Satan."

"Oh dear Lord, cease! I beg of you! I have taken your point, Henrietta. Thus it is only fair that you listen to mine. There must be something in that blasted book about respecting your elders."

"Indeed. It is in Chapter Two. Are you now admitting to being old?"

Sophronia softened and smiled kindly. When she spoke, her voice was soothing and almost sad.

"You have moments of cheekiness, Henrietta. But they are too far and few between. On the whole, you are far too well behaved. Always have been."

Henrietta froze. Hadn't Jack said something to that effect?

"I suppose it is because you are afraid to lose your position here," Sophronia mused. "After all, you have nowhere else to go."

Henrietta sat very still. It was hard to think beyond the pounding of her heart and the gentle whoosh of air in, air out. *Sophronia knew.*

Lightly, on a summer day, she put into words Henrietta's greatest fear.

And then, lightly, on a summer day, she laid it to rest.

"Really, you oughtn't be afraid of that. Honestly, who else would put up with me? We both know there isn't anyone else up to the task."

"I wouldn't say that," Henrietta croaked. What of this Miss Cowdrey?

"My point, Henrietta, is that you have security simply because no one else will take it. And when I'm gone—because I won't live forever, much to my dismay—I have ensured that you will be taken care of."

Henrietta remained very still, save for one thick salty tear that slid down her cheek. She would be taken care of. A weight lifted from her shoulders. It meant she was free to search for the ring—and that her livelihood perhaps wasn't at stake if it weren't found. It meant she was free to kiss Jack again. She could live, just a little more than she'd been doing.

"Thank you, Sophronia." Henrietta whispered the words. "I don't know how to express my gratitude."

"But only on the condition that you do your job, which is to entertain me. And I'd be far more entertained by stories of flirtation and courtship with that rogue Jack by Lady Stewart-Bore-Me's book on proper behavior."

Henrietta cracked a smile, even as there were still tears in her eyes.

"Now be off with you," Sophronia said with a dismissive wave of her hand. "If you haven't kissed him already, do so by nightfall. The deuced wedding is just days away, and rogues have very little reason to visit Dorset."

# CHAPTER SEVEN

*Jack cracked the whip, urging his horses to run faster. Inconvenient as it was to be followed, it did give him a chance to see just what glorious speeds Hippolyta was capable of.*

Five days before the wedding

Instead of an assignation with that rogue Jack, Henrietta found herself among the other wedding guests seeking shade under awnings while watching games of bowls. She wished to be off with Jack kissing *searching* for the ring. But instead, she was prevented from even fetching cakes for Lady Sophronia by the inane conversation of Miss Jane Howell.

While Miss Howell went on and on, Henrietta spied Sophronia in conversation with the duke and his mother and—

Oh, dear! It seemed Lady Sophronia had brought her weaponry despite Henrietta's protests that they would have no need to defend their virtue at a game of bowls.

Henrietta excused herself. If she wasn't going to be kissing *searching* for the ring with Jack, then she at least wanted to find and make the acquaintance of this Miss Cowdrey who possessed much more spirit. At the very least, she should keep Lady Sophronia from terrifying the other guests.

Having failed on all counts—finding the ring, finding Jack, finding Miss Cowdrey, and keeping Sophronia out of trouble—Henrietta determined to seize the first opportunity to be alone with Jack. The moment required her to be bold.

It happened in the drawing room later that evening, after dinner, when a cluster of young ladies took turns playing the pianoforte and singing songs for the guests. At the conclusion of one song, she excused herself and made her way through the seats to the terrace. On the way, Henrietta found Jack, who was conversing with Wessex.

*Notice me. Notice me. Notice me.*

Jack caught her eye. His lips upturned into a smile. Her heart fluttered. Then, remembering her plan, she gave him a Look that was meant to convey *I need to speak with you urgently on the terrace. And then when we're done speaking I'd like to not speak at all.*

A moment later, Jack and Henrietta were alone on the terrace.

"I don't suppose you found the ring," she said.

"No," he said softly. Strangely, she bit back the words, *I'm glad.* She truly wanted to find the ring, save the wedding, and keep her place with Lady Sophronia. But she also wanted more moments like these with Jack. Would they end when they found the ring? Or when the wedding concluded and he returned to London? She bit her lip, not wanting to plague him with such questions and ruin the moment.

Not that she had the ability to speak when he was gazing at her so intently.

"What is it?" she asked.

"You're wearing your hair differently," he said. He'd noticed! Instead of her usual practical and spinsterish style, she'd had one of the maids do one of those elaborate arrangements with ribbons and curls that the other ladies wore. It required an hour's time, hot irons, and twenty minutes debating the exact shade of ribbon to use with Sophronia. But it had been worth it, if Jack noticed.

Jack reached out and gave one of the curls a gentle tug.

"You rogue!" she protested faintly.

"Just like old times, Hen," he said, grinning.

"If it were just like old times I would bash you on the head with a china breakfast plate," she replied.

"We can forgo that part of it," he said. And then in a low, husky voice he asked, "So tell me, Hen, why did you beckon me out onto the terrace?"

"I think we should send a footman to search for the ring," she said, the words coming out in a rush because the sooner they had this Very Important Conversation about the ring, the sooner they could proceed to the kissing.

"Excellent idea," he murmured, leaning in close enough to brush his lips against hers. "Is that all?"

"We need someone to search the road," she murmured.

"Of course," he whispered. Their lips met slightly, briefly.

"All the way from here to London," she added softly.

Jack pulled back and looked at her curiously. Yes, it was a ridiculous errand, but what choice did they have?

"Jack, we only have four more days before the wedding. Neither of us can go missing for that long. Sophronia is already commenting about my absences."

"I'll speak to one of the footmen," Jack said.

"Thank you. Perhaps he could take Hippolyta," she suggested, to which Jack burst out laughing. "Or not," she added.

"We'll find the ring in time for the wedding, Hen," Jack murmured as he drew her close. "In the meantime ..."

When Jack's lips brushed against hers, everything else ceased to matter. The loss of the ring, her uncertain future ... she was far too distracted by the delicious warmth, and the wicked way he deepened the kiss. She clenched her fists in the fabric of his shirt as her knees felt unsteady. Jack wrapped his arms around her, pulling her against him. She'd never felt so wanted, so desired, and so utterly, wonderfully reckless. Just when she was about to discover how reckless Jack inspired her to be, the sound of voices intruded. Reluctantly, Henrietta turned to see who was ruining this perfect moment for her.

"Oh goodness, it's Jane Howell," she whispered. "We must go. Immediately."

# CHAPTER EIGHT

*Jack lost him—whoever that nefarious cretin was—a mile or
so later. Honestly, what kind of fool tried to race Hippolyta?*

The ball

Three days before the wedding

Finally, finally, finally Henrietta managed to steal Jack for a
moment alone. It had taken her days to manage it. Yesterday there
had been a cricket game on the lawn that had kept him occupied for
hours. (And she had, admittedly, been diverted for a spell, watching
him play). She'd hoped to speak to him before dinner last night, but
he'd spent the time flirting with a throng of young ladies, including
Miss Rosanne Lacy, who managed to secure his escort into the dining
room. Whilst sulking on the far side of the drawing room, Henrietta
noticed she wasn't the only one vexed by this coupling. It seemed
Lord Bruton and Mr. Newnham were, too.

At the ball, she finally managed to find Jack and pull him aside.
They lingered in the foyer outside of the double doors leading into
the ballroom where all the guests were celebrating.

For a moment, she forgot what she had to ask him, for she was
distracted by how handsome he looked in his evening attire. The
stark black and white of his clothes set off his sun-kissed skin. When
he smiled at her, she quite forgot how to breathe.

"Have you heard from the footman?" she asked, taking care to
keep her voice quiet.

"You look beautiful tonight, Hen," he said softly, giving a gentle tug to one of the curls in her hair. The affectionate gesture brought a smile to her lips and an extra beat to her heart.

"Thank you," she said softly, momentarily swept up in the moment. But then she remembered and her expression became serious. "Jack, the footman. Have you any news from him?"

"None yet," Jack said, smiling and gazing into her eyes. "But I'm sure the ring will turn up."

"I do hope so," Henrietta whispered.

So focused was she on the handsome man before her that neither she nor Jack noticed the Duchess of Wessex until it was too late.

"I beg your pardon," the duchess said with a tight-lipped smile.

While Henrietta was struck momentarily dumb from the shock and terror of the Duchess of Wessex arriving unexpectedly and quite likely overhearing the bad news about the ring, Jack just smiled that smile of his.

"Good evening, Your Grace," he said, bowing. "I was just saying to Henrietta that you have outdone yourself with this house party."

"Thank you, Jack," she said, softening. "I'm glad to find you both together for once. I wanted to inquire about the wedding ring."

Henrietta forced a smile. Jack looked confused.

"Did Henrietta not give it to you?" he asked, discreetly elbowing her in the side. Then he gave her a Look.

"Jack, I thought you were going to!" Henrietta replied.

"A thousand apologies, Your Grace," Jack said smoothly. Again, he flashed that smile. "We shall deliver it on the morrow. For now, it seems Sophronia is calling to Henrietta. We mustn't leave her unattended. Who knows what havoc she might bring?" Then lowering his voice to a confidential tone, he said, "I hear she is harboring an American in her chambers."

The duchess just sighed; Jack *was* impossible. She gave Henrietta a look suggesting she ought to know better. But as far as Henrietta was concerned, there was no one better than Jack, flaws and all.

"Enjoy the ball," she said. "And *please*, bring the ring to me first thing in the morning."

After the duchess turned and walked away, Jack and Henrietta held serious expressions for as long as they were able—admittedly, it was not very long—before bursting into laughter. Even though nothing about this situation was funny. At all.

45

They'd but three days to find the ring—or else. Seeming to sense her distress, Jack linked his arm in hers.

"That was quite nearly a disaster," Henrietta said. "She must know we do not have it."

"We do have it," he said confidently. "We just don't know *where* we have it."

It took a moment for Henrietta to puzzle over that. Then she just gave up.

"I have an idea," he said with a wicked gleam in his eye. She tilted her head curiously. "Let's waltz."

"I like this idea," Henrietta said with a smile. She didn't say that her heartbeat raced faster at just the thought.

"And then let's waltz out onto the terrace and down to the stables," Jack added as they strolled into the ballroom arm-in-arm.

"Even better."

"We shall search Hippolyta while everyone is enjoying the ball," he said, pulling her into his arms for the waltz.

"I'd love that." And then Henrietta couldn't say much else, between trying to recall the steps and simply marveling at the loveliness of this moment. She didn't waltz very often and never had done so with such a handsome man. Especially one she might be falling in love with.

Even though it was *Jack*.

He spun her around then pulled her even closer, pressing his palm against her lower back and clasping her hand just a bit tighter, as if he couldn't get close enough to her. Truth be told, she felt the same. She wanted more of him.

She was sorry they hadn't found the ring.

But she wasn't very distressed that it had gone missing. If that made sense.

Either way, she knew there would not be much searching once they arrived at the stables. Closer and closer they danced their way across the ballroom before Jack spun her dramatically through the French doors leading onto the terrace.

Henrietta took one last whirl, marveling in the stars and the solitude and Jack's smile. Finally, they had a moment alone.

But it was not to be, for the duke had found them.

"Willoughby. Miss Black. I trust you are enjoying yourselves this evening."

"Indeed we are. Are you ready for your big day, Wessex?"

The duke quirked one brow. "I don't know, Jack. Am I?"

"Only you can answer that," Jack replied. "For what it's worth, Miss Grey is a lovely woman. She'll be the perfect duchess."

"Yes," Wessex said, distracted. Henrietta followed his gaze ... to ... *not* Miss Grey. Turning back to them he said, "Mother wanted me to inquire with you about the ring."

"We already spoke with her about it," Henrietta said. "Fear not, Your Grace, we have everything under control."

"Excellent. If you'll excuse me." The duke bid them a good evening and went off to mingle with his other guests, many of whom unfortunately decided to enjoy a spot of fresh air. The terrace no longer offered the solitude they sought.

Jack cursed inwardly as it seemed that every guest at the party decided to come gaze at the stars and breathe fresh air at that moment. Didn't they know they were quite possibly ruining the wedding? At the very least, they were ruining his moment. It was imperative that he and Hen find the ring. But it was even more essential that he kiss her passionately and, preferably, immediately.

"We'll never make it down to the stables without being seen," she said. Was it wrong that he was thrilled at how forlorn she sounded? It meant that she was possibly of the same mind as he.

"Let's wait a moment," he said, entwining their fingers and hiding the affectionate gesture behind the folds of her skirts.

"We cannot," Henrietta said, now sounding very put out. "Lady Grey is coming this way. She has been pestering me about the ring. And Kingstag. And everything her daughter will soon become mistress of."

"Then we'd better be off," Jack said gallantly. Tugging Hen along, he guided them through the guests on the terrace, through the ballroom, and into the refreshments room, where he spied an opportunity. There was a door to a small chamber that was too small and intimate to be opened up during a ball. However, it had been the perfect place to hide as children. He suspected it would be the perfect spot to steal a moment alone with Hen.

Jack, thinking wicked thoughts, opened the door. There was a burst of candlelight and—

He quickly shut the door. He wasn't the only one seeking a moment alone with a woman.

"What was that?" Henrietta asked, peering around him.

"Who was that is more like it," he murmured, linking his arm with Hen's and leading her away.

"Where are we going?" she asked.

"Where else should we search?" he replied, lifting his brow questioningly. He had an idea, but it was definitely ungentlemanly of him to suggest it. But if it were her idea ... well, a gentleman ought to oblige a lady.

"We've done everything, I think," Henrietta said, furrowing her brow.

"Any place we should search for a second time?" he asked. Ridiculously, his heart was thudding hard. Fortunately no one would hear it, especially not over the din of the ballroom. It was just ... anticipation. Of Henrietta. Whom he was definitely falling for.

"Well if not the stables ... your bedroom?" She said this softly, and an adorable blush suffused her cheeks.

"We did not search there very thoroughly at first," he replied evenly.

"No, we did not," she replied. "We just took a cursory glance, really."

He glanced at her. She glanced back with a sly smile on her lips.

"It wouldn't do to ruin Wessex's wedding," he added.

"Absolutely not," she said. "I could never live with myself."

"Well in that case ..." They had reached the doors of the ballroom, leading into the foyer. "Wait a moment."

Jack held her back while Lord Bruton, who seemed to have been brooding against the wall all evening, gave up and retired. While waiting for Lord Bruton to ascend the stairs and return to his bedchamber, Jack and Hen were interrupted. Again.

This time it was Lady Sophronia. He winked at her. She only smiled wanly back at him.

"Sorry, Willoughby, not tonight. I have a headache," Sophronia replied. "Henrietta, I do hate to spoil whatever scandalous antics you two were about to engage in, but my head is absolutely pounding. Would you escort me back to our rooms?"

"Of course," Henrietta said, immediately concerned and linking her arm with Sophronia's. Jack was sad to lose her for the evening, but there was something about seeing how she cared for others that made him fall for her even more.

"Willoughby, the gents in the card room were asking for you."

# CHAPTER NINE

*It seemed safe to answer nature's call. Or so Jack had thought.*
*That carriage caught up with him ... and slowed down ... and...*

The following evening

Two days before the wedding

The footman dispatched to search the entire road from London to Kingstag in search of the ring had not yet returned, and Henrietta was growing increasingly anxious. Logic and good sense dictated that they continue to search for the ring *just in case* it was lying about somewhere. Henrietta always adhered to logic and good sense. Especially when it dictated that she should team up with Jack to search Hippolyta once more.

She had a feeling their attentions would stray. At least, she desperately hoped so. There'd been a growing heat in her belly and sensitivity on her skin whenever she thought of him and whenever she daydreamed of kissing him, both of which she had begun to do with an alarming regularity.

He had brought her the most stunning and lovely bouquet of flowers.

He had arranged all manner of assignations and rendezvous.

Best of all, he brought out a side of her she'd never known she possessed. For the first time, she felt like a happy, beautiful, carefree girl. She didn't want it to end.

She'd known that rogue Jack forever. She'd always envied his easy manner, his enthusiasm for everything, and his charming grin. Lucky her for finally being able to enjoy it.

As long as she didn't forget the purpose of their rendezvous tonight: finding the ring.

But could she help it if she felt a shiver of excitement as she made her way to the stables? Or was it just a shiver from the chill in the night air because she had deliberately left her shawl behind? For once, Henrietta would try to stifle her practical and proper nature for a possibly romantic encounter. A shawl would be just one more frustrating layer in between his bare skin and hers. *That* thought brought on another shiver of anticipation and she quickened her steps to get there sooner.

The hour was late.

It was a starlit evening.

The house was aglow, full of guests celebrating the upcoming wedding. There was champagne and laughter. But an even lovelier night awaited her in the stables.

*The stables*

**T**he hour wasn't that late. Everyone was still socializing in the drawing room. In London at this hour, he'd only just be dressing on his way out for the evening. Things were different in the country. And things were different with Henrietta.

*Good old Henrietta.*

Miss Henrietta Black.

When he thought of her now, she was just Hen. His partner in crime, his constant companion, his girl.

Jack felt his heartbeat quicken in anticipation of meeting Henrietta secretly at this hour. They had a mission. A purpose. A Noble Quest. Ravishment was not it. But still, his thoughts strayed to *her* and all the deliciously wicked things that tended to happen when a man and woman met, alone, in a secluded spot, with the cover of darkness.

But not too much darkness. Jack started to light a few candles. He did adore the way Hen's skin glowed in candlelight. Also, it would facilitate the search for the ring. Unfortunately, the candlelight also revealed through the adjoining door how the tack room had been transformed.

Before he had a chance to move the candles or close the tack room door, Henrietta arrived. She looked so lovely—so nervous, but excited—that he wanted to pull her into his arms and never let go.

She smiled at him. But it wasn't long before her gaze found the tack room door, taking in the table and chairs, and the bar.

Perhaps the candles had not been a good idea.

"I had wondered why all the gentlemen spent so much time in the stables marveling at your carriage—nice as it is. And now I see," she remarked.

"Don't let Hippolyta hear you disparage her," Jack said. "She believes she has kept dozens of men captivated for days."

"Is that a settee? And a game of dice?"

"No," he replied quickly. But it was.

"No?" She quirked up one eyebrow.

"Can you blame us for avoiding all the wedding madness in the house?"

"It's not fair that the men should have an escape, whereas I ..." She heaved the most heartfelt sigh. "Well, if it weren't for the missing ring, I'd be agonizing over different shades of white for the hair ribbons and other ridiculous things. But never mind that."

"One must take one's pleasures where one may."

"Indeed," she replied softly.

"Let's find the ring," he said. Because once that was out of the way, there would be nothing between them.

Her lips parted as if to say something. But then she murmured her agreement. They started searching the floor around the carriage. But he kept finding his attention drawn to Henrietta. He couldn't focus on the missing ring, because he couldn't think of anything other than Hen.

When it was clear that the ring had not fallen to the stable floors and been brushed aside, Jack suggested searching the carriage once more. He helped her up and climbed in after her.

"It's not in some crevice in the upholstery," Henrietta muttered.

"Nor did I place it in the secret compartment," Jack said after checking it.

"It doesn't seem to be here at all. It doesn't seem to be *anywhere*," she said, her voice rising in panic. "We've been searching for an hour, at least. For a week now!"

"What do we do now, Hen?" He didn't know. He wished he knew. The only thing he was sure of was that Henrietta would know.

"We probably ought to go back before anyone notices we are missing. Then we should confess to the duke."

"You're right, we probably ought to go back," Jack murmured. But he really, really didn't want to. He had another idea instead. "Or we could ..."

"Yes?" Hen whispered. She peered up at him, lips slightly parted.

"We could do this," he murmured, before claiming her mouth for the sort of kiss that made a man forget about everything, even the need to breathe. He had no idea how much time passed, only that he hadn't yet spent enough time kissing Henrietta. Her delicate, artless sighs and moans were driving him mad. Her touch—tentative at first, but becoming bolder with his encouragement—was driving him wild. He wanted to remove all the infernal layers of clothing separating them from true satisfaction. He wanted to make love to her. Desperately.

However, Jack made an unpleasant discovery. While phaetons were excellent for many things—racing along at a reckless pace, impressing women, inciting the jealousy of other men, and generally showing off—they were not very comfortable for making love.

In spite of being a well-sprung carriage, Hippolyta creaked. Every move caused a loud squeaky, creaky noise that was hardly the stuff of romance. The seat was not large enough to recline and the back was far too upright. The damned carriage was deuced uncomfortable.

None of these were sufficient deterrents to Jack. He had started to discover Henrietta and he would not—could not—rest until he knew the exact softness of the skin of her belly and a million other deeply intimate details.

Other things that ought to have been deterrents oddly were not: Henrietta was an unmarried woman. He had rules about that sort of thing, especially since he was not the marrying kind. He didn't have the attention span, for one thing.

They had other matters on which they ought to fix their attentions: that deuced ring. Or concocting an excellent excuse for why he didn't have it. They should be celebrating the impending nuptials with the other guests.

Henrietta sighed and leaned in more. The kiss deepened. His pleasure intensified.

No, there was nothing else they ought to be doing.

Nothing compared to the softness of Henrietta's lips or how sweet she tasted.

With just one touch and just one taste, Jack forgot all else.

In most things, he had an admittedly short attention span, but he could spend hours, days, entire fortnights kissing her, making love to her, bringing her to heights of pleasure neither of them had ever known before.

He'd wager on it.

If he could tear himself away.

"**J**ack ..." Henrietta murmured his name. She thought she heard the sound of people coming. But she couldn't be sure, for her every nerve and all of her senses were attuned to Jack and the mad pleasure she experienced from his every touch.

"Hen, oh Hen," he murmured her name. She sighed. She did so like being "Hen" instead of "Henrietta" or "Miss Black."

She thought she might have heard angels singing, so dazed by his kiss and touch was she.

"Jack," she murmured again, trying to pull back but finding herself drawn to him like a magnet.

But no, that was the sound of men singing. For a second, she considered it *was* the sound of angels singing. But angels would certainly never sing lyrics like "A country John in the village of late/courted young Dorothy, Bridget, and Kate."

The gentlemen must be making their way to the stables to visit with Hippolyta.

And they would see Henrietta and Jack locked in an embrace. Her hair was surely a mess. His cravat was certainly askew.

The implications of discovery hit her like a bucket of cold water. There wouldn't just be one wedding—but two. Imagine that—she and Jack bound together in holy matrimony *forever.*

Henrietta hesitated.

She hesitated!

Eligible gentlemen did not often make their way to Dorset. Lord knew, she wasn't getting any younger and neither was Sophronia. This might be her one and only chance at marriage. But it was *Jack*.

Who was always so distracted. Who was currently so transfixed by her kiss that their imminent discovery hadn't occurred to him.

Who lost the priceless family heirloom. Who spent days and nights searching for it with her.

Who had never paid her much attention, other than to tease. Who brought her a glorious bouquet of flowers that he had risked his life to collect for her.

Who could have any woman he wanted. But who probably needed a woman like her.

He didn't deserve to be trapped into marriage. Neither did she.

"Jack," she said in a frantic whisper. "We have to go."

"Is that singing?" Finally he seemed to realize they were about to be caught in a very compromising position by a very loud, drunken chorus of men.

"We have to go, Jack. *Now*."

Hand in hand they dashed toward the other exit of the stables—but Jack had another idea. He stopped before a ladder leading up to the loft.

"Climb," he said.

"Are you mad?"

"I am mad with desire for you and want to finish what we started."

Henrietta climbed the ladder. Promptly.

Jack swiftly followed.

With hardly a second to spare, the mob of carousing gentlemen burst into the stables. "Hippolyta!" they cried.

"Now, where were we?" Jack asked, sweeping Henrietta into his arms for another kiss that made her knees weak, her thoughts flee, warmth smolder in her belly, and wicked desire take over her.

"Come with me," he whispered. She followed his gaze and noted the soft pile of hay in the corner. Her heart was thudding with the anticipation of an actual roll in the hay.

Finally, life was starting to happen for her. Little old Henrietta, about to have an illicit assignation with a notorious rogue. At least, that's how the others would see it (not that they must ever know). She could only think of Jack and wanting more of him.

There was just one problem.

There were lots of low beams in the hayloft and little light to see them by. Especially when one was glancing over his shoulder and treating her to a wicked smile that promised all sorts of pleasure, except ...

"Jack!"

*Thud.*

"Oh my God, Jack!" Henrietta fell over his body. After hitting his head, he had fallen to the ground. His eyes were closed. She could not tell if he was breathing or if his heart was beating. Did he live? Or had she just discovered love only to lose it so soon?

Love. She loved him.

And he lay dying in her arms. In a hayloft.

Oh, goodness! She couldn't go for help—not without revealing their tryst. She would be ruined, for Jack would be too dead to marry her! A tear slid down her cheek. Then another, and another. It was too cruel that he should be taken from her so soon!

"Hen ..."

"Oh! Jack! You're alive!"

He stirred in her arms. Then he opened his eyes.

"I remember where I put the ring."

# CHAPTER TEN

*... and that damned carriage happened to reappear at the Red Lion when Jack arrived later that night, intent on an ale and a bed. He felt in his pocket for the ring. Safe.*

Somewhere on the road to Dorchester

At dawn

It was one thing to see Hippolyta parked in the stables, but Henrietta had to admit that it was quite another to see her majestically roll along the country roads at a clip. The horses were especially animated this morning, as if they sensed the urgency of this mission. Henrietta, decked in that atrocious bonnet, sat beside Jack.

"Are you certain of this?" Henrietta asked.

She did not usually take impromptu journeys, especially ones that were the result of a blow on the head.

"I am as certain as the last seven times you asked that question," Jack replied.

"No need to be smart about it," she muttered.

"Your nerves. You are overset."

"My nerves are fine," she ground out, though she gripped the carriage rail until her fingers were white.

Tomorrow. The wedding was tomorrow. They were on a mad journey—a race against time!—to find this ring. Also, she might have fallen in love. Her nerves were not fine. Not at all.

"Why don't you close your eyes and try to sleep," Jack suggested.

"I couldn't possibly sleep on this death trap of a machine," she replied.

"Don't speak that way about Hippolyta," he said, defensively.

"You men and your curricles," she sighed.

"High-flying phaeton," he corrected.

"Carriages. Whatever. It's what got us into this debacle in the first place."

"And what will save us. In any other vehicle we wouldn't have a prayer of getting to town and back in time for supper."

"I'm sure we could afford to slow down a little, at least around the turns," Henrietta said. In fact, as another turn approached, she nervously clutched his arm for fear of tumbling right out onto the road. Also, because she hadn't quite finished being affectionate with him.

"Have some fun, Hen," he urged. "Take off your ridiculous bonnet. Let the sun shine on your face and the wind blow through your hair. We're on an adventure."

"Tell me again where we are going and why?" she asked. Last night he'd hit his head and this morning they were dashing along at a breakneck speed.

Nevertheless, she started working on her bonnet strings to loosen them. It was early yet. The roads were deserted. It'd be nice to be free of such a vexing piece of millinery.

"Back in London all anyone can talk about is the duke's wedding," Jack explained. "It's in all the gossip columns, especially."

"Which I shall avidly read about in three weeks' time when they make their way out here to Dorset."

"Indeed. No detail was too insignificant. The papers reported on the bride's attire from her veil to her shoes. They even reported on what the duke would wear. Of course, they went on and on about the Duke's ancient and impeccable lineage and the bride's scandalous sister. The type of cake served at the wedding breakfast was even the matter of a wager in the White's betting book. Not that I should be telling you that."

"Very well, but what does this have to do with the ring? And wherever it is that we are going?"

"The papers also mentioned the ring and that Gold & Son's Jewelers was tasked with resetting and fixing up the blasted thing. Apparently after a few generations it was starting to show signs of wear. Only the best for Wessex brides," Jack said. He glanced down at Hen. The absurdly large bonnet lay in her lap.

"Go on then," she urged. "Eventually you'll get to the point about the ring, right?"

"I thought nothing of it when I read it, and I thought nothing more when I went to collect it. I did notice a peculiar man outside who seemed a bit nefarious. But again, that is just London folks for you."

"I'll have to take your word for it," Henrietta murmured.

"But when I was a few miles outside of the city, I stopped to answer nature's call, if you will."

"Do tell me more," she said dryly.

"I'll tell you what you need to know, which is that another carriage was approaching. I caught just a glimpse of the driver's face as he slowed down to pass me—mind you, I was facing away from the road, staring off at the lovely countryside—and I noticed he wore a ridiculous purple waistcoat."

"Who was it?"

"I wasn't sure. The fellow seemed vaguely familiar. And I didn't think much of it until supper at the Red Lion."

"Was he there?"

"Not only was he there, but I happened to overhear his conversation. Something about a surefire plan for a fortune and catching the next boat to America. I didn't think anything of it until I realized I'd seen him at the jeweler's in London and on the road to Dorchester. And then I remembered that I had a ring worth a bloody fortune in my pocket. I put two and two together and thought I'd better make sure the ring was safe."

"Do you really think this man was following you, intent on stealing the ring and fleeing to America?" Henrietta asked with a gasp.

"And let's face it, there aren't many reasons to venture out to Dorset, other than for the duke's wedding. Or his wedding ring."

"Oh, God! Do you think he stole the ring already? He could be halfway across the Atlantic by now!"

"No, because I anticipated that he would try to steal it. So I hid it," Jack said proudly. Henrietta felt a rush of relief. He had the ring. It was safely hidden away. Within hours this whole debacle would be resolved.

"Where did you hide it?"

"That's the thing. I don't quite remember," Jack said. He gave her a sheepish version of his famous grin. It did not make her swoon. Not at all.

"I'm going to close my eyes, take a deep breath, count backward from ten, and ask that question again. I hope to have a better answer. Please, Jack."

"I may have had a few, so I'm not sure exactly, but I think I stuck it in a low beam in my room at the inn. The good news is, I don't think he stole it."

"One hopes. One very desperately hopes."

# CHAPTER ELEVEN

*"Marriage is an abhorrent institution that stifles the liberty of man!" Jack cried out. A pub full of drunk blokes cried out in agreement. "Hear! Hear!"*

*"Don't tell the duke I said that," Jack mumbled. Annie just rolled her eyes. Not that Jack noticed; he'd been looking at her breasts.*

*"On the way to the duke's wedding are ya?" Jack turned and looked at a small man who had taken the seat beside him.*

*"What business is it to you?" Jack slurred.*

*"The duke's wedding. Has a ring to it," the man said flashing a grin that would not sell a single bottle of Smythson's Smelling Salts. "Say, I heard a rumor about the ring ..."*

The Red Lion Inn

They arrived at the inn around midday—far later than expected after some wrong turns and some bickering over asking for directions. Their nerves were frayed. This time tomorrow the wedding would be taking place. Jack didn't even want to think about what would happen if the ring was not here.

The Red Lion was just as Jack vaguely remembered it. There was a large parlor with tables and chairs, a very well-endowed maid serving mugs of warm ale, and a very short, very rotund, and very bald innkeeper.

"Welcome back, my lord!" The innkeeper, who went by the name of Jenkins, greeted him warmly, which gave Jack an uneasy impression that he'd spent far too much money on his last visit, which meant he'd had far too much to drink.

"My wife and I would like a room," Jack told him.

"Your wife?" Jenkins burst into such uproarious laughter his face reddened to a shade akin to a bottle of Bordeaux.

"Wife?" Henrietta asked as she tilted her head curiously. Jack cringed and stifled the urge to explain that they couldn't enter a rented bedchamber together otherwise.

"Were you not here the other night, declaring that marriage was an abhorrent institution that stifled the liberty of free men?"

Though it was likely true on both counts, Jack said smoothly, "You must have me confused with someone else."

"No, I swear it was you!" Jenkins exclaimed. "On the way to the duke's wedding, you were. It's coming back to me now. You said that a man's leg wasn't the only thing getting shackled."

"What ever—?" Henrietta had Questions. Jack had a rising temper.

*What if Henrietta really was his wife?* Then this old, pudgy, small-town innkeeper was likely ruining their holy union. Henrietta deserved so much better. She did not deserve to be a part of this scene.

Neither did Jack. And he did not want to describe his comment on leg shackling to Hen.

"I insist that you are mistaken," Jack said forcefully. But damn, he felt ridiculous arguing with a man who was probably only half as tall.

"Then you led the whole barroom in singing that old ballad, "I Hope I Die a Bachelor." Then, calling out to the buxom barmaid, Jenkins called, "Remember that, Annie?"

"Aye," she said. Judging by her expression, she did not remember the incident fondly.

"My wife and I would like a room. For the hour," Jack repeated firmly.

"You and your *'wife'* would like a room for an hour?" The evil little innkeeper gave another laugh that someone else might have described as jolly, but Jack was not in the mood.

"Preferably the same room ... that is ..."

Jenkins handed over the keys, smirking all the while.

"Second door on the left. As I'm sure you'll recall."

—✺—

*In the room*

Jack looked around the small, clean chamber. Dormer windows overlooked the high street. The high-pitched ceiling was supported by lower, exposed beams. The walls were white, the floor an uneven wood paneling. The only furnishings consisted of a bed, an armoire, and a nightstand.

*Look for the ring.* But all he saw was the bed. He was far too aware that Henrietta was near, a bundle of nervous energy already looking around the room for the cursed piece of jewelry. Try as he might, he couldn't regret having misplaced it. For then he wouldn't have fallen in love with Henrietta.

Had he—?

Jack pushed his fingers through his hair.

Henrietta peered under the bed.

Jack exhaled and paced. *Did he love her?*

She methodically searched the armoire drawers, one by one.

He certainly *needed* her.

Without her help, he would have just admitted the loss and prayed that his grin was enough to earn the forgiveness of the duke, the new duchess, and the dowager duchess. He might have lost his best friend and family over his absentmindedness. Aye, he needed her.

Yet as Jack watched her contort into an odd position so she might peer into the fireplace and up the chimney, he realized that yes, indeed, he truly loved her and he would not be happy without her as his wife.

Also, he *had* said everything Jenkins had accused him of, though he no longer meant a word of it. Not one.

He loved Henrietta. He wanted to marry Henrietta.

But there was just something he had to do before he proposed.

"If I recall correctly ..." he mused.

"What are you doing?"

Jack stretched and reached up to one of the beams across the ceiling. The man following him had been short, like the innkeeper, so Jack concluded that a high place, like a crevice in the gnarled old wood, was the best spot for the ring.

He slid his hands along the rough wood. Splinters. Damn.

Henrietta's gaze was intent upon him. *Don't cock this up, Jack.* Oh, he cared about the duke and his bride and their perfect day and the family heirloom. But he truly cared about Hen's good opinion of him.

And then ... oh God ... and then ... his fingers skimmed across something smooth. Something like gold, studded with priceless gemstones. The ring.

Jack grinned. Oh, did he grin. Because happily ever after was just around the corner.

With the bauble in his hand, he dropped to one knee before Henrietta.

He held out the ring for her review.

"Oh, it's beautiful," she sighed, slipping the ring onto her finger and holding it up to admire it in the light.

"Hen ..."

"You found it, Jack!" She beamed at him. He would have felt like the luckiest man in the world if she weren't utterly missing the fact that he was trying to propose.

"Henrietta ..."

"Oh, goodness! I am so relieved!" She kissed him briefly on the lips and started toward the door. Jack remained on one knee while she chattered on, oblivious. "For a moment there, I feared that all was lost, but—"

"Miss Henrietta Black," he said firmly.

"Jack? Whatever are you doing?"

"I'm trying to propose, Hen."

Slowly, she turned. She took a few steps toward him. They clasped hands. All the feelings he wasn't sure how to convey managed to arrange themselves into words.

"It's simple, really. We suit—in spite of our vastly different temperaments—or perhaps because of it. I need you to keep me focused and you need me to help you be a bit more adventurous. But most of all, Hen, I have fallen in love with you. Will you do me the honor of becoming my beloved wife?"

# CHAPTER TWELVE

*Do not lose the ring. Do not ruin the wedding.*

*—Jack's drunken thoughts the night he hid the ring*

Henrietta was, quite simply, speechless. She had never imagined anyone would propose to her, let alone a man like Jack. He was handsome, kind, made her heart wildly skip beats and lud, the way that man kissed a girl!

But what of Sophronia?

She relied on Henrietta. And even though she'd given her blessing to indulge with a rogue, she hadn't said anything about marrying one. And leaving her. Alone. In her old age.

And they had to get back to the house soon. Dinner would be in a few hours and everyone probably noticed she had gone missing and—

Actually, they probably hadn't noticed her absence at all. Henrietta spent most of her life in Sophronia's apartments, keeping the old lady company and generally keeping out of the way of the duke and his family. No one really paid much attention to her.

Except that rogue Jack, who had caused her tremendous amounts of trouble. Yet he'd also given her tremendous amounts of pleasure.

Jack, Lord Willoughby.

Was proposing. Marriage. To her.

Any second now, her heart would resume beating and she would remember how to breathe. Then her brain could work and she could reply.

"Yes," she said breathlessly. "Yes, I'll marry you."

He swept her into his arms, and Henrietta knew this was the right thing to do. Sophronia would understand Henrietta wanting love and a family of her own. Or perhaps they could have a long engagement, or perhaps ...

Later. Henrietta would worry about that later. Right now she was being thoroughly kissed and loved by this rogue. Just a moment after that, her clothes were finding their way to the floor one layer at a time. It wasn't long before she was once again treated to the glorious sight of Jack in very little clothing.

And a moment after *that* Henrietta discovered that, in some things, Jack's attention span did not waver at all. He kissed her deeply as they lay on the bed and she surrendered to the great pleasure of his hot, bare skin against hers. She threaded her fingers through his hair and held him close, never wanting to let him go. Exquisite moments passed while he lavished attention on her breasts—his strong, warm hands and his hot mouth doing things that had her gasping in pleasure. Jack then explored her belly, the curve of her hips, and the outrageous sensitivity of the soft skin of her inner thighs.

He glanced up at her. His eyes darkened. Focused. Determined. She sighed.

And then with his mouth and his hands he did wicked things, such that she'd never imagined. He touched her there, stroking until she was wet and teasing her until she was writhing and quite nearly begging for something she instinctively craved.

"Wait for me, Hen," he whispered as he lay above her, settling his weight on hers and enveloping her in tremendous warmth. He found her hands, interlacing their fingers together. She held on tight as she felt him at her entrance.

There was so much she didn't know. But there was so much more she wanted. And above all she trusted Jack not to hurt her. She just had no idea how much pleasure he'd bring to her ...

"I want you," she whispered, gazing into his darkened eyes. He claimed her mouth for a kiss as he slowly thrust into her. Her breath caught in her throat at this strange, new, wildly pleasurable sensation of him inside of her. And then he began to move in a steady rhythm that seemed designed to drive her mad with desire. Jack, too. She felt his hands grip hers and she heard him groan in pleasure. She heard him gasp and it only made her want him *more*. They moved together, a tangle of limbs. She wasn't sure where she ended and he began. When he drove into her harder, she bucked her hips to meet his because ... because ... he reached down between them and stroked her there. It took but a moment before she cried out in a pleasure she'd never dreamt of. Jack, too, seemed to hit the same dizzying heights, calling her name as he reached his climax. Through it all, he never let her go.

# CHAPTER THIRTEEN

*Ring—check. Beautiful and beloved betrothed—check. What could possibly go wrong?*

*—Jack's innermost thoughts on the drive back to Kingstag*

Jack and Henrietta were jolted from their lovely reverie by church bells ringing, indicating the hour had grown late. Quickly and haphazardly they helped each other dress. It became quite plain that while Jack might have a future as a lady's maid, Henrietta would never be hired as a valet. She could not tie a cravat if her life depended on it. But there was no time to bother. They needed to hurry back to Kingstag.

"Just an *hour?* With your *wife?*" Jenkins called out after them.

Jack stifled a devilishly long string of curses.

"We will not be honeymooning at the Red Lion in Dorchester," he muttered.

"Honeymoon! Married!" Henrietta was in a bit of a daze. Still, she remembered to check that yes, the ring was snug on her finger. The gorgeous, sparkling diamond-and-sapphire heirloom was impossibly beautiful. The new duchess, Miss Grey, was one lucky woman. Or she would be, once they returned safely to the house with the ring in their possession.

Hippolyta was brought round and they climbed in and drove off. It wasn't long before they left the town and were all alone on an open country road.

"Do you think we'll make it back in time for supper?" she asked.

"As long as nothing goes wrong," Jack replied. "We know the route now."

"And we have the ring." Again, she held out her hand to admire the way it sparkled in the late afternoon sun.

"The horses have rested," Jack added. Indeed, the beasts were animated and eager to run.

"And we're in Hippolyta, the most terrifyingly fast carriage in England," Henrietta said, with a death grip on the rail and on Jack too for good measure.

"What could possibly go wrong?" Jack mused, gazing down loving at Hen before guiding the horses through a curve in the road.

"That!" Henrietta shrieked, and pointed to a carriage stopped ahead.

"Whoa!" Jack pulled hard on the horses, urging them to slow.

"Stand and deliver!"

A man stood in the carriage parked in the center of the road. It would be too dangerous to attempt to drive around him, especially since he brandished two pistols. Henrietta shrieked. Again.

"You!" Jack seethed, recognizing the man who'd followed him all the way down from London. It was the hideous purple waistcoat that gave him away.

"The ring, if you please."

"No!" Jack shouted. The man aimed his guns at Jack.

"No!" Henrietta shouted.

The man trained his pistols on Henrietta. On his betrothed. On the love of his life. Jack felt his heart stop for a moment. *What could possibly go wrong?* Why did he have to *say* that? He couldn't breathe. He couldn't think. His heart was lodged in his throat. Now that he'd found Henrietta, he couldn't lose her.

"Give him the ring, Hen," Jack said. Wessex would understand, surely. The magistrate would recover it later. It was just a stupid piece of jewelry. It paled in comparison to his lovely Henrietta.

"I will do no such thing," she huffed. The nefarious man tilted his head curiously at the slip of a girl refusing the man with two locked and loaded pistols in hand. "Do you know what we have gone through to get this ring?" she hollered at him. Truly, Sophronia had rubbed off on her.

"Do you know what *I* have gone through?" the man cried out.

"But it *belongs to us*," Henrietta said.

"You probably shouldn't argue with the man with the pistols," Jack urged.

"You probably want to listen to your companion," the man said. Then he trained his pistols on Jack. Henrietta's eyes went wide and she gasped.

"Very well, you can have the ring," Henrietta said. "Come and get it."

Keeping the guns pointed at Jack, the man jumped down from his carriage. He ambled over as if he had all the time in the world.

"Hold on, Hen," Jack said under his breath. And then, with a crack of his whip, the horses shot off at a gallop.

"Come back here!" The man's shouts were lost in the wind. He didn't stand a chance. Not when he was on foot and had to rush back to his hired hack and the tired old brood mares pulling it. Hippolyta flew onward.

"It's a good thing you did that," Henrietta said.

"It was a damned risky thing I did," Jack said, finally able to breathe again. "But I had to get you away from danger."

"Just as well. I daresay we wouldn't have survived if he'd gotten close and discovered that I cannot get the ring off."

# CHAPTER FOURTEEN

*The important thing was that they had the ring. The most*
*important thing was that Henrietta agreed to keep him from*
*disasters like this for the rest of their lives together.*

—*Jack's deliriously happy thoughts*

Kingstag Castle

Early evening, before dinner

**H**enrietta and Jack arrived home to find the house in an uproar.
One of the duke's young sisters fainted on seeing them and there was
a frantic call for Smythson's Smelling Salts, which were procured
immediately from the reticule of Lady Grey.

"Smythson's Smelling Salts to the rescue," exclaimed Miss
Rosanne Lacy.

"I told you lot they'd run off together!" Sophronia declared,
cackling gleefully. Henrietta and her companion shared a smile.

"*She* has not needed smelling salts," said the younger Miss Lacy.

"Where have you two been?" the duke queried.

"We were in such a state after we realized you two were missing,"
the duchess said. "Wherever did you go? And why?"

"The important thing is that we have the ring," Jack said. "Please,
keep that in mind."

Henrietta held up her hand with the ring firmly stuck on her
finger. She managed a faint smile. As long as no one asked her for
the ring, everything would be fine.

"Oh, let's do have a look at it," Lady Grey exclaimed, tugging Henrietta's hand forward so she could get a better view. "Helen, come look at your magnificent betrothal ring."

"It's lovely," Helen said faintly, not seeming to be remotely interested in it.

"Try it on," Lady Grey urged.

"Oh, that's not necessary," Helen said. "It's already been fitted for me. I'm sure it's fine."

"Yes. What she said," Henrietta added. She saw that Jack had taken the duke aside, probably to explain about the mad criminal in the vicinity. Footmen would be dispatched along with the magistrate, the man would be apprehended, and then the wedding would proceed as planned. *If only Henrietta could get the blasted ring off her finger.*

"Is the ring stuck on your finger, Miss Black?" The duchess narrowed her eyes. Lady Grey advanced toward her. The pack of young girls surged forward, intent upon a close-up view of the scene that was about to unfold.

"Give me your hand," Lady Grey said, reaching out.

Henrietta glanced desperately at Jack. He had to save her from the onslaught of wedding-minded-mamas.

"The other important thing to remember is that we're engaged," Jack said loudly. Then he pulled Henrietta into an embrace and pressed a kissed upon her lips. In front of everyone. The matter of the ring was quickly forgotten. For the moment.

# EPILOGUE

Henrietta and Jack were married in a simple ceremony one month later. The duke and his new duchess were in attendance, along with Sophronia, of course, and other dear friends who had met and fallen in love at the same house party. There was not a dry eye in the room as the unexpected couple promised to love and cherish each other forever.

"With this ring—" Henrietta said, her voice wavering. This was more happiness than she had ever hoped for. "—I thee wed."

"With this ring, which I promise not to lose or misplace—" Jack said, to the amusement of everyone in attendance. Though truly, they had no idea. "—I thee wed. *Forever*."

# ABOUT THE AUTHOR

Maya Rodale began reading romance novels in college at her mother's insistence and is now the author of numerous smart and sassy romances. A champion of the romance genre and its readers, she is also the author of the non-fiction book *Dangerous Books For Girls: The Bad Reputation Of Romance Novels, Explained* and a co-founder of Lady Jane's Salon, a national reading series devoted to romantic fiction. Maya lives in New York City with her darling dog and a rogue of her own. To discover more of her books, visit her on the web at www.MayaRodale.com.

### ~ALSO BY MAYA RODALE~
THE WICKED WALLFLOWER
THE BAD BAD BOY BILLIONAIRE'S WICKED ARRANGEMENT
WALLFLOWER GONE WILD
THE BAD BAD BOY BILLIONAIRE'S GIRL GONE WILD

### ~THE WRITING GIRLS~
A GROOM OF ONE'S OWN
A TALE OF TWO LOVERS
THE TATTOOED DUKE
SEDUCING MR. KNIGHTLY
THREE SCHEMES AND A SCANDAL

### ~THE NEGLIGENT CHAPERONES~
THE HEIR AND THE SPARE
THE ROGUE AND THE RIVAL

# P.S. I LOVE YOU

Miranda Neville

# CHAPTER ONE

A group of officers invaded the common room of the Horse Guards in a clatter of spurs, drawing Captain Christian Lord Bruton from the quiet pleasure of a good book.

That was the trouble with belonging to a fashionable regiment permanently stationed in the middle of London. Too many sprigs of the nobility and gentry, large and clumsy like a pack of half-grown dogs—though well-bred dogs—sucking the air from the room and braying about their tedious concerns to those who cared not a whit. Well-oiled by quantities of after-dinner port, they were off to make the rounds of the evening's assemblies, followed by a visit to a house inhabited by ladies of lower birth and looser morals.

"Are you coming, Frank?" someone asked Lieutenant Newnham, the most popular man in the regiment, who'd been sitting quietly, minding his own business. "What about you, Bruton?" another fellow said, with much less enthusiasm and a note of doubt that indicated a modicum of intelligence.

Christian would rather be broken on a rack than expose himself to Lady Beaufetheringstone's ball. "No, thank you. I'll take in the last act at Drury Lane before my supper engagement with Miss Clara Morris."

A solidly built subaltern of extreme youth loomed over him. "Nice for you, Lord Cicatrix, being able to afford the prettiest dancer in London." His side whiskers, barely grown, twitched.

The room fell into an anticipatory silence. In the past Christian would have called him out, but when he advanced to the rank of captain he'd foresworn duels and vowed to defend himself with words alone. Christian guessed the newest officer had uttered the nickname on a dare from his fellows, who eagerly awaited the lad's destruction by one of his infamous volleys of sarcasm. Not in the mood to indulge the idiot mob, he let the insult pass. After all, the man had a point. Miss Morris would love him—if and when they came to an arrangement—for his deep purse and high rank and only if she could bring herself to tolerate his ruined face.

"I believe Miss Morris appreciates my conversation," he said mildly. "Please, take Frank with you and leave me in peace."

"Go without me, fellows," Frank said. "I have something to do."

As the officers clomped out, Christian raised a forefinger to summon his would-be tormentor, who edged forward looking suitably nervous. "Lieutenant," he said softly. "There's no need for fancy words. The slash across my face is a scar. A simple, descriptive, unambiguous word. A scar. If you would like one of your own to mar the softness of your downy cheeks I would be happy to oblige." The youngster appeared likely to soil himself. "But this time, because I'm in an exceptionally mellow mood, I shall let you go. I advise you to remove yourself quickly before I change my mind."

A minute later the room was blessedly quiet, leaving Christian in the sole company of one of the few officers whose company he positively enjoyed. There wasn't a better man in the world, let alone the Household Cavalry, than Lieutenant Francis Newnham. The ladies of London idolized his handsome face and splendid figure and forgave his lack of conversation. Men admired him as a bruising rider, a good fencer, a fearless boxer, and an excellent shot. His unfailing cheerfulness and good humor made him universally loved. Even Christian, not a man given to tolerance of human frailty, held his first cousin in unwavering affection.

"Are you quite well, Frank? Not like you to miss an evening's entertainment. You're not on duty, are you?"

Frank shook his head. "I have to write a letter."

"What brings about this unnatural ambition? Has Aunt Cecilia been complaining again?"

"Mama? No. She's in town. Called on her this morning." Helping himself to another glass of brandy, Frank sat down at the desk provided for officers of the regiment overcome by the urge for written communication.

Christian watched in some amusement as his cousin, betraying his lack of practice, made a hash of sharpening his pen. He returned to his book but found his enjoyment of Byron's latest cantos marred by Frank's gusty sighs, punctuated by hopeful glances in his direction.

"If you can't get on with it, go away. What is wrong with you?"

"I'm in love."

"For God's sake! Dancer or actress?" Frank's intimate relations had so far been confined to the demimonde. "Either way, she isn't going to want you for your literary skills."

"You don't understand. I'm truly in love this time." An expression of deep fatuity settled on Frank's symmetrical features. "With Miss Rosanne Lacy."

"Warnford's daughter? Are you thinking of *marriage?*"

"She's the most beautiful girl in the world. I met her staying with Norton in Leicestershire and—" His face turned from idiocy to panic. "—I asked her father's permission to write to her."

"What made you do such a foolish thing?"

"How else will I make an impression? You know what I'm like, Chris. A man of action. Never can think of much to say to a woman. I'd be happy to fight a duel or save her from a villain, but there never seems to be an opportunity."

"Very true. In these civilized times, the daughters of peers rarely fall into the clutches of criminals. Such a shame."

"I knew you'd understand," Frank said, with the bashful smile that made marriage-minded misses melt while their mamas invited him to dinner and would probably have done his washing had he so asked. "Trouble is, I can't think of anything to say."

Christian looked cynically at Frank's ridiculously perfect face. "I hardly think it matters. She's probably halfway in love with you. I take it she doesn't live in London?"

"Dorset. She spent the season here some years ago, I think, but her family don't care for London."

Christian nodded sagely. "She must be a desperate spinster. She'll have you."

Incapable of taking offense, Frank ignored the aspersion cast on the object of his fascination. "Miss Lacy has turned down dozens of suitors. I told you she's a beauty. Clever too. I'm a fool to think she'll accept me."

One of Frank's virtues was an astonishing lack of vanity. He had no idea that he was the handsomest man in London—no, in England—in the estimation of several enamored ladies. "What do you want to say?" Christian asked, giving up his plan for a couple of hours of quiet reading.

"I don't *want* to say anything. Give me an idea."

"Tell her what you admire about her."

Tweaking his nose with the end of the quill, Frank relapsed into deep thought. "I can't," he said. "It wouldn't be proper to tell a young lady I like her ..." He traced a curvy shape with his free hand.

"Fine, are they?"

"Very fine. Wait! I can't discuss my future bride's bosom with you."

"Nor with her, apparently. Start with the eyes. Women always like that. What color are they?"

"Blue, maybe brown. Darkish."

"Avoid being specific. It wouldn't do to get it wrong."

"Christian," Frank said after another fruitless minute spent staring at a blank page. "You're good at words. Would you ...?"

Really, Frank was hopeless. Even the cynical Earl of Bruton wasn't impervious to the distress of a man in dire need. "Very well. I'll dictate. *Dear Miss Lacy ...*"

"Dash it, Chris. Do I have to write it myself?"

"You intend to marry the girl, right? Despite your aversion to pens, you are not going to be able to live with her for fifty years or more without her ever seeing your handwriting. *Dear Miss Lacy. As I sit in my gloomy barracks ...*"

"The barracks of the Royal Horse Guards are not gloomy. Best in the whole army."

"Don't be so literal and write it down. *As I sit in my gloomy barracks, the thought of you is a beacon of light, an unflickering candle glimpsed through a storm. I sink into the dark pools of your lovely eyes ...*"

**R**osanne Lacy planned to slip out after breakfast and seek the privacy of her favorite spot in the garden. She wanted to read her letter away from the hopeful eyes of her mother and the curiosity of her sister. Only the first goal proved achievable; not for the first time had she underestimated Kate's persistence.

"Where are you going?" Kate caught her at the garden door.

"Outside. You'll catch cold, and as your elder I order you to stay in by the fire."

The little pest had been ignoring her advice since she learned to walk and talk. "It's a lovely day for March. I'm coming with you."

"It's windy. You hate wind."

"In that case you should stay inside, too. The pages of your letter may blow away."

"What letter?"

Kate cast her eyes to the iron-gray sky. "Please, Rosie! I made Thompson show me the post when it arrived today. You have a letter from *him*. Already."

Three days ago, Lord and Lady Warnford and their elder daughter had returned from a house party near Melton Mowbray. Seventeen-year-old Kate, bored at being left at home, must have detected the whiff of excitement in their mama and wormed the truth out of her.

"Yes," Rosanne said. "I have a letter from Mr. Newnham. Papa gave him permission to write to me." She stepped firmly out onto the terrace with Kate at her heels. Giving up the fruitless effort to shake off her sister, she examined the unopened letter. "He must have written soon after he reached London."

"If he is so enamored, why did he leave Melton before you?"

"He has his military duties to attend to. That speaks well of him, I think."

"It would be better if, desperate with love, he disobeyed the orders of his commanding officer and pursued you to the ends of the earth. Or at least to Little Mickledon."

"He might be court marshaled and disgraced."

"Then he would beg you to flee the country with him and live like gypsies, evading the clutches of the army. Think how much fun that would be!"

"Think how uncomfortable! You should stop reading novels; you take them too seriously."

"What else am I supposed to do for entertainment?"

Kate had a point. Lord and Lady Warnford, apart from the occasional country house visit like their recent Leicestershire trip, preferred to remain cozily in Dorset with their daughters and their country neighbors. Much as Rosanne loved her family, it sometimes, even in winter, felt like being drowned in a warm bath.

"The sooner Mama and Papa take us to London the better, although I dread to think what you'll get up to, unleashed on the unsuspecting ton. It's worth getting married just so I won't have to witness your notion of taking the town by storm. And take the blame when you get into trouble."

"While I can see you'd want to be wed to avoid being cast into the shade by me—" Kate scampered backward to avoid a sisterly swat. "—I'd like to know what made Lieutenant Newnham turn your head when every man in southwest England has failed."

Rosanne had asked herself the same thing. She was only half joking when she claimed she'd prefer not to share Kate's debut season. She'd rejected half a dozen suitors without the slightest regret. Going through a London season as the lively Kate's spinster sister didn't distress her precisely, but it did make her think about the future. It was time to have an establishment and a life of her own. Also, her mother was driving her mad.

"I'm twenty-two. Some people—and by 'some people' I mean Mama—think I'm almost on the shelf."

"It would have to be a tall shelf, or your feet will reach the ground."

"I trust my feet will always remain the ground. One flibbertigibbet in the family is quite enough. Also, for your information, Mr. Newnham is taller than me by a good six inches."

"Aren't you going to see what he has to say for himself?"

"Something, I hope. He's not a great one for conversation."

"Speaking for myself, I have no objection to silence in a man, as long as he listens to me. But you? You're always complaining about gentlemen being dull-witted. What did you see in him?"

Rosanne drew her shawl around her shoulders and recalled the moment that she first encountered the splendor that was Frank Newnham. When he sauntered into the Melton Assembly Room there had been a collective gasp from every woman in the place, followed by a reverent hush.

"It was at a ball," she said.

"Did he stride across the room, thrust aside your partner, and sweep you onto the floor?"

"Quite the opposite. There are always plenty of sporting gentlemen in Melton, but many of them refuse to dance, especially with the less pretty girls. Lizzie Norton is not only pale and thin, she's also very shy. When he was presented to us, he immediately asked her to stand up with him. I never saw her so happy."

"He snubbed you!"

"Not at all. He danced with me later, twice. He said he'd wanted to immediately but his mother had told him the prettiest girls never want for partners and he must be sure to make sure that *all* the young ladies enjoy themselves. Don't you think that's sweet?"

Kate, possessed of overweening self-confidence and no fear that she would ever be a wallflower, was unimpressed. "Sounds like nonsense to me, not to mention the kind of thing our mother would say. I would prefer a man who broods in the corner, disdaining the company and refusing to dance with anyone until he laid eyes on *me*. Your Mr. Newnham sounds a bit dull."

"Oh no! He is the most delightful man. I do think kindness and good nature are the most important qualities in a husband." Kate shook her head in patent disdain. "You wouldn't know because you aren't out, but the handsomest men are often overly conceited and quite disagreeable."

"Handsome, is he?"

"Lord, Kate!" Rosanne gave up attempting to appear high-minded. "I never laid eyes on a better-looking man. I believe he must be the pinnacle of masculine beauty. Such a face and figure as you wouldn't believe. I could look at him forever. But of good character, you understand. Without a good character, looks are nothing."

"Oh no. Nothing at all."

"I am not so shallow."

"Absolutely not. Describe the paragon."

"Tall, of course. He's a cavalry officer, so very strong and muscular. Fair hair, side whiskers, but not long ones I'm glad to say, a firm chin, a straight nose of exactly the right size. And best of all, his eyes! Blue as a summer sky ..." Rosanne closed her eyes and relived the dizziness of sharing a country dance with Frank Newnham.

"You look like an idiot. Stop daydreaming and read the letter, or I shall."

Rosanne broke the seal to reveal a page covered with large, rather careless writing.

"Goodness," she said finally. "Gracious." And because she knew Kate would persuade her in the end and she needed another opinion, even that of her giddy sister, she read it again, aloud. "*Dear Miss Lacy. As I sit in my gloomy barracks the thought of you is a beacon of light, an unflickering candle glimpsed through a storm. I sink into the dark pools of your lovely eyes, feast my gaze in contemplation of your perfect countenance. I curse the duty that forces us apart. My only consolation is the hope that you will assuage the longing of your poor admirer with a few words. I shall remain in painful diffidence until I hear from you. I beg you, tell me what you do, what you read, whom you see! I am jealous of the pen, clasped by your slender hand, but will treasure the paper that reveals your precious thoughts. Until then, Miss Lacy, I remain your humble and respectful servant, Francis Newnham."*

For at least half a minute only birdsong disturbed the spring morning. If nothing else, the letter had rendered Kate speechless. "What do you think?" Rosanne asked.

"I think you'd better not show the letter to Mama."

"No, indeed. She'll either forbid the correspondence or demand an immediate marriage."

"He seems to admire you excessively." Kate's lips twitched at the corners.

"From anyone else, I would think it a joke." She perused the lines closely, searching for truth. "Mr. Newnham did not seem the sort of man to make a jest of me. Yet I wouldn't have expected he would express himself in such ... florid language." A vision of the author, splendid in scarlet regimentals, danced in her brain. "You know, it is quite flattering to be addressed with such fervor. And there is a certain elegance to his prose, however overwrought."

"If you say so."

"Perhaps he was nervous." That was it. "I'm sure he was."

"What shall you do?"

"I shall write back, of course."

"**W**hy the frown?" Christian asked. Frank had been reading the letter for a good quarter of an hour. "Do you need help deciphering the mysteries of your lady love's thoughts?"

"I think she may not have liked your letter."

"Your letter, my boy. *Your* letter. And it was a fine letter, designed to flatter and cajole, therefore bound to appeal to any female."

"Listen to this. *I confess to no little astonishment at being addressed in such terms so early in our acquaintance.*"

"If she's so easily shocked, you're better off without her."

"I cannot make out the next bit," Frank said, his noble brow forming perfect ridges. "*I'm also both worried and confused about your claim to sink into the dark pools of my eyes. Firstly, because my eyes are a light gray. Secondly, if you are under water you cannot see my countenance.* What can she mean?"

Having previously regarded Frank's infatuation and his own assistance with the letter as an insignificant joke, Christian discovered a glimmer of interest in Miss Lacy. "Either she has a very literal mind or a sense of humor. Perhaps both. By God, she chides me for my metaphors and she has a point. What else does she have to say?"

Frank handed him the letter. "Read it yourself."

Miss Lacy wrote in evenly formed characters with an elegant forward slant.

> *In answer to your questions, I am enjoying the charms of Little Mickledon Hall. I have the company of twenty thousand daffodils, three dogs, a cat, a flock of ducks, and my parents and sister. The former you met, the latter did not accompany us to Leicestershire, since she is Not Yet Out. Though almost eighteen, Kate will not, to her considerable distress, make her debut this year. Mama and Papa prefer country life and secretly hope that she will find a husband before she persuades them to take her to London next year. Or else convert to Rome and elope to a convent.*
>
> *You would think that being so busy with ducks, daffodils, etc. I would have little time to read. But somehow I manage to consume prodigious quantities of books because I am a firm believer that reading improves the mind. Dedicated perusal of the novels contained in Dorchester's circulating library have improved my mind to such an extent that I am in danger of becoming a bluestocking. You have been duly warned, and I shall not hold it against you should you prefer to cut the connection and cease this correspondence. If you reply, I would be interested in hearing how you undertake mental improvement.*
>
> *Yours sincerely, Rosanne Lacy*

Lowering the sheet, Christian felt a rare grin stretch the scar on his cheek. "You *must* marry this girl, Frank. She will brighten up our family gatherings."

"I knew you'd like her. How shall I reply?" His voice held a note of panic. "About the mental improvement thing."

"She wants to know what kind of books you like."

Frank shifted uneasily. "Not a great reader, as you know, Chris. I often take a look at *The Morning Post*, avoiding the political reports, of course. And *The Sporting Calendar*. Lots of useful stuff in there."

"That's a good start. Then we'll burnish your credentials a little."

---

*Dear Miss Lacy,*

*Beauty is in the eye of the beholder. This beholder drowns in your eyes day and night, and at night the pool is dark. I concede that under those circumstance your countenance may not be easily regarded. Not to mention that a remarkable contortion would be needed to see your face while swimming around in your eyes. Your criticism of my prose was well deserved and I have saved you the trouble of finishing the job. The fact that you will not soon be traveling to London distresses me so much that I have been forced to take solace in much-needed mental improvement. Having exhausted the charms of* The Sporting Calendar *and* The Morning Post, *I resort to poetry. Your crowd of daffodils directed me to Wordsworth, yet somehow the joy of your letter put me in a less contemplative mood. The adventures of* The Giaour *have enlivened my dull existence these past days. If you have not yet had this work (I assume you, like every lady of my acquaintance, have sighed over* Childe Harold*) I will send it to you. What do you think of Byron? To my mind ...*

---

*Dear Mr. Newnham,*

*Will you despise me if I admit that I am no great lover of poetry? I like Byron more for his wit than his lyricism. I prefer my reading without rhymes. If I cannot find a work that offers believable and amiable characters and a story that ends well (such works are rarer than I would wish), I happily devour the narrative excesses of Minerva Press novels. But please lend me The Giaour because I would enjoy discussing it with you.*

———⟨∞⟩———

Dear Miss Lacy,

*I take the liberty of enclosing a newly published work by A Lady. I believe it satisfies your requirements ...*

———⟨∞⟩———

Dear Mr. Newnham,

*I apologize for my delay in writing, but I could not put the book down, and as soon as I finished I read it again. Pride and Prejudice is the best thing I ever encountered. Please tell me that the author has written a hundred such works ...*

———⟨∞⟩———

**T**wo months and sixteen letters later ...

"*Dear Mr. Newnham. The weather has reduced me to banality, so I will say only that this uncommonly wet and cold spring makes me more grateful for your letters. I have never regretted so much that my father refuses to go to London for the season. How can life at Little Mickledon compare with the diversions of the capital? You describe the performance of Kean in Othello and all I have to amuse you is the performance of a fox who broke into the henhouse two nights ago and rendered us short of eggs. My father's distress at the loss of his morning omelet is certainly histrionic but doesn't carry the same dramatic force as the unfortunate Moor possessed by the green-eyed monster. Neither can the parade in the Little Mickledon churchyard (I shall spare you an account of the bonnets since I know gentlemen have little patience for such important matters) compare to the trooping of your regiment. How I should like to see it! You must look splendid on your horse, galloping with saber brandished, ready to repel invaders.*"

Frank stopped reading and chuckled. "Miss Lacy has quite the wrong idea about the Household Cavalry. Wouldn't like to hear what the colonel had to say if I galloped around London with a drawn sword. Besides, Boney's on the run. Not likely to turn up now. Do you think we should explain?"

"I could be mistaken," Christian said, "but I believe she is being mildly ironic."

"Is that a good thing?"

"*I* think so."

Frank grinned. "Glad you approve."

"Remind me, Frank, why you fell in love with her? Apart from her physical perfections, that is."

"I don't know, really. The moment I saw her, I knew she was the one for me."

"That sounds unwise. She might have turned out to be beautiful but stupid. Or ill-tempered, or cruel."

"But she didn't, did she? Rosanne is the cleverest and kindest lady in the world, as well as the most beautiful."

Christian couldn't argue. Though not able to opine on Miss Lacy's appearance, her letters suggested that she was in every other way worthy of his cousin. While Frank read the remainder of the letter, he wondered if his cousin was worthy of her. He didn't think Frank appreciated her letters on the same level that Christian did.

But if Frank wanted her, Christian owed him every assistance. He pushed him over to the desk and handed him a pen that he had sharpened himself.

"Do you think we could keep the letters shorter?" Frank said. "Damn it, Chris, my wrist gets tired when you make me write page after page."

"Nonsense. Miss Lacy is not a young lady to be impressed by slim platitudes. Chin up, man. It's time to move forward a step. *Dear Rosanne. I am presumptuous, I know, but Rosanne is how I think of you. Beautiful Rosanne. Rosanne of the kind words and clever wit. Rosanne of my heart. You consume my every thought, haunt my waking hours, and disturb my dreams. There, I have challenged propriety and said what I should not but I cannot help it. I must speak.*"

"Slow down." Frank scribbled frantically. "*Speak.* There. I knew I was right to have you compose the letters. I could never come up with anything so fine on my own. This is exactly how I feel. What next?"

Christian cleared his throat. *"For weeks, your letters have been my only comfort, but they no longer suffice. I wish to see you, hear you—dare I say it?— touch you. I yearn for your presence. In a month I have leave from the regiment, and I hope you will receive me kindly if I should happen to be in the neighborhood of Dorset."*

Frank put down his pen and shook his wrist. "Do I have leave?"

"I spoke to the colonel today. We both have the month of June free. You must have noticed her hints that she would like to see you. I don't believe Edmund Kean is the only reason she wishes she were in London."

"I want to see her, too. I'm going to Wessex's wedding, and Little Mickledon's only twenty miles or so from Kingstag. I could do it."

"Sooner you than me. I intend to decline my invitation, but I grant that the timing is fortuitous for you."

It occurred to Christian that Frank might—would—have difficulty maintaining the quality of his discourse once in the presence of his beloved. He'd just have to bowl her over with the potency of his physical presence. When confronted with the glory of his person, Rosanne would be too befuddled to notice his lack of wit. Women never did, Christian thought, absent-mindedly fingering the livid scar that slashed down his cheek and disappeared into his collar.


Rosanne tore through the topiary walk to her secret place, the stone bench next to the ornamental pond, well out of sight of the house. She was in no state to deal with Kate's mischievous nonsense, her mother's determined cheerfulness, or, Heaven forbid, her father in any mood.

*How could he?* How could her mother bear it?

She had been brought up to suppress any hint of temper as unsuitable for a lady. A lady must be calm. A lady must refrain from embarrassing herself and distressing others with unseemly displays of emotion. A lady must be happy, because then those around her would be happy too. At moments like this, Rosanne feared she was no lady.

Her recent discovery made her want to scream, very loudly indeed. Since this might attract the attention of the gardener, she seized a handful of gravel from the path and flung it into the water. The stones were too small to make a satisfying splash and succeeded only in alarming the carp that lived in the pond. The fact that letting her anger harm the innocent—albeit only fish—supported her mother's precepts didn't make her feel better. She wished she were a hundred miles away from Little Mickledon and anyone by the name of Lacy.

A new letter from Frank, her obvious means of escape, rested in her pocket. But he was all breezy good humor, although his letters often displayed an ironic edge that she'd never detected in the few days they'd spent together. Today she didn't want affability. She'd rather read something dark and dreadful and filled with passion.

Perching on the bench she unfolded a single sheet. A shorter letter than usual, but a wonderful one. Not dark and dreadful, but the passion was there. Frank loved her! He didn't say it in so many words, but surely that was what he meant.

*Rosanne of my heart.*

Her own heart soared and her pain receded, to be replaced with a new and raw emotion.

He loved her and she had an overwhelming desire to see him, to feel his arms around her. She read the letter again, relishing every word. Did he linger over each sentence? She rather thought not. It was more like the dashing cavalry officer to attack the business of composition with impetuous zest. She imagined the words pouring from brain to pen. Tracing the careless trails of ink with her forefinger, she felt a physical connection to their author and a shivery excitement.

*I wish to touch you.*

In recent weeks, curiosity about the intimate side of marriage, and a kind of yearning, had possessed her. It was another reason to put an end to spinsterhood. Closing her eyes and envisioning Frank Newnham's handsome face and magnificent figure, she longed for it. Gentlemen were habitually swathed with cloth and buttoned to the throat. They didn't show their necks and bosoms as women did. The only bits of Frank she'd ever seen uncovered were his hands and face. It didn't seem quite fair. She'd like to start with the neck cloth, unwind it ...

She started at her unruly thoughts. Today, of all days, she mustn't forget the darker side of male desire. A darker side that her father had succumbed to. She still could hardly believe that the bluff, plain-spoken, affectionate man had betrayed his wife. She wondered how she would react if it happened to her. Well, it would not. She wouldn't allow it. Besides, she trusted Frank. He was a good man and he loved her.

Only by trusting him with the feelings she couldn't share with her own family might she elicit the reassurance she needed.

Christian experienced an unusual attack of nerves when the reply came from Rosanne. Had he advised his cousin badly? Would he—Frank—be answered with disdain for his bold declaration? Forcing his arms to his sides when he wanted to throttle Frank and tell him to hurry up, he hid his anxiety as Frank fumbled with the seal.

"My word. Listen to how the letter opens!" Frank said. *"Dear Mr. Newnham, Frank. Yes, Frank, for that is how I think of you.* How about that?"

"Go on." This was splendid news, just the response they'd hoped for. The sinking in Christian's stomach was merely relief.

*"I write today in an agitation of spirits, for I learned something dreadful. Oh, Frank! In the months we have exchanged letters, I have come to feel such affection and friendship for you that now I can confide a most distressing secret. I don't have to tell you that these words are for your eyes alone and must go no further."*

"You shouldn't be reading this." Christian and Frank spoke in unison, then the latter goggled at his cousin.

"It's addressed to me," Frank said. "As a gentleman I can't go blabbing what she tells me in confidence."

"Don't be an ass. I'm a gentleman too, and I'll keep Rosanne's confidence to the death. But I wrote those letters and I have a right to know what she says."

Frank was as unhappy as Christian had ever seen him. "I don't think you should call Miss Lacy Rosanne," he said stiffly.

"How are we going to answer the letter if you won't tell me what it says?"

*Go on, Frank. Tell me to go to hell and you'll write your own damn letter.* That's what he ought to say, but Christian hoped he wouldn't. He wanted to know what had upset her. Perhaps there was something he could do to help. "Come on, Frank. We're like brothers. You can trust me as well as she can trust you."

"You're right, Chris. I'm sorry to doubt you."

91

"No apology needed. Now let's find out what Miss Lacy has to say."

*"I have two sisters. Kate, of course, as you know from my letters, but also another. I fear I have begun the story at the end so let me arrange my disordered thoughts. For several years a Miss Mary Birch, who is now ten years old, has visited us for a month every summer. She's a sweet child and I enjoy her visits. We were always told that she was the daughter of a friend of my father and came to us for country air while her widowed mother enjoyed a holiday. Now that I know the truth, I see how absurd the story is. She and her mother live in Dorchester, a mere ten miles from Little Mickledon and scarcely a smoke-filled metropolis. Today, as a result of unintentional eavesdropping, I learned that Mary is my father's natural daughter. Oh Frank! Now that I know, I see signs of our kinship: she had light brown curls like me, Kate's blue eyes, and my father's smile. Like me, she enjoys stories, and I have often read fairy tales to her in the nursery. I now understand my mother's air of disapproval whenever I mention little Mary. I should not burden you with these unsavory family affairs, but you are the only one I feel I can tell. Thank you for reading this. Next time I write, I shall be myself again and full of news about books and spring flowers and the local assembly and the mad things Kate says. For now, my dearest friend, I offer only a sad adieu. P.S. I do not blame little Mary. She is innocent in the whole affair. She will always be my sister, even if forever unacknowledged."*

Frank's voice cracked as he read the last sentence. "What a decent girl she is, my Rosanne. Not many ladies would be so kind."

Christian agreed. He also wanted to pummel Rosanne's father into the ground.

"You have to answer her at once," he said. "You must set her mind at rest."

"I don't understand you."

"Miss Lacy fears that you would behave like her father."

"She doesn't say so, does she?" Frank peered at the letter.

"Women do not always say what they mean."

"I don't see it, but I expect you are right. You would know better than I how she'd feel in this case. Of course, I wouldn't ever look at another woman if I were lucky enough to win Rosanne. How shall I tell her? Seems a bit awkward to bring it up."

"Subtlety, my dear boy. Now, write."

As Christian dictated the reply, he felt a twinge of regret that the recipient would never know how much it came from his own heart.

*"My dear Rosanne, I am honored that you shared your trouble with me. Your generosity of spirit touches me, and I have no doubt that you bring your little sister as much joy as you bring me with every word you write. But Rosanne, my dear, I feel for your unhappiness at discovering your father's behavior. Common enough, I fear, but distressing to a man's family and abhorrent to me that a man should so betray his vows. I'll say no more but if you wish for a sympathetic ear, I am here."*

**R**osanne's reply arrived by return of post. Frank was on duty all day and the missive sat in his box in the officers' quarters. It was all Christian could do not to rip it open. Their last letter worried him. Frank, as usual, had taken dictation like a lamb, never questioning his cousin's words. Pressing her to speak further of her father's sins was bold, indelicate even. Christian had his reasons for thinking Rosanne might want to talk about it. Suppose he was wrong and she was insulted? Suppose she broke off the correspondence?

Frank would be devastated.

He'd better go and get changed for his dinner engagement with Clara, who wasn't dancing that night. But as his servant helped him out of his uniform and into evening dress, he discovered a complete lack of interest in either dining with Clara or bedding her. There was nothing wrong with her. A perfectly pleasant companion and skilled lover. But their liaison, after only a couple of months, bored him. He wrote her a note and went downstairs to dine with the regiment.

Frank arrived only as the meal started, so Christian had to suffer through several excellent courses—the Guards did themselves proud in the mess—and endless toasts. At long last, he got Frank settled in the common room with brandy and Rosanne's letter.

"Why are you hovering over me like that?" Frank asked as, maddeningly, he sipped instead of reading.

Christian sank into the embrace of an armchair and took a deep breath, forcing himself to wait patiently for Frank to break the seal and unfold the sheet of fine, hot-pressed paper favored by Rosanne.

*"I am so happy that you think as I do on the subject. I did not like to say more in my last letter, but it is a relief to write of feelings that I cannot share with anyone else. I know my father is not the first gentleman to behave thus, and I do not know if Papa continues his relations with Mary's mother. He visits Dorchester frequently, as do we all. I know that he called on Mrs. Birch when she*

*was ill. I suppose it is right for a man to visit his former mistress (hateful word) to ask after her health. But suppose she is not former but present? In my disappointment with my father I've found it difficult to look him in the eye this past week. I honor him for looking after his child, but I cannot understand why my mother tolerates her visits. I suppose she must have forgiven him. For myself I would find it impossible. I have a horror of deception and dishonesty."*

Frank stopped reading when Christian groaned. "What?" he asked. "What's the matter?"

Frank, the poor dolt, didn't see the problem.

"It occurs to me, dear cousin, that Miss Rosanne may be a little upset should she ever learn that the tender letters she has read are not, in fact, the products of your own genius."

It took a few moments for Frank to understand. Not the gentle insult in the question. Frank never expected unkindness because he never suffered from it. He wafted through life on a cloud of approval. Christian rarely unleashed his tongue on Frank but Rosanne's letter had made him ... prickly.

The handsome numbskull nodded slowly. "She'd better not find out."

"No, she must not. In future you shall write your own letters. And keep hers to yourself." It hurt to say so, but it was the right thing to do. He was too invested in the vicarious correspondence and feared he'd managed to harm Frank rather than help him.

"Never mind. Listen to this."

Christian raised his eyebrows in warning.

"Nothing here anyone shouldn't hear. *I hope that your promised visit in June will not coincide with the wedding of the Duke of Wessex, whose marriage to Miss Helen Grey is to be celebrated with a very large party. Very large indeed, if we are invited. The duke is only a distant connection, but Mama surmises that we've been asked since we live in the same county. We shall be at Kingstag for a week.*"

That was it, then. Frank would speak to Rosanne's father at Kingstag, make his offer, and be accepted. Future correspondence would be minimal and quite within Frank's capabilities. Rosanne would never learn, must never learn, of the part Christian had played in her courtship. She must never discover just how much he knew about her.

They would meet at her wedding as strangers, about to be cousins. Frank would want him to stand up with him in church.

Damn. He hated weddings.

"You have to come with me to Dorset, Chris. I can't meet her again without your support. What shall I say to her? I need you."

"Frank," he replied with more patience than he felt. "She loves you. She knows you're no chatterbox. Just be yourself."

"Please."

Just as Christian hated weddings, he also detested large gatherings of the ton. At least a London ball was only one evening. But a weeklong celebration in a house crammed with people, many of whom were his own relations? Possibly even his own parents? He couldn't face his father's blustering demands that he leave the regiment, settle down to his duties on the estate, and produce an heir or two. Or his mother's careless assurances that he needn't worry about his scar because any woman would be happy to marry the heir to the Marquess of Glastonbury.

She should know; she'd done so herself, and look how well that marriage had worked.

Very likely the marquess and his wife would decide not to attend, since they rarely occupied the same house at the same time. But there would be no avoiding the stares and covert whispers inspired by Christian's appearance.

Put in the balance against this was that *she* would be there. Would she stare and whisper? Would she be repelled by the sight of him? He could not believe that Rosanne was so shallow. She wasn't like other women.

And although he knew it was a bad idea, he wanted to meet her.

# CHAPTER TWO

In the years since she came out Rosanne had stayed in many country houses, but none as magnificent, as imposing, as just plain grand as Kingstag Castle. She'd been here once, for an open day, but that wasn't at all the same as being received as a guest in the lofty hall by the Duke of Wessex, his mother the duchess, and his bride-to-be, the incredibly beautiful Miss Grey. Kate, who'd persuaded Lord and Lady Warnford to let her attend the ducal wedding, seemed unintimidated by the vast halls, herds of liveried servants, profuse gilt, and endless passages. As soon as she'd changed out of her travel clothes into a demure white muslin gown, she set out to explore. Rosanne kept their maid tweaking her curls, showing a demand for perfection that surprised the girl.

Kate burst back into the room. "I met the duke's sisters, all three of them, and Lady Charlotte Ascot."

"What are they like?"

"Very friendly. They told me Mr. Newnham arrived hours ago. Aren't you ready yet?"

"I suppose so." Instead of setting forth with Kate to join the house party, she picked up her modest string of pearls and held them up to her neck. "Do you think these look better than the gold cross and chain?"

"Who cares? Aren't you dying to see Frank?"

"I'm afraid I won't be able to think of anything to say to him. I liked him when we met before, but I had no idea how clever and eloquent and wonderful he is. I'll disappoint him, I know."

"Nonsense," Kate said with complete lack of sympathy. "You can't stay up here all day. If you don't hurry, Mama will come looking for us and you'll have to see him for the first time with her watching."

Faced with the prospect of finally getting a daughter off her hands, Lady Warnford was almost as excited about the coming reunion with Mr. Newnham as Rosanne, and much more vocal about it. Rosanne shuddered, picked up a light shawl, and made for the door, trying to ignore the fluttering in her stomach.

"I haven't told you the best thing." Kate bounced at her heels, chattering away. "Lord Bruton is with him. Lady Serena says he's frightening, but I think it would be splendid if I could attach him. I can see myself a future marchioness."

"Please try to behave properly, Kate. I'm nervous enough without you setting your cap at Frank's cousin."

"I have no intention of waiting to marry until I am practically decrepit."

Rosanne's hands flew to her face. "Do I look all right? Am I getting wrinkles?"

"Maybe one on your forehead. And very faint crow's feet around your eyes. No one will notice, I'm sure."

"Ka-ate!"

Kate stopped teasing her. "I've never seen you in such a state. Mr. Newnham admired you a few months ago, and you haven't changed. You are still beautiful. And he wouldn't have kept writing so many letters if he didn't love you."

This was no comfort but rather the source of her unease. After she confided her father's sin, something had changed. Frank's letters changed. They were shorter, for a start, and somehow less thoughtful, less intimate. He wrote only of inconsequential matters: his regimental duties and ventures into London society. While she couldn't believe he would blame her for Lord Warnford's behavior, she feared her indelicacy in mentioning it had disgusted him. He had been so kind to her over the matter, but ...

She set down the pearls, checked the mirror once more (no crow's feet), and walked smartly to the door. "Let's go," she said. No point letting her mind gnaw at the question until she was on the brink of insanity. Soon she would see Frank and judge his feelings for herself.

On the ground floor, a footman directed them to the saloon where the party was gathered for a light collation. Taking a deep breath and a firmer grip on her sister's arm, Rosanne stepped toward the double-doored entry.

"Rosanne, Kate. Stop!" Unfortunately they couldn't ignore their mother. "We'll all go in together."

"Where's Papa? Shouldn't you wait for him?" Kate asked, bless her. "I'll keep Rosanne company."

Lady Warnford smiled wryly and shook her head. She, too, had taken special care with her coiffure, and she looked pretty and young. How could Papa? "Some gentlemen have gone to look at a phaeton that is said to be the most marvelous carriage ever built." No further explanation was necessary. "I daresay most of the company at nuncheon will be ladies, unless a certain lieutenant cannot wait to see you." Her avid expression did not bode well for the chances of tactful restraint when they encountered the gentleman.

"You look very lovely, Rosanne," she said approvingly. "Take my arms, my loves. The doors are wide enough for the three of us to enter together." When she turned to Kate, a shriek of horror saved Rosanne from her fate. "What are you thinking? You cannot wear that gown in the morning without a chemisette high to the neck. And is that rouge on your lips? What were *you* thinking, Rosanne, to let your sister leave the room dressed like that?"

"Rosanne was distracted," Kate said, without a trace of repentance. "I think I look quite fetching."

"I knew I shouldn't have let you come with us to Kingstag. You are not ready to be presented. Go back and change at once. No, we'll come with you."

"I see Miss Black. I will join her." The threat of her mother's presence had removed any reluctance to face Frank. With luck she could get over the first awkwardness without maternal observation and comment.

The crowd of guests made the spacious saloon appear small. As Lady Warnford had guessed, there was a preponderance of ladies, but a number of men had eschewed the delights of advancement in the art of carriage construction. Trying not to appear too obvious about it, Rosanne picked her way through chattering groups, craning her neck for a glimpse of one tall gentleman who would stand out as the handsomest, most distinguished man in the room.

"Hey, gal! Are you looking for someone?" An extraordinary old lady, dressed in the style of her youth with an abundance of very improbable red hair, stood in her way. Rosanne recognized Lady Sophronia from her previous visit to Kingstag, when the old eccentric had berated the open-day crowds as ignorant gawkers before being tactfully led away by her companion, Miss Henrietta Black.

"My lady," she said, dropping a polite curtsey. "I wondered if Lieutenant Frank Newnham was in the room."

"He's an idiot. All the Newnhams are. Take after their father."

"Mr. Newnham is very clever," Rosanne said. "It is unfair to demean a man's brain just because he is handsome."

Judging by her cackle, the old woman took no offence at being contradicted. "He's pretty enough, I'll grant you that. If that's sufficient for you, I won't argue. And why not? Marriage lasts a long time, and one may as well have something nice to look at when conversation palls."

"Lady Sophronia!" A pretty, rather harassed young woman joined them. "Miss Lacy, isn't it?"

"A pleasure to see you again, Miss Black. Now if you'll excuse me ..."

Rosanne managed to escape, but two uneasy circuits of the vast room failed to reveal Frank's presence. Apprehension turned to a touch of pique that he wasn't waiting anxiously to see her. But perhaps he was looking for her in the same way and they missed each other milling around.

In a spot near a window, she had a good view of the room, with the advantage that a monstrous baroque stand crowned with a massive floral arrangement offered shelter from the eyes of her mother, who would be looking for her once she'd dealt with Kate's wardrobe transgression.

Three ladies and a gentleman, none of them known to her, were gathered a few feet away. The man presented a striking profile: inky black hair, a prominent but perfectly straight nose, and slashing cheekbones that set off a wide mouth curved into a derisive twist. Skillfully tailored to show off an excellent figure, he stood poker-straight and silent, radiating an unmistakable tension. To amuse herself, Rosanne wondered whether this was his habitual expression or whether his companions were the source of his disgust. As she strained her ears to distinguish the group's conversation through the ambient buzz, he turned his head to reveal that his other cheek was marred by a jagged scar, a puckered puce line that descended from just below his eye, over his chin, and all the way down into the frothy folds of his neck cloth. Combined with his forbidding expression, it made him a sinister presence, like a villain in the silliest novel. Try as she might, she couldn't keep her eyes off it, and neither, she realized, could the other ladies, whose glances kept darting to the poor man's ruined face.

How horrid it must be to be the object of vulgar curiosity. Not to mention the pain that must have accompanied such a grievous wound. Thinking about it made her cringe.

Christian had no idea how he'd managed to get himself maneuvered into a conversation with as inane a group of women as he'd ever encountered. He could have gone to look at the phaeton with Frank, but he'd seen that design at the carriage maker's when he ordered a new curricle. And whom was he fooling? He was dying to lay eyes on Rosanne Lacy. The trouble was, he had little idea what she looked like, aside from grey eyes and a well-endowed bosom. Frank was as inarticulate in the description of his lady love as he was at writing to her.

Christian allowed himself to be introduced to what felt like every female in the room—and promptly forgot their names once he learned they weren't called Lacy. They would remember him, all right. Their reactions were all the same: a moment of pleasure at meeting the heir to the Marquess of Glastonbury, followed by intakes of shocked breath, some better disguised than others, at his monstrous face. Then the continual stolen glances. Why was a scar so fascinating, anyway? He should never have come to this damnable event.

The silly creatures were talking about the wedding. Of course. Women were all enthralled by marriage.

"Miss Grey will make the most beautiful bride."

"She is very pretty," agreed the youngest of them. "I wonder what she will wear for the ceremony. Her sister Mrs. Barrows dresses strikingly. The quality of her cloth and trimmings is very fine, though the colors are too bold. Still, I should like to know where she found that canary silk twill."

"My dear! Don't you know that Mrs. Barrows owns a shop?"

Christian let the ill-natured gossip float over his head. He was wondering how long he had to put up with this nightmare when his opinion was sought, not, thank God, on the question of silk twill.

"What do you think, Lord Bruton? Don't you think every man should marry?"

"Certainly," he said. Even he wasn't rude enough to ignore a direct question. "I agree with Socrates. If you get a good wife you'll be happy, and if you get a bad one you'll become a philosopher. I have always aspired to be a philosopher."

The girl wrinkled her sweet little forehead, not sure how to take it. "How interesting," she murmured. "I do like quotations."

"You should embroider that one on a sampler," he said. "Or how about this: *Marriage is a desperate thing*. Or, if you prefer the highest authority: *O curse of marriage, that we call these delicate creatures ours.*"

"Is that from the Bible?"

Before he could say something cutting, one of the older ladies, perhaps the ingénue's mother, claimed to see an acquaintance across the room with whom they needed to speak immediately. The trio scurried off in a swish of petticoats. Having scared off the flock of nervous hens, he folded his arms and glared, daring anyone else to approach him. Then he heard a voice. A musical voice, low and lush, with a lilt of laughter.

*"Let me not to the marriage of true minds admit impediments."*

He swiveled to discover a young woman peering at him from behind a vase of flowers. A very beautiful young woman. "I beg your pardon?"

"If you're going to quote Shakespeare as your authority on marriage, I don't think it's fair to use Othello. I present a different point of view. You insulted that poor young lady, you know."

"By quoting poetry?"

"No, by suggesting she sew a sampler. Only schoolgirls do that. She is undoubtedly out."

"I don't pretend to comprehend the subtleties of female education. Or the female mind."

"That explains why you are standing alone and scowling instead of mingling with the company." Quite a bold piece, she was, and apparently unalarmed by his repellant appearance and demeanor.

"I don't see you doing much mingling yourself, hiding behind those flowers. Are you shy or merely avoiding someone?"

Why was he bandying words with this girl? He never bandied, especially not with women, even pretty ones. She was smiling at him, a big, generous smile. Perhaps she hadn't noticed the scar. He turned to squarely present the ruined left side of his face so there could be no mistake. His reward was a discernible flinch.

"I'm not avoiding anyone except my mother," she said, recovering quickly from the horrible sight.

"A good decision. I always avoid mine."

"Not that I'm not fond of her, but I have a particular reason at the moment. I'm also looking for someone. Do you know Lieutenant Newnham?"

It couldn't be. It must be.

"Are you Miss Lacy, by any chance, Miss Rosanne Lacy?"

Frank was an idiot. Her eyes weren't dark at all. They were a smoky blue with darker circles about the edges. And he, Christian, had been unwittingly right. A man could drown in them.

"I am," she said with obvious surprise.

"I thought you didn't much care for poetry."

Those fabulous eyes widened. "Shakespeare doesn't count. He's in a category of his own. But how did you know?"

"Frank told me. He is my cousin."

"You must be Lord Bruton, then. I had no idea." She flushed, a faint tinge of rose on creamy cheeks, and he knew why. She hadn't expected the scar. "Frank has written so warmly of you. He says you are the very best of men, a true friend whom he can rely upon to the end."

That must have been in one of the recent letters, after Christian resigned as his alter ego. He was rather touched to have inspired his cousin, with his scores of friends and intimates, to such praise. Christian hadn't thought he held the same place in Frank's regard as Frank did in his.

"I've heard about you, too," he said, "and I must say that Frank is no hand when it comes to describing a person." He hadn't expected her tall, slender grace, the fine features beneath shining brown curls, the eyes. And yes, she had a spectacular bosom, which, like any gentleman, he had the skill to examine without being obvious about it.

"Frank's eloquence is saved for the written word," she said with a fond smile.

"If you say so."

"Oh yes! He writes the most wonderful letters."

"I didn't know," he said, schooling his features to hide any hint of gratification. "Since we live in the same quarters, he doesn't have much occasion to write to me."

"Are you in his regiment? I'm surprised a gentleman in your position would be in the military."

"My father wasn't pleased when I decided to join the Guards, but a man must have something to do."

She nodded with obvious approval. "Were you injured in battle?"

Men had been verbally eviscerated for asking such a question; ladies avoided the subject. He took a deep breath to dislodge the instinctive lump of anger in his chest.

"I beg your pardon if I upset you," she said. "I tend to ask too many questions. Please be frank with me if you would rather not discuss it."

He had indeed been *Frank* with her, but she must never know that he was the author of those "wonderful letters." The irony would slay him.

An anxious little frown, forming a pair of faint creases between her brows, did nothing to diminish her beauty. His own discomfort dissipated, and he realized that the tension he usually felt in this kind of social gathering had disappeared in her presence. They'd corresponded with some intimacy for months and he knew her well, knew her curiosity wasn't inspired by malice or a desire for sensation.

"The Royal Horse Guards remain in London to guard the King. Mere Hyde Park soldiers."

"I'm sure Hyde Park offers many dangers. I know I was alarmed by all those disapproving ladies at the fashionable hour."

"Anyone who had the temerity to disapprove of you, Miss Lacy, deserves to be run through with a saber."

His compliment elicited a new kind of smile, a wry pursing of the lips. Riveted, he stared at the generous mouth and thought about kissing her, a startling idea and one that could never be acted on.

"You are kind, Lord Bruton, to offer to slay my dragons."

"Frank will do that for you," he said firmly before he got any ideas about protecting her from mythical monsters or more mundane perils. He had no right.

"Where is Frank?"

"A group of men went to the stables to look at Willoughby's new phaeton."

"Oh. I thought he would be here."

He lied to spare her disappointment. "He believed you hadn't arrived yet. He'll be devastated to miss even a few minutes of your company."

"It doesn't matter. He'll be here soon." Her eyes roamed hungrily about the saloon.

*Look at me*, he wanted to say. *Give me your attention for a little longer before my handsome cousin usurps me.*

"Oh, look! There he is."

And there he was. Tall and fair, exuding good-humored confidence as he strode across the room. A dozen people, men and women, spoke to him, and he gave each a smile and a word or two before continuing his determined progress toward them. Frank might not be articulate, but he possessed the social ease and popularity Christian lacked. Rosanne observed his approach with adoring eagerness and radiated joy as she held out her hand. It was impossible to imagine a handsomer or better matched pair. Christian backed away a step. His grotesque face and dark mind had no place in such luminous company.

"I'm so glad to see you," she said without a hint of missish restraint. She wore her heart on her sleeve. "I've been waiting for you for ages."

"I see you've met Chris."

"Chris? Oh, Lord Bruton. Yes. I was happy to meet your cousin. And even happier now that you are here."

"Splendid," Frank said. "You look splendid." He flushed, opened his mouth, then closed it again.

"Did you have a good journey?"

"Splendid."

"How was the phaeton?" she asked after a silence that was only a few seconds short of awkward.

"Splendid." Apparently months of correspondence hadn't rendered Frank any less mute in the presence of the adored one. He darted a panicked look at Christian, who offered only a lift of the eyebrows. Perhaps realizing his cousin could hardly speak for him in the flesh as he did on paper, Frank made a visible cogitative effort and found inspiration. "I saw your father at the stable. Spoke to him." He touched a forefinger to his nose. "If you know what I mean."

Christian did, and so did Rosanne. She blushed becomingly and made no effort to disguise her satisfaction at the imminent proposal of marriage. The besotted pair stood and gazed at each other. Perhaps it didn't matter if they couldn't speak.

Christian had enjoyed satisfactory, though temporary, liaisons with mistresses in which conversation was the lesser component of the relationship by a long way. His own parents rarely exchanged more than a few words in passing when they happened to run into each other at the huge London house and the even more expansive spread of Bruton Hall. Not that they were exactly pattern cards of wedded bliss. Still, he could imagine a marriage that was both happy and largely silent. Unlike the marquess, Frank was a good man and would never give his bride reason to doubt him. He adored Rosanne and would do anything for her. In fact, he would let her do whatever she wanted.

Yet he would have expected Rosanne to expect more.

Women. They were either drearily predictable or completely incomprehensible. And in the case of this particular house party, far too numerous. A couple of them, Rosanne's mother and sister, came over to be introduced.

Lady Warnford wasn't bad. A pretty woman who looked too young to be the mother of two grown-up daughters, she greeted him without shock at his scar or excessive deference to his rank. She was far more interested in Frank, who merited a delighted smile very like her elder daughter's.

"Mr. Newnham! How charming to see you again."

The demands of good manners restored Frank's voice, at least beyond total incoherence. "Your servant, ma'am. I hope you had a good journey."

"Quite comfortable, thank you. It's a mere step. We were sorry when you had to leave Leicestershire so soon. I hope you intend to remain in Dorset longer."

"And this is Kate," Rosanne said hastily. Christian wondered why she seemed anxious to put a stop to her mother's conversation with Frank.

"I've heard a lot about you, Miss Kate," Frank said.

"And I've heard a lot about you," the girl said with a saucy smile and turned her attention to Christian. "How do you do, my lord. I look forward to hearing a lot about you, too. As Mr. Newnham's cousin, of course." She was exactly as her sister's letters had conveyed: chirpy.

Rosanne broke in again. "I've been longing to hear what you thought of Kean's Shylock."

Frank, who had been dragged to Drury Lane by Christian the previous week, gulped. "Very fine performance. I liked the farce better."

"Really? You never told me you enjoyed comedy."

"Er ..."

"Frank loves all drama," Christian said helpfully. "But a discussion of Shakespeare is more likely to impress a lady."

"Oh Frank! There's no need for that. You must always tell me exactly what you think. Besides, I love to laugh, too. I'm sure I would have enjoyed the farce."

Christian's unholy amusement at his cousin's discomfort was quelled when Frank, showing unwonted presence of mind, offered to escort the ladies to the refreshment table. But instead of leaving him in peace, Miss Kate Lacy hung back. She had that look in her eye Christian sometimes encountered and interpreted as the desire to catch the heir to a marquisate, no matter how hideous. She seemed a nice enough girl and resembled her sister, which was a point in her favor—a shorter, darker, curlier, less beautiful version of Rosanne. But she was seventeen years old and, my God, did she chatter. All the time.

Christian wasn't in the market for a noisy child bride, or any other.

# CHAPTER THREE

Frank was the perfect suitor: attentive, devoted, and oh so handsome. Whatever she needed—be it a glass of ratafia or an arm to lean on during a walk—he leaped to provide. His only drawback was his general popularity. Young ladies crowded around him and didn't seem to understand that the most attractive man at the house party belonged to her. He was also much in demand among the gentlemen, who kept disappearing together to do Lord knew what. All in all, the first two days of their much anticipated reunion disappointed her.

Distinctly disgruntled at the discovery that he'd left her to take part in a game of battledore and shuttlecock on the main lawn, Rosanne set off for a different part of the gardens, where she met Lord Bruton.

He was often alone, appearing to regard the entire wedding and its attendant festivities with a dismissive scorn demonstrated by a sinister curl of the lip. She had spent quite a bit of time in his company. Frank always invited his cousin to join their group and Kate, not easily repelled, tagged along too, chattering. Even her irrepressible sister was beginning to lose interest in the face of Bruton's patent lack of response. She claimed to prefer a few smiles with her silence. But Rosanne rather liked him, and not only because he was Frank's friend.

"Miss Lacy," he said with a bow, his graceful bearing in contrast to his harsh face. "You are alone this morning." He looked warily at the path behind her.

"Kate has become great friends with the duke's sisters," she said. "She is busy with them."

"Oh good. That she has made friends, I mean."

"I'm afraid it means you will be deprived of her presence this morning."

"I am devastated," he said gravely, but his lips twitched. She liked the fact that *she* could make him smile. "Will you walk with me?"

"I warn you I won't be good company. When I'm in a bad temper I don't inflict myself on others."

"I am the same way, which is why I spend so much time alone. You may either join me in taciturn discontent or I'll let you go on your way."

"That's an invitation I can't resist," she said, taking his arm. "How pleasant to meet someone who understands me. There's nothing more tiresome than making polite conversation when one isn't in the mood."

"I'm rarely in the mood."

They set forth along a tree-lined path that meandered toward the lake, and in ten minutes of brisk walking she felt her irritation slip away. She was wondering whether it would be intrusive to break their companionable silence when an unusual sight caught her eye: a gentleman attempting to manage a huge armful of flowers while warding off an attack by a bee.

"Why are you laughing?" Bruton asked.

"I don't often see gentlemen gathering their own bouquets."

Bruton shielded his eyes from the sun and frowned. "It's Willoughby." They watched the man wrestle with the stem of a peony, sending up a shower of pink petals, then heard a sharp oath as he pricked his finger on a rose thorn. "I trust whichever of his flirts is destined to receive this tribute appreciates what the poor fellow is suffering."

"Perhaps he's picking them for his own bedchamber," Rosanne suggested. "I'm sure there are some men who prefer the fruits of horticulture to more sporting pursuits."

They looked at each other and smiled. "No," they said in unison.

As Willoughby swore again and dropped a thistle, they continued their walk.

"I feel comfortable with you, Lord Bruton," she said. "I have come to value your friendship." At once she felt a tensing of muscles beneath her hand and it occurred to her that he was just as strong as Frank, despite a less brawny physique. She noticed a tightening around his mouth. "I'm sorry. Do you find me forward?"

"Not at all, Miss Lacy. I am honored to have won your esteem."

"Honored, perhaps, but you do not seem pleased."

"Not true. I'm not a charming fellow like Frank. I have a good deal of sympathy for Mr. Darcy in *Pride and Prejudice*."

"I loved that book! Did you read it, too? Did Frank lend it to you?"

"I believe I read it first."

"In that case I must thank you for the recommendation. The park here makes me think of Pemberley. I don't believe I've ever seen a place so beautiful." She felt a little flustered, recalling the meeting between Elizabeth Bennet and Darcy at the latter's house. Lord Bruton could easily be a Darcy, whom she'd found quite wonderful. So upright and proud, with an affectionate heart buried by reserve. A sudden thrill of attraction to her companion must only be the result of remembering the book. "Perhaps Lord Willoughby would lend us his phaeton for a tour," she said, striving for lightness.

"I am told it has yellow wheels. I wouldn't be seen dead in such a vulgar conveyance. Especially one with a name."

"Hippolyta! He must be a classical scholar." Her laughter sounded forced to herself. She was suddenly terribly aware of Lord Bruton's nearness and couldn't account for her jumpiness.

She retreated ignominiously to the topic of the weather. "Isn't it a glorious day? I'm feeling rather warm even though I am wearing muslin. You poor gentlemen must feel the heat badly. Wouldn't you like to strip off and dive into the lake?" Oh, God! Had she really said that? What would he think?

"Another time, Miss Lacy." His voice sounded strangled.

"Much as I love this park," she said, steering the conversation into less provocative waters, "the size of the house daunts me. It sounds silly, but I believe that I prefer Little Mickledon Manor. Where is your home, Lord Bruton? Is it very large?"

"My father's principal seat, Bruton Hall, is in Somerset, and it is neither as big nor as grand as Kingstag. I'm fond of the place, I suppose, though I spend little time there."

Rosanne regarded him curiously. It wasn't the first time she'd detected a caustic note in his voice at a reference to his family. "I've been trying to count the number of guests here," she said, "but it's impossible. I do believe the duke must have invited everyone he ever met, right down to distant connections like us. I'm glad we were invited because it gives me a chance to see Frank." Her sense of ill-usage returned. "When he isn't at the stables looking at that phaeton again. What can be so fascinating about a carriage? My father has been spending a good deal of time there, too. I suppose he can get up to no mischief among the gentlemen guests."

"Why would he?"

She blushed but was glad to note that he had no reason to read any deeper meaning into her words. Frank had kept her confidence, as she had expected, and not mentioned Lord Warnford's infidelity. Ever since she learned of it, she had been suspicious when her father spoke to a lady other than her mother. She only wished she could be certain he was in the stables and not slipping off to meet his mistress in Dorchester.

"I shouldn't resent the masculine obsession with the stables," she said with a sigh, "even though it leaves the ladies to amuse ourselves."

Lord Bruton placed a hand on hers, a fleeting touch that surprised and agitated her again. He was not a man who went in for empty gestures. "When the neglected lady is you," he said, "I convict the gentlemen only of stupidity." Another surprise. In most men, the words would be flirtatious, but Lord Bruton emphatically did not flirt. She had on occasion caught him looking at her bosom, but she was used to that from all males over the age of thirteen who weren't closely related.

"Thank you," she said, a faint heat in her cheeks. "I am glad today for the chance to speak to you alone. As Frank's cousin and closest friend, I beg you to advise me."

"Whatever can be the matter? I've never seen a man more smitten than Frank, and I understand your parents favor the match."

"He won't *talk* to me," she said, her frustration pouring out. "Since we met here, we've spent hours together and only exchanged words on the most trivial of subjects."

"Frank has always been very shy with ladies. He isn't a great talker, even among men. I believe he finds women intimidating."

"But surely not me? At first, yes, but after we exchanged letters I was sure we would be comfortable together."

"What makes you think he isn't at ease with you?" Lord Bruton asked in measured tones. "He always looks happy in your presence."

"You're right. He does. As happy as I am. And the odd thing is that I am scarcely more eloquent than he. I'm not at all shy, with members of either sex. Look at the way I talk to you. It must be love." Bruton looked startled. What an idiot she was. "Oh, not you," she said with a nervous laugh. "Don't worry that I'll be chasing you. I love Frank, and apparently it has rendered me inarticulate. All I can do is gaze at him."

About to rave about Frank's glorious looks, Rosanne stopped. It really wasn't kind when poor Lord Bruton was so damaged. She liked him so much she hardly noticed the scar. No, that wasn't true, she realized as she looked sideways at him. Combined with his dark eyes and sculpted features, it gave him a beauty all his own. It was disconcerting to find him attractive when she was in love with another man.

"That's all right then," he said, happily unaware of her wayward thoughts. "You will live together in devoted silence. Speech as a means of communication is overrated."

"You're teasing me! I love to exchange ideas, as Frank and I did in our letters. Since arriving here, we haven't talked about a single book, or anything of much interest at all. I've had better conversations with you. How shall we manage if he makes me an offer and we marry?"

"You'll have to discuss everything of importance by post."

"You are very funny, but it won't do. Frank and I must overcome this tendency to muteness. We can't just stare at each other for the rest of our lives."

"Perhaps things would go better in the dark."

The thought of what they would do at night made her blush, until she grasped his meaning. "Lord Bruton, you are brilliant! I knew you would have the answer. Frank and I shall meet outside tonight and everything will be fine."

Christian couldn't believe he was doing this. "How have I let myself be dragged into this piece of folly? Rosanne will undoubtedly recognize my voice. She has probably heard it more than she's heard yours."

Frank had come up with his most absurd plan yet, in answer to Rosanne's request for a clandestine meeting at eleven o'clock that night.

"We sound alike," he said. "People often remark on it. All you have to do is pitch your voice a little higher. You very likely won't have to say a word. I feel full of courage tonight. You're simply coming with me in case of emergency. As soon as I signal that all is well, you may leave us alone."

Strongly suspecting that Frank's courage was three parts composed of claret, Christian had let himself be persuaded. He couldn't bear for Rosanne to be disappointed. If worse came to worst, he'd quote a little Shakespeare—he had it all ready—then leave the lovers alone.

The two of them took up their places in a shrubbery, located below a terrace attached to an obscure corner of the house. As a clock chimed the hour through an open window, a pale figure emerged above them in a faint rustle of silk, a slender ghost illuminated by the stars and a fingernail moon.

"Frank?" There was more music in one syllable than an entire orchestra, even when the syllable struck Christian as a particularly discordant one. "Are you there, Frank?"

Frank didn't answer. In the meager light his cousin's mouth opened and shut like a beached fish.

"Frank?" she called, louder.

His cousin's hand grabbed his shoulder in a fervid clasp, but Christian responded to the desperation in Rosanne's voice. He couldn't let her slink back into the house, humiliated because her suitor had panicked.

"Rosanne?" To his ears the word came out somewhere between a squeak and a hiccup.

"Frank ... You are here. Speak to me."

Gulp. "*It is the east, and Juliet is the sun. Arise, fair sun, and kill the envious moon, Who is already sick and pale ...*"

"Oh!" The words from the best balcony scene ever written were supposed to evoke a sigh, but not one that sounded miffed. "Romeo and Juliet. On a balcony. It is a wonderful scene, of course. Very famous."

Christian felt a little miffed himself. Certainly his chosen quotation was hackneyed, but none the worse for that. There was a reason it was so popular.

"*Ill met by moonlight, proud Titania,*" he retorted and was rewarded with an enchanting giggle.

"*Well* met, Oberon."

Frank started mouthing words at him, asking who the hell Oberon was. Thank God he didn't have to reply. To Frank. He wanted to talk to Rosanne. On Frank's behalf, of course. But they couldn't just stand in the dark exchanging snippets of Shakespeare. What would Rosanne and Frank talk about if they were a normal courting couple, not struck silent by shyness and mutual admiration?

"Are you enjoying the house party?" he asked. Normal and utterly commonplace.

"How could I fail to enjoy a week spent in the most beautiful and splendid house in England?"

"The gardens and park are even better, in my opinion."

"I've seen only part of them. There is much to explore. I hear the grotto is remarkable."

If that wasn't an invitation, he didn't know what was. He opened his mouth, summoning smooth words with which to invite Rosanne to set forth into the dusky gardens—and couldn't think of a word to say. Darkness hadn't inspired Frank to eloquence. Instead, it had turned Christian into an idiot. The presence of Rosanne, separated from him only by stone balusters and a few feet of rose-scented air, drove away all intelligence or wit. He wanted to speak from his heart: simple, passionate words that he couldn't articulate even to himself. Even if he could, what was the point? She was Frank's love and it was Frank's heart that should be speaking.

Frank pummeled his upper arm. *Speak for yourself,* he wanted to snap. *Win your own wife.*

"There's something I would like very much." Rosanne said into the uneasy silence. Her voice dropped and sent ripples of anticipation through his belly. "Something a lady should not ask a gentleman."

Frank, the damned man of action, grabbed the baluster rail, hoisted himself up with insolent ease, and swung his legs over. "Rosanne!" he croaked and snatched her into his arms. He'd managed to get out one word, and that was enough.

For a bare moment, Christian watched the shadowy figures join in a passionate kiss. Then he turned and plunged sightlessly across the lawn into the trees, sick with longing and a despicable envy.

Instead of looking forward to seeing her beloved, as might be expected of a lady who had enjoyed a kiss under the stars, Rosanne felt oddly shy the next day. She spent the morning indoors, listening politely to plans for the wedding ceremony discussed by the Duchess of Wessex and Lady Grey, mothers of the bridegroom and bride respectively. She tried to avoid her own mother, who had an ominous sparkle in her eye indicating a desperate desire to discuss her own daughter's nuptials, if only Rosanne would get on with things and become formally betrothed to the charming Lieutenant Newnham.

Eventually the ladies drifted out to watch the sport on Kingstag's bowling green. The duke himself was present, playing a game against his bride's sister, Mrs. Barrows. Of Frank—and most of the other gentlemen, including Lord Bruton—there was no sign.

Accepting a glass of lemonade from a footman, she sat down next to Miss Angela Cowdrey, an American and rather an odd young woman.

"Doesn't it trouble you," she said, "to be in England when our countries are at war?"

Really, her wits had gone begging of late, asking Lord Bruton if he wanted to take off his clothes—she blushed every time she thought of it—and now insulting a fellow guest.

Miss Cowdrey appeared startled. "To be honest," she said, "I haven't given it a thought. No one has mentioned it."

"I shouldn't have."

"It doesn't bother me, as long as you don't want to shoot me or throw me in the lake."

Rosanne laughed. "The French are our real enemies."

"Always up to mischief, those French. Do you know Sir Richard Howell?"

"I've met his daughter. I don't think either is French, but she knows a great deal about Paris fashions. I believe smugglers bring over the latest journals in kegs with the brandy."

Miss Cowdrey nodded intently. "How interesting. I had never thought of fashion plates being part of the illicit wartime trade." She had a strange way of putting things, presumably because of her nationality, but she was quite amusing. Lord Bruton would find her entertaining too.

As the morning turned into afternoon, the remaining gentlemen slipped away, including the duke. They were all off about their fascinating manly affairs, but for once Rosanne could not regret Frank's penchant for masculine company. After last night's moonlit tryst, she was filled with doubts and desperate for advice. She would have liked to consult Lord Bruton, but the subject of her anxiety wasn't one she should discuss with a gentleman. She couldn't ask her mother, either. If Lady Warnford knew what she'd been doing on the terrace, she'd be marched to the altar in five minutes flat—and she was no longer sure she wanted to be.

Which left Kate, as usual surrounded by a gaggle of white-muslin-clad girls. Sometimes it was hard to believe the duke had only three sisters. "We're going for a walk, Rosie," she said. "Do you want to come with us?" The chorus of giggles that accompanied the innocuous invitation gave her to expect more mischief than rational conversation from the expedition.

"Where are we going?"

More giggles. "The stables," Lady Alexandra said. "We want to spy on the gentlemen and find out what's so interesting about this phaeton."

"We strongly suspect," Kate added, "that there's something more than a boring carriage to hold their attention."

Rosanne wondered if she should discourage the younger girls, but it seemed harmless enough. She couldn't believe any gentlemen would bring mistresses to a wedding party. So they circled the lawn in sight of mothers and chaperones, dodged into the shrubbery, and slipped down the side path to the stable block.

"Let them go ahead," she whispered to Kate. "I need to talk to you."

"Pray tell! You were so close-mouthed last night. I suppose you went out to meet Frank."

"I thought we might be able to speak more easily in the dark."

"Speak! Was that what you were doing?"

"For a little bit. And then he kissed me."

"Rosie! Was it wonderful?"

"Not really. At first it was. He vaulted over the balusters and swept me into his arms, and that was wonderful."

"Is he as strong as he looks?"

"Yes. And even in the dim light, he looked splendid doing it. I was looking forward to being kissed. In fact," she added self-consciously, "I sort of asked him to."

"I didn't know you were so bold." Kate's eyes were huge. She was a lot less worldly than she liked to think. "But you didn't enjoy it? What was it like, being kissed?"

"He put his arms about me very tightly, and Grandmother's brooch was crushed into my bosom." She touched the place above her right breast where the pearl ornament had been pinned to the lace trim of her evening gown. "And then he kissed me hard."

"On the lips?"

"Of course."

"Was he rough?"

"Not rough, exactly, but I would say he lacked finesse. And his lips were wet."

"Perhaps he was nervous."

"I'm sure he was, as was I. But still. It's important to enjoy kissing the man you intend to marry."

"Perhaps kissing is always like that."

Rosanne hesitated, wondering if she should really be saying this to her young sister. But Kate had to know at some time. "Kisses can be most enjoyable. I know."

"Rosie! Who?"

"Johnny Peyton."

"No! You kissed *him*? He is quite ineligible and tried to elope with an heiress, as well as being addicted to gaming, or so Mama says."

"I wasn't going to marry him. My fortune is too modest to attract him, anyway. But he caught me in an alcove at the Beltons' Christmas ball and I thought I might as well let him. It was exceedingly pleasant. I quite understood why the heiress became enamored. I also kissed George Belton. Not in the same evening."

"But you turned down Mr. Belton's proposal."

"After he kissed me. He pressed so hard the inside of my lip was bruised by my teeth. I couldn't possibly accept him."

"I can see why. Was Frank so bad?"

"Not as bad as George but not as good as Johnny Peyton."

Kate frowned in perplexity for a moment or two, but she'd never met a problem she couldn't attempt to solve. "Do you suppose Frank has kissed a lot of girls? Mr. Peyton had the heiress and probably others to practice on, but Frank seems a respectable man. You may be the first."

Rosanne could have retorted that so-called respectable men went in for kissing, and much more, with unrespectable women, but there was only so much education she felt up to imparting at once. Besides, Kate might be on to something. Frank was charming to all the ladies, young and old, but she'd never seen him flirt with any of them except herself. He'd said in one of his letters that he'd never been in love with anyone but her, a claim she'd taken with a pinch of salt. If it were true, however, his lovemaking experience might be limited.

"You are right, Kate. I mustn't give up yet. But I am quite determined not to marry a man I don't enjoy kissing."

There were other things she hadn't told her sister. Her closest childhood friend had married two years ago and provided her with detailed information about the activities of the marriage bed. Maria loved her husband and was ecstatic about wedded life. But try as she might—and she'd spent several sleepless hours trying the night before—Rosanne couldn't summon the enthusiasm she needed to indulge in these pleasures with Frank.

The only reason Christian decided to investigate the delights of the Kingstag stables was a determination to avoid Rosanne Lacy. He had nothing to say to her. Not a word. He didn't wish to bask in her smiles, or her thoughts on poetry or novels, or her comments on the other guests, which somehow managed to be both incisive and kind. His own were merely incisive, but when Rosanne smiled at the foolishness of the world, he wanted to love it as much as she did. He wanted to believe that other people were worthy of respect as well as tolerance, because that was the way she thought. He didn't want to be lured into the sunshine of her view of life. And he didn't want her glowing eyes and luscious lips to persuade him that the world was a delightful place—because it wasn't. If he needed evidence beyond his own experience, the very fact of her existence proved it. In a just world, he would not desire a woman who belonged to his cousin.

So he tortured himself by seeking out Frank. To be in the company of his cousin was less painful—by a slim margin—than in Rosanne's. Frank's simple, kindly, handsome face would sharpen the vision of watching him kiss Rosanne. But better that than the agony of seeing her face, of gazing on those lips that could never be his, the sweet body he could never embrace. He needed the reminder that she was not for him, and that he deserved punishment for his disloyalty in even wishing she could be.

As he walked with more doggedness than enthusiasm toward the stable block, he saw three young girls jumping up and down, apparently trying to see through a high window from which faint sounds of merriment emerged. The duke's younger sisters, he fancied, mercifully unaccompanied by Miss Kate Lacy, who was often to be seen in their boisterous company.

Luck was not on his side. Coming up the road from the other direction was Miss Kate, accompanied by the one person in the world he currently wished most to avoid: her sister. A gentle breeze caught the light cloth of her pale yellow gown, emphasizing the curves of her waist and hips. His heart felt as though it would burst from his chest, and his feet, divorced from his brain, began a forward march, just for a second, until he remembered why he was avoiding her.

Hanging back in the thick cover of a large rhododendron, he waited to see what the female party would do next. Without making out their words, he watched the duke's sisters dash back to speak to the Lacys in a chorus of giggling excitement. Rosanne laughed at their report. Too far away to make out the words, from the gestures and reactions of the quartet he gathered that she advised against an invasion of the masculine stronghold. After some argument, the younger girls succumbed to her persuasion and she drove them off, scampering away like chickens under the command of a benign mother hen. He liked the way she'd diverted their indiscretion without arousing resentment. But he liked everything about Rosanne, and therein lay his problem.

And his problem, instead of walking safely away, abandoned her chicks and headed toward him.

"Lord Bruton?"

"Miss Lacy." He stepped forward, embarrassed to be caught lurking in the bushes.

"Are you joining the 'phaeton viewing' party? You too?" Whatever those girls had seen, it wasn't vehicle inspection. She was clearly amused.

"I decided even I needed to see this chariot worthy of Apollo."

"You must tell me about it. Its splendor has rendered Frank speechless." She blushed a little, and he knew they were thinking the same thing but refrained from saying it. It was just one in a long list of things that rendered Frank speechless. As she drew closer, he noticed a shadow of anxiety behind the smiles. She didn't look like a woman aglow with bliss at her first kiss from a lover.

"Is there anything I can do for you, Miss Lacy?"

"I was looking for Frank, but I shouldn't intrude on the gentlemen's fun. Would you give him a message for me?"

"Of course."

"I have heard almost as much about the Kingstag grotto as I have about Lord Willoughby's phaeton. If he is able to escape from his other obligations—" She sounded put out. "—I would like him to come with me. Could you ask him to meet me there in, say, half an hour?" A delicate blush tinged her cheeks and she lowered her gaze.

"I daresay the darkness of the grotto will inspire Frank to eloquence," he said nastily, pierced by a pang of envy.

"Exactly." She looked up, blasting him with the force of her shining eyes. "You are such a good friend to Frank. And to me."

"I am at your service, Miss Lacy," he said stiffly and watched as she tripped off happily. He damned his hopeless yearning and resumed his progress into the stable yard, fingering his scar as he went. Not only was he ugly, but also bitter. A woman like Rosanne might see him as a friend—a testament to her remarkable sweetness—but never as anything more.

In no good frame of mind, he followed the raucous laughter through the carriage house into a tack room filled with men lounging against walls hung with tack or sitting on upholstered chairs, an array of top-booted legs stretched before them. Not to his surprise, every fellow held a tankard or glass.

"Welcome, Bruton, to our woman-free refuge." The Duke of Wessex sat in a corner, brandishing a bottle. Not the sentiment of an eager bridegroom. "Find a glass and let me offer you brandy. Or there's a keg of beer over there if you prefer it."

Christian took a quick inventory of the room, spotting a couple of his former Eton tormenters. It was as bad as the Horse Guards' mess. "Brandy, please, Wessex." A nip of spirits would sharpen his tongue. He downed the first tot in a single gulp and accepted a refill. Excellent quality. Trust Wessex for that. The spirit filled his stomach and fired his brain. Almost disappointed when his former classmates greeted him with polite indifference instead of the old mockery, he found a bare patch of wall near Frank and leaned back.

One of the men was describing, in stupefying detail, a recent horse race at York. "Altsidora won by a mile and I won with handsome odds. Hear Sykes intends to rest her for the St. Leger."

"She'll never beat the colts."

"I bet you a pony she will. Never saw a faster filly. What do you think, Frank?"

"No reason the right one can't run as fast as the lads. My mare Miranda was the best hunter I ever owned. Lots of bottom, and that's what's needed over the St. Leger distance. If she's all you say, I'll put a guinea or two on her."

"In that case, I'll lay off. Never win so much a sixpence when I follow you. Do you remember at Goodwood two years ago when Frank backed the second-place horse six races in a row and came away without his shirt?"

"Good old Frank." The approving sentiment was accompanied by much backslapping and general bonhomie.

Christian wished he liked the company of men en masse other than in the course of his military duties, which he did enjoy. Any of these gentlemen—or half of them, anyway—might be rational in a tête-à-tête, but in large groups their discourse degenerated into pointless anecdotes, crude badinage, and ribald laughter. Frank, however, was in his element: friendly, modest, the best fellow in the world. He never changed, except that in a masculine milieu he was relatively articulate. How would a thoughtful, intelligent woman like Rosanne fit into Frank's world? Yet her father, Lord Warnford, was also present in a group of older men having a very similar kind of conversation. She probably found the average English gentleman normal and acceptable.

On the day Christian told his father he wished to buy a commission, he tried to explain his notions of honor and service to a greater good. Lord Glastonbury brushed him off with the admonition "not to think so much." Perhaps he was right: what good did it do him? He sipped his brandy, let dozens of male voices wash over him, and tried not to think about Rosanne's. But the more he tried to shut off his brain, the more her voice intruded. He closed his eyes and saw hers. And her lips.

The stable clock struck the half hour, and he remembered. He was supposed to deliver a message, which meant getting Frank away from the company because he couldn't publicly announce a tryst. Frank would have to hurry to reach the grotto in time. A massive irritation arose that his cousin, who could have spent the morning in the company of the woman he professed to adore, preferred to wallow in beer and racing stories.

"Frank," he began ...

# CHAPTER FOUR

**R**osanne added unpunctuality to Frank's known list of qualities. Unless Lord Bruton had failed to give him the message—but Bruton didn't seem like an unreliable sort. She'd have sworn he was a man whose word was his bond, even if he had joined almost every other gentleman at the party in a drinking session.

In the heat of the midday sun, the circular entrance to the grotto beckoned. Framed by massive rocks draped in ivy, it was set in a wooded hillside and approached by a path lined with wildflowers. Entirely the work of man, the folly mimicked a cave, an ancient and natural shelter away from the elegant elevations of Kingstag Castle and its careful landscaping. The dark tunnel enticed Rosanne with a promise of unseen hazards.

What nonsense. The place must be kept in a perfect state by Kingstag's many gardeners and presented no risk to the visitor. It was nothing but a playhouse, and she would play at danger. She stepped inside.

Almost immediately, a flight of shallow stone stairs led her down into a small chamber, barely lit by the light from the door above. On each side, a dark passage led further into the grotto. She shivered, from the chill air and the illusion of being in a primitive, uncivilized place.

"Rosanne?" Frank's call came from outside, repeated louder as he reached the entrance. She dodged into the tunnel on the left, following a bend into impenetrable darkness. She stood motionless, hearing her own breath in counterpoint to Frank's husky demand. "Are you there?" He paused and then made the wrong choice. She heard his tread take the opposite passage.

P.S. I Love You

The plop of distant dripping water enhanced the fantasy of having wandered into a gothic novel where a dark, dangerous hero would seize her unawares and sweep her away to his underground realm. How absurd. There was no one who fit the description less than Frank. He was blond and uncomplicated, a creature of sunlight: Apollo, not Hades. She felt a twinge of disappointment and smiled at her folly as she waited for him to realize his mistake.

Her heart skipped a beat at a soft footfall behind her, from inside the tunnel. The passage must be circular. She held her breath and remained still. Let him find her in the dark.

He did, through luck or a catlike ability to see in the dark. A finger ran down her neck and along the line of her gown, provoking a delicious shudder.

"Frank?" she whispered.

"Were you expecting anyone else?" His voice seemed deeper than usual. Every inch of her skin tingled in response, and heat unfurled in her belly. Both his hands rested on her shoulders, and his thumbs descended beneath the muslin to stroke the shoulder blades. She leaned back into a solid body and caught his scent: subtle, clean, and intriguingly unfamiliar. In the absence of light, all her senses seemed heightened. She closed her eyes and emitted a soft moan of encouragement.

"So beautiful," he said.

"You can't see me."

"I would recognize you anyway."

"Even in a dark pool?" The question came out in a gurgle of mirth, quickly smothered by another happy gasp when his lips found her nape.

"You're never going to let me forget that unfortunate line, are you?" His voice buzzed against her skin. "In a dark pool, a thick forest, a mountain top, or in the crush of a ballroom. I will always know you."

"Go on talking."

But he busied his mouth another way, caressing the sensitive skin with lips and breath until she thrummed with desire. Wanting more, she turned around and tilted her head, laughing a little until he touched her cheeks with hands neither soft and smooth like hers, nor rough, and found her mouth.

123

Ah, yes! *This* was a kiss. Not too hard, nor too gentle, but just right. Partly open lips moved over hers, nibbling first the bottom, then the top, then the whole, evoking the most wonderful sensations. She opened to his easy pressure, tasting his breath. He'd indulged at the stable drinking party. Brandy. On a daring impulse, she mimicked the most shocking aspect of the fortune hunter's technique and darted her tongue forward to touch his, with a dramatic result. Their mouths merged into a maelstrom of shared heat, probing, stroking, tangling blissfully.

Apparently a little practice went a long way when it came to kissing the right man. And when other activities offered themselves, conversation was overrated.

One hand descended to her breast. Even through undergarments and gown, her flesh felt swollen at his touch. She wanted to touch him back, urgently, but his chest was too well-covered by the sturdier layers of masculine attire and she wanted skin. She raised her hands but before she could find his face he seized her wrists and whipped them down, securing them behind her back in a compelling hold as he enclosed her, pressing his form into hers, chest, hips, and thighs. She was bound and helpless in the circle of his embrace. At the same time, she'd never felt so powerful, for his rapid breathing and the erratic sounds from his throat told her this large man, this fearless soldier, was as affected as she.

Melting into him, she crushed her breasts against his chest in a frenzy, thrust her hips forward, and felt what must be the ... evidence ... of his desire against her belly. Lord, how she wanted him, wanted to give herself to him in every way and satisfy the new, raging fever that consumed her. The sooner they wed the better, as far as she was concerned, and surely he felt the same way. All in good time. She was loath to stop their crazed kissing and let him speak the words of a proposal.

He was the one to break contact. Keeping her wrists captive in one hand, he stroked her cheek, rested his forehead against hers. "Rosanne," he said, his voice strained and husky. "Oh, Rosanne. What am I to do with you?"

She thought the answer obvious but understood that his wits might have gone begging. Her own were not sharp.

"I don't know, Frank. What do you want to do?"

Instead of taking the hint and proposing, he kissed her again, sending her senses whirling and driving away coherent thought, then broke off and almost thrust her from him, leaving her cold. "You should go," he said through jagged breaths. "Your mother will miss you."

"I suppose so." She groped for the deranged ribbons of her bonnet and did her best to straighten them. Smoothing her skirt with trembling hands, she waited.

Nothing.

"Shall we go?" The path through the park included a tall, hedged walk, perfect for private conversation.

"I have to let you go alone."

"Why?"

"Because I'm in no state to be seen. I need time to recover."

"Oh. I see." At least, she thought she did.

"I shouldn't have done this. Treated you so."

She reached out to caress his cheek, to assure him that she'd wanted this kiss as much as he. She had, after all, invited him to meet her in this secluded spot. Before she could speak he stopped her hand again, firmly placing it at her side. "Go. I will see you later."

# CHAPTER FIVE

The day's entertainment was another impromptu cricket match, stupid game, inspired by the exceptional weather. Thunder, lightning, or a volcanic apocalypse would better have suited Christian's mood. But this was southern England in June, where there was always a chance of a fine day. He took a book and installed himself with his back against a tree trunk in the farthest part of the field, well out of the way. Out of the way of the ladies and older gentlemen who gathered closer to the action and were served lemonade and biscuits.

He'd been avoiding Frank, easy enough so long as he eschewed any manly activities. Keeping away from Rosanne was harder. Good manners demanded he attend dinner and a drawing room evening of musical performances. As long as she was in the same room with him, his eyes found her, having acquired a life of their own beyond the control of his will. He tried to tell himself that her piano playing was no better than adequate and her singing voice—in a duet with her sister—weak. But he didn't give a damn. When she sang she opened her mouth, and he thought only of kissing her again.

Weakened by brandy, he'd rejected the dictates of honor and persuaded himself that if he kissed her—just once—he could die happy. That had been a huge mistake. Now he knew what he was missing, and he'd never felt more miserable in his life.

He was going to read Dibdin's *Metrical History of England* and he wouldn't mind if it killed him. He would not look at Frank, reenacting his role as the leading batsman of the Eton eleven. And he would not even glance at the watching ladies to see if *she* was there.

So successful was he in keeping his nose in his book, taking in at least one out of every ten words, that he missed her approach.

"Lord Bruton?" He'd kissed this woman to the point of madness and she still addressed him by his title. "May I join you?"

He wasn't sure whether her standing before him, the sun creating a halo about her form, was better than having her sit beside him on the grass, where he could sense her warmth and her fragrance. Where a slight movement would let him touch her. His hands clenched and almost cracked the spine of his book.

She dropped in a rustle of petticoats and made herself comfortable on the ground with her knees folded beside her, her skirt—blue today—bright against his black Hessian boots.

"Do you not play cricket?"

"Not since school."

She turned her head to watch Frank, standing in front of the wicket, hit the ball squarely over the boundary. "Frank is very good." She glowed with admiration.

"He always was," he said curtly.

"But you prefer a book?" She peered at the spine. "A history in verse? That sounds like a very bad idea. How is it?"

"I haven't got very far."

"I see you share Frank's tastes."

"Not at all." He was about to deny any interest in *The Sporting Calendar* when he remembered. "Not usually."

"I would never expect military gentlemen to have poetic tastes."

"You must never have read Sir Philip Sidney. He composed a poem while dying from battle wounds."

"Wasn't he the one who gave his water ration to a common soldier because 'thy need is greater than mine'?"

"A great poet and a great man. The example of men like him is what drew me to the army. The ideals of honor and selfless service to a need greater than one's own."

The way he'd failed those ideals, by deceiving her and betraying his cousin, haunted him. There was one way to atone for his sin. If it pained him, so much the better.

"You asked me about my scar—"

"Frank said you don't like to speak of it. There is no need."

"It concerns Frank, and I wish to tell you."

"Surely he wasn't responsible—"

"Nothing like that." He took a deep breath. "It's ugly now—"

127

Again she interrupted him. "It's not so bad. Now I have come to know you, I don't notice it much." She reached out to the jagged line on his cheek. God, how much torture was he expected to bear? "How far does it go down?"

"Far enough." He leaned back to avoid the delicious agony of her touch and she lowered her arm with an apologetic grimace. "When I went to Eton at the age of ten, it was much worse. Scarlet and livid, a temptation for every schoolboy wit and bully. It didn't help that I was small for my years. Without Frank, I'm not sure how I would have survived. He was taller and stronger and backed me up in every fight. Eventually I learned to parry my tormenters with my own wits. And I grew taller."

"The two of you are the same height now."

"To the inch, though Frank is still the stronger. He used his fists and his popularity with our schoolfellows to defend me."

"Everyone loves Frank."

"How could they not? He is the best fellow in the world. After Eton, he decided to buy into the Guards and I joined him."

"And does Frank still protect you?" She smiled fondly.

"I am glad to say that I no longer need his help. But he has my eternal affection and loyalty."

The last statement was for him, not her. To remind him that the lovely woman sitting beside him belonged to his cousin and that to fight for her would be a betrayal. Not that there was any chance of winning, even if he were inclined to try. She was watching the cricketers again, radiant with admiration as Frank ran between the wickets.

"Lord Bruton," she said after a minute or two. "Thank you for telling me about you and Frank. And since you have his best interests at heart and already know so much of our courtship, I wish to confide in you again. I must confess that I had terrible doubts about him. Did you know that we met in the dark two nights ago?"

"Uh ... he did mention it."

"After that I was uncertain about our connection." She pursed her lips, thought a little, then shook her head. "Forgive me for being so bold, but our meeting was not all that I could wish."

Well that was a surprise! Frank, lucky devil, had been as eloquent as he ever was about the joys of kissing Rosanne Lacy.

"I decided to give him another chance when I asked him to meet me in the grotto."

"How did that go?" His heart beat fast enough to cause a seizure.

"It was wonderful. Miraculous. Splendid beyond all my dreams."

He was dumbfounded. She was talking about his kiss. *Their* kiss. The kiss that had seared his soul and destroyed his peace.

"But even more importantly, you have confirmed what a truly noble man he is. I am so happy. He hasn't spoken to me yet, but he asked my father's permission."

His lack of a reply didn't stem her paean of joy.

"It's funny how he seems to have no difficulty talking to gentlemen. He talks to you, and I've seen him taking to other men. He has plenty to say when he's talking to them about that phaeton. But I'm not worried. Eventually he'll feel comfortable enough to speak to me the way he can in his letters. Really, I should be flattered that my presence deprives him of the power of speech. Don't you think?"

"If you say so. I hope you don't mind if I continue reading." Talking was too much of a temptation. He'd be wise to get up and leave, but each time he resolved to do so, his body resisted his will. The delight and agony of her proximity nailed him in place as he stared at meaningless lines of print.


Keeping half her attention on Frank's cricket heroics, Rosanne sat in the sun and made a daisy chain. It had been hard for Lord Bruton to tell her about his school days. She had learned from Frank, and in greater detail from another guest, that the subject of his scar was one a man was wise to avoid. How strange that a man of his birth and talents should care so much for an accidental disfigurement. That side of his face was shocking to the eye at first, but she'd become used to it. In fact, she thought it gave character to his countenance. She was sure most people would feel the same if he would let them know him. But he kept others at bay with fierce looks and haughty reserve, ensuring that they didn't forget the most sinister aspect of an otherwise unexceptional appearance. As she threaded the flower stems together, she stole surreptitious glances at his impassive features, which, she fancied, disguised some inner grief.

She had the urge to comfort him, to hold his dark head between her hands, to kiss the cruel red line ...

Good Lord! What was she thinking? He'd no doubt be appalled at the very idea, and so should she. She was in love with his cousin and friend and would soon be his cousin too. Doubtless that was why he felt comfortable enough to mention the forbidden topic to her. She stole another glance and met his eyes over the top of his book: a hot, dark look that set her pulses racing.

Confused and blushing, she shifted to face the cricket field and put the perplexing man out of her sight. Frank brandished his bat, looking dashing and splendid. Any day now, possibly any hour, this magnificent man would propose to her, she would accept, and they'd plan their wedding. What better time to become betrothed than at a wedding party when love and matrimony were in the air? Yet she felt less rapturous at the prospect than she expected.

He took a mighty swipe, but instead of driving the ball into the distance as he had a dozen times, he missed and the wicket shattered. He accepted his dismissal with his usual good nature. She watched him congratulate the bowler and accept the commiserations of his team. Then he loped gracefully across the field and flung himself onto the ground next to them.

"Well played, Frank," she said.

"Were you watching me?" He grinned bashfully. "I certainly botched that last ball. Went right by me."

"You never could resist a fast one." Apparently Lord Bruton could read and watch cricket at the same time.

"You know my weaknesses." He paused. "Uh, Rosanne. Would you like to come for a walk with me or are you busy?"

"Busy making a daisy chain, that's all." She guessed what was coming and perhaps she needed to wait. Spend more time with Frank before she accepted him. On the other hand, she wouldn't object to another kiss. That should settle her doubts. "Let me finish this. I won't be a minute."

"What are you going to do with it?" Lord Bruton asked. "Crown Frank with the garland?"

"I'd look very silly, but if Rosanne wants me to wear daisies, I will."

Bruton sneered, every bit the man who sent soft-hearted ladies scuttling away in terror. He scowled even more ferociously as Kate ran up to join them.

"Rosanne," she said breathlessly. "Have you seen Papa? I have something particular I want to ask him and I can't find him anywhere."

"Does Mama know? Or perhaps he's at the stables again."

"I know where Lord Warnford is, Miss Kate," Frank said. "He told me this morning he had to go to Dorchester on a matter of business."

"Again?" Kate asked. "He's always going to Dorchester. You'd think he could manage without while we are here."

Rosanne didn't want to ask what her father was doing. She was terribly afraid she knew the answer.

Christian watched as the Lacy sisters exchanged small talk with Frank, whose talk was predictably much smaller than the ladies'. Thank God, Miss Kate was set on some mission of her own that precluded any attentions to him. He had to suffer no more than a winsome twinkle or two in his direction, a pale facsimile of her sister's heart-stopping smile.

Rosanne was not smiling now. As Kate wandered off, she ignored Frank's hand, offered to pull her up from the ground. "Are you coming, Rosanne?" he asked. She blinked back at him as though far away. "Is something the matter?"

She shook her head, still distracted. Christian guessed the cause and sympathized.

"Well that's all right, then," Frank said. "Let's go. Would you like to see the grotto?"

Damn, blast, and ruination. In three seconds Frank would reveal that he had not yet, in fact, seen the grotto in Rosanne's company. "I think I know what is troubling you," Christian said. "I assure you that Lord Warnford has spent most of this house party in the stables. Whatever he has done in the past, he doesn't strike me now as a man who abandons his family for a mistress. And I am in a position to know."

Rosanne jerked her head around and stared at Christian, then she scrambled to her feet and turned on Frank. "How could you, Frank?"

"What?" Frank hadn't yet caught on.

"I wrote to you about my father in the strictest confidence and you betrayed me."

"I would never betray a confidence," Frank said indignantly. An accusation of ungentlemanly conduct was one of the few things likely to upset him. Then he blushed scarlet because he had, of course, done exactly that.

"Did you read my letter, Lord Bruton?" she asked with a glare.

"I would never read another man's letters without being asked," Christian said.

"That doesn't answer the question."

Their case was hopeless and there wasn't a damn thing Christian could do. He couldn't even take the lion's share of the blame for the disaster he'd wrought while trying to avert another. Goddesslike in her anger, Rosanne faced them with hands on hips and sparks erupting from stormy gray eyes. "What do you have to say for yourself, Mr. Newnham?"

Frank, predictably, had nothing to say. His mouth emitted desperate gibberish as he threw Christian a pleading look.

"Nothing? Nothing?" Rosanne's low, musical tones took off into the heavens in an almighty, unladylike screech. "If and when you find your voice, you may tell me the truth."

Christian and Frank watched her stride off, the sun outlining her figure through a cloud of blue muslin.

"That's torn it, old boy," Christian said. "I'm sorry. I truly blundered there." He couldn't tell Frank that he'd been trying to steer the conversation away from the grotto.

"What shall I do?"

"You must offer a groveling apology. Tell her you are accustomed to telling me things, that you know I will never mention the matter to another soul, and swear you'll never do it again. As long as she doesn't find out the words were mine, she'll forgive you."

Frank's expression was a comical mix of misery and panic. "I'll never be able to say all that."

"I certainly can't say it for you. You're on your own this time. Go after her now."

"I'll do it by letter. You tell me what to say and I'll write it."

"Are you serious? That's what got us into this mess in the first place. For God's sake, Frank! At a certain point you have to learn to speak for yourself and it may as well be now."

"Please, Chris. Just this last time."

Christian wavered. Every instinct told him to refuse, not to exacerbate their fault by repetition. Yet was he not more to blame than Frank? They both could have said no to the initial deception. But now he was by far the greater sinner. He'd impersonated Frank to win a kiss and then triggered the present contretemps when he tried to cover it up. He wasn't sure that on some level he hadn't done it on purpose because he wanted Rosanne to know the truth. The greatest betrayal was of his cousin when he'd let himself fall in love with Frank's woman.

He might as well admit it to himself. He loved Rosanne. He was desperately in love with her and without the slightest hope of success. Even if he could steal her from Frank—and that was out of the question—she would never return the love of a monster like him. He had now proven that his character was as ugly as his face.

"She's coming back. Help me, Chris. What shall I do? What shall I say?"

Through his despair, his heart soared at the sight of her, then plummeted. "Just say you are sorry. I know she loves you, so she'll forgive you."

Rosanne's fists clenched at her sides, but she spoke calmly. Too calmly. "What do you think of Miss Elizabeth Bennet?" she asked Frank in a conversational tone laced with frost.

"Do I know her? Is she the red-headed girl who played the harp last night?"

Her answering smile was quite nasty. They were getting a taste of that temper she'd mentioned. "Lord Bruton knows, don't you?"

Christian nodded helplessly. God, she was wonderful.

Frank looked baffled.

"She is a character in a novel called *Pride and Prejudice*. That you gave me."

Frank still looked baffled, and Rosanne looked scornful.

Once it became clear he had nothing to say, she continued. "At first I wondered if you had told your cousin about my father's other daughter to ask his advice. While displeased that you would do so

133

when I explicitly asked you to keep the information to yourself, it was at least reasonable. I tried to understand because I wanted to forgive you." A tapping foot belied her rational tone.

"You do?" Frank blurted out. "I'm sorry, Rosanne. I should never have mentioned the matter to Chris."

She narrowed her eyes. "Wanted, Frank. Wanted to forgive you. Past tense. Not want. I changed my mind. You see, I started thinking about all the letters we had exchanged, wondering if your cousin had been privy to more than one. It seemed to me that in my conversations with Lord Bruton we had covered many of the same topics. Very well, I thought. They are cousins and friends. They have the same tastes. Except that not once have you and I exchanged words in person on any of these matters. I know you are not a great talker, but even your few words have been on very different subjects. I wish to know, and please don't lie to me again, did Lord Bruton write your letters?"

"Uh. They came from my pen."

"I wouldn't be too proud of that," she said with utter disdain. "Your handwriting is execrable."

Christian's lips twitched.

"As for you, my lord, laugh if you like, but this is not funny. Did you dictate the letters to Mr. Newnham? Don't bother to deny it, for I won't believe you."

"In that case, I won't try. Frank needed my help constructing his ideas."

"You mean Frank needed your help having ideas. I believed I knew him through those letters. I thought I loved him. But now I know that I fell in love with a man who doesn't even exist. Good Lord, I kissed a man who doesn't exist. You have made a game of me, the pair of you."

"Never that. I never intended that." Not after the first letter, he added silently. True, it had started as a joke for him, but now the joke was on him. He could tell her that every word had come from his heart and, in speaking for Frank, he'd revealed more of himself than he ever had before. But what was the use?

She glared at each of them in turn, infinitely desirable and quite beyond his reach. "I will never speak to either of you again." She swiped her glistening eyes with the back of her hand then turned and walked away, fury evident in her stiff back and every deliberate step.

# CHAPTER SIX

"**D**id you get too much sun?" Lady Warnford placed her hand on Rosanne's forehead. "Quite cool."

"I just don't feel like going to dinner. I'm not hungry."

"That's no excuse for bad manners. Really, Rosanne. At your age, I would hope you had grown out of these selfish tantrums. Get dressed immediately and remember that you are a guest in this house."

She was tired of being ordered about by Mama, and now there was no prospect of ever escaping. She felt doomed to eternal childhood.

"No one will care if I'm not there," she said sulkily.

"I can think of someone who will." Her mother gave her an arch look that turned shrewd. "Have you quarreled with Mr. Newnham?"

"I will never speak to him again as long as I live."

Lady Warnford sat down on the bed and took her hand. "Don't look so sad, my love. I'm sure you will make it up."

"You are so desperate for me to marry that you don't care what he has done."

"Desperate? You are wrong about that. It is true that I wish you to find a husband. I want you to have a family of your own as happy as ours. But you know that neither your father nor I would ever encourage you to wed someone who doesn't suit you. We love having you at home with us."

She couldn't believe what she was hearing.

"Mr. Newnham is such a nice young man," her mother continued, "that I find it hard to believe he has done anything you cannot forgive."

Rosanne had been biting her lip to hold back her angry retort but this was too much. "You would say that since you forgave Papa. I would not have done so and I will not forgive Frank."

"Whatever do you mean? Your father has his annoying traits—what man does not?—but he has never done anything so very dreadful."

"You don't call keeping a mistress and siring a daughter out of wedlock dreadful?"

"Papa? A mistress? Never! Where did you get such a notion?"

"Mary Birch. I heard you tell the vicar's wife that she is really a Lacy. And you've always been a little, I don't know, disapproving of her visits. I always suspected there was something amiss."

Lady Warnford smiled grimly. "Let this be a lesson against eavesdropping. Mary is not your father's daughter, but your Uncle George's. Papa promised to keep an eye on her, and her mother, while George is in India. I have nothing against the little girl, but I cannot condone the actions of her parents."

"Why does Uncle George not wed Mrs. Birch?"

"Because she is already married, though living apart from her husband."

"I wish you had told me," Rosanne said, feeling the ground lurch beneath her. "I am a grown woman and no longer need to be protected from uncomfortable truths."

Her mother nodded. "You are right. It's hard for me to stop thinking of you as a child, but if you are old enough for marriage, you are old enough to learn that life is not always tidy. I shall do better in future."

"I have made a fool of myself."

"We all do that sometimes, my love. Since we are setting forth on a new road to openness, will you tell me what's wrong between you and your young man? Who knows? I may be able to help."

Rosanne threw her arms around her mother's neck and inhaled the comforting scent of her childhood. The distance that had grown between them, caused by her own discontent at home and her belief that her parent was pressing her to find a husband, melted away. She recounted the whole story, or most of it, omitting the kissing. There was a limit to mother-daughter confidence and she wanted advice, not a lecture.

"So you see, Mama, even though it turns out the thing was over nothing, I am glad it happened because otherwise I might never have found out that Lord Bruton was the author of the letters. How can I forgive him?"

Lady Warnford had listened quietly to the recital. Now she subjected her daughter's face to a shrewd examination. "Forgive Frank or Bruton?"

"Either."

"You seem much angrier with Bruton."

"He is more at fault. Frank would never have done this without him."

"It is strange to me that you are so very angry at a man who means nothing to you, that is all."

Bruton had not been nothing to her. He had been her friend and she trusted him.

"I don't know who either man is now."

Her mother stood up and looked through Rosanne's wardrobe, selecting her favorite blue silk evening gown. "Here," she said. "Let me help you dress. You are not going to find out by staying in your room. If you want my advice, you'll come down to dinner and give each of them a chance to explain himself. And if neither can satisfy you, why, there are other young men."

So there were. Perhaps she would further her acquaintance with Lord Willoughby, owner of the famous phaeton. That would show Bruton. And Frank.

Arriving downstairs for dinner, Rosanne went straight to her father and gave him a quick kiss on the cheek. He seemed surprised, and very pleased. She'd treated him coldly for weeks.

"Tell me about this miraculous carriage you've spent so much time admiring in the stables."

She listened fondly as he described, in exhaustive detail, the shining paintwork, sumptuous upholstery, and superior springs of what must surely be the greatest phaeton ever built. "I'd be happy if either you or Kate caught Lord Willoughby's fancy, puss," he concluded. "It would be a fine thing to have Hippolyta in the family."

"Papa!"

"It'll have to be Kate, eh? You have your heart set on Newnham, and he's an excellent fellow. Good eye for a horse or a set of wheels."

"We'll see, Papa. Things can change." She decided to leave it to her mother to break the news that Frank, whom she had no intention of forgiving, was out of the running. "Lord Willoughby has much to appeal to a lady apart from his equipage." Not quite as handsome as Frank—no one was—but with a charming smile. He also had a reputation as an incorrigible flirt. Just what she needed tonight.

By luck the gentleman in question passed by at that moment. Rosanne managed to beat several enterprising young ladies to his side and there was nothing he could do but offer to take her in to dinner. As she set her hand on his arm, she felt a kind of itch at the back of her neck, a shiver down her spine. Glancing back, she met Bruton's intense gaze. He stood quite alone in his black evening clothes, the scar livid in contrast to the snowy muslin of his elaborate cravat. Unlike the other guests, milling around and finding partners, he was quite alone.

It served him right. Why then, did she have the absurd urge to relinquish the flirtatious Lord Willoughby, who would scarcely miss her with all his admirers, and go over to him? The only reason could be the urge to berate him for his unspeakable conduct.

In the few seconds it took for these thoughts to pass through her mind, a young woman in white, the duke's eldest sister, approached him. A very suitable match for the heir to a marquess. She dared say Lady Serena wouldn't mind a deceiving weasel for a husband as long as he was possessed of rank and fortune. She hoped she could see beyond the scar to the intelligent and thoughtful and ... dastardly man.

She turned back to her companion. "Tell me all about your phaeton, Lord Willoughby."

Willoughby turned out to be quite a disappointment. He had something on his mind, and Rosanne didn't flatter herself that his compliments and badinage were anything but mechanical. He demanded little of her brain, leaving her too much time to dwell on her resentment toward a pair of cousins. Both seated on the same side of the table as she, there was no way of knowing how they enjoyed the long, lavish meal. She imagined Bruton entertaining Lady Serena with amusing, slightly sarcastic insights into life, literature, and poetry and Frank talking to an unknown partner about ... she had no idea. She knew nothing of his thoughts, his interests, or his opinions. He was a beautiful blank sheet of paper.

By the time dinner was over and the gentlemen joined the ladies in the drawing room, her rage had cooled to curiosity about the excuses either man would attempt. Frank was the one who found her. She allowed him to lead her to a settee in a quiet corner, protected by another of the duchess's enormous flower arrangements.

"Rosanne," he said. Then, not to her surprise, he stopped. The lack of his usual easy good humor and an unwonted pallor spoke of unusual agitation. "Rosanne," he repeated, in an agonized plea.

"Yes, Mr. Newnham?" Determined not to help him find his words, she felt as though she were kicking a puppy.

"I am sorry, very sorry. I wanted to please you so much. I never met a girl like you, never fell in love before. I'm a simple man, so I asked Chris to help me. When I said how wonderful you were, I meant it. Only the words were Chris's, not the sentiments. You are much too fine, too clever, and too beautiful for me, but won't you give me a chance?"

Frank had finally found his tongue and she gave him credit for the rough eloquence of his speech, if not for elegance or finesse.

"That's all very well, Frank. I am honored to have inspired such feelings. But I don't know you. I thought I was learning your character and your tastes from your letters, but I am no better acquainted with you than I was when we met at Melton."

He snatched her hand for a fervent kiss. "Give me a chance. There are still three more days until the wedding. Let me spend all the time with you. I'll do anything to change your mind."

His blue eyes glowed with sincerity, and he was still the handsomest man she'd ever met. But he no longer sent her heart tumbling. She regarded his perfect features and felt ... nothing. She found it hard to believe she'd kissed him. Twice. Closing her eyes, she recalled the embrace in the grotto and, for a moment, her body buzzed with the sensations of that momentous embrace. Then she opened them and met his anxious, hangdog gaze. Nothing.

She was over Frank Newnham.

"Well," he said. "May I try to regain your forgiveness and affection?"

"You have my forgiveness. I consider Lord Bruton far more to blame than you. As for the other, I doubt it is possible."

"I will never give up, never."



**F**rank meant it. No more slipping off to the stables for manly company and carriage worship. He dogged her footsteps all morning and he had plenty to say, none of it remarkable. She discovered that he was a very ordinary, even dull, man blessed with extraordinary beauty. His constant presence got on her nerves.

As for Lord Bruton, he appeared to be avoiding her, a fact she found extremely annoying. The man owed her an apology. Finally, frustrated by the earl's failure to grant her a much-deserved grovel, she sought him out and discovered him in the library, reading on a bench behind a pair of giant globes.

He leapt to his feet at her approach and stood before her in stiff military stance, not a muscle of his face or body moving. There was no way of telling if he was too ashamed to speak or simply wished she'd leave him alone. Both, maybe. Clearly he wasn't going to break the awkward silence.

Perching on the bench, she arranged her skirts and indicated that he should sit beside her, an invitation he ignored. "Do you have anything to say to me, my lord?"

"What can I say?"

"How about *I am sorry*?"

"An apology is an indulgence I do not deserve."

"I believe that is for me to decide."

"In that case, I am sorry." Every syllable seemed to pain him.

"You don't sound it," she said. "Frank's apology was more eloquent."

"Good." He walked a few feet to look out of the window, giving her a chance to admire his well-tailored back and note that his hands were clenched into fists. Whatever his thinking, he was not at ease. "Have you forgiven him?" he said.

"I have."

His shoulders slumped almost imperceptibly and he turned to face her. "That's that, then. There is nothing left for me to do but wish you happy."

She gave him a sickly smile, as insincere as his congratulatory grimace. "I didn't say I would marry him."

"Why not? You will never find a better man."

"Still speaking for your cousin, I see. I thought you had learned that lesson."

"I speak for myself too."

"Then for heaven's sake, speak. Why did you do it?"

Her urgency got through to him, and finally he spoke without sounding as though he had a mouth full of rocks. "I began with no motive but to assist Frank, with some reluctance I may add. I suppose I may as well admit that it was a bit of a joke. Then I found I could not resist the pleasure of our correspondence."

"I enjoyed it too," she said softly, not daring to ask about one particular letter, whether he had written the words she'd read so often they were burned into her brain.

*Rosanne of my heart. You consume my every thought, haunt my waking hours, and disturb my dreams.* No, she knew he'd written the words, but had they come from his heart and not Frank's? The desire to know obsessed her, but his face reflected only stoic constraint.

"When you confided your private family business, we both knew we were wrong," he said in a disappointingly reasonable voice. He might as well be giving her directions to the dining room. "The last few letters you received were Frank's alone."

"I see that now. That explains why they were different, and much less enjoyable." An indecipherable flicker of emotion crossed his features. "I prefer your epistolary style, and your conversation."

"Frank is shy with women, doubtless a result of growing up with four brothers and spending far too much time in the officers' mess. It sounds as though he has found his voice with you. You will discover he lacks neither intelligence nor ideas."

Rosanne doubted it, or doubted that Frank possessed the depth of character to appeal to her. She wanted more. Clearly Bruton needed a bit of encouragement.

"Lord Willoughby is a delightful man," she said.

He paced around their corner of the library in some agitation. "That lightweight! He named his carriage."

"A most amusing conceit."

"But of course, he has a pretty face and a charming smile. What else do women want?" Looming over her, he fingered the length of

141

his scar, and her heart ached for him. At the same time she felt a great deal better. She was also filled with a burning curiosity about how far down the blemish reached.

"For God's sake, Rosanne!" He crouched in front of her chair. "If you must care only for a man's appearance, at least let it be Frank, who loves you."

"Do you think we are all so shallow that we care only for the outer man? At first, perhaps. When I first saw Frank, he attracted me, like a peacock who displays his tail to impress the hens. But I fell in love with him because of his letters: his words and the thoughts they expressed. Now I know the words weren't his, and I doubt the thoughts were either."

His eyes bored into hers, making her dizzy.

"I wondered," she said carefully, "if perhaps some of those letters came from your heart." It was as close as she dared come to the question she wanted to ask. She could hardly throw herself at the man.

"My feelings are irrelevant."

"So you wish me to make up my differences with Frank."

"For his sake, I must," he said hoarsely, averting his eyes and not sounding at all like a man heartily endorsing the pretensions of his friend. "To do otherwise would be the height of dishonor."

How could she break through his rigid sense of honor? Convincing him that his looks did not repel her would be easier. Her fingers itched to touch the ruined cheek, to assure him that he was beautiful. With his face only a couple of feet away, she could do it. Before she could talk herself out of it, she raised the hands that had rested in her lap throughout the conversation and extended her arms, only to have him snatch her wrists and wrest them to her side.

"Don't," he said.

And then she knew. In the grotto, a man had seized her wrists rather than let her touch his face. It hadn't been Frank. Joy surged through her. The kiss in the grotto that marked the moment when she had truly fallen in love had come from this man.

To the Devil with honor, guilt, and any of the dozen other masculine reasons he had come up with to prevent his wooing her, as she was now confident he wished to. She loved Lord Bruton—Christian—and she was going to have him.

# CHAPTER SEVEN

As if life wasn't hellish enough, the duchess had organized a ball to entertain the wedding guests and made it clear that the occasion merited everyone's best clothes. The only thing Christian wanted to do was change into his oldest riding gear and gallop off into the hills until he and his horse were exhausted and he was too tired to think. Instead, while they got into their dress uniforms in their shared room, he had to listen to Frank bumble on about his plans for winning back Rosanne.

"You'll help me, won't you, Chris?"

"I don't see what I can do. You'll have to rely on the magic of your *beaux yeux* and skill on the dance floor."

"You could put in a good word for me. I know Rosanne likes you."

"I already did what I could when I apologized for our ruse. She says she's forgiven you, and now it's up to you to woo her. I'm staying out of it."

He meant it, too. The most he would do was leave the field open for Frank to try to win back Rosanne's affections. Given how splendid his cousin always looked in regimentals, he might very well succeed. And if he did not? Christian wasn't ready to face where that left him. He dared not indulge the mad hopes aroused that afternoon. It had taken every bit of strength he possessed not to sweep her into his arms. He'd been saved from foolishness by fear of her disgust. She hadn't seemed horrified when he crouched in front of her, close enough to drown in her gaze, but he was too accustomed to suppressed revulsion in the eyes of women. If a miracle occurred and he was ever again in the position to make love to Rosanne, he'd make sure he did it in the dark.

"You are right, Chris," Frank said. "I must win her myself. And I believe I can. This morning I found I could talk to her quite easily. It proves that she is the right woman for me."

If he were a better man, he would be glad his cousin had overcome his diffidence. Instead, he stood at the edge of the ballroom in despair as Frank and Rosanne, the picture of youthful beauty, moved in harmony though the steps of a quadrille. Frank was talking and she was laughing.

He could have danced with her. Both she and her sister had made it clear that they would welcome an invitation from him. Sticking to his resolve to give Frank every chance, he'd come up with a story about turning his ankle on the cobblestones of the stable yard. Since he didn't, thank God, have to dance with anyone else either, and unable to bear watching Frank's hopes come to fruition and his own float off into the night, he slipped away. No one would miss him.

**R**osanne knew the minute Christian left the ballroom. She'd kept an eye on him brooding against the wall, exuding a dark cloud that repelled anyone foolish enough to approach him. She also knew he'd been watching her. At the end of the quadrille, she excused herself and questioned a footman in the hall. Hoping that Christian had stepped outside—another encounter in the grotto would suit her very well—she found the news that he'd asked for his valet to be sent to his room rather daunting.

She quickly formed a different and riskier plan. An hour later, having retired to her room with the excuse of a headache, she dismissed her maid, wrapped her largest shawl around her nightgown, and set out for a spot of passage creeping. The gentlemen were housed in a different part of the house, well away from the single ladies. Her maid had told her the servants were holding their own celebration of the duke's forthcoming nuptials in the staff quarters, so she was able to traverse the dimly lit corridors and reach the bachelors' floor without encountering so much as a stray valet. All was quiet as she crept up to what she hoped was the right door. Peering through the keyhole revealed only that the room was lit. An ear to the aperture yielded a more promising sound: that of a page turning. Trusting that no other gentleman had decided to forego the joys of the ballroom for a book, she ignored the hammering of her heart and turned the handle, cracked open the door, and peered around it.

He looked up as she stepped all the way in. "Good God! Rosanne. What are you doing here?"

She closed the door behind her and leaned against it, clutching her shawl to her bosom. "I wanted to see how far down the scar goes," she said, more airily than she felt.

And now she knew. He sat up in bed bare-chested, revealing that the blemish extended to just below the collarbone. Even more remarkable were the contours of his shoulders and chest, the latter sprinkled with black hair. Really, it was a pity gentlemen always went out covered up to the neck. She felt a bloom of heat in her belly that she recognized as desire.

"Now that your curiosity has been satisfied," he said, the words emerging from deep in his throat, "you must leave. At once."

"No." The single syllable was all she could manage. She had become as inarticulate as Frank.

He started to rise, then stopped. "Damn. I can't even get out of bed while you are here. Turn your back."

How interesting. Now she had him where she wanted him. "No," she said again, with a provocative smile.

"Think of your reputation!"

"No one saw me," she said with a bravado she almost felt. "They are all dancing. Why did you leave the ball?"

"I preferred to read."

She sauntered over to the bed, removed the volume from his nerveless hands, and scanned the page of poetry. "*I could not love thee, dear, so much, loved I not honor more,*" she read. "What nonsense."

His throat rippled. "Not to me. It is the tenet by which I try to live."

To break down his barriers, she had to dare. Having come this far, there was nothing to do but demand the truth—and hope for the best. "Do you love me?"

The words fell into an unnerving silence. She was about to conclude she'd made an utter fool of herself when he replied in a low rasp. "God help me, I do. I have betrayed my best friend."

Joy and relief flooded her, tempered by an edge of pique. "This isn't just between you and Frank, you know. What about me? Do I have no say in the matter? I love *you*, Christian." The blaze in his dark eyes turned her knees to water, but his face otherwise remained carved in stone. She had more work to do before the much-anticipated reward of kisses and embraces.

"Nothing you or Frank can do will change that fact," she said. "I didn't intend to fall in love any more than you did, but it happened. To both of us."

With trembling fingers she touched the gash on his cheek, made livid by his pallor. She shook off his restraining hand. "I love your scar because it is part of you. It makes you even more beautiful to my eyes. You wouldn't let me touch your face in the grotto, but now I want to feel it." She ran her fingertips along the ridge of skin, down his cheek and neck. "Will you kiss me again, as you did that day?"

"How did you know it was me?"

"I guessed."

"Of all the things I have ever done, that was the most dishonorable." His hands, tanned against the white sheets, clenched in his lap.

"If our happiness is dependent on the dictates of honor, let me ask you this: Which is more important to you, Christian? Your honor or mine? I am alone with you in your bedchamber. I am wearing my nightdress and you, as far as I can tell, nothing at all. If anyone finds out, I shall be ruined. Will you save my honor?"

"You don't play fair."

"I am not an officer and a gentleman. However, if you wish, now that I have said what I came to say, I shall leave and hope no one sees me."

For endless seconds the outcome hung in the balance. Finally, with a groan that might have been misery but Rosanne preferred to interpret as joy to match her own, he seized her by the waist, drew her down with him so she lay across his chest and—at long last—brought her mouth to his.

Her lips opened to his on a sigh and heat spread through her body, unfurled by his kiss.

"Rosanne," he murmured, the word a mere puff of warm breath. Her heart was fit to burst with happiness. She had won and he was hers.

They kissed until she was dizzy and feverish. His bare skin burned through her linen, her breasts yearned for his touch, and lower down she ached and ached. His hands tangled in her hair, caressed her scalp. Neck, shoulders, and every other inch of her throbbed in vain, but he made no further move. She'd come here wanting and expecting to be kissed, and it wasn't enough.

Instead he lifted her head away and turned his own aside.

**I**t killed him to stop. In the space of a quarter of an hour, dull despair had turned to shattering happiness such as he'd never hoped to experience. That Rosanne loved him was more than he could logically take in. At any moment he expected to wake up and find he'd imagined the whole incredible encounter. He closed his eyes for a few seconds, and when he looked again, she was still there.

"I should let you go," he said.

She scrambled onto her knees but otherwise made no move to leave him. Straddling his thighs, she regarded him with a tenderness that sent his heart crashing and sucked the air from his lungs. He couldn't resist unwinding her hair from the imperfect restraints of a loose plait hanging over her breast, combing the locks smooth with his fingers, and arranging it over her shoulder.

"You are a goddess. Do you have any idea how beautiful you are?" His throat felt thick.

Her answering smile held a riveting blend of innocence and passion. Then she took his hand and held it against her breast. Blood roared into his cock. Through her nightgown her flesh was warm and lush beneath his fingers. Not for the first time he pictured the magnificence he'd never dared hope to see and touch in the flesh. Soon. Tomorrow he would ask for her father's permission to address her. Reluctantly he removed his hand.

"You are beautiful too," she said. "Never believe otherwise."

"If you mean that, I can only rejoice in your blindness and my good fortune."

When she again traced the line of his scar with a satin finger tip he almost stopped breathing. The touch of her lips on the spot where the red line narrowed to a point above his breast slew him. He stroked her hair and prayed for strength.

"You skin is warm," she said, "and a little bit salty."

He groaned. She smiled.

147

"Do you know what will happen if you do not leave this room immediately?"

"Yes. I want it. I want *you*."

When it came down to it, there was only so much his sense of honor could resist.

Laying her down on the mattress, he set about ensuring that she wouldn't regret the gift she offered in entrusting herself to him. Accustomed as he was to pleasing women to make up for his ugliness, he determined to do even better with the one who didn't find him a monster. With some misgivings, he left the candles alight, but seeing Rosanne without her nightgown, all rosy and cream, drove away his inhibitions.

He explored her body in a way that would give her as much pleasure as she gave him by the very fact of her existence. With complete focus, he noticed every minute reaction, each heightened breath, each gasp, each happy movement, as his lips and mouth worshipped the silken skin of neck and shoulders, the firm softness of her gorgeous breasts.

"Oh yes! Don't stop," she whispered, as he applied his mouth to a tight nipple, and arched her back when he sucked it hard.

So he didn't stop but let his hands descend over the gentle hill of her belly and into her core.

"Oh, Lord! What are you doing?"

"Hush, darling. You will like this."

And she did. He took it slowly, letting her arousal mount until she was bucking with delight and frustration.

"Relax," he coaxed. "Let me see to you."

Then he kissed her again, mimicking the rhythm of his fingers with his tongue, swallowing her joyful moans, feeling her accelerated breathing against his own racing heart. The only thing better than sensing her sex grow wet and hot and clench around his fingers would be to see it for himself and taste her. His own urgency, he ignored. His only wish was for her pleasure and when, after a long climb, she exploded in quivers of joy, he had never known anything more beautiful. He watched her head tilt back and heard her low keen. He hoped that would always be the sound of her fulfillment. He would have years to find out and that incredible fact made his heart swell to the point of explosion.

Whispering every endearment he knew, he held her close as the waves of passion abated and continued to caress her body, to keep her arousal simmering while his own strained against her stomach.

She smiled at him with huge and dreamy eyes. "Amazing. But I know there is more."

"There is," he agreed. "I'm afraid this bit will be more enjoyable for me than for you."

She stroked his hair and cheek. "That seems only fair since what just happened was more enjoyable for me."

"You are wrong. Seeing you in ecstasy was the best thing that ever happened to me."

A wriggle of her hips elicited a groan. He was now beyond conversation, needing all his energy to take her on the next step of the journey with due care and deliberation. Propped up on his arms, he flexed his hips and slid his rigid cock along the crease of her sex.

"Oh!" she said. "That's wonderful."

After maintaining the movement as long as he could, he reached down to confirm that she was as wet and slippery as he thought. Sliding into her with all the patience he could muster, he halted when her happy murmurs ceased with a sharp intake of breath. "All right, sweetheart?"

Her response was a gallant smile and a thrust of her own that took him all the way into heaven. Raining kisses on her face, he let her adjust to his size before he began to move with long, steady strokes, adoring her, adoring shared congress with the one he loved. With astonished joy, he sensed her renewed response and all coherent thought ceased. Joined in a swirling eddy of heat and sweat, of soft moans and eager breaths, they drowned in pure sensation until he felt her climax and, for the second time, heard her particular cry of bliss. Only then did he let himself go, tense every muscle and toss back his head in a silent shout of triumph before shuddering into his own orgasm and collapsing, utterly spent, into her welcoming arms.

She had expected it to be good, but the whole experience defied her moderately informed expectations and most hyperbolic imaginings. And now she felt wonderfully, perfectly splendid, with no further ambition than to pass the rest of her life in Christian's company, doing it again as often as possible. Every inch of her skin, every ounce of her flesh, every drop of her blood, and every thought in her head was focused on how much she loved him.

She stroked the damp black hair resting on her breast. She had just done the one thing she knew a lady should never, ever do outside of marriage. She wasn't worried. He hadn't mentioned the word, but she trusted Christian completely for his sense of honor and the fundamental decency of his character.

Once his heaving breaths slowed to normal, he rolled onto his back, eyes still closed, wearing an expression of supreme satisfaction that became him well. Leaning on her elbow, she drank in his beloved face and waited. When at last he raised his lids, they gazed at each other foolishly with matching idiotic grins.

"We shouldn't have done that," he said, turning serious. "We should have waited until after the wedding."

"Oh! Is there to be a wedding?" She could barely suppress giggles of glee.

"There had better be."

She turned over and sat up, folding her knees back, and tried to look prim, rather difficult when she was naked on a mattress with an equally naked man stretched gorgeously before her. "I do not believe I heard a proposal. Though I grant I may have missed it, being distracted by other things."

He grinned again, a younger and joyful Christian she'd never seen before. Her heart turned over and all she wanted was to hurl herself onto him again. But first things first. Her mother would insist on it. Her lips twitched.

"Miss Lacy. Will you marry me? If you consent to be my wife, I will be the happiest of men." The formal words seemed odd delivered from a reclining position but nonetheless beautiful.

"On one condition." He raised his brows, the action no longer sardonic, but happily amused. "That you kiss me again, immediately."

"I believe that could be arranged. Anything else?"

His heated look raised a blush she could feel from forehead to ... lower down. "We already did that," she whispered.

"We can do it again." Good Lord! His male ... part was expanding before her fascinated gaze. "But first you have to say yes."

"Yes." The syllable was barely uttered before he pulled her down to join him, enveloping her in his strength and taking her lips in another kiss, soft and lingering without the explosive hunger of their first joining. She fancied it the kiss of two people in love, exploring each other physically as they would in other ways over the years, and recognized the expansive fluttering in her chest as pure joy. Instead of deepening his embrace, he held back, not letting their fever rise. Finally, with a sigh, he released her mouth, settling her loosely in his arms.

"Why not?" She didn't mind. Lying with Christian like this was a delightful aspect of a shared bed. She tucked her head into the angle of his neck, reveling in the intimacy of their nakedness, both relaxed and marvelously alive.

"You are new to this and once is enough. I don't want to hurt you."

She did feel a little sore. "I love your body," she said, stroking his chest and running her thumb along the ridge of his collarbone.

He returned the favor, idly plucking at her nipples with his finger tips. "Not as much as I love yours."

"Even though I suspect this is an argument neither of us can lose, I can't be bothered now." She took a deep breath. "I am too happy all over. I wish I could define the feeling."

"It's why I read poetry. At its best, it puts our deepest emotions into words."

"I could learn to like verse myself if it does that. I cannot describe the sensations that seem to spread from my heart, but now I know how love feels."

"You put it very well," he said, his voice deep and thick.

They lay in silence for a minute or two, and her questing finger found his scar. "Christian," she said, "won't you tell me how you got it? Everyone has been speculating on what heroics you must have performed."

"Idiots," he said, without rancor.

"A duel is the most popular theory, but I doubt you called anyone out at the age of ten."

"There were no heroics. I fell off a horse."

"Most of us have, at some time. How did you come to suffer such a terrible injury?"

His muscles tensed beneath her hand and for a moment she thought, despite everything, that he wouldn't confide in her. But he answered readily enough.

"I was showing off for my father and tried to jump a brute of a hedge, too wide and too tall for my mount. The pony refused at the last second and I went head first into the obstacle, catching a stiff branch that sliced me open. Only by a miracle did I keep my eyesight."

Rosanne closed her eyes to squeeze out the vision of the child's tender flesh being cruelly ripped. "Why didn't your father stop you doing something so rash?"

His voice hardened. "I doubt he noticed what I was doing. It was and still is a rare occasion that we are under the same roof. We'd never ridden together before, and I wanted to impress him. What a wasted effort."

"I don't understand. How could he not care about his son? His only child?"

Only a tightening of his arms belied the studied flatness of his tone. "I am his son and, more to the point, his heir. But I am not his only child. I had no idea why he cared so little for me. Only later did I learn that my father had a mistress and children before he wed my mother. Theirs was a purely dynastic arrangement. He was upset by my accident only because, had I been killed, he would have to return to his wife's bed to get another heir. His true family lives comfortably in Kensington, and that's where he spends most of his time."

"I'm so sorry, my love. I see why you understood my distress over little Mary."

"You father may have strayed, but at least he loves you, and your sister. I have watched you together and I know."

Now that she knew the truth about Christian's family life, she felt almost ashamed of believing ill of her father, who had never spared his daughters either affection or attention.

"He does love me," she said, "and you were right when you doubted he was that kind of man." She told him what she'd learned from her mother. "So you see, my confidence was unnecessary. I cannot be sorry, however, for I might not have guessed that you wrote Frank's letters, or only discovered it too late."

"I am not looking forward to breaking the news to Frank that I have stolen his beloved."

He mustn't be allowed to let guilt shade their happiness. "I wasn't Frank's to steal," she said firmly. "He never proposed to me and I never accepted."

"I promised I'd give him the chance to change your mind."

"Nothing he could do would have succeeded. I knew I did not love him, even before I knew I loved you. Even before I discovered that the letters that meant so much to me were yours. He was disappointing in person."

"Frank's person has never disappointed anyone."

"Are you fishing for another compliment?" She ogled him outrageously from his elegant feet, the length of his muscular legs, past his powerful member, and all the way to the scar that added such character to his face. "Here's one. You are a much better kisser. You must have felt unbearably smug when I told you about my feelings after the grotto."

"Unbearably stupid, rather. Hoist with my own petard."

"I could have a few choice words to say about that particular episode, but I've decided to put it all behind me and think only of the future, which will, I am confident, be quite delightful."

"I love you, Rosanne," he said, "but I fear I do not deserve you. I am not a sweet-tempered man."

"Good. I'm not a sweet-tempered woman. I've always been told that a lady doesn't show anger, doesn't *feel* anger. Since I am to wed a curmudgeon, I take it as permission to indulge my annoyances and voice my displeasure."

"You need never dissemble your feelings with me."

"Nor you. I shall see your bouts of melancholy as a challenge to dispel." She extended her exploration of his body below the chest, discovering the muscles over his ribs, the firm, flat belly and the masculine hip bones. "How are you feeling now?"

"Quite sweet-tempered."

Her hand moved lower. "And now?"

A firm grasp on her wrist stayed further descent. "Unfortunately, we need to stop. You must return to your room before the party disperses. And before Frank comes back."

"You share this room with Frank?" She chuckled, and clearly Christian was feeling far from curmudgeonly, for he joined her in mirth. "Thank heavens I had no idea or I would never have come here, and that would have been a great shame."

# CHAPTER EIGHT

**C**hristian trusted that Rosanne had reached her room without being seen, at least in the bachelors' wing. Letting her go had been a wrench. The muscles of his face ached with unwonted smiling as he contemplated a time when he could keep her in his bed all night. Only the thought of his cousin cast a shadow over a joy that was more delightful for being utterly foreign.

They had decided that Rosanne would tell Frank she would not marry him, firmly denying any chance of a reconciliation. Their own engagement would remain a secret until after the duke's wedding. Then Christian would break the news to Frank that he wished to court Rosanne himself and follow her to her own home after the house party dispersed.

He didn't like lying to Frank. Even more, he hated that he couldn't publicly claim Rosanne as his own, announce his triumph to the world, and spend every second of every day at her side, basking in her smiles and her conversation, and finding ways to get her alone ...

There was absolutely no chance he could be interested in poetry again that night, nor any other book. Neither would he sleep. So he dressed and went downstairs to look for company. Furthering his acquaintance with Lord Warnford wouldn't be a bad idea. If he couldn't spend the night in Rosanne's arms, he could amuse himself by searching her father's face for a resemblance. The lack of music from the ballroom and the procession of guests–mostly female–up the main staircase told him that the evening was over for most.

He was heading out of the billiards room, which contained a crowd of men, but not Warnford, when James Blair, the duke's cousin, hailed him. "Bruton! Just the fellow we need to make a fourth at whist. The ladies are all taking to their beds and the night is but a pup."

Why not? He enjoyed an occasional game and was in a mellow enough mood to put up with almost anything. He followed Blair to a small antechamber set up for cards. The other two players turned out to be the two people in the world he least wanted to see at this moment: Frank and Lord Willoughby. Not that he had any reason to resent the latter now. But he was not so magnanimous as to welcome the company of any man who had the temerity to flirt with Rosanne. He hoped he'd draw Blair as his partner.

"Look whom I've found," Blair announced. "You know Bruton better than I, Newnham. Is he a player you can trust not to trump his partner's ace?"

Frank appeared a little the worse for wear, with his scarlet jacket unbuttoned, his hair awry, and his face flushed. The reason for this unsoldierly disorder was apparent as he poured a full glass of wine down his throat and reached for the decanter. Finding it almost empty, he scowled at the mouthful that remained and sloshed it into his glass. Though Frank usually drank in a spirit of happy conviviality, the belligerent glare he aimed at his cousin made Christian's neck prickle.

"You don't want to bet against Bruton," he said, not sounding as intoxicated as he looked. "He always has an ace up his sleeve."

Blair and Willoughby exchanged uneasy glances. Was this a jest?

Christian hastened to lighten the awkward moment. "And you, Frank, my boy, have a glass too many in your belly. Careful these gentlemen don't misunderstand you."

Blair forced out a laugh and Willoughby flashed his accursedly brilliant smile. "We're all friends here. Come and cut the cards. I fancy our chances against Blair and Bruton, even if they are clever fellows."

Frank brushed off a well-intentioned effort to get him into a chair. "Very clever, is Captain Lord Bruton. You need to watch him carefully, or he'll rob you blind." Christian hadn't known that Frank could curl his lip—that was more his own style—but he curled it now. Fixing Christian with a gaze filled with pain and betrayal, he enunciated his words carefully. "Let me be very clear. Lord Bruton doesn't play with the officers of our regiment because he's a damn cheat."

This was arrant nonsense, and both men looking on in appalled silence knew it. However slight their acquaintance with Christian, the reputation of the Horse Guards endorsed him. The famous regiment would never tolerate a card cheat in its ranks.

Frank *knew.*

Outwardly composed to disguise his sinking heart, Christian walked forward and stopped a couple of feet from Frank, who had taken up an aggressive fighter's stance. "Gentlemen, I think it would be better if you left us alone to settle our differences."

"Don't go," Frank said. "Your services will be needed." And he tossed the remains of his wine into Christian's face. "That will improve your hideous scar, Lord Cicatrix."

Never in all their years of friendship had Frank used the hated nickname. "You're drunk. Let us go somewhere and talk."

"You're a damn coward, Bruton, and I demand satisfaction."

"I think that's up to Bruton," Willoughby interjected. "He's the one who's been insulted. I know he doesn't hold with dueling, but I don't see what else he can do, do you James?"

"I think there's a good deal too much senseless quarreling at this gathering," Blair replied. "Newnham should apologize. He's drunk as a lord."

"I shall never apologize, but I'll be happy to let Lord Bruton defend his *honor* the way a *gentleman* does."

The last thing Christian wanted was to break his vow against dueling to fight Frank, of all people. Yet he couldn't explain to two near-strangers that Frank must have walked into their bedchamber and discovered Christian with the woman Frank loved, a young lady of spotless reputation. Damn and blast! Why had he given in to his own weakness? He should have sent Rosanne scurrying back to her room and waited to quench his endless desire for her until they were lawfully wed. He should have been strong. He'd behaved with dishonor and ended up in disaster.

There was only one thing to do.

He bowed crisply. "Choose your weapons, Lieutenant Newnham."

He did it to protect Rosanne, and also because he owed it to Frank. The accusation of cheating was a mere pretext, and Christian couldn't find it in his heart to blame him for the subterfuge. Under the circumstances, he'd have done the same. He owed Frank the chance to beat the Devil out of him.

"**W**ake up, Rosanne!"

Pulled unwillingly from a delicious dream, she opened her eyes to a flickering candle flame in an ocean of darkness. "Christian?" she murmured. Unlike in her dream there was no warm body beside her, but perhaps that could be remedied. Her hand emerged from the covers and found an arm. Not the sinewy masculine limb lightly sprinkled with hair that she yearned for but a smooth, slender one, capped by a puffed sleeve. Kate. Rosanne sank back into the nest of blankets and tried to resume the interesting events of her sleeping state.

It was not to be. "Hah!" Kate said, far too loudly as she grasped her sister's shoulders. "Now I understand. Wake up immediately. Frank and Lord Bruton are fighting a duel."

Where shouting and shaking failed, this news had her fully awake. "What?" She sat bolt upright. "When? How?"

"At dawn."

She leaped out of bed and ran to draw the heavy curtains. "It's still dark. Do you know where they are meeting?" she demanded, making a mare's nest of the wardrobe as she rustled through clothing in the feeble light.

"In the meadow on the other side of the lake. Lord Willoughby says it's out of sight of the house."

"Willoughby? What does he have to do with it? How do you know, anyway?"

"Bridget told us." By "us" Kate meant the duke's sisters and other young girls. Dazed with happiness, Rosanne hadn't paid much attention to the fact that Kate hadn't come to bed, merely been grateful that she wasn't there when she returned from Christian's room.

"Do up my stays, will you?" she asked. "Have you been downstairs all this time?"

"We were having a midnight feast in the day nursery. Alexandra managed to hide a bottle of wine and some sweetmeats under her shawl and we were safe up there because the head nurse sleeps like a log. We could hear her snoring all the way down the passage."

"Christian and Frank were in the nursery?" Rosanne asked, quite confused.

"Of course not. Bridget stole downstairs when everyone was dancing and hid behind the tapestry in one of the card rooms because she wanted to find out if Mr. Blair was meeting Miss Grey."

"You cannot be serious? Never mind that now. Then what?"

"She came up to tell us what she heard. Keep still." Rosanne almost screamed with impatience as Kate fumbled the lacing. "Frank accused Lord Bruton of cheating at cards."

She swiveled round, almost knocking her sister to the floor. "Christian would never cheat!"

"*Christian* again. I'd like to know when Lord Bruton became *Christian*. A couple of days ago you were madly kissing Frank in the grotto."

Rosanne snatched up a gown at random. "I have no time to explain now," she said, mumbling through the muslin. "Button me up and keep telling me about the duel."

"Mr. Blair is to be Lord Bruton's second and Willoughby will be Frank's." Kate tugged at the apron front of the gown. "This must be mine. It's too small for your bosom."

Rosanne swallowed a scream of frustration just in time to prevent awakening the whole floor. The next garment she laid hands on was a silk evening gown, but she didn't care. "Since they're both soldiers, do you suppose they'll fight each other to a standstill? I know they both practice fencing a lot."

"It's pistols."

"Oh, heavens! One of them will be killed and it's all my fault. We have to stop it." She grabbed a shawl to cover the gaping back of her gown and thrust her bare feet into a pair of slippers. "There's no time to lose. I'm going."

"I'm coming too."

The long descent through the silent mansion put an end to further conversation. They tiptoed through the great hall, where a dozing footman remained on duty all night, and wasted precious minutes that felt like hours looking for a door they could unlock on the garden front. By the time they found one, Kate's candle had burned to the socket and Rosanne made an appalling discovery. "The blasted rosy fingers of dawn," she said with a groan. "It was dark when we left our room."

"Our room faces west."

"You could have pointed that out before," she said and took off at a run through the endless levels of garden. Why did the Duke of Wessex have to live in such a ridiculously large place?

What did "at dawn" mean, she wondered as she panted step by endless step in the growing light. Would the duel start at dawn, or was that when the combatants arrived at the meeting place? There wasn't a soul to be seen as she reached the treeless lawn descending to the lake.

"How are you going to stop them?" Kate yelled at her elbow.

She wished she knew. How they had been discovered she had no idea, but the accusation of cheating was a pretext. And Christian, already feeling guilty about betraying Frank, wouldn't turn down the challenge. They had to be stopped.

Damn, stupid men. And stupid her, too. By going to Christian's room, she'd played with his elevated sense of honor. The notion of him being badly injured or killed was too appalling to even contemplate. And supposing he won? She wasn't familiar with the laws of dueling, but she was fairly certain that if you killed an opponent you had to flee the country. And she didn't want Frank to be hurt either.

With her heart pumping from fear and exertion, she felt hot tears on cheeks cooled by the early morning chill. She tripped, almost fell headlong into the damp grass, and had to stop to adjust the unfastened gown that was slipping off her shoulders. Deciding this wasn't a moment for modesty, she hitched the silken skirts above her bare knees and increased her pace, ignoring Kate's cries of "Wait for me!"

Ahead of her, the arched stone bridge spanning the lake emerged from the mist. Dawn had definitely broken. She must be on time. She must. Gathering air into her burning lungs and summoning a final surge of strength, she streaked across the lake and into the copse that screened the meadow. Through the trees, she glimpsed the swath of green tinged by pale sunlight and heard male voices. With the rising sun in her eyes, she saw a fair man in a red coat raise a pistol and take aim.

"Stop!" she cried and prayed she was on time.

When Frank had demanded "Pistols at fifteen paces," Christian knew he was serious. Christian was the better swordsman, and Frank held a bare edge in the boxing ring. They'd fought each other many times, always in friendly bouts. But as a marksman Frank was a nonpareil. If he intended to hit a man at fifteen paces, he could do it easily, and it was by no means certain that Christian could hit him back. If Frank wanted to kill him, he could.

When Christian contemplated joining a regiment fighting the war in the Peninsula, he'd known death was a possibility and it hadn't troubled him. Now, he had something he desperately wanted to live for. To lose his future with Rosanne by Frank's hand held a certain poetic justice, but for once he wasn't in the mood for poetry.

Frank had disappeared with Willoughby, his second, without another word, giving Christian no chance to argue him back to sense. For his own part, Christian had spurned the offer of wine and company from Blair. While grateful to the man for agreeing to act for him, he had no wish to spend what might be his last night on earth making conversation with a virtual stranger. He'd retreated to the library to brood and wish he could be in Rosanne's bed, in her arms. The best night of his life had turned into a nightmare.

Apparently Frank hadn't returned to their room last night, either. Like Christian, he still wore his dress uniform, the scarlet cloth a shocking splash of color amid the muted greens of the park at dawn. Blair and Willoughby checked the pistols while Frank avoided Christian's eye. His cousin's expression was a new one: grave, still, intent. *Like a man about to go into battle*, Christian thought, and wondered if he looked the same.

"It is our duty as seconds," Willoughby said in a solemn voice but exchanging a look with Blair that said he couldn't believe he was doing this, "to attempt to effect a reconciliation." He turned to Frank. "Mr. Newnham, will you apologize to Lord Bruton?"

Frank's features remained cold and steadfast. Under other circumstances—if it were indeed the onset of battle—Christian would have been proud of him. "I will not," he said.

"Lord Bruton." Blair took his turn. "Will you withdraw your challenge?"

At any sign of softening, Christian would back down. For a second, Frank's eyes displayed a flicker of emotion, but his face remained stony.

"I cannot," Christian said. "I demand satisfaction."

It wasn't his own satisfaction he sought, but Frank's. If shooting at him would make Frank feel better about losing Rosanne, he was ready to give him the chance. Though the seconds didn't know it, he was the offending party in this duel, guilty of stealing the affections of his cousin's beloved, and he didn't regret it a bit. There was no way short of death that he would ever give her up. He trusted it wouldn't come to that.

"Stay here," Blair said. "Jack and I will select a suitable piece of ground and pace out the distance. There are a devil of a lot of molehills and we wouldn't want you to trip."

Through the copse of elms, mist rose from the lake, droplets of water glistening in the rising sun. It was as lovely a morning as one ever saw in England and should have been Christian's happiest. His opponent stood at attention beside him, watching the seconds work.

"Frank," he said softly. "I'm sorry."

"You were kissing her. On the bed." At least things hadn't progressed too far when Frank made his unnoticed appearance. "You ruined her."

"I'm going to marry her. I love her and she loves me. We planned to tell you."

Frank gulped. "I trusted you," was all he said. He was never good at expressing himself, which was what had got them into this damnable mess in the first place. Another thing Christian should, but did not, regret.

"I didn't intend it to happen. It just did. Does it have to come to this foolishness?"

Frank turned his back on him.

The ground selected, the seconds returned and gravely handed them their pistols. Mantons, which meant their aim should be true, though shooting an unfamiliar gun was always risky. As Wessex's secretary, Blair would have had access to the best contents of the duke's gun room, and the chasing on the barrel was particularly fine. Not that it mattered, but time had slowed to a trickle and every little thing, however irrelevant, took on massive significance. Each blade of grass in his path, each clinging drop of dew looked painted by the hand of a master. A handkerchief, stark white against the greensward, marked the place where Christian would turn and aim a deadly bullet at his oldest friend. His dearest friend, who would aim back at him. His favorite cousin, who was far more likely to do damage at this distance than he was.

"Cock your pistols. March."

It was time. Time to consider what he would do, a decision he'd avoided throughout his sleepless night. His instinct was to fire in the air, but deloping in a duel could mean one of two things: admitting that he was at fault and a cheat, or showing disrespect for his opponent. He wished to do neither. He decided to aim wide, but not insultingly so, and trust his shooting was good enough not to hit Frank by mistake. What Frank would do was out of his control. He patted the pocket of his tunic and hoped that Frank wouldn't shoot him right through the neatly folded square of his final letter to Rosanne, lying next to his heart.

He checked the ground and found the seconds had chosen well. No molehills or hummocks, though tufts of long grass were unavoidable in the summer meadow. He noted a particularly thick one and avoided it in his stance. Due south, so neither had to aim into the rising sun, Frank was already in place. He looked as he always did, incuriously content with whatever life offered.

"Ready?" Blair shouted.

Christian nodded and he supposed Frank did too.

"Fire at will," Willoughby commanded.

The elaborate gold facings on Frank's dress uniform glittered, making an easy target. As did his own, of course. He took careful aim at least a yard to Frank's left.

Three things happened in succession, so quickly that he could never tell in what order.

A feminine shriek of "Stop."

Two shots.

He waited for the pain of a wound. Nothing. Examining his body gingerly he concluded that he was unharmed. But Frank had pitched forward and lay on his side, knees awkwardly folded. Rosanne tore across the grass, hair streaming behind her, her gown falling off her shoulders, and her skirts hitched up to display far more leg than should be seen by any man but himself.

"Frank!" she cried, kneeling beside him. "Are you all right?"

Willoughby and Blair hastened to the scene and Christian joined them at a run. The blasted red uniforms didn't show blood, which was all very well for maintaining battlefield morale but almost gave him a seizure as he waited to see where he'd wounded Frank and how badly.

"Oh, Frank!" Rosanne wailed. "I'm so sorry. I didn't mean this to happen."

Christian tore off his jacket, losing a button or two, and draped it over her shoulders. A nasty knot in his stomach told him he might be about to lose both his friend and his bride, judging by her agonized tears. The least he could do was protect her from the insolent gaze of Jack-bloody-Willoughby. "What are you waiting for?" he yelled at Willoughby. "Fetch a doctor. He could be bleeding to death."

He fell on his knees next to Rosanne, nudging her out of the way. "Let me see."

"How could you shoot him?" she asked through a sob. "Why did you do anything so terrible?"

"I didn't mean to." He leaned over his cousin, feeling his chest and limbs for a wound. Thank God his heartbeat seemed strong and he was breathing deeply, almost panting. "Damnation, Frank. By what miracle did I hit you while you missed? The pistols must have been off."

"Newnham fired into the air," either Blair or Willoughby said.

He had deloped. The knot in Christian's stomach dissolved into nausea. "Wake up, Frank. Tell me where I hit you."

Frank rolled over. "Hell's teeth, man. You missed me by a yard. Can't you do better than that? Good thing you aren't in a foot regiment."

"He's all right!" Rosanne burst into tears and threw herself into Christian's arms. "Thank God!"

Her relief, expressed in shuddering sobs, could hardly exceed Christian's own. Now that he knew he hadn't shot Frank, the joy of holding Rosanne engulfed him. In the shelter of his jacket he found her slender waist and drew her close, murmuring incoherent words of love into her disordered hair.

"I thought he was dead," she said into his chest.

"No one is happier than I that I didn't hurt him." Lifting her chin, he kissed her eyelids, wiped the salty tears from her cheeks with his thumb, then took her lips. Even under these circumstances their kiss was perfection, as it always would be. When her hands touched his face, he realized he would never again give a damn about the scar.

"Ahem."

Someone's cough released him from a blissful trance. What he did care about was that his coat had fallen off and her undergarments were on display to the interested gaze of no fewer than three gentlemen. Helping her up, he rearranged the red tunic about her shoulders and met Frank's gaze.

"Will you accept my apology now, Frank?" He offered his hand, searching for softening and seeing only a dull pain.

His cousin nodded despondently. "I wish you both happiness."

"Thank you," Rosanne said softly. "I am sorry I hurt you."

"You picked the better man."

"No," she replied. "Not better, but the right one for me."

An uneasy silence fell, broken by the arrival of a limping Kate Lacy. "I turned my ankle and missed the whole thing. I heard shots but as far as I can see no one was hit. What happened?"

"What did happen?" asked Blair, who had been standing with Willoughby at a short distance from the trio.

Frank's face turned sheepish, a welcome return to a familiar look. "When Rosanne arrived shrieking, my attention wavered and I tripped on a thick tuft of grass. My fault. First rule of dueling is examine your ground. Lucky I was aiming high or I might have hit Chris by mistake."

"So neither of you meant to shoot the other?" Rosanne asked.

"Of course not," Frank replied. "We're cousins."

Kate threw up her hands. "Then why fight a duel at all?"

Christian and Frank traded infinitesimal smiles. "Shall I answer that?" Frank nodded. "It's because we are gentlemen."

It was the sisters' turn to exchange glances, of utter incomprehension, while Frank finally took Christian's hand then seized him into a hug. "Are you going to be all right?" Christian asked.

"Yes," Frank said with his usual eloquence and Christian knew what it was like not to have a care in the world.

"I don't know about you," Willoughby said, "but I'm hungry. Besides, I have something important to look for—er—to do."

The party moved back toward the house, Kate hopping along, hanging onto Frank's arm and chattering like a magpie.

Christian and Rosanne let the others go ahead. "You know," she said, "Kate claims to like a silent man."

"She certainly talks enough for two. Perhaps Frank and I will end up brothers-in-law."

"That would be splendid." With wild hair, reddened eyes, and her gown falling off, she had never looked more beautiful, and she smiled as though, miraculously, she felt the same way about him. He drew her into the shadow of a sturdy tree.

"Right now," he said, "I'm not interested in anyone's marriage but ours."

"Not even the duke's?"

"Especially not his."

A long, delicious kiss later, he reluctantly set her aside. "How soon can we be married? Tomorrow?"

"My mother will want to organize a big wedding and introduce you to our friends and relations. Also to all the neighbors she most dislikes, so that she can show off having a daughter married at last." She laughed at his heartfelt groan.

"I look forward to getting to know your family, and I don't even mind impressing the neighbors. But I'd rather do it as a married man."

She gave him a saucy look through lowered eyelids. "I hear the Archbishop of Canterbury is arriving today."

"I shall speak to him about a special license. Then my career as a good-tempered, sociable man can begin. Now turn around and let me fasten your gown."

"I don't want you to change one little bit." She cast a delightfully lascivious glance over her shoulder that set him sizzling to his core. "I dreamed of you last night and wished you were in bed with me."

"The sooner I am, all night and every night, the better."

# ABOUT THE AUTHOR

Miranda Neville grew up in England, loving the books of Georgette Heyer and other Regency romances. She now lives in Vermont with her daughter and an immensely talented cat who made a book trailer for her novel *The Importance of Being Wicked*. Her historical romances published by Avon include the popular Burgundy Club series, about Regency book collectors, and The Wild Quartet. *P.S. I Love You* was inspired by Cyrano de Bergerac and her very talented fellow authors.

For more information about Miranda and her books, and a link to the fabulous feline book trailer, visit her website www.MirandaNeville.com. She loves hearing from readers via email, Facebook or Twitter.

# WHEN I MET MY DUCHESS

Caroline Linden

# CHAPTER ONE

It was going to be a terrific storm.

Gareth Cavendish, Duke of Wessex, surveyed the rapidly darkening sky as he stood on the steps of his country estate. Gray-violet clouds boiled up in angry billows and every few seconds thunder rumbled, as if the storm were clearing its throat, preparing to roar. But so far not a drop had fallen.

"I do hope they're near," he murmured, scanning the pristine landscape of his property. "The clouds may burst at any moment."

The man behind him shifted his weight. "Sir William is a very punctual man."

"Yes." Gareth narrowed his gaze upon a far-off puff of dust, just visible beyond the stately oaks that lined the road leading to Kingstag Castle. A servant had been sent out to watch for the visitors' arrival, but it was still over a mile from the main gates to the house. A moment later, a traveling chaise-and-four emerged around the last turn. "There. Just as you said, Blair. Very punctual."

His secretary murmured a vague reply.

The carriage bowled smartly down the drive, drawing nearer. He stood a little straighter. It wasn't every day a man welcomed his bride-to-be to his home. Miss Helen Grey, younger daughter of Sir William Grey and the toast of the Season, would be the Duchess of Wessex by the end of the month. Gareth was very pleased with the match. Her father's best property marched with one of his smaller estates, and according to the marriage settlements, that land would be his one day, as Grey had no sons. It was a good match as well, for the Greys were an old and respected family, even if they had fallen on rather hard times of late. And the young lady herself was ideal: a serene, gracious manner, a lovely face and form, and a beautiful voice. Helen Grey would make the perfect Duchess of Wessex.

Gareth glanced again at the sky. He hoped the storm broke soon and blew over quickly. Guests were to begin arriving the next day, and he shuddered to imagine the chaos if everyone was kept indoors for the next week.

"Let us hope there are no lightning strikes, hmm?" He half-turned to flash a faint smile at his secretary, who nodded, stony-faced. Gareth took another look at the man who was not merely his secretary. James Blair was his distant cousin from a poorer branch of the family and superbly competent. He relied on him like he relied on his right arm. Normally they worked together in perfect tandem, Blair anticipating his thoughts and Gareth relying on his cousin's uncommonly good judgment in all matters. No one was more closely acquainted with his business concerns or personal matters, nor a better friend. He trusted the man completely.

But now his secretary looked as though a funeral train were approaching instead of a bridal party. "All right, Blair?" he asked curiously.

Blair stared straight ahead, his eyes flat. "Yes."

He glanced toward the approaching chaise as an awful thought struck him. Good Lord. There couldn't be something about this marriage giving him pause, could there? Blair had conducted the marriage settlement negotiations on his behalf while estate business had kept Gareth in the country. Naturally, he must have seen Miss Grey and her family a fair amount. Alarm stirred in his chest. Perhaps Blair has seen something troubling but hesitated to bring it up now that the documents had been signed and the engagement announced. Blair would notice. Blair also would not want to embarrass him.

He cleared his throat. "You seem quiet. No reservations about the bride, I hope?"

At last Blair looked at him, albeit reluctantly. "No. Miss Grey is a very suitable choice."

That seemed an evasive answer. "Were there any problems with Sir William?" he asked, lowering his voice even further. Blair shook his head. "Come, man, what is it?" he prodded. "You look positively grim."

Blair's chest filled as if he would speak, and then he sighed. "My apologies, Wessex," he muttered. "It must be the storm."

Gareth closed his eyes and mentally smacked himself on the forehead; he'd completely forgotten Blair had been frightened of storms as a boy. Perhaps he still was, and now Gareth had just gone and forced him to admit it aloud. "Of course," he murmured quickly.

"I wish you and Miss Grey every happiness," added his secretary with a forced smile.

Gareth nodded, happy to let the conversation lapse. The carriage was almost to the steps, and for a second he wondered what he might have done if Blair had confessed some wariness about Miss Grey or the marriage in general. He couldn't very well just send her home, but it would have been gravely alarming had James found her wanting.

There was a rustle of silk behind him. "I hope I'm not late," said his mother as she stepped up beside him.

"Your timing is perfect," he said. "I presume Bridget had something to do with it."

"As ever," she replied under her breath.

Gareth shot his mother a quick glance. All three of his sisters were beside themselves with excitement over the impending celebrations and desperately eager to meet Miss Grey, the reigning toast of London. But while Serena and Alexandra were capable of proper, dignified behavior, the youngest had a true genius for trouble. If anything were to break, go missing, or inexplicably wind up on the roof, Bridget was sure to be found nearby, protesting—with a perfectly straight face—that the most incredible circumstances had caused it. Normally he took Bridget's mishaps in stride, but he would be eternally grateful if she managed to behave properly for the next fortnight. Perhaps he ought to tell Withers, the butler, to post footmen outside the guest rooms to make certain Bridget didn't accidentally inflict a broken leg or a black eye on the bride.

"She'll be on her best behavior, won't she?" he asked, praying that would be good enough.

"Yes." The duchess gave him a confident smile. "I've told her she will be excluded from all the wedding festivities if she is not. For now, I've sent her to help Henrietta entertain Sophronia."

His shoulders eased. "A masterstroke." The only person more capable than Bridget of causing trouble was Sophronia, his great-great-aunt. Or was she a great-great-great-aunt? He tended to think of her in the same vein as the statues in the garden: ancient, crumbling, and utterly impervious to anything. Normally Sophronia kept to her own apartments with her companion, Henrietta Black, but if she and Bridget could occupy each other tonight, so much the better for everyone.

"Never let it be said I don't know my children." His mother turned to face him and her gaze sharpened. "Do you love this girl, Gareth?"

She only called him Gareth when she wanted to get his attention. His eyes narrowed, but he spoke calmly. "What has love got to do with marriage?" He knew it existed and that it was pleasant to find it in marriage, but he'd never met a woman who stirred him, even slightly, the way poets and romantics sighed about: the world upended, walking on air, being struck by lightning from a clear blue sky. Rubbish. Whatever else Gareth might have been amenable to, he preferred to keep his feet on the ground, and he most certainly didn't want to be hit by lightning. If such a force even existed, he was just as happy not to know about it. His marriage to Miss Grey would be elegant, refined, and sensible: in a word, perfect.

"Don't scoff," said his parent. "You know I only ask out of concern. You've persuaded me the match is advantageous for both parties, but you've hardly said one word about your feelings for the lady herself."

"She's lovely. She'll make a very suitable duchess and mother. You'll adore her."

"I wasn't worried about adoring her myself," replied the duchess. "I worry about *you* adoring her."

His jaw tightened. What a time to ask that question. "I have the utmost respect for her, and I trust we shall be very content with one another."

His mother only sighed.

Irked at her and at Blair for ruffling what had promised to be a perfectly smooth welcoming, he descended the steps as the carriage reached the gravel and slowed to a more decorous speed. There was nothing to reproach in his actions. He was a sensible man who made logical decisions. He thought he'd chosen quite well, despite his mother's sentimental disquiet and his secretary's grim silence. If they had some objection to this marriage, he thought darkly, they had better speak soon or forever hold their peace.

But this was not the moment to brood about that. Straightening his shoulders, he prepared to welcome his future wife and her family. Miss Grey, her parents, and her elder sister would spend the next fortnight at Kingstag, preparing for the wedding at the end of that time. Behind him, the butler, housekeeper, and a few servants waited at the ready to greet their soon-to-be mistress. The house had been cleaned and polished to a bright shine over the last month to appear at its best for the wedding. He darted a quick glance at his mother, but she silently stepped up beside him, her serene smile back in place, and he breathed a sigh of relief.

The sky growled again as the coach pulled to a halt. A dust-covered servant jumped down to open the door, and Sir William alighted first. The baronet fairly radiated triumph. "A very great pleasure, Your Grace," he boomed, sweeping a bow as the servant turned to help Lady Grey down.

"The pleasure is mine, sir. Welcome." Gareth greeted the older gentleman. "May I present my mother, the Duchess of Wessex?" His mother stepped forward and graciously greeted the baronet.

Gareth turned his attention to Lady Grey. "Welcome to Kingstag Castle, madam." He bowed over her hand.

Her pleased eyes climbed the façade of the house before she turned a beaming smile on him. "A pleasure it is to be here, sir. And for such a happy occasion!" She laughed, a little trill of delight. He smiled, then stepped forward to help his betrothed down from the carriage himself.

Helen Grey was lovely, he thought approvingly as she stepped down, her small hand nestled in his. He'd thought so from the moment he met her. Her dark hair was arranged in the latest style, her dress the picture of elegance. She looked as fresh and beautiful as the roses in his mother's garden. The Greys must have stopped so she could change and refresh herself before arriving. "Welcome to my home, Miss Grey." He raised her hand to his lips as he bowed.

She blushed, her cheeks a perfect soft pink. Her dark eyes glowed as she gave a little curtsey. "Thank you, Your Grace. I'm delighted to arrive at last."

Gareth smiled in satisfaction. She truly was the perfect bride. Her voice was just as lovely as he remembered, and her person even lovelier. Her manner was gentle and sweet. What more could a man ask for in a wife? He presented her to the duchess, pleased to see his mother greet her as warmly and graciously as ever. He knew she would never be rude or crass, but he wouldn't put it past her to probe—in that delicate, almost imperceptible way she had—into Miss Grey's feelings as well.

"How fortunate you arrived before the storm broke," he said to Sir William. "It's been threatening all day."

"Yes!" exclaimed Lady Grey, fanning herself. "We were quite worried we would be caught in a downpour."

"It looks to be a bad one," observed Sir William, squinting at the sky.

"Indeed. Shall we proceed inside?" Gareth paused, remembering something. "But did you not say your eldest daughter would also be accompanying you?"

A moment of silence passed over the group. Sir William and Lady Grey exchanged a glance. Miss Grey wet her lips. "Yes. My sister did come. She wanted a moment to repair her appearance, I believe."

"Ah." Gareth nodded, and turned toward the carriage again, wishing the sister would hurry up and get down so they could step inside before the rain came and soaked them all. How long did she need to repair herself, anyway? Miss Grey managed to look as neat and elegant as any lady in town.

"I'm coming," said a voice from the carriage. "Just a moment!" She appeared in the door of the carriage, her face hidden by a dark red bonnet. She gathered up her vibrant yellow skirt in one hand and reached out to take the hand of the footman waiting to assist her. "So sorry to keep everyone waiting," she said a bit breathlessly as she jumped down and faced them all.

She looked like her sister, but different. Where Helen Grey's face was tranquil and composed, this woman's face was lively and expressive. Her eyes sparkled and danced. Her features were sharper than Helen's and her figure was fuller, almost lush. And as she tipped up her pointed chin and looked at Gareth with openly interested brown eyes, lightning struck.

# CHAPTER TWO

Everyone jumped at the thunderous crash and the burst of light that burned a streak across the sky. "Gracious!" cried Lady Grey, clapping a hand to her heart. "I thought it would strike us all dead on the spot!"

Helen's sister turned her face to the sky as the first sharp drops of rain hit the ground. "It looks to be a good show," she said mischievously.

"Indeed not, Cleo," said her mother in an undertone. "Behave yourself!"

Gareth heard all this dimly, around the introduction. Mrs. Cleopatra Barrows, Sir William was saying, his eldest daughter. He thought he made the polite response but couldn't be sure; once he took her gloved hand in his, he wasn't quite sure what else went on in the world around him. It wouldn't surprise him if his hair were standing on end, and he was most likely staring like an idiot. Mrs. Barrows put on a polite smile and curtseyed, but that excitement that sprang into her face at the crack of lightning stuck in his mind.

A soft noise behind him finally broke whatever spell he'd fallen under. He stepped back, remembering himself. "I'm delighted you've arrived at last. You remember Mr. Blair, of course?" Blair stepped forward and bowed.

"Capital to see you, sir," said Sir William courteously, and Lady Grey gave him a benevolent smile.

"Mr. Blair," murmured Miss Grey.

"Mrs. Barrows," said the duchess, coming toward her. "What a delight to make your acquaintance. Welcome to Kingstag Castle."

"Thank you, Your Grace." She dropped a graceful curtsy.

"And you must meet Mr. Blair," his mother continued, looking at Blair, who obediently stepped to her side. "He is Wessex's secretary as well as our cousin."

"How do you do, sir?" Mrs. Barrows gave Blair a sunny smile, and Gareth's stomach clenched. He had to make himself turn away from her, unnerved by his reaction.

"Come, let us go inside," he said, offering Lady Grey his arm. "The guests will begin arriving tomorrow. I thought you might like a day to explore the castle on your own before they lay siege to the place."

Lady Grey gave her trilling little laugh again as she fell in step beside him. "How kind of you to arrange it so, sir! We are thoroughly delighted to be invited for such a stay, and to meet your mother and sisters! I vow, Kingstag Castle is every bit as lovely as I'd heard ..."

She chattered on as they walked inside. Gareth was aware of Mrs. Barrows walking behind him with Blair. In the doorway he stole a glance back, catching sight of his cousin's smile at something she said. Miss Grey followed, listening soberly to his mother, but her sister chatted quite amiably with Blair.

He felt a strange stab of discontent in his chest. Logically, he should hope Mrs. Barrows could revive Blair from whatever melancholy he'd sunk into lately. He should hope his cousin took a great enough liking to Mrs. Barrows to entertain her for the next fortnight, leaving Miss Grey to him.

Somehow, he didn't.

The housekeeper stepped forward to show the guests to their rooms to refresh themselves and rest. Although, as Mrs. Barrows passed him with a swish of her brilliant skirt, he couldn't help but think that the Greys didn't look in great need of refreshing. Gareth watched as they climbed the stairs, Lady Grey in the lead with the housekeeper and his mother, followed by Miss Grey and Mrs. Barrows.

"Just as lovely as you remembered?" asked Blair quietly, coming up beside him.

Gareth tore his gaze off Mrs. Barrows's figure, trying to shake off the unpleasant feeling of having been knocked sideways. "Yes."

Blair exhaled. He still looked a little ill, his mouth tight and his eyes shadowed. "That is a great relief."

Gareth breathed deeply. The ladies had reached the turn of the stairs, and he watched Mrs. Barrows trail one gloved hand along the banister appreciatively. "Yes. It is, isn't it? I can hardly stop the marriage now."

Blair shook his head slowly, still watching the women climb the stairs. "No. I don't suppose you can."


"**G**racious, Helen, you never said he was so handsome!"

Cleo burst into her sister's room, too full of energy to rest. Helen was lying obediently on the bed, but at Cleo's entrance she sat up at once, just as she had since they were girls. Of course, this time their nurse wouldn't come scold them for not resting like proper young ladies, thought Cleo with a grin, since she was a widowed lady and her sister was about to become a duchess.

"Do you really think so?" Helen's face lit up with a luminous smile.

Cleo laughed. "Of course! Such broad shoulders! Such brooding eyes! Such a lovely home!" She laughed again. "Did Mama see Kingstag Castle before you accepted his offer, or after? I thought she would swoon with delight when the house came into view."

Helen sighed, her glow fading. "After. You well know she would have liked him had the house been a fright. He's a duke, Cleo, and very wealthy," she said in perfect imitation of their mother's voice. "What more does a girl want?"

"Mmm, and handsome, too," Cleo added. "A mother might want a title and a fortune, but a girl wants a handsome face."

Helen tried, and failed, to repress her grin. "Cleo, you're wicked."

"Of course I am," she exclaimed. "That's why you love to have me about. But hush—" She lowered her voice and glanced around. "I did promise to be on my best behavior this fortnight," she whispered. "So you mustn't let on when I'm my usual awful self, or Papa will send me packing."

Helen's smile disappeared. "It was dreadful that Papa said that to you," she said in a low tone. "You are not awful."

Cleo lifted one shoulder. "To them I am. The stench of trade, you know. I suppose someday I might give away all my money and take up embroidery or some other suitable pursuit and live out my days in respectable poverty." She gave a theatrical sigh and collapsed backward on the chaise as if in a swoon, throwing up one arm over her head in a fit of drama. "Perhaps then I'll be acceptable. Poor and dull, but acceptable."

"You could never be dull," said her sister. "I'm ever so glad you've come, because if you're here, at least it won't be dull." She shuddered.

Cleo uncovered her face and looked at Helen curiously. "Do you think it will be? Why? You're reunited at last with your betrothed husband, about to meet his family and become his wife."

Helen rolled her lower lip between her teeth and plucked at the lace on her sleeve. "I don't know him that well, Cleo," she confessed. "I've only seen him a few times this year. And last year ... well, he didn't distinguish himself from my other suitors in any real way. It seems odd, doesn't it, that I'm to marry him in two weeks' time and I barely know his name."

"Gareth Anthony Michael Cavendish," said Cleo. "How could you not know his name, when Mama's been practicing saying it every day? 'Their Graces, the Duke and Duchess of Wessex,'" she mimicked her mother, just as well as Helen had done. "'Wessex of Kingstag Castle.' 'My son-in-law, the duke.' 'My daughter, the Duchess of Wessex.'"

Helen laughed again. "Stop! Perhaps I do know his name, but otherwise ..." She shook her head. "The wedding just seems so near, all of a sudden."

This time Cleo looked more closely at her sister. It had been clear to her that Helen was nervous their entire journey, but she'd thought it was only bridal nerves. Helen wasn't usually a nervous sort, though. "Don't you want to marry him?"

Her sister's face turned bright pink. "Of course. Who would not?"

Cleo couldn't argue with that, and yet ... "Perhaps he invited us early to get to know you better," she suggested. "To steal away into the garden with you and kiss you senseless." Helen's eyes went wide. Cleo grinned, trying to lighten the mood. "Oh, don't be like that. It's not at all a trial to be whisked into the shrubbery for a clandestine kiss from a handsome man."

Helen's smile was a trifle wistful. "Isn't it?"

"No doubt you'll soon find out." Cleo leaned forward, unable to resist prying a little. She didn't see her sister very much anymore, and she missed her. She and Helen had never had secrets from each other, once upon a time, before Cleo's marriage and subsequent widowhood had horrified her parents and made visits to the family home uncomfortable. "Don't you want him to?"

Before Helen could answer, there was a tap on the door, closely followed by the entrance of their mother. "Oh, girls," she whispered in ecstasy. "Isn't this the loveliest house? Isn't His Grace the handsomest gentleman? Oh, Helen, my darling, you are a very, very lucky girl!" She bustled over to kiss Helen's forehead. Watching her sister, Cleo thought there was a flicker of panic in Helen's eyes before she smiled at their mother.

"Thank you, Mama. I thought you were resting."

Millicent Grey waved a hand. "Pooh! As if I could sleep away my first hours at Kingstag Castle. It's one of the most beautiful estates in all of England! And my daughter will be mistress of it in just a few days' time!" She swept Helen into another embrace. Cleo draped her arms over the end of the chaise and rested her chin on her arms, watching. It had been a long time since she'd seen such an outpouring of maternal affection.

"Now, are you feeling well?" Millicent placed her hand on Helen's forehead. "Shall I send for a tonic? Luckily we've brought our own Rivers, I can have her prepare my special tonic at once."

Helen clasped her mother's wrist and smiled. "I'm fine, Mama. I don't need a tonic."

"A bath?" pressed Millicent. "I wager the duke's staff can have one ready in no time. I hear he even had pipes installed to bring in the water! Have you ever heard of such a thing? Let's send for a bath and find out."

Cleo couldn't resist rolling her eyes. Hadn't they just stopped at an inn barely three miles distant so Helen could wash and change her dress? Of course she must look lovely for her future husband—Cleo didn't argue with that—but this was silly, pretending to rest when none of them could close their eyes and wanting a bath just to discover if there really were pipes for the water.

"I'm fine, Mama." Helen pushed her mother's hand away and dodged it when Millicent would have reached out to smooth her hair. "Really, I'm quite recovered from the trip. Cleo and I were just talking about the duke."

Millicent paused, clearly caught between the excitement of gossiping about their host and wariness of whatever Cleo might have said. "Indeed?" she asked with a too-bright smile. "What did you decide?"

"That he's a very handsome gentleman," said Cleo dutifully.

"Of course he is!" Their mother beamed, relieved.

"But Helen doesn't know him all that well, does she?" Cleo went on, unable to ignore the devil inside her. "How long was his courtship?"

Millicent glared daggers at her. "It was all very proper," she said sternly. "He contacted your father, most properly, and made a very pretty proposal—"

"Before he'd spoken to Helen?" Cleo was genuinely shocked—she hadn't known that—and looked to Helen for confirmation. Her sister frowned and looked down, picking at her sleeve again.

"And his secretary—no, his *cousin*, Mr. Blair, came every week to pay his respects and make the arrangements!" Millicent lifted her chin.

"Didn't His Grace call on you, Helen?" Cleo asked, ignoring her mother.

Helen said nothing.

"Of course he did!" said Millicent indignantly. "Last Season! Several times! And twice this year!"

This was all news to Cleo. When Helen had said she didn't know the Duke of Wessex well, Cleo had thought it was due to a short but typical courtship, not one conducted by proxy. "And he sent his cousin to *propose?*"

"He did—That is—Not everyone must run wild and elope like you did, miss!" Millicent's temper got away from her, and Cleo could almost see smoke coming from her mother's ears. Behind Millicent, her sister was ripping the lace from her sleeve, her head bent.

She relented. Helen had accepted Wessex's marriage proposal, and it was her choice. She said she was happy to be marrying him. Cleo had no right to make her sister more nervous than she already was.

"No, Mama," she said soothingly. "They mustn't. And I am very happy for Helen."

Millicent opened her mouth, then closed it, as if she'd been ready for more argument. "Of course you are," she finally said, accepting the truce. "We all are. But Helen! You must rest!" Cleo watched her mother press Helen back down, fluttering around her like an excited bird. This must be a dream come to life for Millicent, marrying her most beautiful daughter to a duke, especially after the disappointment Cleo had been.

She wondered if her mother had ever had the same hopes for her, before she proved herself difficult and rebellious. She wasn't *completely* unlike Helen. She was pretty enough, though not beautiful like her sister. She'd been told she was intelligent and clever, but with an appalling tendency to speak too strongly and be too opinionated. Her great failing, though, had been her willingness to marry a man in trade, thereby drawing shame and discredit upon all her family. Millicent, the daughter of a squire and wife of a baronet, had dreamt of having a titled son-in-law her whole life. For Cleo to saddle her with a merchant son-in-law was intolerable.

Of course, her mother's reaction to her marriage had been kind and warm compared to her father's response.

From across the room, Helen's eyes met hers, reluctantly amused and resigned. She'd always been the obedient daughter, and today was no different. Cleo would have wagered a guinea Helen would end up taking both a nap and a bath to please their mother.

She jumped to her feet. "I'm going to take a walk in the garden." It might not be the nicest thing to leave Helen at their mother's mercy, but she didn't think she could take all the smothering maternal affection. She whisked out the door and back to her own room for a shawl, then went in search of the outdoors.

Despite the lightning, the storm was mild. Only a light mist was falling when a servant directed her to the gardens behind the house. She let her skirt drag in the wet grass, lifting her face to the sky. It felt good to be outside after two entire days in the carriage with her parents. If she could have managed it, Cleo would have hired her own carriage just for herself and Helen, leaving the elder Greys to congratulate themselves on Helen's triumph all the way to Dorset. Their mother, of course, had wanted Helen nearby in case a spasm of delight overcame her again and she needed to smother her daughter in an embrace. Their father hadn't trusted Cleo not to put "radical and absurd" ideas into Helen's head. He'd watched her warily the entire trip, and Cleo had nearly bitten her tongue off a dozen times keeping her silence. And his final warning, delivered even as they drove up the sweeping drive of Kingstag, had almost been too much. She'd had to sit in the carriage a minute and compose herself before getting out.

But she *would* keep her composure, come what may. It was only for a fortnight, and it was for Helen and her wedding. She was aware that her parents had invited her only because Helen wanted her to come. Her father might be ashamed of her and her mother might think her unnatural, but her sister still loved her, and she wouldn't repay that by causing strife and discord.

She slowed down as she reached the gravel paths of the garden. The Duke of Wessex, no matter that he might be remote and cool when it came to courting a wife, had a lovely garden. She stopped to examine all the plants, marveling at the profusion of greenery and blooms. How on earth did they get them to grow so thickly? Her own house had only a small garden, and nothing seemed to thrive. But these roses! They were everywhere, lush globes of pink and yellow petals that smelled divine. Cleo stuck her face into the flowery bower and sniffed, in paradise. What she wouldn't give for her garden to look like this ...

And this would be her sister's home. She touched another fragrant rose, spilling a cascade of raindrops onto her skirt. The Duke of Wessex wasn't at all what she had expected. From Helen's description of him, she'd imagined an older man, very elegant and urbane. The man she'd met today was far more masculine. Thick waves of dark hair threatened to tumble over his high forehead, which gave him a somewhat wild look that was at odds with his surprisingly sensual mouth. He was undeniably handsome, but there was an implacable strength in his face as well. Cleo fancied he was a man of strong passions and great control, the sort of man who wouldn't be denied anything he set his heart on.

Then she shook her head at how ridiculous she was, imputing an entire personality to a man she'd only just met. No doubt he'd turn out to be much as Helen described him, once she got to know him a little better. Dukes were far out of her ordinary acquaintance.

She bent down to sniff a peony, trying to squash the seed of worry that had sprouted when Helen confessed to nerves. Her sister was gentle and kind-hearted, and Cleo wasn't at all certain Helen would be able to stand up to a man as intimidating as the duke.

It worried her that Wessex had only called on Helen a few times. How could one marry on such short acquaintance? She could forgive her sister, who had, no doubt, been dazzled by his rank and broad shoulders and very handsome face, but she hoped the duke hadn't chosen Helen because she was beautiful, demure, and dutiful. He must be a very busy man, and if he didn't spend time with his bride, he would never know how wonderful Helen was. And if he made Helen miserable ...

She sighed and walked on toward the irises. As strong as her instinct was to protect Helen, this was not her battle. Helen had chosen him, and she must have had her reasons. Again her father's warning echoed in her mind: *Hold your tongue or you will be dead to all of us.*

The rain grew a little harder, and she shook out her shawl, intending to drape it over her head. She had two weeks to take the duke's measure. The duke had two weeks to recognize what a jewel Helen was.

"Are you well?"

She jumped at the sound of the voice, dropping her shawl in the process. The man she had just been thinking of stood behind her. "No, no," she said, flustered, then corrected herself. "That is, I'm quite well, thank you. I was just admiring the roses."

The Duke of Wessex stooped to retrieve her shawl. "My mother is a passionate gardener. She'll be pleased you admire her work."

"Very much so," she said with enthusiasm. "They're superb!"

"She does dote upon them," he agreed.

"Everything beautiful must be nurtured and loved." Cleo reached toward a pink rose that climbed up a nearby wall. "Nothing could bloom this profusely without a great deal of care."

He cleared his throat. "And a large contingent of gardeners."

She laughed. "I am sure they help as well, but this is a garden of love. Don't you agree?"

The duke didn't move. "Love?"

Cleo vaguely knew she ought to mention her sister, but the intensity in his dark eyes jangled her thoughts. "Yes. Love for the plants ... although also a place where one might be moved to steal a kiss in the shrubbery."

She had shocked him. His eyes darkened, and he opened his mouth to speak only to close it again. Oh dear; she'd let her mouth run away from her already.

"Indeed. You may be correct," said the duke before she could apologize. "Forgive me if I interrupted your study of the roses and the—er—shrubbery. I was on my way to see a tree."

"A tree?" she echoed, grasping at a new topic gratefully.

"It was struck by lightning, or so I was told."

Cleo remembered the tremendous crack of lightning when they first arrived. "Oh, yes! I almost fell off the carriage step, it startled me so. I hope the tree didn't damage anything."

His expression was as calm as ever, but his eyes were piercing as he looked at her. "Likely not. We are positively overrun with oaks at Kingstag. I expect we'll all be glad of the lightning when the tree is fueling our fires."

She grinned in surprise, not having expected a duke to pay attention to what went into his fireplaces. "How very practical."

For a moment his gaze seemed to snag on her smile. Cleo wiped it away at once. Oh dear, had her impulsive nature already managed to offend? But all he said was, "Quite."

She wet her lips. The rain was growing harder now, although the duke didn't seem to mind. "I think I ought to go back to the house now. The rain ..." She held up one hand as if to catch the drops falling around them.

He looked up as if just noticing the rain. "Of course. And here I am, holding your shawl." He handed it back to her.

"Thank you, Your Grace. Until dinner?"

He thrust one hand through his hair, sweeping the wild locks back over his forehead. It exposed his sharp cheekbones and firm jaw more starkly. Cleo was impressed in spite of herself. Gracious, how could Helen *not* want him to whisk her into the shrubbery? "Until dinner, Mrs. Barrows." He bowed and walked on, his boots crunching on the gravel.

Cleo flung the tail of her shawl over her head and hurried toward the house. Suddenly, two weeks didn't seem so long after all.

# CHAPTER THREE

It was an eternity before the dinner hour finally arrived.

Gareth delayed going to the drawing room. He smoothed his cravat and tugged at his jacket, trying not to notice how his heart seemed to be thudding very hard against his ribs. He hadn't seen his bride since the Greys arrived. That was perfectly expected; no doubt she had wanted a chance to rest from the journey and refresh herself. The fact that he kept picturing Mrs. Barrows—instead of Miss Grey, his chosen bride—reclining against the pillows of her bed was surely just a result of the lightning strike. It must have been closer than he'd thought and disordered his brain. No doubt as soon as he saw her at dinner, he would realize how mistaken that first electrifying impression had been.

Of course, he'd met her for a moment in the garden and nothing had happened to change it. On the contrary; she'd called it a garden of love and mentioned kissing in the shrubbery, and his mind had almost ceased working.

But now it was time to see her, along with his bride and her parents and even—God help him—all his family. His sisters were wildly excited to meet Miss Grey, and his mother had deemed dinner the proper time. Perhaps some of his bride's quiet self-possession would wear off on Bridget especially, he thought, trying not to think how Mrs. Barrows's lively nature was far more like his siblings'.

He took a deep breath. What was the matter with him? It *must* have been the lightning. Once he met the lady in proper, dignified circumstances, he would revert to his usual sane, rational self. Surely a longer acquaintance would confirm what he truly believed, that Helen Grey was the best possible choice for his duchess. She would be an excellent hostess, a kind mother, and a good role model for his sisters. She would look beautiful on his arm. He would have her dowry property, which he had long coveted. Just thinking through the logical, sane reasons why he wanted this match had a calming effect. He had made the right choice, and his odd fascination with her sister was merely a passing flight of fancy.

The door opened behind him and James Blair came in. The storm had blown away, and Blair's expression was once more calm and equable. He would be at dinner tonight as well, as he often was at family dinners or when there was an unescorted lady present. Gareth had even excused him from most of his duties for the next fortnight; Blair had spent a great deal of time around the Greys this spring, and he could help smooth any awkward moments that might arrive as the families mingled. "Ah, there you are. I was beginning to fear you'd left me to face the ladies all by myself."

"Sir William would be there."

"I had hoped for more," said Gareth dryly.

"And here I am." Blair made a grimace. "In desperate need of a drink, I'm afraid."

"Yes." Gareth seized on the word. Now that his cousin mentioned it, a drink sounded like just the thing. "A brilliant idea." He went to the cabinet in the corner and poured two measures of brandy, glad of something to do.

"I've decided to grant your wish regarding Mrs. Barrows," said Blair then, with no warning at all.

The brandy bottle seemed to lurch in his hand, spilling liquor on the silver tray beneath the glass. "What do you mean?" he asked, keeping his back to his cousin as he hastily mopped up the liquid.

"That I act as her escort this fortnight."

"Ah yes." Gareth had forgotten that request. It had seemed a natural one to make a week ago, when all he knew was that Helen Grey's older widowed sister would be part of the party. Blair had already agreed to do that; why did he have to bring it up now? "I thought we'd settled that a week ago."

"I was uncertain." Blair accepted a glass of brandy. "But after meeting her today, I believe I may enjoy her company a great deal."

Gareth was struck motionless. "Why?" was all he managed to ask. Had Blair also met her in the garden? Hadn't he been cowed by the threat of lightning? For some reason, Gareth was wildly irked that his cousin might have seen her with raindrops glistening on her skin.

Damn it, maybe they'd better go in to dinner at once, so he could take another long look at her and cure his irrational interest right away.

Blair seemed not to notice his tension. "I suspect she is the source of some tension in the family. There was something about the way she pressed her lips together when she stepped out of the carriage."

He pictured her mouth and took a gulp of his drink. "She's a widow with her own home. Perhaps there's something in her own life, and not her family's, that gave her pause."

"No doubt. She married a shopkeeper when she was only seventeen, and she still owns and runs the shop."

A shopkeeper's wife. Gareth either hadn't paid attention to that part of James's report on the Grey family or hadn't cared enough to remember. "Where is the shop?" he asked, instantly chagrined that he had done so. Why did that matter?

"In Melchester, near Grey's property. A rather large draper's shop."

A draper's shop. He pictured her running her fingers over bolts of brilliant silks, gauzy laces, satin ribbons. He tossed back the last of his brandy. Why did she run the shop? Ladies did no such thing; his mother would have fainted away at the thought of managing a shop. "How independent. What do you suspect, Blair?" He tried to get back to the main topic, which was ... oh yes. Mrs. Barrows's secrets. The way she pressed her lips together. "Is this shop a dark family secret?"

Blair shook his head. "No, although you won't hear a word about it from Sir William. The man has a supremely inflated sense of himself, and I doubt he approves."

"No, I expect not." Gareth's one overriding impression of his soon-to-be in-laws was pride. Sir William clung to it, and Lady Grey couldn't hide her delight in having a connection to Wessex. He rather doubted a merchant in the family had been as agreeable to the Greys. "Why did she marry a shopkeeper?" he murmured, almost to himself.

"Apparently she loved him." Blair's faint grin returned. "I told you: impulsive, bold, and passionate. She's a woman who isn't afraid to pursue what she wants."

Oh, Lord. He raised his glass and realized it was already empty. "Do you think that might be causing this tension you noticed?" he asked, grasping at Blair's earlier comment.

"I'm not certain." Blair spoke slowly. "Didn't you remark it? I wasn't aware of it earlier, in London, but it was almost palpable when they arrived."

Gareth frowned. He hadn't noticed anything amiss—well, he hadn't noticed much of anything beyond Mrs. Barrows's mouth and eyes and the way her skirt swayed as she climbed the stairs, none of which had struck him as remotely amiss. "I wonder why. Could it be the wedding?" He lowered his voice, watching his cousin closely. "Do you think Miss Grey or her parents want to break the engagement?"

Blair seemed startled. He turned to Gareth, a frown creasing his forehead. "I highly doubt it, Wessex. What made you say that?"

Yes, what *had* made him say that? He had no idea. This morning he had been highly pleased with his impending marriage and his choice of bride. Not one wisp of hesitation had clouded his mind, not even his mother's gentle chiding about love and affection. Then a woman—the wrong woman—looked up at him with sparkling brown eyes and it seemed as though all his logical decisions had been made hastily and foolishly, based on air. Now he had just asked, without any forethought at all, if his bride might be planning to jilt him. Even worse, there had been a thread of hope in his question.

What was wrong with him tonight? His mother had planned a wedding celebration that would be spoken of for years to come. Dozens of guests would be arriving in a matter of days. The marriage contract was signed. The bride was upstairs, probably already planning how she would redecorate when the duchess's suite was hers. The marriage was going to happen. Gareth must have lost his mind to contemplate—let alone contemplate with equanimity—anything else.

"Nothing," he said, telling himself it was true. "You made it sound very ominous, and that was the most alarming thing I could think of on the spot. The wedding is in a fortnight, after all."

Blair's shoulders eased. "Of course."

He cleared his throat. "Yes. Right. Well, thank you for sharing your concern with me. If anything particular comes up, do let me know."

"Of course I will. I shall do my best to learn Mrs. Barrows's secrets."

For some reason, that didn't sit too well with Gareth. He cast a longing glance at the brandy decanter but resolutely set down his glass. "Shall we go to dinner?"

"Indeed," murmured Blair. "Time to face the enemy."

That fit a little too well with Gareth's own feeling, so he said nothing. They went to the drawing room, where much of the family had already gathered. His sisters had clustered around Miss Grey, chattering with various degrees of animation. Serena and Alexandra, he was pleased to see, were achieving some level of decorum, but Bridget, as feared, was louder and more boisterous than ever. For her part, Miss Grey seemed a little cowed by them. Her smile was uncertain, and she wasn't saying much, although in fairness, it must have been rather intimidating to have three girls discussing every detail of her dress and pelting her with queries about London.

His mother was conversing with Sir William and Lady Grey, who looked up with twin expressions of rapture at his entrance. Gareth joined them as Blair headed for the younger ladies. He had a way with Bridget, and Gareth hoped Blair could calm his sister down so she wouldn't frighten poor Miss Grey to death.

"Good evening, Your Grace, good evening!" Sir William almost preened in his satisfaction. "Delightful house."

"Oh yes," gushed his wife. "I've never seen one finer!"

"How very good of you to say so." He inclined his head, keeping one eye on the door. A quick survey of the room had revealed the absence of Mrs. Barrows.

"If you'll pardon me, I shall have a word with the butler about dinner." His mother lowered her voice as she passed him. "Sophronia has deigned to join us this evening."

"Has she?" Gareth shot her a look. "How generous of her."

"Don't start," she murmured, edging past him. "I tried to dissuade her."

Everyone knew that was hopeless. Nothing dissuaded Sophronia once she set her mind on something. Still, it gave him something to think about as Lady Grey's effusions of delight over Kingstag Castle continued. Everything was perfection, in her opinion, and she seemed determined to list each point. It grew to be a bit much, to tell the truth. Gareth appreciated his home and was pleased to hear it admired, but she went on and on as though praising a gift he had given her. As soon as he could, he excused himself and went to Miss Grey, who appeared more at ease now. Blair had channeled the discussion into the diversions planned for the next fortnight.

"Good evening, Miss Grey." He bowed, and she curtseyed. Very proper. Very reserved. "How have you found Kingstag Castle thus far?"

She smiled. "It is lovely, sir. I look forward to seeing the grounds. Your sisters have described them so well."

"We're going to take her around to see everything!" put in Bridget, beaming. "The lake, the grotto, everything! Only, she doesn't ride terribly well, so James will have to drive us in the barouche."

"I never promised," Blair said with a smile.

"But near enough! I shall be on my best behavior. Please?" she begged.

"Perhaps Wessex will want to show Miss Grey the grounds himself," replied Blair with a glance at Gareth.

"If she wishes," he said. "We shall ride out to see as much as you care to see, Miss Grey."

She lowered her eyes and curtseyed again. "That is very kind of you, sir."

Blair drew the younger girls aside, saying he had an idea for an entertainment later, and they retreated to a corner of the room, although the giggles and whispers were audible to all. Gareth looked at his bride-to-be, and she looked at him. He suddenly realized he had no idea what to say to her, and from the expression on her face, she probably felt the same.

"Your sisters are charming," said Miss Grey.

"They are indeed—and they have been positively wild to make your acquaintance." He watched Alexandra whisper something in Serena's ear, and a slight smile curved his lips at the delight in Bridget's face over whatever they were plotting. His sisters were exhausting, but he did love them. "I hope they haven't been impertinent."

"Not at all." Miss Grey paused. "Sisters are important. I shall be glad to have some more."

"I shall be glad to share them." Gareth repressed the urge to glance at the door yet again at the mention of her sister. He must not allow himself to think what was teasing the edges of his mind. If their conversations were always rather dull, it must be his fault and not hers. When they were better acquainted, they would know what to talk about and not end up in these awkward silences.

"Good evening," said a bright voice behind him. He turned, tamping down the quick spurt of anticipation. This time he was prepared. This time she wouldn't catch him off guard, the earth would remain firmly and motionlessly lodged beneath his feet, and he wouldn't feel as though he'd been hit over the head by a falling tree branch.

Instead he felt as though the breath had been sucked right out of his lungs. Mrs. Barrows wore a gauzy white dress that swirled and clung to her body with every step. A long, narrow shawl of vivid blue looped around her bare arms. Ropes of delicate gold chain looped around her bodice, jingling with little gold coins. Her sable hair was twisted up on her head, more gold chain running through it, and on her feet—her bare feet—were dainty leather sandals. She looked like a Roman goddess, he thought numbly: Venus, the goddess of desire.

"Oh, Cleo, how lovely you look," said Miss Grey warmly.

"Thank you, Helen. The minute the chain came into the shop, I thought to wear it." Mrs. Barrows beamed at her sister as she joined them. "Although I don't think I can compare to you!"

Gareth turned his head to look at his fiancé. He hadn't even noticed what she was wearing. A pale pink dress, very fashionable and very ordinary. His feet had never left the ground once while looking at her.

"Good evening, Your Grace." Mrs. Barrows dipped a curtsey. The little coins tinkled softly as she moved.

"Good evening." His tongue had trouble forming the words.

"Mrs. Barrows." Blair appeared at her elbow with a pleased smile. "Good evening. What an original gown."

She smiled. "Very unoriginal, you mean! I fell in love with an illustration in one of my father's books and longed to recreate it for myself. This design must be two thousand years old."

"But surely even better now," he replied. Blair was looking at her with far too much appreciation, thought Gareth testily. "Don't you agree, Wessex?"

"Er— Yes," he said. At least the question gave him an excuse for staring at her.

191

She looked directly at him then, her dark eyes sparkling. A little smile curved her mouth into a perfectly kissable shape. Gareth felt a cold sweat break out on the back of his neck. He might need another brandy. "Thank you, Your Grace. You flatter me."

The door opened, and Gareth's mother returned, thank God—although with Sophronia and Henrietta Black in her wake. Sophronia looked as eccentric as ever tonight, in a gown thirty years out of date and her henna-colored hair tied up in a bewildering assortment of braids and knots, but her gaze was as keen and ruthless as ever. Unconsciously Gareth braced himself, sensing that she had decided to join them in order to stir up trouble in some way. "Isn't it time to eat?" she asked loudly, confirming his suspicions. Her companion, Henrietta, tried to murmur something in her ear, but Sophronia waved her away. "I'm half-starved after the long walk down here."

"Nearly," said the duchess calmly, guiding her across the room. "Come meet our guests. Here are Sir William and Lady Grey. Wessex is to marry their daughter. Sir William, Lady Grey, may I present you to Lady Sophronia Cavendish?"

"A great honor, madam." Sir William bowed.

"Oh yes, indeed!" trilled his wife, fluttering her hands as though she couldn't contain herself. "A singular pleasure, my lady!"

Sophronia gave the woman a hard stare, then turned away. The duchess quickly intervened. "You must meet the bride!" She gave Gareth a look as Sophronia tottered toward him, and he made the introductions.

Sophronia baldly looked Miss Grey up and down, then did the same to Mrs. Barrows. "Are you the bride?"

Mrs. Barrows blinked. "No, my sister has that happy honor."

The older woman grunted. "She doesn't look honored."

"Sophronia," murmured the duchess in a warning way.

"Oh, but she is!" put in Lady Grey. "Who would not be honored to become the Duchess of Wessex, mistress of Kingstag Castle? I assure you, madam, my daughter feels her honor very, very well!"

"She doesn't show it." The elderly lady's keen eye landed on Mrs. Barrows again. "Already married, are you?"

"No, my lady. I'm a widow." Mrs. Barrows seemed amused by Sophronia. She shot her sister a glance full of impudent amusement. Her mouth twitched as if to keep from laughing. Gareth wondered what her laugh sounded like. What her lips felt like. What she wore underneath that slip of a gown.

God help him.

"You don't dress like one," remarked Sophronia. Once again she was coming perilously close to rudeness, and as usual, no one seemed to know quite how to deflect her. She peered closer at Mrs. Barrows's gown. "Where did you get that chain? It's quite unusual."

"Oh my heavens!" burst out Lady Grey. Everyone looked at her and her face seemed to fill with panic for a moment. "I—I beg your pardon, Your Grace, I have just remembered something I must tell my daughter."

"Yes, Mama," murmured Miss Grey, stepping forward.

"No, Helen dear." Her mother's voice was high and strained. "Your sister."

Miss Grey's eyes flickered to Mrs. Barrows's. Something passed between them, but Gareth wasn't sure what. Suddenly he understood what Blair had meant about a tension in the Grey family. Even Mrs. Barrows's supple mouth looked flat. "We're about to go in to dinner, Mama," she said, her voice quiet and reserved. There was none of the warmth and humor she had shown before.

Lady Grey's face pinched. "It will only take a moment, Cleo. Come here."

"Well, Alice, is it time to eat or isn't it? I never had the patience to stand around waiting for my dinner." Sophronia turned to the duchess, who began to look a little strained as well.

"Yes, dinner is ready." The duchess nodded at one of the footmen, who swept open the doors.

"Thank goodness," declared Bridget, bounding across the room. Alexandra and Serena followed more sedately. "I'm so hungry!"

"That's my girl," said Sophronia with approval as the duchess closed her eyes in despair. "Who's going to escort me? I see you haven't got nearly enough gentlemen tonight, Wessex."

"The guests will begin arriving tomorrow," he replied. "Blair will give you his arm tonight." He nodded at his cousin.

Sophronia grunted. "I suppose he'll do." She put out her hand, and Blair obediently gave her his arm.

The duchess smiled at the rest of them. "Since we are just family tonight, I thought we could all go in together. I hope you will forgive the informality."

There was a murmur of assent. Gareth turned to Lady Grey, still hovering behind him. What the devil had she wanted to tell Mrs. Barrows so urgently? And why had it banished the light from the lady's eyes? Even now, she was staring fixedly at the carpet, her lower lip caught between her teeth. He felt again the oddest sensation of falling. He wanted to shake her mother—her own mother—for dampening her spirits. He must be going mad. "May I escort you, madam?"

Lady Grey hesitated, but after exchanging a glance with her husband, she took Gareth's arm. "Why yes, how kind, Your Grace! I have heard such reports of your chef at Kingstag, I expect dinner shall be utterly incomparable ..." She went on, but he barely heard her. His sisters fell in step with Miss Grey behind them, and they followed his mother into the dining room.

But when he reached the dining room and seated Lady Grey, he discovered that Mrs. Barrows and Sir William had not followed them.

# CHAPTER FOUR

"**S**tay a moment," growled Sir William at his older daughter as the others left the room. Cleo waited, burning with humiliation. The momentary relief she'd felt when the Duke of Wessex intercepted her mother had quickly been replaced by dread when her father gave her a black look behind the duke's back. For a moment there, she'd been blessing the duke with all her might, but of course the coming confrontation couldn't be avoided.

Her father waited until everyone else had left, then stared fiercely at the footman until the servant closed the door, leaving them in complete privacy. Even then, he spoke in a harsh whisper. "You think very highly of yourself, don't you? When will you cease trying to humiliate us at every turn by bringing up your wretched little trade?"

"It is not wretched," she said quietly.

He snorted. "It is indeed! My own daughter, laboring in a shop like some baseborn chit. It is intolerable, I tell you, *intolerable*. The very least you could do is remember your place here and kindly keep your idle thoughts and opinions to yourself."

"What is my place?" she asked before she could stop herself. Perhaps he wouldn't be able to tell her. Perhaps he had some trace of affection left for her.

"A tradesman's widow," he said with a snort. "Utterly beneath your ancestors! Your sister will be a duchess, and you stand in her drawing room and loudly proclaim yourself little better than a common servant!" Cleo's mouth opened in shock, and he went on. "Sometimes I wonder precisely who you think you are, miss!"

"You named me for a queen," she said. "Who do you think I am?"

He harrumphed. "What a laughable mistake. Cleopatra was born to royalty and she knew her place. Don't think so highly of yourself, miss."

"But she led her country," Cleo reminded him. "I daresay someone thought that wasn't her place."

Her father glowered at her. "She did not go against her parents' wishes and lower herself to go into trade."

"She lowered herself to marrying her brother," Cleo murmured. "Although I suppose that was at her parents' wish."

He closed his eyes and exhaled, then shot her another sharp glance. "You've done as you wished, and I have not disowned you. But don't think I'm proud of your actions. You're only welcome here because your sister wished it. It is her wedding—she, at least, will take her proper place in society, while you have done precious little for our family."

Cleo shifted her weight back and forth, setting her skirt to swirling about her ankles. The tiny coins clinked softly. "I paid for Helen's wardrobe."

"Shh!" hissed her father, glancing around anxiously, as though the duke might hear her words all the way in the dining room. "Don't tell everyone!" He gave a snort. "Bad enough that my daughter has to operate a shop like a common merchant. You'd tell the world I must accept your charity, too."

"It's not charity," she protested. "I wanted to help! Helen is my sister."

"Then mind your tongue," he snapped. "Do you want to embarrass her in front of her future husband? Do you want him to think us a pack of penniless, hysterical fools?"

Cleo watched the coins settle into silence again. "No, Papa. I'm sorry."

"You should be." With that, he brushed past her, only waiting at the door to offer his arm. As angry as he was with everything she did, he would never break protocol and leave her to walk into the dining room alone. *We must keep up appearances, after all*, Cleo thought, pasting a wooden smile on her face, feeling oddly detached from her father even as her hand rested on his arm.

She knew her parents hadn't understood when she and Matthew eloped; she hadn't expected them to. The years of her marriage had been rather cool ones between her and her parents, but still civil.

Cleo knew why; her mother had once outright admitted that if she had to be the wife of a shopkeeper, at least she was the wife of a very prosperous shopkeeper. At the time, she'd wondered who her parents thought she would marry. The Greys had had no money for as long as she could remember, and no connections of consequence. Suitors had been rare in their house.

But whatever their initial hopes for her, it was clear that all the burden of making a great match had descended upon Helen. Cleo felt sorry for that. She had been so happy with Matthew and wished the same for her sister, whether it was with a duke or a lowly tailor. She got some glimpse of what her sister must have endured after Matthew died. Her father had tried to insist that she sell her shop and return home. Unspoken was the presumption that she would make a better match the second time, now that she was a widow of some modest fortune. After that conversation, Cleo had made only the briefest visits home. She had no desire to settle into a ladylike uselessness in her widowhood. Working in the shop reminded her of Matthew, and Cleo liked being responsible for herself. She could support herself, it turned out, so why shouldn't she? Without the shop, she would have precious little of her own: no children, no husband, no income ... nothing to keep her mind occupied. What else was she to do with herself?

The unfairness of her father's feelings made her want to scream. Never mind that her shop, which he hated, supplied her money, which he somehow managed to accept. At times she had been almost determined to stop offering it, since the source of the income was so hateful to both her parents. Perhaps they would be more appreciative if they felt the lack of her "common merchant" funds. But cutting them off would mean cutting off Helen as well. Helen was the dearest person in the world to her; Helen had wished her joy when she married Matthew. And now she had made a splendid match to the illustrious Duke of Wessex—even if he did seem awfully reticent and reserved—and Cleo would never regret helping her sister find happiness.

That was the thought she must keep in the forefront of her mind for the next few weeks. Stirring up an argument with either one of her parents would only cause Helen anxiety, and she had absolutely no wish to embarrass her sister in front of the Cavendish family.

# CHAPTER FIVE

The guests began to arrive the next day. The house came alive with trills of female voices, and the jangle of harnesses was almost constant. Cleo had marveled at the size of the castle when they arrived, but after a while she began to wonder where all these guests would stay. Surely even Kingstag Castle couldn't hold them all.

Helen, of course, had to greet everyone, welcoming them at the duchess's side. Cleo joined her, losing herself in the excitement of meeting new people, none of whom seemed to recoil at the sight of her, common merchant though she was. Perhaps that was because she said nothing at all about herself, speaking only of her sister and the wedding and how lovely the castle was.

"I'm starting to sound like Mama," she whispered to her sister after a while. "All I can speak of is Kingstag!"

Helen sighed. "There is a great deal to say about it."

"Well, it truly is magnificent." Cleo craned her neck to admire the vaulted ceiling of the hall, which put her in mind of a cathedral. The house was full of modern improvements—there was indeed piping for water inside the house—but it retained much of its ancient air as well. "To think, you'll be mistress of this in a few days! Do you remember when we used to dream of living in a castle?"

Her sister smiled. "Yes. But even then I never dreamt of one this enormous."

"All the more to explore!" Cleo grinned, but finally realized how pale her sister had become. "Helen, are you well?" she asked in concern. "You should sit down."

There was a distant rattle of wheels on gravel. Helen turned toward the open door. "I can't. Someone else is arriving."

"Let Her Grace greet them. Come," she urged. "I'm sure the duke wouldn't want his guests to first see you passed out on the floor."

"No, indeed," said a male voice behind them.

Cleo jerked around. The Duke of Wessex stood there, watching in his intent way. His wasn't a merry, fond countenance, but she had the feeling that he paid closer attention than most people. Even in this trifling circumstance, she felt the force of his regard in every fiber of her being. No wonder he was such a powerful man. She could barely drag her eyes away from his.

"Your Grace." Helen dipped a graceful curtsey. "We did not expect you."

"I had some pressing business to attend to this morning; my apologies." He barely glanced at her. "What makes you think your sister is about to faint, Mrs. Barrows?"

Cleo wet her lips and darted a wary glance at her sister. Helen might have been a statue, from all the emotion or energy she conveyed. "She looks pale to me, Your Grace, but perhaps I'm imagining things."

"I would never discount the keen eye of a loving sister." He turned the blast of his regard upon Helen, who seemed to waver on her feet under it. "I agree with Mrs. Barrows, my dear. You must sit down."

"As you wish, Your Grace."

Cleo rolled her eyes. Now that the mighty Wessex had given his approval, Helen would sit. Still, she wasn't one to cast aside help, so she merely took her sister's arm and helped her into the nearby morning parlor, where a pair of elegant settees stood in front of the windows. Helen sank onto one, and Cleo perched on the edge of the facing settee. In the bright sunlight, her sister's face looked drawn and lined, as if she had aged since they arrived. It was distinctly odd, and Cleo frowned in worry. Her sister should be glowing with happiness, or at least contentment. Instead she looked like she had come down with some wasting disease.

Wessex followed. He rang the servants' bell, then closed the door. He came and seated himself next to Cleo, opposite his bride. "Why are you unwell, my dear?"

"I'm only a little tired, Your Grace," said Helen. "A few moments' rest, and I shall return to greeting guests with Her Grace, your mother."

"Nonsense," said Cleo. "You need to eat something; you hardly ate a bite of breakfast. There is no color in your cheeks at all."

Wessex glanced at her. "Is this true, Miss Grey? Was breakfast not to your liking?"

Helen's eyes widened in alarm. "Oh, it was delicious, Your Grace—I simply couldn't choose ..."

"Perhaps a tot of brandy will restore you," he suggested.

Without thinking, Cleo snorted. "Don't be ridiculous! She's hardly eaten. Brandy will make her faint dead away."

Slowly he turned to her. "What?"

"Tea would be better. Tea and some muffins. Ladies don't normally drink brandy, sir."

"I see," he murmured, still watching her. "A pity, that."

Yes, it was a pity, in Cleo's opinion. She liked a little nip of brandy now and then—never enough to make her head spin, just a small amount after dinner in the winter or perhaps a drop in her tea on especially trying days. Still, her mother would have an apoplexy if she admitted that to the duke, so she merely smiled. "I think the muffins are particularly important. There were some delicious ones at breakfast this morning. May I send for some for my sister?"

"Of course." As if on cue, a servant slipped into the room. Wessex arched one brow at Cleo. "What shall we send for?"

"Tea, please, with milk and muffins. And if there is any of that superb gooseberry jam, that would be lovely." Cleo smiled at the servant, who bowed and hurried off. "Are the guests to arrive all day, Your Grace?"

"I've no idea," he said without a trace of concern. "My mother will know, but she's also quite capable of greeting them herself. I believe the first arrivals were to be family, in any event."

She had to purse her lips to keep from grinning. "And you've no desire to see your family?"

"They will be here for a fortnight at the least." He sounded resigned. "I will see them quite enough."

"Perhaps some of the other guests will prove more diverting." She couldn't resist a naughty smile at his measuring look. "What are guests for, if not to provide entertainment?"

For the first time, his mouth curved. With his head tipped thoughtfully to one side, and that slow, slight grin, he looked sly and devastatingly attractive. "I devoutly hope you are correct."

"I have great expectations," she told him. "Your cousin in particular has promise."

"Ah—you must mean Jack." The duke's grin grew wider. "I believe he inspired a formulation of smelling salts. I would suggest that you tease him about it, but he cannot be teased; on the contrary, he is quite proud of it."

"Yes, *very* promising," repeated Cleo with enthusiasm. "Dare I ask what he did to inspire smelling salts?"

"I don't recall all the details." The duke made a bored grimace even though his eyes shone with amusement. "It began with a wager, naturally, and took place during one of the most elegant balls of the season, but I never knew why there was a bow and arrow involved. And as for the monkey ... well, the less said about the monkey, the better."

"A real monkey?" she asked, trying not to laugh.

"Pungently real," he confirmed. "Lady Hartington swore it took a month to get the smell out of her house."

Cleo laughed. She had a strong feeling Wessex almost envied his cousin. Goodness, he was far from the stuffy duke she had thought him yesterday. He had a dry wit that charmed her, and he was devilishly appealing when he grinned. "No wonder he's famous!"

"Infamous," said the duke, though that slight grin still curved his mouth. "But even Lady Hartington forgave him. Apparently he has this way of smiling at ladies that makes them forgive and forget, even when he looses a monkey in their homes. It prompted some wit to declare that there ought to be a smelling salt to combat the effects of that smile, and thus a legend was born."

Opposite her, Helen sighed, and she abruptly remembered herself. "Not that I think Lord Willoughby will upset the wedding! Indeed, he had better not, or I shall take measures—and I will neither forgive nor forget," she added with a quick laugh. "Never fear, Helen, nothing shall mar your wedding day."

Her sister smiled wanly, glancing at the duke. "I never thought it would."

"Jack is a bit of a rogue, but he's to stand up with me," Wessex assured them. "I would never have asked him if I couldn't rely on him."

"I would never question your judgment, Your Grace," Helen murmured. "See, Cleo, there is nothing to fear."

The duke's grin faded. "No. Nothing at all."

An awkward silence fell over the room. Cleo looked down at her hands, shaken to realize she really liked Wessex's smile. Not merely in the manner of a woman gratified to see some warmth and humor in her sister's future husband. No, her thoughts had not touched on Helen at all. For a moment, she had quite forgotten why they were there, and her appreciation had been purely female. Which was wrong in so many ways.

It was a relief when the servant returned with a tray. Cleo busied herself with fixing a cup for Helen, keeping her attention firmly on the tea and her sister. Wessex said nothing, but she could feel him watching her. She steadfastly resisted the urge to watch him back. She had a terrible feeling it would be hard to look away again. After a few moments, the duke wished Helen well again and excused himself. When the door clicked closed behind him, she almost wilted.

"Thank you, Cleo," said Helen before she could speak. "I don't know what I would do without you here."

She smiled uneasily. "Live in less anxiety that I'll offend the duke?"

"He didn't appear offended by anything you said." Helen sipped the tea. Some color was already coming back into her cheeks. "He didn't appear bored, either, as he always does when I speak to him."

"Nonsense!"

"If not bored, then he looks as though his mind is elsewhere."

"You mustn't let him do that ..."

"How can I stop him?" Helen sighed. "He finds me dull."

Cleo sat in tense silence for a moment. She had a terrible feeling it was the truth. Wessex had barely looked at Helen while he sat with them; he had looked at *her*, and she had liked it. That must be corrected at once. "He had better begin to pay you more attention. Then he'll see how sweet and charming and lovely you are."

"Oh, Cleo." Her sister smiled wistfully. "Not everyone sees me as you do. I'm not vivacious and capable of speaking to anyone, as you are."

"Which makes you a far better companion, since you never say anything hurtful or rash, as I do."

Helen stared into her tea. "I am sure, after a few years, the duke and I will have learnt how to get on with each other. I will learn what pleases him, and he has already been so solicitous of me. We will learn."

"Er ... yes." She worked to keep the frown from her face. Every time she talked with her sister, it became less and less clear why Helen had accepted his proposal. Did her sister merely want to be a duchess? Was he simply too eligible, too handsome, too wealthy to refuse? Had Papa forced her to accept? Cleo wasn't sure she even wanted to know if the last was true. Her father would never forgive her if she stirred up trouble, and yet ... "Are—are you pleased with this marriage, Helen?" Her sister looked up warily. Cleo wet her lips. "I presumed you were, when you accepted His Grace's proposal, but ... I cannot help but notice how listless you are. It's as if something you dread is approaching, rather than something joyful."

For a long moment Helen said nothing. "My marriage won't be like yours," she finally whispered. "His Grace doesn't love me as Matthew loved you. I don't expect him to—I daresay most men of his rank don't love their wives—and I knew that when I accepted his proposal. I suppose it's just becoming real to me now, that he and I will be married in a few days."

"You don't have to marry him." It popped out of her mouth before Cleo could stop it.

Helen's dark eyes widened in alarm. "Don't say such a thing! Of course I do. The guests are arriving! I couldn't possibly jilt His Grace."

*You could if you really didn't want to marry him,* thought Cleo. She bit her lip, hard, to keep the thought unspoken.

"It's just nerves," went on Helen, a bit more firmly. She took a sip of tea. "Becoming mistress of this house, part of this family, a duchess ... It's very overwhelming, but I shall do my best. Please don't tell Papa anything."

"No," Cleo said after a pause. "I wouldn't." She hardly wanted to speak to her father at all, especially with this new suspicion in her mind that he had browbeaten Helen into accepting Wessex. She took a deep breath and shook off her worries. Perhaps it was just bridal nerves. Helen was reserved, but she was no shrinking violet. She would find her way; the Cavendish family was warm and welcoming, and he wasn't unkind or cold at all. Cleo thought it would be very easy to fall in love with the duke. And surely once Wessex spent more time with Helen, he would see what a lovely person she was and fall deeply in love with her. It was impossible not to love Helen, once one knew her.

And if an opportunity presented itself to nudge His Grace a little closer to that happy state, Cleo would be prepared to take it.

Gareth left the house, avoiding the front of the castle where yet another carriage was arriving. His mother had planned the wedding and guest list, and as far as he was concerned, she could welcome every distant cousin and acquaintance who came. Normally he would be busy as usual, off in his study or out riding the estate. If he had any discipline, he'd return to his study now. Or more accurately, if he had any discipline, he never would have left it and gone down to the hall where he knew his bride and her sister were greeting guests. He knew because Blair had mentioned it as they sat down to work. And if his cousin had deliberately set out to destroy Gareth's peace of mind, he couldn't have done a better job. Within an hour Gareth had admitted defeat and gone to see for himself.

He didn't want to think about why.

The contrast between the two sisters couldn't have been sharper. Helen, his future wife, held herself with perfect poise, her hands clasped in front of her. Her smile was polite, her manner reserved. She was lovely, from the top of her glossy dark curls to the tips of her pink slippers peeking out from beneath her snow-white skirts. She was every inch the perfect duchess.

Mrs. Barrows, on the other hand, was like a bolt of light in the dark expanse of the hall. Her dress was blue, with bold embroidery on the skirt and—God help him for noticing—all over the bodice. Her smile was wide and warm. She greeted the arriving guests as though she were truly delighted to meet them, her hands as animated as her face. He lurked at the back of the hall and watched her laugh with his cousin Jack Willoughby, and a tendril of something like jealousy circled his gut.

Speaking to her, though, hadn't helped at all. He'd been spurred forward by an apparent argument between the sisters, and he'd told himself he was being a solicitous fiancé, urging his bride to sit down and rest, as she did look rather pale. But then her sister spoke to him, and he'd almost forgotten his future wife was in the room.

Cleopatra. She was well named. Gareth could easily see men being willing to fight and die for her. How could two sisters be so unlike? And why, by all that was sane and reasonable, was he so mesmerized by the wrong one?

He had to stop this. He must think of Miss Grey—Helen. Perhaps if he called her by name, he would feel closer to her. Helen, Helen, Helen.

He walked down the gravel path that led to the stables. One of the ancient oaks that grew along the path had been felled, split right to the roots by lightning in the recent storm. It had fallen away from the carriage lane, but it would take weeks to clear the debris. There would be firewood for a year from that tree. Several men were working on it and doffed their caps as he walked by. Gareth nodded at them and walked on.

The Kingstag stables were spacious, laid out with a small courtyard in the center. The stalls could house almost eighty horses at a time, although in recent years they had rarely done so. Since Gareth's father's death, his mother had chosen to remain quietly in the country while raising her young daughters. Now he supposed there would be more entertaining at Kingstag; not only would he have a wife but his sisters would be making their debuts soon, which would necessitate balls and parties and all manner of visitors. He suspected his mother was looking forward to it, given her enthusiasm for the wedding plans. He remembered how much she had loved hosting parties and soirees when he was young. It was the only reason he had agreed to a large wedding celebration. Left to his own devices, he would have been happy to wed in the bishop's private quarters.

He wondered what Helen wanted. He hoped his mother had consulted her.

A shiny black phaeton with startling yellow wheels currently stood in the stable courtyard. Grooms were unhitching a pair of large black stallions, although their actions were slowed by the awestruck glances they kept bestowing on the carriage. It must be Jack's. If it wasn't, Gareth would wager half his estate it *would* be Jack's by the end of the week. His cousin was drawn to beauty like a bee to a flower, and this phaeton cast all others into the shade.

"Did you win it, steal it, or borrow it?" he asked loudly.

Jack Willoughby stepped out from behind his carriage. "I'm wounded. Naturally I bought her. Had to borrow a bit, but she's mine."

"She?"

"Hippolyta." Jack whispered the name with the reverence of a lover. He reached out and rubbed a spot of dirt from the gleaming wheels. "Hippolyta, my beauty."

"You named your phaeton." Gareth shook his head. "Of course you did."

"Just look at her, Wessex! Such curves, such elegance! Have you ever seen a female finer than this?"

Cleo Barrows's laughing face flashed into his mind. Gareth exhaled. "As a matter of fact, yes."

His cousin grimaced. "You always did do things the right way. Besotted with your bride already!"

He closed his eyes. God, he needed a drink—and it wasn't even noon. "You brought the ring?"

"Of course." Jack had gone back to gazing lovingly at Hippolyta. "Got it from the jeweler yesterday."

For a moment there, he'd been almost hopeful Jack would have forgotten it. Lost it. Wagered it away in a card game. The ring was a family heirloom, sent off to a London jeweler to be sized and cleaned. If Jack had forgotten it ... But the ring was here, so the wedding wouldn't be delayed by the need to procure another one.

"Excellent," Gareth murmured. "Are you headed up to the house?"

"Not yet." Jack took out his handkerchief and reached up to polish another spot on the carriage. "Too many girls in white dresses, giggling like mad. I may spend the next week here in your stables."

"I'll send Withers out with some port and a blanket."

Jack grinned. "Very sporting of you, Wessex."

Gareth nodded and left. He turned away from the house; if Jack wasn't going back, neither was he. There was nothing at the house but trial and temptation right now, as long as Helen and Cleo would be standing in the hall, the contrast between them sharpened by their proximity. He had to cure himself of this unwanted fascination. He was the Duke of Wessex. He'd had his pick of women in England and he'd chosen Helen. He wished he could return to that certainty that she was the one. He wished he could feel any sort of contentment about his rapidly approaching marriage to her. He would even be glad just to be less attracted to Cleo; then he would be able to persuade himself that all would work out right in the end, that he would come to care for Helen, that they would all be happy eventually.

Instead ... all he felt was dread, growing stronger by the hour.

# CHAPTER SIX

When they had been at Kingstag several days, Cleo decided to catch up on her correspondence. She'd been away from her shop for several days now, and although she'd left Mr. Mabry, her most trusted clerk, in charge, there were decisions only she could make. A packet of reports and letters had arrived from Mabry the previous day, and she needed to read them.

Reading them would also, she hoped, restore her sense. A week at Kingstag had been both wonderful and a trial. Wonderful, because it truly was the loveliest estate she'd ever seen, from the sprawling splendor of the house to the grounds that seemed to encompass every beauty to be found in England. The food was superb, the servants were well trained, and even the guests were interesting and pleasant for the most part.

And yet it was a trial, because everywhere she saw the duke. Just a glimpse of him across the dining room was enough to make her heart skip a beat. She told herself it was just the awe of meeting a duke; she'd once been presented to a viscount, but nobility had been rare in her corner of the world before this week.

The correspondence, on the other hand, was her life—bills from the silk warehouses, requests from customers, and overdue accounts. A fortnight at Kingstag was an interlude, not a permanent change. She was very much out of place here and always would be.

She gathered her writing case and letters and set out in search of a quiet spot. It was too beautiful a day to remain indoors, bright and extremely warm. Thinking the lake might offer a secluded spot as well as some breeze, she headed down the shaded path along the side of the back lawn, pausing to marvel at the remains of the giant oak that lay beside the path. The trunk was charred black in places and looked as though it had been ripped from the ground. One of the men working to cut it up told her it had been hit by lightning a few days before. That must be the tree the duke had mentioned going to see when she met him in the garden. She was still shaking her head over it as she passed the path to the stables, when the one man she hoped to avoid stepped out in front of her.

"Good morning, Mrs. Barrows."

Just the sound of his voice made her heart jump. "Good morning," she replied. "I was setting out to explore your magnificent estate a little, if I may."

"You must treat it as your own home." His eye dropped to the writing case she carried. "May I carry that for you?"

Oh dear. Cleo tried to smother the little frisson of anticipation that shot through her veins. He had clearly just come back from riding and was even more appealingly masculine in riding clothes than in his evening wear. "You must have a dozen things to do ..."

He glanced over his shoulder down the path to the stables, where male voices could dimly be heard shouting "Huzzah!" "On the contrary. I would like nothing better than a bit of a walk. Unless, of course, you preferred to walk alone."

He was her host. It was only polite to accept, which must explain why she accepted at once. "Not at all! I would be honored." She surrendered the writing case with a smile.

"How have you found Kingstag?" he asked as they strolled along the lane.

"It's magnificent," she said. "My mother hasn't exaggerated in the slightest."

"I'm not certain angels dwell in the attics," he said dryly, "but I'm delighted you've found it comfortable and welcoming."

"Did she really say angels in the attics?" Cleo tried and failed to bite back a laugh. "Well, she's very pleased by it, and the excitement might have gone to her head a little."

"I could seat her next to Sophronia, who would point out every draught and inconvenience of the house."

Cleo shook her head. "It would make no difference. My mother is determined to see no fault, even if the ceiling should collapse before her eyes. She would only exclaim over how rustic it looked to have a pile of rubble in the dining room."

He laughed. "That would be too rustic for me. I prefer solid walls and ceilings."

"As do I. The grounds may actually be perfect, though," she went on, shading her eyes with one hand to survey the lake, sparkling in the distance. Willow fronds waved above their heads, dappling the path with sunlight, and the scent of honeysuckle sweetened the air. "I don't know how anyone even notices the house in these surroundings."

"My mother deserves much of the credit. She created the landscape as much as the gardens." He glanced at her, and Cleo felt her face warm. Not just a garden of love, but a whole landscape. "In fact, I seem to recall a nuncheon for the ladies in the garden today."

She smiled uneasily at the veiled question. Nuncheon in the garden would include her mother. For the first few days, it had been enough for Millicent to bask in her role as mother of the bride, which was trying but not unexpected. Lately, though, Millicent had become almost unbearable in her delight, and when she wasn't praising Kingstag in some way, she was fretting at Cleo about being proper and respectable. In the decade since she'd left home Cleo had got used to her freedom, and her patience for her mother's anxious, inane chatter was wearing thin. And if her mother knew that the Duke of Wessex was carrying the drapery shop correspondence from Mr. Mabry at this moment, she'd probably faint dead away. "I have some letters to write and thought I might get a bit of exercise as well. I miss the outdoors."

The duke nodded. "Your shop, I suppose, keeps you indoors a great deal."

Cleo jerked, glancing at him in alarm. She wasn't to talk about her shop at all, not to anyone, but especially not to him. But he was watching her with those dark, dark eyes, and she felt compelled to answer.

"Yes," she murmured. "It does."

"Mr. Blair tells me it's quite a prosperous business," he went on. Cleo couldn't resist a quick glance over her shoulder, half expecting her mother to be lurking nearby, but they were quite alone. "Quite an achievement."

"Yes, for a woman," she said, too late hearing the edge in her voice. She forced a smile as he looked at her, his eyebrows raised. "My apologies," she said hastily. "I shouldn't have spoken so."

"No," he corrected her. "You should speak as you feel."

Cleo fastened her eyes on the path in front of them and they walked in silence for a few minutes. "I was wrong," she said when her voice was even and calm again. "I shouldn't have spoiled our walk."

"I don't think it's been spoiled at all." He was remarkably unruffled. "It's a draper's shop, I believe?"

"Yes," she said politely. There seemed no reason to lie about it.

"Is it a large one? I have little experience of draper's shops."

Cleo was torn. On one hand, he sounded genuinely interested, and she was proud enough of her business to want to talk about it. On the other hand, her parents would have an apoplexy if they discovered it. "Moderately," she said, erring on the side of modesty.

"And yet you manage it on your own?"

"Does that surprise you?"

He tipped his head in contemplation. "I confess I have no idea what's required to run a draper's shop. I imagine it's a great deal of effort, though. When my sisters descend upon the shop in Dorchester they are gone for hours, and one can only pity the poor proprietor, worn out from being sent back and forth for ribbons and lace and bolts of every sort of fabric sold in England." He grimaced as Cleo almost choked on her laughter.

"It's never that dreadful," she protested. "Many aspects are quite enjoyable. Every year I travel to London to visit the warehouses and order the latest fabrics before anyone else has seen them. Nothing is more satisfying than spotting a beautiful piece of silk and knowing exactly which customer it will suit. My clerks do most of the fetching in the shop, but I quite like helping ladies choose the right colors and trimmings. A fine gown is a significant expense and ought to please the wearer for years to come. Most ladies are very grateful to have another woman's approval before making the purchase. Men should understand; I know perfectly well most of the gentlemen here have spent a great deal of time in the stables admiring a carriage." He gave her a sideways glance, and she grinned. "That, and drinking the many bottles of port I saw a footman carrying to the stables."

Wessex coughed. "And a new gown is like a carriage?"

"To most ladies, a new gown is far, far more important than any carriage," she confirmed.

The duke chuckled. "You have illuminated one of the great mysteries of life. I begin to see why Alexandra was reduced to tears when Bridget mocked her bonnet."

"Well, mocking is never kind. She might have suggested a different ribbon, or less trimming."

"Bridget's way is rarely diplomatic," he said in resignation.

Cleo, who rather liked the impetuous girl, waved one hand. "She has time to learn. I was very like her when I was younger, and we all endure difficult ages only to come out the better for them."

"That is very encouraging," he said. "Bridget is ... a challenge."

"Lady Alexandra and Lady Serena are very poised young ladies. I'm sure Lady Bridget will grow into it." She paused, remembering the disputes and heartfelt conversations with her own sister when they were girls. Without Helen, she didn't know what she would have done. "They are fortunate to have each other. They seem quite close, your sisters."

"Devilishly." He stopped and turned. "In fact ... Serena?" he called.

First one girl, then another, and so on until no fewer than five young ladies emerged from behind a nearby hedge, looking guilty. "Yes, Wessex?" asked the eldest, a girl with auburn hair and the same intense dark eyes as the duke.

"You're far from the house," he remarked.

"We're not doing anything wrong," blurted out Bridget Cavendish. "It's that horrid pest Henry—"

"Shh!" hissed Charlotte Ascot—sister to the horrid pest, if Cleo remembered correctly. "I swear he can hear his name from a mile away."

"We're just out for a walk," said Serena with a bright smile. "As are you, I see." She curtseyed to Cleo. "I hope you are enjoying your visit to Kingstag, Mrs. Barrows."

"Very much so," she replied warmly. "I simply had to see more of it and walked out in search of adventure."

"Capital!" declared Bridget with a beaming smile. "Would you like to see the grotto? James was supposed to drive us on a tour but he's disappeared."

"*All* the gentlemen have disappeared," muttered Kate Lacy with a very fetching pout. "They only turn up when there's a cricket match."

"Or a game of battledore," put in Charlotte. "Which is even less entertaining to watch, even if that handsome Mr. Newnham is playing."

"No, I much prefer to watch Lord Everett play cricket," said Miss Lacy with a dreamy look on her face.

"They can't have all disappeared into thin air!" burst out Bridget. "We just have to keep looking—" She froze, looking at her brother in alarm.

Wessex, though, merely grinned. "I can hardly turn traitor on my fellow man, can I?"

"And will you tell Mama?" asked Alexandra cautiously.

"We aren't doing anything wrong!" cried Bridget again. "We're just ... just—" She glanced at her companions. "—just trying to be good hostesses. What if the gentlemen have disappeared because they're bored to death of Kingstag and need reviving from their stupors?"

The duke glanced at Cleo, mirth glinting in his gaze. "No one accused you of doing wrong. But I doubt you'll need to revive anyone from a stupor—not until the ball, that is."

A chorus of protests went up. "No! The ball is the only worthy event!" "Who could fall into a stupor at a ball?" "The gentlemen wouldn't dare try to miss the ball, would they, Wessex? Mama would be furious!"

The duke held up his hands. "I'm sure they'll all be at the ball. Just as I'm sure you ought not to wander too far away. If Mama misses you, nothing I say will save you. It would be a terrible shame to miss the ball as punishment ..."

He let his suggestion trail off as the girls stared at him in shocked horror. Without a word they turned toward the house, although as she passed Cleo, Bridget did whisper once more, "You really ought to see the grotto!"

Cleo laughed and waved farewell. For a moment she and the duke stood and watched them go, some with steps dragging and some putting their heads together to whisper.

"So that's why the men have congregated in the stables," she remarked. "Not merely the lure of a top-notch phaeton."

He cleared his throat. "I don't know anything about that."

Cleo laughed again.

"Although—" Wessex glanced at his sisters' retreating figures. "—one does sympathize."

"Frightened by a group of girls?" she asked mischievously.

A faint smile crossed his face. "When Bridget is one of their number? Yes."

On impulse, she added, "Where is the grotto?"

The duke looked at her, his eyebrows slightly raised. For a moment everything seemed to fade away but the two of them. Cleo felt again the mixture of attraction and alarm that had tugged at her in the parlor the other day. She wet her lips. "That's twice now that Lady Bridget has mentioned it. I've never seen a grotto. Is it very dark and mysterious?"

His gaze dropped to her mouth. "Yes."

Oh no. No, no, no. She held out her hand and forced a shaky smile to her lips. "Excellent! Perhaps I shall visit it some other day, after I've written my letters."

He hesitated, then handed her the writing case. The weight of it seemed to help hold her feet to the ground; she was a lowly merchant, not someone a duke would find fascinating. She would take her bills and inventory reports, and he would go back to his castle. "You might find a quiet spot by the lake. There are blankets in the boathouse."

She nodded. "Thank you."

He looked as though he might say something else, but after a moment he merely bowed. "Good day, Mrs. Barrows." He turned and walked back the way they had come, without looking back.

Cleo knew, because she watched him until he disappeared from sight.

# CHAPTER SEVEN

Gareth joined Blair on the way to the bowling green a couple of days later. He hadn't planned to go when his mother told him she had planned a day of bowls, but by now he conceded that he was unable to concentrate as usual. *Besides, it is the proper thing for a host to join his guests*, he told himself as he caught sight of the green, some distance from the house. The ladies reposed under the awnings, enjoying refreshments. A pair of young boys were on the green, arguing over something with fingers pointed and an occasional stamp of a foot. But otherwise there was something decidedly off about the scene.

"Where are the gentlemen?" he asked.

"In the stables."

"All of them?" exclaimed Gareth.

Blair grinned. "Willoughby's refuge has proven enormously popular."

"That damned phaeton." Gareth shook his head. He knew several men had joined Jack in the stables, but they had still come to his mother's planned entertainments—until now.

"It really is the finest thing on four wheels I've ever seen," agreed Blair warmly. "And as fast as the wind, he assured us all."

He glanced sideways at his cousin. "So you're a member of his band of refugees?"

"I was merely investigating where all the port seemed to have disappeared to," replied Blair with a perfectly straight face.

"He took the best spirits, didn't he?" That explained things a bit more.

Blair just grinned again.

215

Gareth shook his head. "God help the woman Jack marries. She had better be made of stern stuff."

His cousin coughed. "We cannot all be as fortunate as you, Wessex, to marry a lady as agreeable as Miss Grey."

Gareth had nothing to say to that. Helen Grey *was* agreeable—perfectly, completely, alarmingly agreeable. Whatever he said to her, she agreed with. Whatever he suggested, she did. He was developing the oddest feeling that she was afraid of him. Even Withers opposed him from time to time, and Withers was his employee. He reminded himself to pay attention to her today—and then felt guilty that he was in any danger of overlooking her.

Perhaps if he had no interest in any of the women, he wouldn't feel that way. Unfortunately, Cleo Barrows had come to the wedding, and he was not only uninterested in his actual bride, he was fascinated by her sister. It was wrong. It was almost immoral. He wanted it to stop and yet felt helpless to do so when his eyes seemed to follow her of their own volition and his ears seemed more attuned to the sound of her voice than to any other's.

They reached the largest of the awnings, set on a gentle rise overlooking the bowling green. His mother came to meet them. "What a lovely surprise!"

"Isn't it my duty as a host?" Gareth kissed her cheek even as he covertly scanned the tent. He saw Cleo Barrows first, sending his heart leaping. She was speaking to another lady ... whom he recognized a moment later as his betrothed bride. Not a promising beginning.

"I merely remembered that you told me you would be busy until the ball," his mother murmured, linking her arm through his. "I'm very pleased to see you were drawn out earlier." They strolled among the guests, pausing now and then to speak to someone. If Jack had assembled a gentlemen's retreat in the stables, it seemed his mother had created one under the awnings for the ladies. Round tables held pitchers of lemonade, plates of cakes and biscuits, and pots of tea, constantly refreshed by servants. The seating included small settees and benches, although Sophronia was sitting in a large upholstered chair, like a monarch on a throne, slicing a cheese with her sharp little knife.

"Finally come to see the girl, Wessex?" The old lady fixed her gleaming gaze upon him. "You've hardly spoken to your bride."

"Sophronia," said the duchess. "Really!"

"I came to see you," Gareth said before his mother could go on. He leaned down to kiss her cheek, which she presented with the regal detachment of a queen. "How are you, old dear?"

"Bored," Sophronia replied. "Everyone here is too polite. There's no trouble. No scandal."

"Do we really want that?" he asked mildly. It only encouraged Sophronia when people gasped and swooned at her outbursts.

"It's dull," announced the old lady, pointing her dirk at him. "What good is a house party if everyone's going to behave? I got my hopes raised when you invited that scamp, Jack Willoughby, but he's barely shown his face around here! And even worse, he's been a horrible distraction to Henrietta, and I have to let some parlor maid help me. I'm astonished to see her here today." She glanced over at Henrietta, who was holding a plate of cakes and listening with obviously strained patience to a very earnest-looking young woman. "She still hasn't brought my cake, though. I wager she'd bring it quickly enough if Willoughby wandered in."

"I will speak to Henrietta," began the duchess quickly, but Sophronia waved her off.

"Oh, let her have some fun. I'm sure they're up to something scandalous. I'd pay a shilling to watch them torment each other, but they keep disappearing and Henrietta refuses to tell me what they get up to, the vexing creature," she finished sourly, as if Jack and Henrietta had purposely schemed to deprive her of entertainment. "If she's going to desert me, she might as well tell me how naughty he can be."

"I'm not certain I can help," Gareth said. He doubted Jack would be flushed out of the stables by anything less than a duel.

"I daresay you can't," she grumbled. "Too upstanding by half. And your bride—Miss Grey! I never met such a polite, proper girl in my life. At least the party includes a few interesting people. Have you met Angela?"

Gareth glanced at his mother, who looked nonplussed. "I don't recall anyone by that name," she murmured.

"Oh! I invited her. The daughter of a very distant relation—not your side of the family, Alice. Very intriguing girl. She must have slipped off somewhere, but you'll meet her eventually." There was a hint of relish in the old lady's voice that made Gareth wonder what trouble this distant relation Angela might unleash.

"But Sophronia," said the duchess delicately. "The house is very full. I'm afraid we haven't any rooms to spare. If you had informed me earlier you wished to invite someone—"

"Don't worry about that," interrupted Sophronia. "Angela is staying with me. I need someone to talk to, now that Henrietta's set her cap for Willoughby." She scowled. "And if he doesn't recognize her for the prize she is, I shall take my dirk to him. He won't make a fool of my companion, no matter how charming his smile!" She stabbed her knife into the cheese for emphasis.

Gareth bit his cheek to keep from roaring with laughter at the image of Sophronia pursuing Jack with her dagger drawn. It was almost as entertaining as the thought of Jack falling for Henrietta, who was everything Jack was not: organized, responsible, and punctual.

He excused himself and made his way toward Helen, determinedly keeping his gaze fixed on her. She looked far livelier today, laughing and talking with obvious pleasure. She was truly lovely; her eyes glowed and there was a very handsome blush on her cheeks. She fluttered her hands about, as though portraying birds, and Gareth made the mistake of letting his eyes follow one graceful hand as she fluttered it over to rest on her sister's arm. Her sister, sitting very close to James Blair on the bench.

He almost missed his footing at the expression on Cleo Barrows's face. Her face was scrunched up with laughter—she had even wrinkled her nose—as she shook her head at whatever her sister said. Her curls bounced and threatened to topple down her back; one had already come loose and brushed the nape of her neck. Her sister was beautiful, but Cleo ... she was captivating.

He had the growing feeling that he was doomed. The harder he tried to find a reason why she was undesirable in any way, the less success he had. He wanted to wind that loose curl around his fingers. He wanted to press his lips to the back of her neck, and the base of her throat. He wanted to talk to her, to have those sparkling brown eyes fixed on him, to see that impish grin directed his way. Instead he watched Blair receive all that and more when she turned to his cousin, put her hand on his arm, and leaned close to whisper something that made Blair throw back his head and shout with laughter.

"I'm delighted to see Miss Grey looking well again," said his mother. "I do believe Mrs. Barrows could make anyone smile, though."

He watched the way she tipped her head to one side, and for a single heartbeat their gazes met. "Indeed."

"James seems quite taken with her," his mother went on. "I understand she's a widow with a pretty income. He could certainly do worse, if he's thinking of marrying."

This time there was no mistaking the feeling oozing through his veins. It was jealousy, raw and bitter. It was utterly irrational and yet undeniable. He forced it down. "I suppose," he replied, in what he hoped was an offhand voice. "Has he said anything to you about her?"

"Of course not. Do you think I should encourage him?"

He gritted his teeth. "I think he's a grown man capable of deciding such a thing himself." Without waiting for her reply, he went down to join the boys still arguing over bowls. The only other male about seemed to be Blair, and Gareth found he had no patience to watch his cousin flirt with Cleo.

And he didn't swerve from his course when he saw the lady in question stroll down to the green ahead of him.

To Cleo's immense relief, Helen seemed like herself again when they walked down to the awnings the morning of the bowling party. Anyone's nerves would have been strained by their mother's incessant chattering about how grand and elegant everything—and everyone—was at the party. Cleo had long since grown content with what she could afford, but Helen had never been allowed to do the same. Sir William refused to acknowledge his straitened circumstances, and Millicent was incapable of economy; they had relied on Helen making a marvelous marriage to restore their fortunes. Cleo was fairly certain that burden had put the faint lines around her sister's mouth and brought a shadow to her eyes.

But the bowling party had revived her. Perhaps it was the weather, which had been nothing short of perfect. A group of young ladies, including the duke's sisters, had amused them for some time before Lady Sophronia came to grace them with her presence. Helen obviously found the old lady somewhat intimidating, but Cleo thought she was splendid. Sophronia spoke her mind and did as she pleased. When she'd had enough conversation, she simply announced that she was leaving.

"I see a fine cheese over there and want to secure it before someone else makes off with it," she confided. "The guests at these parties are like wolves, eating up every crumb in sight."

"Oh! May I fetch it for you?" Cleo offered, privately entertained by the description of the aristocratic guests as hungry scavengers.

"No, no. I can take care of myself." Lady Sophronia drew—of all things—a small pointed dagger from her pocket. "A memento of my third fiancé, Malcolm MacBride," she said fondly, showing them the knife. "I was very sad when the consumption took him. Still, it's a very useful dirk—that's what the Scots call it. I recommend you get one. No one interferes with a lady who is armed."

"No, I imagine not." Cleo's voice shook as the old lady nodded to them and hobbled after her cheese. She glanced at her sister and saw Helen's eyes tearing up. "Shall I give you a knife as a wedding gift, Helen?" she asked mischievously. "I don't want you to lose out on any fine cheese ..."

Helen covered her face. "Oh, my," she gasped, fighting back giggles. "I can only imagine what Mama would say!" They were still shaking with suppressed laughter when Mr. Blair joined them. He immediately inquired what had made them laugh so hard, and Helen told him with animation and spirit, laughing anew at Sophronia's concern for her cheese. It made Cleo's heart lift to see her sister happy again. The only thing that might have pleased her more was if Wessex himself had joined them. He had arrived at the party with Mr. Blair, but was intercepted by the duchess. Cleo kept stealing glances at him, willing him to come over to them. He was looking fondly at Sophronia, and it was hard not to notice how attractive it made him. She wondered if he knew about Sophronia's dirk.

Then, by chance, their eyes met. It was just a passing glance, no more than a moment, but it sent a little shock through her. He was smiling, his dark eyes bright with mirth, and it transformed his face from handsome to mesmerizing. Cleo turned instantly back to Mr. Blair, but she could feel the duke's gaze upon her. It made her heart beat a little faster even as it reminded her of her vow to be quiet and discreet around His Grace. Helen had been right about one thing the other day: Cleo was more ebullient than her sister. She tended to attract people's attention. Therefore, she must absent herself when the duke and Helen met, so there could be nothing to distract Wessex from falling in love with Helen.

If it also kept Cleo from becoming more attracted to him, she would be immensely relieved.

When she caught the duke and his mother watching their little group, she murmured an excuse and slipped away. Mr. Blair was charming and had already brought a wide smile to Helen's face with an amusing story about Lady Sophronia; apparently, the dirk was not her only memento of a former suitor. Cleo knew her sister looked her best today, and if she left, the duke would be able to sit next to Helen and notice how enchanting she was.

Cleo walked down the gentle slope toward the bowling green, where two boys had been arguing for some time. "It seems you're in need of an umpire," she said as she reached them. "May I serve?"

"He put his foot in front of my bowl," said the younger boy at once. He was sturdy and blond, with the look of a boy who spent hours outdoors. "His bowl is dead and I ought to be allowed to replay mine."

"I did not!" Henry Ascot's eyes glittered with tears. "I never touched your bowl! It stopped on its own!"

"You did," accused the other. "And now you're trying to cheat!"

"I am not a cheat." His voice quivered, and Cleo could see how desperately he was trying to contain himself.

"'Cheat' is a dangerous word," she admonished them both. "One should never cast it about without proof. Do you have proof that he impeded your bowl? I presume you've measured every cast so far."

The first boy clamped his mouth shut and dropped the bowl in his hand. "Beg pardon, ma'am. I guess we ought not to play anymore." He ducked his head and walked away.

Cleo stooped to pick up the discarded bowl, giving Henry a moment to collect himself. He was tall and a bit gangly, with an uncompromisingly square brow and dark hair. Lady Bridget had called him a horrid pest, but he didn't look very dreadful now. "I hope there wasn't a wager riding on the match," she said.

He sniffed. "No. Not one I could win, at any rate." She glanced at him through her eyelashes. The poor boy looked thoroughly dejected. "I never win at bowls," he added softly.

"There's more to life than bowls."

"I know. There's boxing and racing and quoits and all manner of sport where I can be a disappointment to my father."

Cleo bit her lip. She knew more than a little about that herself. Before she could reply, though, someone else did.

"Every man has his talents, Henry. I daresay yours will turn out to be of far greater import than bowls."

Henry looked warily at the Duke of Wessex, who had walked up behind Cleo. "Do you really think so, sir?"

"I wouldn't say so otherwise."

"Of course not." The boy blushed. He shifted his weight, then awkwardly offered Cleo the bowl in his hand. "Thank you, ma'am, for settling things. I think I'd rather take a walk. Do—do you happen to know where my sister Charlotte's gone?"

"I'm sorry, no," said Cleo. Charlotte had disappeared with the rest of the young ladies some time ago, very soon after Henry and the other boy had reached the green.

"Toward the lake," said the duke. "I believe she was with my sisters."

Henry's dark eyes lit up, and Cleo got the idea he'd be quite a handsome fellow in a few years. "Thank you, sir!" He hurried off with a spring in his step.

"What a devoted brother, wanting to see his sister," she said lightly.

"Perhaps," replied the duke with a wry look. "I suspect it's more of an urge to torment. After I sent them back to the house the other day, Bridget came to me to lodge an indignant complaint that he had thrown mud on them."

"The things a man will do for love." Cleo heaved a dramatic sigh. "I'll wager a shilling he has a bad case of calf love for one of them."

"It had better not be Bridget." Wessex shuddered. "I had to order her not to put treacle in his bed. She didn't take it well when he ruined her favorite dress."

Cleo laughed. She started down the green to collect the abandoned bowls. "Have they really gone toward the lake?"

"I did see a group of young ladies in the general vicinity of the lake today," he confirmed, walking beside her. "It might have been some time ago ..." Cleo laughed again. "But a long walk will do him good. He ought to clear his mind before he finds them. I've rarely seen one girl this week without three or four others nearby; the poor lad will be severely outnumbered."

"It builds character," she said.

"He'll need it if he fancies Bridget. I daresay she'll make Sophronia look demure and quiet."

"Yes. Lady Sophronia showed me her dirk." Cleo grinned at the way he cast his eyes upward and sighed. "A rather unusual remembrance of an old love."

"There are many unusual things about Sophronia."

"She is your great-aunt, I understand?"

The duke paused. "Great-great-aunt. Perhaps. I'm not entirely certain. I think I inherited her along with the house."

Cleo snorted with laughter, and this time he laughed, too. Something seemed to melt inside her at the sound. His laugh was a rough rumble, as if he didn't use it often. She stooped to retrieve a pair of bowls, holding them to her chest. When she rose, Wessex was holding the jack. He gave it a little toss, catching it easily in one hand. "Would you fancy a match, Mrs. Barrows?"

Cleo watched his fingers curve around the bowl. Good heavens, he had fine hands. "I haven't played bowls in a very long time."

"Neither have I," he said. "But it's a fine day out, and the greens are marked."

She glanced at the awning on the hill above as they walked to the head of the green. Helen was still in conversation with Mr. Blair, but she raised her hand and gave a cheery wave. Cleo was torn. It was a fine day, and she wouldn't mind a lighthearted game in the sun. Since the duke had invited her, surely not even her father would find it objectionable. She could suggest inviting Helen and Mr. Blair to join them, except that she knew her sister hated bowls. And perhaps this was her chance to determine the duke's feelings for Helen.

"Very well. But we must have stakes." She grinned at his raised brow. "Not money! After each cast, the winner must share something of himself or herself. After all, we shall be family within the week, and we ought to become acquainted, don't you think?"

He looked at her for a long moment. In the sunlight, his hair seemed to have a hint of auburn; the breeze had ruffled it until he looked quite tousled. And his eyes were so dark, unfathomably deep as he regarded her. Cleo heard the echo of her own words—*we shall be family*—and felt her heart sink a little. Oh, why had he followed her, thwarting her intent to avoid him? He ought to be sitting beside Helen right now, gazing at Helen, making Helen yearn to smooth his wild mane and imagine his large hands on her skin.

"Of course." Wessex bowed his head. "Will you set the jack?"

Unnerved, she turned toward the green and pitched the jack. It didn't roll far enough, and she clenched her hands as he strode out to get it. She had to wrench her gaze away as he bent over to pick it up; good heavens, he was a finely made man, from all angles. And he would be her brother. Sisters did not look on their brothers so admiringly.

The second time she managed to set the mark appropriately, and the duke stepped to the footer to cast his first bowl. "Were you a good bowls player, when you last played?"

Cleo laughed. "Oh, my. I certainly thought so, but I was a girl then." She delivered her first bowl, pleased to see it roll to within a respectable distance of the jack. Nearer than his, in fact. "I suppose you're far more accomplished, given that you have a bowling green within sight of your house."

He made his next shot. "Merely having a green doesn't make one skilled." His bowl wobbled off the green into the ditch.

"It takes a while to learn the bias of the bowls," she said diplomatically, hefting her own. It was smooth and dark, shaped more like a fat egg than a round ball. This time she misjudged, and the bowl came to rest at the edge of the green.

They played the rest of the end and then walked down together to score it. "One point to you," said Wessex, collecting the bowls. "What secret do you want to tell me?"

"Se-Secret?" she stammered, laughing nervously. "Oh, no, I didn't mean a secret—"

"But we've only just met," he said, watching her in that too-intent way he had. "Everything about you is a mystery."

"Helen and I had a game, as children," she said after a moment. "We would choose a play—one of the great works of antiquity, most often—and act out every part. It nearly killed my father when we performed *Lysistrata*, even though Helen and I had very little idea what it was about."

"How old were you?" he asked, looking a little incredulous.

"About twelve," she said airily. "And Helen only eight."

Wessex coughed, then he laughed. "I would pay a fortune to have seen your father's face. He doesn't seem the type to take it well."

Her father didn't take most things she did well. Cleo's smile faded. "I was a bad influence even then," she murmured before she could stop herself. The duke gave her a keen glance but said nothing.

They bowled another end, and this time Wessex won a point. Cleo shook her head as she retrieved two of her bowls from the ditch but was glad that it was his turn to reveal something. "I inherited my title when I was sixteen," he said. "Barely older than young Henry." Her eyes rounded in shock. "My sisters were infants, my mother was heartbroken, and I was responsible for everything." He turned to face the house, squinting against the sun. "I was deathly afraid of letting my father down by making a hash of it."

"I'm sure he would be very proud!" Impulsively she laid her hand on his arm. "Kingstag is beautifully maintained. Your sisters are lovely young ladies, and it's clear to all that they adore you. No man can be a failure if his family loves him."

His arm flexed under her fingers. "Thank you," he said quietly. "My sisters' happiness is very important to me." He paused. "As is, I think, your sister's to you."

Cleo snatched her hand away. "Yes, very important." She went back to the mat, trying to ignore the faint question in his voice at the end. Helen's happiness *was* very important to her, and yet here she was, almost flirting with her sister's fiancé. She turned toward the awning again, both relieved and disconcerted to see Helen still absorbed in conversation with Mr. Blair. It should be Wessex sitting there with his head next to Helen's, bringing that glowing smile to her face. He should want to be there, instead of here in the sun with Cleo. But when the duke joined her, bowls in hand, she didn't say anything. She put her foot on the mat and bowled.

Wessex won another point. They walked to retrieve the bowls and she was glad again she didn't have to say anything. "What can I tell you?" he murmured, facing her thoughtfully. "Hmm."

"Something from when you were young," she suggested, thinking it would be safer. "A fond memory."

"Ah." He grinned. The wind lifted his hair from his forehead, and he looked boyish for a moment. "Blair came to Kingstag when he was about ten. His family fell on hard times and my mother invited him; his mother is her cousin. As you might imagine, we had a grand time, two boys with all this to explore." He swept one hand in a wide arc to encompass all of Kingstag. "One day I conceived a plan to go boating on the lake. Blair wasn't as eager but he went along with it, and we soon were in the middle of the lake, two sporting gentlemen at leisure." He shook his head. "Imagine my shock when I looked down to see an inch of water in the bottom of the boat. We neither of us wanted to swim—my mother would have punished us for spoiling our clothes and boots, to say nothing of taking out an old, leaky boat—so Blair bailed water with his hands while I rowed ferociously. We managed to come within a few feet of the shore before it sank entirely. Both of us had the most incredible blisters."

"That's your fond memory?" Cleo smiled. "Blisters!"

"No, it was the thrill of saving ourselves from disaster."

"That I can understand, particularly if you didn't get caught."

"We didn't," he assured her, his eyes twinkling. "Blair and I have always backed each other up."

She laughed. "All the sweeter!"

"Indeed. It was one of the few times I truly escaped responsibility." He met her gaze. "Today seems like another. I can't say when I've enjoyed myself so much."

Cleo's heart felt warm and light even as she tried to tell herself he was just being polite. "Nor I, Your Grace."

"Wessex," he said. "Please."

Now her face felt warm. "Very well. But you must call me Cleo. After all, we shall be family." Perhaps if she reminded herself of that, forcefully and frequently, it would blunt the attraction she felt.

The expression on his face certainly didn't. If anything, it made things worse. Wessex had a way of looking at her that made the breath almost stop in her chest. "Very well, if you wish," he said after a moment. "Cleo."

She shouldn't have. She'd made a mistake. It sounded too familiar, too tender when he said it. Cleo glanced back at her sister in despair. Helen hadn't looked at Wessex any more than Wessex had looked at Helen. Not only had Cleo failed to discover the duke's feelings for her sister, she had only succeeded in making her own feelings worse.

If she didn't catch herself soon, she would find herself utterly in love with him.

As soon as possible, Gareth excused himself and went in search of oblivion. He found it in the stables. His cousin had the right idea, avoiding all the females. Some of the men looked a trifle guilty— Lord Warnford hastily hid a pair of dice behind his back—but Gareth just raised his hand in greeting and retired to a corner to contemplate the trouble he was in, a bottle in hand.

He brooded over his brandy while a tedious conversation about a horse race occupied the other men. The only person who appeared less interested in the race was the Earl of Bruton, who arrived shortly after he did and looked as grim as Gareth felt. He caught his old friend's eye and invited him to have a drink, not surprised to see Bruton here. With that slashing scar down his face, the earl had long avoided the ladies.

"Thank God for Willoughby," cried one decidedly drunk fellow all of a sudden. "He's saved us all with this refuge from the ladies."

"Hear, hear!" cheered the rest of the company.

"No offense intended, Wessex," added the man, still swinging his tankard of ale in one hand. "Felicitations on your marriage."

God help him; even drinking in the stables couldn't save him from that topic. He nodded in acknowledgement and poured another gulp of brandy down his throat, wondering if he could drink enough to purge the sound of Cleopatra Barrows's laughter from his mind. He could still feel the touch of her hand on his arm.

He left the stables, handing his bottle to Lord Everett as he went. If they raised a toast to his bride, he might be ill. There was one inescapable thought circling his brain, and he didn't know how to address it.

He was marrying the wrong woman.

# CHAPTER EIGHT

Cleo went downstairs early two mornings before the wedding, which was finally almost at hand. After their match of bowls, she had taken care only to cross the Duke of Wessex's path in company. Even at the ball last night, she had determinedly kept her distance. It hadn't kept her from noticing how very attractive he was, or how kind and good-humored he was with his sisters, or even how gallant he was to Sophronia. How could one dislike a man who was so wonderful? Cleo had clung to her sister's side and tried to interest herself in the wedding plans, but that had difficulties of its own. She thought she might scream if she didn't escape her mother's hawk-like watch for a few hours. As the wedding drew nearer, so apparently did her fear that Cleo would say or do something unacceptable.

Since Cleo knew very well that she was doing something unpardonable, it was hard to argue with her mother. She had diligently avoided talking about her shop except when directly asked, but her real sin was far worse, even though her mother could have no idea. She had tried everything to keep her wicked thoughts in check, to no avail, and now she had only one option left: avoidance. If she spent her time wandering alone over the estate and secluded herself in her room the rest of the time, she could endure until the wedding was over. Then it would be perfectly acceptable to make her excuses and return home to her little shop, where she couldn't ruin anyone's life but her own.

She paused before a mirror in the hall to tie her bonnet ribbons. The castle was still almost silent, populated only by the servants moving quietly about. Everyone would probably sleep late after the ball the previous night. In spite of everything, she would be sorry to leave Kingstag. It really was a wonderful place.

"Good morning," said a voice behind her.

Cleo jumped. The one voice she'd been trying to avoid but somehow still longed to hear. "Good morning, Your Grace," she managed to say, knotting her ribbons before facing him. "I was just setting out to indulge myself with a long walk."

"As was I." He wore a long coat and carried a rather battered hat. Cleo's pulse leaped as he pushed one bare hand through his thick dark hair. "I rarely have the time to step out later in the day."

"Oh! Please don't let me disturb you," she began, but he raised one hand.

"On the contrary. I didn't expect to meet anyone this morning, but it would be a pleasure to have company."

She should say no. She drew an unsteady breath. "I hate to disoblige you ..."

"Please," he said, and Cleo closed her mouth. Without another word she put her hand on the arm he offered, and together they walked out the door.

A blanket of mist covered the ground, lending an unearthly air to the scene. Cleo drew in a delighted breath, loving the cool, earthy scent of the country. They strolled along the gravel, heading toward the lake, which lay still and quiet beyond the fog. "How beautiful," she sighed. "I rarely see such a sight in town."

"Are you always an early riser?"

She blushed. She had to be awake early to open the shop. "Yes. I love the morning light."

"My sisters and mother prefer not to rise until the sun is high in the sky."

"I'm sure they have good reason, particularly today," she said lightly. "It would be very hard to rise early when there are guests and entertainments every evening."

He smiled. "They are creatures of candlelight, even when there are no guests."

"As long as they are all the same, I see no cause for worry. If Bridget were to favor the morning while the others did not ..." She shook her head and sighed as the duke chuckled. "It's lovely to see sisters so close."

"Barely three years separate them. My father was away for much of my childhood as a diplomat." Wessex slanted her a look. "My mother was quite joyous at his return."

Cleo sighed, but with a smile. "How lovely to find a married couple in love."

"And how sad when they are parted too soon," he murmured.

She said nothing. It was true. The last time she had walked arm-in-arm with a man had been two years ago, before Matthew was cut down by an inflammation in his lungs. Not since then had she ever once felt the same easy companionship she seemed to have fallen into overnight with the Duke of Wessex. He was nothing like Matthew and yet ... in some ways he reminded her of her husband. He had a wry way of putting things. He was even-tempered with everyone, from his ebullient sister Bridget to Cleo's own flighty mother; even querulous Lady Sophronia never ruffled him. And he had a way of looking at her that made her feel every lonely minute of her widowhood.

"I understand you know too well how sad that is," he said quietly. "Forgive me for mentioning—"

"No!" She squeezed his arm lightly. "I have nothing but happy memories of my husband."

"Does that make it better or worse?" He cleared his throat. "To have loved and lost, I mean. My mother was destroyed when my father died. I was only a boy, but I became utterly convinced she would have been far happier if she hadn't loved him."

"I suspect she would disagree," Cleo murmured. "Love is worth the risk."

"Yes," he said after a moment. "I am beginning to agree with that."

"I am as sure of that as I am sure the sun will rise in the east. I took a great risk and suffered a great loss, but I would do it all again. Real love is very much worth it."

"A great risk," he echoed, sounding pensive. "What do you mean?"

"I suppose there's no reason not to tell you," she said, keeping her gaze fixed on something in the distance. She was under orders not to tell him and yet the words spilled out. "Helen knows, after all, so you would be sure to hear of it eventually. I eloped when I was seventeen. My parents have never forgiven me."

He stopped, and she had to stop, too. Cleo realized how far she had to tilt her head back to meet his eyes. "As bad as that?"

The concern in his voice made her flush. He wasn't haughty and arrogant, looking down on her for keeping a shop—unlike her parents. The temptation was too much. "Oh, yes," she said with a rueful smile. "I'm only here on sufferance."

"Oh?" His voice was soft and warm, comforting and seductive.

"Yes," she barreled on. "He wasn't enormously wealthy, titled, or extremely famous; he was a merchant. And my parents have never recovered from the shame."

"I see." He leaned forward a little. "Why did you do it, then?"

She smiled wistfully. "Because I loved him. He made me laugh."

The duke seemed mesmerized for a moment. His face was so still and yet rapt.

Cleo supposed she had just displayed her common nature, impulsive and reckless, and gave a little shrug. "There is so much of life that must conform to duty or polite behavior, but I don't know how people endure it all if they aren't *happy*, or at least content. My parents were horrified that I would run off like a hoyden with no care for how it reflected on my family. I suppose they only wanted better for me, but I ... I was happy. For that, I could endure any discomforts life brought."

"Yes," he said, as though very struck by her words. "How very wise you are."

"Oh! Not really." She blushed at the look he gave her, direct and probing. "Headstrong. Willful." Those had been two of the kinder words her father used.

"What is headstrong and willful in a woman is often called decisive and bold in a man." He took a deep breath. "I wish we had had this conversation several months ago. You have shown me a multitude of errors on my part."

They had passed the bowling green by now, the awnings still standing like lonely sentinels over the bare rinks. Cleo felt again the way her heart had turned over when Wessex grinned at her over the bowls, the breeze ruffling his hair. Why did it have to be her sister's fiancé who made her heart leap? "I'm sorry," she said softly. "That wasn't my desire."

"No!" He shook his head. "On the contrary. I've never shied away from my mistakes. I made a great many of them, inheriting a dukedom at so young an age. Humiliation is a powerful teacher. But I fear it also taught me some lessons too well, lessons I've only just realized were all wrong."

She fixed her gaze upon the ground, afraid of what he would say next and yet desperate to know. "How so?"

"My parents were devoted to each other. My father's death ... it seemed to shatter my mother. To my horrified young eyes, all that love seemed to have turned into soul-rending anguish. I was sure I wanted no part of that in my own marriage, and I never met anyone who changed my mind—until you."

"Love in marriage is vital," she whispered. Her heart thudded dangerously.

"I am more and more persuaded of that." He stopped walking. "You must understand ... I had the best of intentions when I courted your sister. I don't love her, but I fully expected to be an honorable, faithful husband to her—"

"Stop." Cleo put her hand over his mouth to stop him. Tears prickled in her eyes. "Don't say anything else. You can love her—you *will*. Helen is the most wonderful girl, it's impossible not to love her—"

Gently, tenderly, he covered her hand with his, moving her palm to his cheek. His eyes closed for a moment and he inhaled a long slow breath as he leaned into her touch. "But not in the right way." He opened his eyes and looked at her, his face stark with yearning.

Cleo wavered on her feet at the longing that stabbed through her. If he had been anyone else in the world, she would be in his arms right now. God help her, she still wanted to be. But Helen—Helen, her beloved sister—even if Helen didn't love him and he didn't love her, Cleo couldn't betray her sister that way.

"You have to try," she said, her voice trembling.

"I have." He sounded helpless.

She pulled away from him, recoiling a step even though he made no move to stop her. "Keep trying. You've not spent enough time with her—it's just a bit of madness—we've only just met—"

"I don't think a lifetime will be enough to change my feelings so dramatically."

"Nor mine." The words slipped out before she could stop them. She raised a trembling hand to her mouth as if to recall them, but it was too late; he had heard.

If Gareth hadn't understood his own feelings before then, there was no doubting them now. He had thought—suspected—that Cleo was as attracted as he was, but he hadn't known if she felt more. But as her words lingered in the air, confirming what he yearned for, it seemed as though the earth finally went still beneath his feet again. After days of being off balance, caught between disbelief and alarm that he was falling in love when it was almost too late, he found he finally knew what he wanted.

He had tried to love Helen, he really had. After the bowling match, he'd kept his distance from Cleo and paid more attention to his betrothed. It hadn't helped—if anything, it had only convinced him he'd made a terrible error. Helen was as lovely and sweet-tempered as he had originally thought, but she was also far quieter. She was reserved and polite with the guests, and more than once he saw her glance longingly out the window, as if she couldn't wait to escape the room. For the life of him he couldn't remember why he'd thought she would make a good duchess; of course one could learn it and grow into it, and his mother was ready and able to teach her, but he suspected it would take years for Helen to feel at ease as the Duchess of Wessex and mistress of Kingstag Castle.

But when he looked at Cleo, more and more he saw someone who would be a splendid duchess from the beginning. She knew all the guests within days. His mother remarked on her effortless conversation. His sisters, who had been so eager to meet Helen, had quickly switched their adoration to Cleo, with her bold and unusual clothes and friendly manner. Even Sophronia liked her, and Sophronia was the harshest critic Gareth had ever met. What's more, she was used to running a large business, overseeing more than a dozen men, and managing her own finances—much the same skills that would be required to run Kingstag. He doubted anything would daunt her, including him in his worst temper.

And then there was the way she made him feel. When she smiled at him, Gareth would swear he could still feel the electric tingle in the air, as if lightning had struck him anew. When she laughed, he wanted to kiss her. When she took his arm, he wanted to carry her off into the shrubbery. And when she put her fingers on his lips, he wanted to fall to his knees and make love to her on the spot.

But deciding what he wanted was only part of the difficulty. He knew what he would have to do, somehow. It would be unpleasant, no doubt, and he didn't quite know how to go about it, but this was a risk that was definitely worth the reward.

"Cleo." He took a step toward her. She turned her face away, biting her lip, but otherwise she didn't move. He took another step and reached for her hand. "Tell me what you want," he murmured.

"It doesn't matter what I want."

"It does to me." He edged a step closer. She smelled of roses, soft and beautiful. "I didn't believe in love, let alone love at first sight. I am torn in two, caught between what I want and what I've promised. Tell me what you want, darling, and I will move heaven and earth to do it."

"I want my sister to be happy."

"Only your sister?"

A shudder went through her. "No," she whispered despondently. "But how can this end well for everyone?"

His fingers tightened on hers. "I promise it will."

"How can you promise that?" She shook her head. She pulled her hand loose and finally turned to face him. There was no sparkle in her dark eyes now, no teasing curve to her lips. It was all he could do to keep from touching her. He wanted to hold her close and swear that everything would fall in place. Her unhappiness gutted him. "My parents—my sister—what will they think if you cry off? How could I cause such humiliation for my own wicked desires? Do you know what people will say about me, if you desert Helen for me? I can't, Your Grace."

"And what will your sister think of me if I marry her strictly out of duty?"

For a long moment she said nothing. "I hope you won't—I hope you'll be happy with her, and she with you. But I won't interfere in my sister's marriage." She turned and hurried away, her footsteps muffled in the fog.

Gareth watched until she disappeared around the trees before cursing under his breath. He had to think; he had to find a solution to please everyone. He had learned to be a duke at age sixteen, responsible for solving his problems and everyone else's. This was no different ... merely his entire future happiness was at stake.

He was startled out of his thoughts by Blair, who came trudging across the lawn with a pistol case in hand. His cousin stopped short when he saw Gareth. "Wessex."

"Blair." Gareth stared at the case. "You look like a man on his way to a duel."

"The duel was at dawn." Blair looked troubled. "Bruton and Newnham."

"They're cousins," said Gareth in shock. "And the best of friends—or so I thought. What did they duel over?"

"Rosanne Lacy. Newnham was courting her, but judging from what I just witnessed, Bruton will be marrying her."

"What you just witnessed," he repeated.

"Miss Lacy flying across the field, barely dressed and sobbing as if her heart would break." Blair's face twisted. "She flung herself into Bruton's arms and I could see it in Newnham's face. He loved her and yet knew he'd lost her. It takes a strong man to watch the woman you love marry another man."

He heard again Cleo's anguished voice, asking what her sister would think if he jilted Helen for her. Cleo loved him, but she couldn't betray her sister.

On the other hand, the notoriously aloof Earl of Bruton had somehow fallen in love with the girl his cousin was courting, and he'd found a way to marry her. Gareth ignored the matter of the duel and focused on the result, which was that Bruton was marrying the right woman for him.

Somehow Gareth had to do the same.

"I trust no one was hurt," he said. When Blair shook his head, Gareth added, "Excellent. Then it seems everything has worked out for the best."

His cousin jerked up his head and gave him a strange look. "You really think so?"

He nodded. "Absolutely. I must remember to wish Bruton happy. He certainly deserves it."

"I expect he and Miss Lacy will be very happy," said Blair slowly.

"Yes." Gareth grinned. "I expect so, too."

# CHAPTER NINE

Cleo took the long way back to the house before shutting herself in her room for the rest of the day. The conversation with Wessex whirled round and round her brain until her head ached. Every accusation her father had hurled at her seemed to be proven: she *was* wicked and reckless and dangerous to her family. Not only had she fallen in love with her sister's fiancé, she had only by the very thinnest of threads held herself back from kissing him. She never should have walked out into the mist with him. She never should have bowled with him. She never should have come to Kingstag at all. She ate dinner in her room and sent for her trunk to begin packing, so she could leave as soon as the wedding was over.

She only ventured out of her room late at night, when the house was quiet at last. She couldn't sleep and thought a turn in the garden might soothe her spirits. It must be beautiful in the moonlight. But a muffled sound caught her ear as she passed her sister's room, and before she could reconsider, she tapped gently on the door. "Helen!" she whispered into the jamb. "Let me in!"

The door jerked open and Helen stared at her with wide, wet eyes. She turned her face away, swiping her handkerchief over her face. "Cleo. You're still awake."

She felt a chill of guilt. The duke had hinted that he didn't want to go through with the wedding, and now Helen was crying. She stepped into the room and closed the door. "What's wrong?"

"Nothing!" Her sister folded the handkerchief into her pocket and went to sit on the sofa. She looked up, a wobbly smile on her face. "Nothing at all."

"I can see very well that something is wrong." She sat next to her sister. "Why are you crying?" A sudden fear gripped her. "His Grace didn't make you cry, did he?"

"I haven't seen him all day," said Helen, wringing her handkerchief and missing Cleo's breath of relief. "How could I, when Mama kept me in this room all day with the dressmaker fussing over my gown, and had Rivers put up my hair three different ways to see which was most flattering, and wouldn't even let me go down to dinner because she thought I looked pale? She told me I must keep up my strength because I'm to be mistress of a castle." Her face began to crumple.

"Oh my dear." Cleo bit her lip. "What brought all this on?"

Helen gripped her hands together in her lap. "The wedding, of course. She's determined that everything must be perfect, because otherwise His Grace will be disappointed or ashamed of me. I don't think I can be perfect anymore. I don't know if I can do ... this." She waved one hand around the beautiful room, but obviously including everything about Kingstag.

In spite of herself, a poisonous weed of hope sprouted in Cleo's heart. "What do you mean, you don't know if you can do ... this?" She waved one hand around as Helen had done.

Her sister sighed. "Being a duchess sounded so delightful: beautiful clothes and jewels, the highest society, never worrying about money or being received or given the cut direct. And it made Mama and Papa so happy—I cannot tell you how it eased their minds about everything when I accepted Wessex. I don't think I've ever seen them happier."

Cleo pressed her lips together. She was growing thoroughly tired of her parents' feelings. What sort of people grew happier at the cost of their children's joy? Because it was clear to see that Helen, whatever her original feelings about her marriage, was decidedly not happy now. And if Helen wasn't happy, perhaps she oughtn't to marry Wessex. She couldn't bring herself to say such a thing, afraid of persuading her sister to do something she'd regret just because it suited Cleo's own wishes. But neither could she advise her sister to forge ahead regardless of her feelings. "But you are not happy."

Helen jumped up and paced away. "I know I should be. Most of the time, I've wanted to run into the woods and hide, even as everyone tells me how fortunate I am."

"Many brides have nerves," murmured Cleo.

Her sister nodded, nibbling her bottom lip. "Were you nervous, when you married? Are all brides?"

"All brides should be happy," said Cleo diplomatically. She hadn't been nervous, she'd been eager. Why, if she were in Helen's shoes, about to marry Wessex ...

But she wasn't.

"Do you think I will be?"

She blinked at the question. "What?"

"Do you think I will be happy?" repeated her sister. "Married to the duke. Mama sees no other possibility—who could be unhappy, married to one of the richest dukes in England?—but you've always been honest with me. What do you think of him, Cleo?"

She sat like a woman turned to stone. How could she possibly answer that, after the traitorous longing that still stained her soul? Wessex was everything she thought a man ought to be, and more. He was the friend she longed for, the companion she had been without for so long, the lover she dreamt of at night. But he would never be hers. "He's very kind," she managed to say. "Handsome. Charming, in a wry sort of way. I think he'll be a good husband."

"But do you think I can be happy with him?" Helen seized her arm, her fingernails digging into Cleo's flesh. "Do you?"

Her heart broke at her sister's expression, anxious and yet hopeful. She swallowed hard. "It doesn't matter what I think," she said quietly. "Only you can know what your heart compels you to do. Your happiness is in your hands."

Helen's gaze bored into her. "Yes," she murmured. Her grip loosened on Cleo's arm as she turned away, her eyes growing distant. "Yes, it is. If I tell him—if I make him understand how I feel—he will have to listen. He did ask me to marry him, and a man doesn't do that lightly, does he? If I persuade him that all this is too much ... Yes, I think he will understand. It's not too late, is it?"

"You mean ... the wedding?" Cleo frowned a little. "Has it simply overwhelmed you?"

"Has it!" Helen gave a disbelieving laugh. "To no end! I have no idea who half these guests are, and if I have to listen much longer to Mama talk about how perfect Kingstag is and what an honor it is to be mistress of it, I may scream. You were so clever to elope, you know. You spared yourself immense aggravation." She stopped, looking startled, then flashed a cautious grin. "I shouldn't have said that, should I? Well, I think I'm done with doing what I ought to do."

"Oh," said Cleo, disconcerted. "Good."

Her sister laughed again. "It *is* good—or rather, it will be, thanks to you."

"I just want you to be happy," Cleo repeated. And she would do whatever it took, including going away and never visiting her sister and her too-tempting husband again. Wessex was not hers to lose; he was Helen's. And Helen certainly wouldn't lose him to Cleo.

Helen smiled. Tears still glittered in the corners of her eyes, but they no longer ran down her cheeks. "You do, don't you? Oh, Cleo, I think I would have gone mad without you. Sometimes I feel as if you are the only one who truly understands me." She flung her arms around Cleo, and Cleo hugged her back, heartsick. If Helen really hadn't wanted to marry Wessex, there might have been a chance ... but it was foolish to have let the thought cross her mind. Firmly she smothered it, renewing her silent vow to leave as soon as the wedding took place.

"There," she said, patting Helen's back. "Dry your eyes. You only have one more day before your wedding." The words were like a blow to her heart. "It's finally upon us," she said, her voice only breaking a little at the end.

Helen laughed, swiping at her eyes. "Yes. So it is—and I am ready for it at last," she said. Her doubts seemed to have been allayed, which meant they couldn't have been very serious doubts. Cleo told herself that was a good sign. "Thank you for coming. You've done me a world of good."

Helen mustn't know that her conscience was only just holding back the longing she felt. Helen didn't know her sister was thinking impure thoughts about her future husband. Cleo gave a shaky smile. "I'm delighted to be of help, any help I can be."

"Believe me," said Helen earnestly, "you've been more help than you know."


**G**areth realized two truths that day.

First, he couldn't marry Helen Grey. Not only did he not love her—and suspect she did not love him—but the mere mention of

Cleo made him forget the very existence of his betrothed bride. Just a glimpse of her snared his attention, and the very sound of her voice made him deaf to anything and anyone else around him. Everything she did persuaded him she would be perfect as his duchess—not a biddable ornament but a true partner. Gareth had little choice but to admit he was utterly lost.

But second, Cleo would never do anything to hurt her sister, even if she did want him as badly as he wanted her. What could he say to that? Gareth had sisters, too. He would never want to hurt them. Still, it would hurt Helen far worse to end up married to the wrong man, and he knew he must speak to her. Somehow—without mentioning Cleo—he would persuade her to break it off. It would be a great surprise to all the guests, but he was sure his family would support him, particularly when he revealed his true affection to them.

But there his plans were thwarted. For the rest of that day, Helen seemed to have gone into hiding. He finally located Sir William and inquired, only to be told Helen was busy with her mother, having her dress fitted. Mention of the wedding gown only made Gareth more anxious to see her, but she wasn't at dinner. Neither was Cleo. He went to bed determined to see both of them the next day.

He hadn't counted on his own mother and sisters, who surprised him with a private family breakfast the next morning in the duchess's sitting room. "After today you will belong with your wife," his mother told him with a smile as they lingered over coffee, "but we wanted you to ourselves one last time."

"I refuse to give you all up," he replied. "Surely you're not planning to leave after tomorrow?"

Serena laughed. "Of course not! But you won't want us about anymore, when you have Miss Grey."

Gareth had to bite his tongue to keep from correcting her. "I shall always want you about. Who else will protect me from Sophronia? She was threatening Jack with her dirk the other day."

Bridget hooted. "Perhaps Mrs. Barrows will! She's not frightened of Sophronia."

*An excellent idea*, thought Gareth, sipping his coffee to hide his reaction to her name. He quite liked the idea of Cleo defending him.

"Come, girls." The duchess rose from her chair. "Your brother has a great deal to do before the wedding tomorrow. We must leave him in peace." They protested a little, but bade him farewell with much laughing and teasing.

He turned to his mother as the girls trooped out. "May I ask a question, Mother?"

"Of course," she said in surprise.

Gareth took a deep breath. "Would you have married Father if you had known how little time you would have together?"

Her lips parted. "Oh, my. Without a doubt. I loved him too much. A year with him made me happier than a lifetime with any other man could have done."

He nodded. "For years I thought otherwise, you know; that the pain of losing him was so great, you must have wished you had never loved him at all."

She put her hands on his arms and studied his face. "No. The love was greater than the pain." She hesitated. "I wish you every bit as much happiness, Gareth, and for many more years than I had."

"I thought you might say that." He kissed her cheek. "Thank you, Mother." He ought to have listened to her from the start, he realized, and set off to make her wish come true.

Unfortunately, his luck was no better this day than the last. By the time he found Helen and was able to manage a quiet word with her alone, everyone had gathered for dinner.

He drew her aside before they went into the dining room. "I must speak to you tonight."

She ducked her head. "Is it about tomorrow?"

"Er—yes."

Helen put her hand on his arm. Gareth remembered Cleo doing the same thing, although her touch had sent a shock of awareness through him, while Helen's only made him tense. "Your Grace, I want to speak to you as well. I think tomorrow will be difficult for us both, but you must know that I'm confident it will be for the best. I've been worried about the wedding, you see, but my sister helped me understand that it will lead to great happiness."

"Ah—yes. About that ..."

"I want you to be happy," she said wistfully. "As much as I want my own happiness."

This was not going well. Gareth cleared his throat. "Will you meet me later tonight, then?"

She hesitated, and her mother swooped in. "Helen dearest! Oh, Your Grace!" She curtseyed, beaming from ear to ear. Gareth remembered the veiled hurt in Cleo's voice when she spoke of her parents and could barely bring himself to nod at Lady Grey. "What a lovely couple," she gushed. "I was just telling Lady Warnford how handsome you look together. I'm sure Sir William will hire a painter to capture your likenesses so we might always remember how perfect a pair you form!"

"There's no need to rush to do so. Mama, His Grace has just invited me to walk out after dinner. May I?"

Lady Grey gasped. "Indeed not! It's the night before the wedding! Not only is it bad luck, you need your rest, my dear! Please understand, Your Grace," she hastened to add. "You will have her every night after tonight!"

Gareth clenched his jaw as Helen demurely bowed her head. "Yes, Mama. I am sorry, Your Grace."

"Quite right," he said bitterly. How the bloody hell was he supposed to talk to her? He was the Duke of Wessex, damn it, and if he wanted to see his bride ... in order to persuade her to jilt him ... he ought to have the right to do so.

He barely paid attention at dinner, working out in his mind how best to present the problem. Cleo wasn't there again, for which he was grateful. There was still a stir over the engagement yesterday of Miss Rosanne Lacy to the Earl of Bruton, although no mention of the duel. Even Jack Willoughby's shocking announcement that he and Henrietta Black had agreed to marry only diverted Gareth for a moment. There were several rounds of toasts, and Sophronia declared that she'd suspected that match all along, but Gareth only saw the ring. After making a blushing Henrietta stand up with him, Jack had presented Gareth with the Cavendish heirloom ring that had been sent to London for cleaning and sizing. He was supposed to put that ring on Helen Grey's finger tomorrow morning. It sat on the table in front of him, taunting him through the port and the ribald conversation of the other gentlemen when the ladies had left. Every man here seemed pleased to be getting married except him.

By the time he extricated himself from the guests, Gareth was almost wild with impatience. He had to do this tonight. In the morning it would be too late; the bride would be dressing for a wedding he no longer wanted to happen. He finally decided to wait until the house was quiet and then go to her room. It was improper, but he didn't see any other way. He couldn't stand at the altar tomorrow beside Helen, all the while wishing it were Cleo standing beside him instead, Cleo with his ring on her finger, Cleo in his bed that night. Although if it were Cleo next to him, Gareth was quite certain she would be in his bed long before night. His mother could entertain the guests at the wedding breakfast, and he could entertain Cleo upstairs.

He retreated to his study and dropped into his chair with a sigh, letting his head fall back. He poured a generous glass of brandy and let his mind run wild with all sorts of schemes, in case he couldn't persuade Helen. He could pay Sir William to break the betrothal. At this point, any amount of money would be a small price to pay. He could invent some crisis in London he must attend to at once and literally flee the scene. He could shoot himself in some harmless place to buy time; a man with a bullet in his leg could hardly stand up in church. Gareth set down his empty glass with a thunk when he realized he was willing to cripple himself to avoid a wedding he had once sought. He glanced at the clock and cursed; he should wait another hour at least before seeking out Helen. He'd have no choice but to marry her if people saw him going into her bedchamber.

He lifted the glass, intending at least one more drink, and a letter came with it, stuck to the bottom. He pulled it off and started to toss it back on the desk when the direction caught his eye. It was to him, in Blair's hand. Gareth frowned. It hadn't been here earlier in the day. Blair hadn't said a word to him at dinner, or after. Gareth had bade him good-night barely an hour earlier. What would his cousin write that he couldn't say aloud? He broke the seal and unfolded the letter.

He read it three times before the meaning sank in. And then he began to smile. He read the letter again, just to reassure himself he understood it, then laughed out loud. What a prize Blair was! And what an idiot *he* was; if he hadn't been knocked senseless by Cleo's sly little smile, he surely would have noticed something earlier and deduced what had made Blair so quiet and bitter lately.

But how to proceed now? Gareth thought carefully for a moment, absently rotating the empty glass under his fingers. This would solve all his troubles, if handled properly, and not merely his own troubles. At last he got to his feet, folded the letter carefully into his pocket, and poured another drink, smaller this time. He raised the glass to the portrait of his father above the mantel. "To Cleopatra, your future daughter-in-law," he told the painting. "And to James Blair, the finest man I know."

# CHAPTER TEN

The wedding day dawned cool and misty. Awake since before first light, Cleo lay staring at the ceiling until the maid brought warm water for her to wash. There would be dark circles under her eyes, but the last two days of solitary contemplation had been good for her, in a way. She had nothing to regret; she had lost nothing that had been hers. What she felt for Gareth ... it was unnatural, besides being wrong. People couldn't fall in love so quickly, she told herself. It was not love; it was merely desire, or perhaps a hidden longing to be married again emerging with all the fuss over Helen's wedding. It would pass, she told herself, trying to believe it. Sooner or later. The important thing was that she hadn't acted on any of those mad, wicked impulses and betrayed her beloved sister.

She dressed slowly, carefully. Her mother had dictated her gown for the day, and Cleo had rolled her eyes behind her mother's back at the volume of lace and the bland shade of gray. It would have been entirely appropriate for elderly Lady Sophronia—or rather, for someone of Lady Sophronia's age, for Sophronia would probably have sliced the gray dress into pieces with her little Scottish dirk. Normally Cleo would feel the same way; Matthew had even made her swear not to wear mourning for him. He didn't want her to be old before her time, he had said. But this morning Cleo put on the gray dress without complaint. Today she felt old and mournful, and might as well look it.

She drank the tea the maid brought, then just sat by the window, staring blindly at the grounds. The carriages were to come at ten o'clock to carry them to the Kingstag chapel. It was only a little past eight, although if Cleo knew her mother, the carriages would be waiting at least half an hour. Millicent was incapable of being on time to anything.

A maid interrupted her morose thoughts. "Your pardon, ma'am, but your mother, Lady Grey, requests you come to her."

Cleo's eyebrows went up, but she went without question. No doubt she would provide an audience to her mother's raptures over Helen's gown and hair and shoes. With something as momentous as this, Millicent would need someone to boast to, and Cleo was the only person who would listen and not think her crass. She braced herself and tapped at Helen's door.

It opened and her mother seized her arm, whisking her inside before closing the door behind her. Cleo rubbed her arm, startled. "Why must you do that, Mama?"

"Shh!" Millicent pressed a handkerchief to her lips before her face crumpled. "Something awful has happened."

Her heart stopped. "What? Is Helen ill?"

"Helen," said her mother in tragic tones, "is not here."

"What do you mean? Of course she's here, somewhere at Kingstag." Cleo was astonished. "When did you discover she wasn't in her room? We must look for her—"

Millicent waved her handkerchief as if to dispel the words. "Don't say that! Would you have us run up and down the corridors calling her name? What would people think?"

"They'll notice if she doesn't come to her own wedding." Cleo tried to tame her thoughts into order. "Chances are she woke early from nerves and went for a walk. Have you checked the garden?"

"Of course we did!" snapped her father, pacing in front of the fireplace. "What kind of fool do you think I am? I went there first thing."

"But she's not there—her bed hasn't been slept in—she never rang for her maid—she's gone and run off and we'll all be humiliated when His Grace discovers it!" Millicent burst into loud weeping. Cleo patted her mother's shoulder numbly, not knowing what to think. Where could Helen be? Had she truly run off?

Her heart took a mad leap at the thought; perhaps her sister didn't wish to marry Wessex after all. Perhaps there was a chance for Cleo to have him without hurting her sister and causing a scandal. She was a wicked woman for thinking it, but she did think it.

"We must tell His Grace," she began, only to be cut off by her father.

"We most certainly must not! What will he think?"

"He'll think Helen's not here," said Cleo, "which is true. Mama, we must tell him," she insisted as her mother shook her head and burst into tears again. "We cannot conceal her absence! He'll notice his bride is missing."

Millicent clutched at her arms. "You must find her," she begged. "Please look—you and she were always thick as thieves. We'll be a laughingstock if she jilts the Duke of Wessex at the altar!"

Cleo ignored that. She rather thought the duke wouldn't mind being jilted, but there might be another reason Helen had gone missing. "I'll go look for Helen, but I have to tell the duke. He has a right to know," she said, raising her voice as her mother began to moan softly. "Let me change my shoes and get a pelisse."

"Yes! Yes, you must go." Her mother retreated to the sofa. "Oh, where are my Smythson's Smelling Salts?"

Cleo went back to her own room and kicked off her gray satin slippers. Her sister might have gone for a walk and fallen; she could be lying hurt somewhere on the vast estate. Walking boots in hand, Cleo sat down at the dressing table, not bothering to ring for her maid to change her dress. Until she knew Helen was at least safe, there was no time to lose. She laced up one boot, combing her memory for any place Helen might have wandered. Where could she be?

The answer stared her in the face when she reached for the second boot.

Cleo seized the note tucked partly under a box of face powder. It was folded small and bore her initials in Helen's delicate writing. Unfolding it with shaking fingers, she read. Then she read again. She laughed a little madly, then stopped at once, glancing around the room in guilt. People would think she was mad, and Helen, too.

Oh, God. What a twist.

On shaking legs she went back to her mother's room. Her parents were where she had left them, alone, thank God. She closed the room door behind her, and cleared her throat.

"What is it?" barked her father.

"I've found a note," she said, "from Helen."

That roused even Millicent. "What does it say?" Sir William strode across the room to snatch the paper from Cleo's hand before she could read it. His eyes skimmed it, then his face blanched, and he thrust it back at her as if it burned him. "You!" he croaked. "You did this!"

"No!" she gasped. "No! I did nothing!"

"What?" cried Millicent, struggling off the sofa. "What has happened to poor Helen?"

"Poor Helen," spat Sir William, "has disgraced us all! Disgraced and ruined us! And you—" He shook his finger at Cleo. "—you are responsible!"

"I most certainly am not!" Cleo's temper finally snapped at his unjust accusation. She had held her tongue about her shop and endured his suspicion without a word, but now she had had enough. "You are, Papa, if anyone is. You and Mama both."

He reared back. "How dare you!"

"Helen has been unhappy and anxious since we arrived, and neither of you paid any attention because you were so pleased she was marrying a duke. I knew she was unhappy, but she insisted it was just nerves—which you, Mama, made worse with your incessant talk of how glorious Kingstag is and what an honor it will be to preside over it."

"But it's a castle," protested her mother. "Helen needs to know—"

Cleo threw up one hand. "Helen needed to know her future husband cared for her. She needed to know she would be happy with him. It doesn't matter what sort of house he has if she's miserable!"

"This is the match of the season!" said her father furiously. "A brilliant marriage! You tempted your sister away from following her duty, prompting her into some hysterical fit. I knew it was a mistake to let you come."

She shook her head. "Why is it Helen's duty to replenish your fortune, Papa? Why wasn't it your duty to make economies or learn investments or do anything at all to support your family? Instead you've been content to live off your daughters, taking the money I earned in my hateful little shop and now selling Helen in marriage, regardless of her feelings in the matter."

Sir William's face was purple. "You are dead to me now."

Cleo just lifted one shoulder sadly. "I know. I've been dead to you for years. But now I think you shall be dead to me as well, if you cannot forgive Helen for what she's done. Being happy is more important than being a duchess." She turned to go.

"Cleo!" Her mother's anxious voice stopped her. "You—you will still try to find her, won't you? To make sure she's not hurt, and—" Millicent cast an anxious glance at her husband. Cleo's heart started to soften toward her mother. Perhaps one parent would be made to see reason; surely her mother still cared about more than Helen's status. "And perhaps," Millicent went on hesitantly, "perhaps she might reconsider ..."

"Yes, Mama," she said, and left the room, closing the door on her parents. Her heart thudded, both with disbelief that she had finally been so blunt with them and with surprisingly little regret. She had borne it because she believed that, deep down, they loved her and Helen; she had told herself they were simply unable to conquer their disappointment in her marriage to Matthew. A shopkeeper was a distinct step down, and she had excused them that. But finally she accepted that it was excessive pride, indifferent affection, and arrogance. They wanted their daughters to marry well so they might live more comfortably and trade on their daughters' connections. Her actions, like Helen's today, mattered to them only as a reflection on their own state.

And if Helen had finally taken charge of her own life and happiness, there was nothing at all to stop Cleo from doing the same. She didn't know where Wessex's rooms were, but she found the butler and told him she must speak to the duke urgently. He directed her to the study at the back of the house, overlooking the gardens.

At the door she took a deep breath and knocked. Just the sound of his muffled voice made her pulse jump. She let herself in, glancing quickly around to be certain there was no one else in the room.

He was alone, standing in front of the window with his hands clasped behind his back. Just the sight of him made her dizzy with yearning and hope. She unfolded Helen's note. "I have something to tell you, Your Grace. It is about my sister."

His attention was fixed on her. "Oh?"

"Yes." She checked that the door was securely closed. "My sister left me a note, which I only discovered a few minutes ago. May I share it with you?" He inclined his head, and she wet her lips, then read Helen's note. "*Dearest Cleo: By the time you read this, I shall be gone from Kingstag Castle. I am writing to you because you are the only one who will understand why: James and I are eloping. We hope to make Gretna Green by the end of the week.*"

Her voice faltered. She swallowed, and read on. "*I am very sorry to do such a thing to His Grace. He honored me greatly with his offer of marriage, and I did accept him honestly. But I feel it would be an even greater disservice to him if I were to go through with a marriage I no longer want, and could not be happy in, while I loved another man. Comfort him, Cleo, and tell him I am sorry. Your loving sister, Helen.*"

For a long moment there was silence. Cleo folded the note, unsure what to do next.

He crossed the room to her. "May I see it?" She gave it to him, trembling a little as his fingers brushed hers. Wessex unfolded the note and read it before letting it fall to the ground. "So I've been jilted."

"I believe you have been." Her heart beat so hard it hurt. He wasn't going to marry Helen, sang the wicked voice inside her head. Some remnant of duty obliged her to add, "My parents are distraught that Helen would do such a thing."

"Yes, I imagine they are," he murmured. "Are you?"

"Well—I wish my sister had confided in someone before disappearing in the night and giving us a great fright ..."

"James Blair is the most capable man I know. If she's with him, she is perfectly well."

She just nodded, overwhelmed by the jumble of hope and uncertainty inside her. He was taking the news very calmly, but also without any show of the relief she felt that now he—like Cleo—was free to follow his heart. Perhaps his heart had reconsidered; perhaps he couldn't stomach the thought of anything to do with her family after Helen's action. She was a common merchant, after all, hardly a likely duchess. Perhaps she had been all wrong ...

"And have you come to do as your sister asked?" He rested one hand against the door above her shoulder. "Have you come to console me, Cleo?"

The way he said her name was almost a caress. "If there is any way I can."

A smile bent his mouth as his eyes darkened. "I think I may require excessive consolation after this most distressing fortnight."

"And being jilted," she whispered.

His smile grew darker, more intimate. "My darling," he said, "being jilted has been the best part—thus far."

Cleo's knees went weak. She hadn't been wrong at all. She laid her hand on his chest. He was wonderfully big and warm beneath her palm, his heartbeat steady and strong. "Your heart doesn't seem broken."

He laid his hand over hers, pressing it against his silk waistcoat. "On the contrary—I think it has only just begun to beat with purpose, now that you are here."

She listed toward him. "Why is that?"

He smoothed a wisp of hair away from her temple, then curved his hand around her nape. "Because I can finally do this," he said, and kissed her.

She melted against him, opening her mouth and meeting his tongue with her own. She gripped his jacket, holding him to her, and then she forced the lapels wide, trying to peel it off him. With a harsh exclamation, he pulled his arms free of the jacket and let it fall to the floor behind him before gathering her close. She pressed against him, her cheek on his chest, listening to the rapid thump of his heart. She could feel the warmth of his skin through his shirtsleeves.

"Cleo," he murmured against her hair. "If there is any reason ... any objection you have to me making love to you, tell me now."

"No," she gasped, catching his shoulders as his hands slid down around her bottom, lifting her up onto her toes, dragging her against his rigid arousal.

"No? I should stop?" He tugged her earlobe between his teeth.

Cleo whimpered. "Don't stop," she moaned. "Don't ever stop."

His hand slipped behind her back, pulling loose the tiny pearl buttons of her gown. The demure bodice slid down, and then he pulled it further down until her breasts were almost exposed. She shuddered at the cool air on her flesh, her head falling back against the door behind her. His hand cupped her breast, his mouth was hot on her neck. "Wessex," she gasped, dimly thinking they ought to find a more comfortable location.

"Gareth." He pulled at her bodice again, and there was a sound of cloth ripping. "My God, you're beautiful in every way." He lowered his head to her breast and Cleo abandoned all thought of moving. She plowed her fingers into his thick dark hair and gave herself up to the pleasure of his lips on her skin, his teeth scraping over her taut nipple, his tongue playing along the delicate flesh of her bosom.

He drew up the skirt of her gown, and she shifted her feet to allow him to press ever closer to her. He raised one eyebrow as his boot bumped against hers. Cleo blushed; in her hurry she'd run through the house wearing only one shoe. Gareth simply grinned as he fell to his knee, unlaced the boot, and tossed it aside, and then his hands were exploring the length of her legs. His fingers skimmed her silk stockings, plucked at her garters, and then roamed higher. She gasped aloud in pent-up desire when he finally touched the aching folds between her legs.

Even she, who had eloped at seventeen, had never been so careless of propriety and restraint. With inarticulate words and sighs she urged him on, clasping his head to her bosom as he stroked her and teased her. When her legs threatened to give out beneath her, she managed to tug at his hair. "Gareth," she gasped, her heart thundering and her breath ragged. "Gareth, please ..."

He shuddered. "When you say my name that way ..." He lurched to his feet, tearing at his trousers. "Put your arms around my neck," he commanded, his voice rough. Cleo obeyed, glad he put his own arm around her waist. She might have stumbled and fallen if he hadn't. "Now tell me ..." He caught her knee and pulled, hooking it around his hip to hold her skirt out of the way. "Say you want me, Cleo ... Please, darling ..."

"I want you madly." She strained against him. "I want you now."

"Thank God." He cupped his hand around her bottom and held her as he fitted himself against her and pushed home. Cleo made a faint gasp of delight and surprise. It felt so good, so right, to have him inside her. She tightened her grip on his neck and pressed her forehead against his shoulder. Every nerve felt alive as he held her so easily, so securely, so intimately. He seemed as moved as she was. His chest heaved and his arms trembled. "At last," she thought he whispered, and then he began to move.

Whatever making love against a door might lack in finesse and comfort, Cleo thought she might prefer it to any other kind. She curled herself around Gareth, meeting each hard thrust with a little arch of her back. He held her easily, he knew right where to touch her, and when it all culminated in a fierce climax, she almost burst into tears. Gareth caught his breath and rested his forehead against hers as his hips jerked a few more times in his own release, and then he kissed her, leisurely and thoroughly.

And then there came a soft tap at the door. Cleo started in spite of the hazy contentment that enveloped her. She could feel the knock through the wood at her back, and the thought of what the person on the other side would think, if he knew what was just inches from him, made laughter bubble up in her throat. Lips pressed shut to hold it back, she looked up at Gareth, her eyes tearing.

He grinned lazily down at her. "Yes?" he called.

There was a pause, then the butler's voice came through the door, low and rushed, as if he were whispering through the crack of the doorjamb. "Your Grace, Mr. Blair wishes to see you at once."

The laughter stuck in her throat died. Cleo didn't move, her fingers clenching in the folds of Gareth's shirt. Mr. Blair had returned, which meant Helen must have as well.

Oh, Lord.

Gareth just kept smiling down at her. "Does he? Excellent. Where is he waiting?"

"In the stables, Your Grace. With Miss Grey."

"Ah. Tell them I shall be with them directly."

"Yes, sir." Cleo could hear his footsteps faintly, going down the hall. Gareth still wore the slight grin of a cat who knew where the cream was hidden, and she didn't know why. Part of her longed to run out to the stables and hug Helen close before shaking her and demanding an explanation, and part of her didn't want to face her sister for years. She had just made love to her sister's fiancé. Even though Helen hadn't wanted to marry him, she might still be shocked and horrified to hear how quickly he had turned to Cleo.

And now there wasn't much time for her to talk to Gareth before facing Helen. What did he want from her? Making love was one thing, but there were no promises between them. Cleo wanted more. She didn't want to give him up to anyone, ever again.

She wet her lips. He was still inside her, his hand still curved around her hip. With a little wriggle, she unhooked her leg from around his, easing her weight back to the ground. With a soft sigh, he slid free of her, his hands steadying her waist as her knees wobbled. She smiled uneasily, smoothing down the skirts of her gown as Gareth repaired his own clothing. She wasn't sure she could stand under her own power. Even now, aftershocks of pleasure left her muscles lax.

"Cleo." His hand cupped her face, making her look at him. Gareth smiled. "You look so grim, darling. Was I that rough?"

Her mouth fell open. "No! You know you weren't. It was wonderful. But Gareth—" He cut her off with a long kiss, and when he lifted his head Cleo had forgotten what she'd been saying.

"All will be well," he said. "Trust me." She gazed up at him, afraid to ask. "You look as though a great problem troubles you," he added.

She was surprised into a weak laugh. "A great problem! This is a rather out-of-the-ordinary problem, I think ..."

"Yes, I might have ruined this gown beyond repair." He gave it a frown. "Although it's not my favorite."

She blushed. "My mother chose it."

"No wonder," he muttered. "I won't apologize for ripping it, then." Still, he turned her around and fastened what buttons remained. "Will you come with me? I expect your sister will want to see you."

"What are you going to say to them?" she asked softly. His fingers moving so gently over her back had sapped her will to argue.

"I think your sister and my cousin explained themselves very well in the notes they left. I can't think what they might have to add to that."

Cleo blinked and whirled around. "Your cousin left you a note as well?"

"He did."

"Then you knew before I told you that Helen had run off?"

"I did."

"You might have told me," she protested.

He grinned. "But I desperately wanted comforting, darling." He kissed her. "Let's go see what they have to tell us, shall we?"

## CHAPTER ELEVEN

Gareth felt at great charity with the world as he and Cleo walked toward the stables. He held her hand in his; she had looked a bit self-conscious at first, but she made no effort to pull away. There was a beautiful flush on her cheeks, and her eyes sparkled as they had the morning she first arrived at Kingstag, when lightning had seemed to strike him in the head.

A servant lingering near the front gate ran forward to meet them and say that Mr. Blair was waiting in the rear tack room, where Jack Willoughby had established his gentlemen's refuge earlier. As they headed there, they passed Jack's shiny black phaeton, now covered with dust and being fussed over by a number of grooms. Cleo darted a curious look at him, but Gareth just shrugged. He had a feeling Hippolyta had helped the lovers in their escape and in their inexplicable return.

The instant they stepped through the door, Helen Grey jumped up from the bench. She was wearing traveling clothes, her hair swung in a braid down her back, and her eyes were haunted. On the bench behind her, James Blair sat with his hands on his knees, his head hanging as if exhausted. Helen took a hesitant step forward, eyeing them almost fearfully.

Without a word, Cleo opened her arms, and Helen fell into them, breaking into ragged weeping. The sisters held each other close. Blair's expression twisted in anguish before he averted his face. Both were the picture of misery.

"I'm sorry," Helen sobbed. "I'm so sorry, Cleo. I didn't mean to cause trouble, but I was so unhappy and it seemed like the best idea ..."

"Are you hurt?" Cleo pulled back to scrutinize her sister's face, red and puffy and tear-stained. "Are you well?"

She nodded. "I'm fine. We—James and I—we're both well. It's just—it's just—"

James Blair rose to his feet. "We both knew it to be wrong," he said, his voice hoarse. "Wessex—Mrs. Barrows—I cannot apologize enough for what we've put you through. It was entirely my doing. I convinced Miss Grey—"

"No! I convinced him!" Helen grasped her sister's hands. "It was my idea, all mine! I couldn't go through with it. Cleo, you told me my happiness was in my hands and you were right, you truly were. I found James yesterday and forced him to take me away last night—"

"You did no such thing," said Blair tenderly but wearily. "Helen ..."

"It seems to me," Gareth said mildly, interrupting them, "that the more important question is why one of you had this idea, and why the other consented."

Helen raised her chin as she finally faced him, but he could see her hands shaking. "I am very sorry, Your Grace," she said haltingly. "I ... that is, I had a—a change of heart. I ... fancied myself in love with Mr. Blair ..."

"It was the duel," Blair interrupted. "Bruton was willing to let his cousin shoot him rather than give up the girl he loved. I was his second, Wessex, and it went to my head—seeing his joy and relief when Miss Lacy threw herself into his arms ... And when you said you would wish Bruton well, I lost my grip on reason." He gave Helen another hopeless look. "I've been in agony since the Greys arrived. I tried to forget my feelings, and I never wanted to betray you, but after the duel ... I didn't know how I could bear to see you marry Helen."

"And running off was much safer and preferable to a duel, don't you see?" Helen pleaded. "I couldn't let him risk being shot."

"Indeed not. Blair is a capital fellow, and I would hate to see him wounded," agreed Gareth. "He's quite the most decent man I know. I congratulate you on your excellent taste."

Helen glanced at Blair in bewilderment. He seemed equally dumbstruck. Gareth wanted to shout with laughter at the look on his cousin's face.

Helen wet her lips. "But it was an abominable thing to do to you ..."

"Not when weighed against the ills of marrying a man you could never love." He paused. "You couldn't, could you?" It was more a statement than a question, and Helen's eyes welled up again as she slowly shook her head. "Then you've done us all a great favor," he said gently. That had been his last trace of worry, that Helen might somehow have honestly regretted running off. If she had declared she was ready to carry on with the wedding, he would have had the very devil of a time.

"You're not angry?" asked Blair in disbelief. "Wessex, I ..." Words seemed to fail him; he shook his head in stunned silence.

Gareth smiled, darted a warm glance toward Cleo. "Angry? Not at all. In fact, I have rarely been happier. And it is all due to you, Miss Grey, for having the courage to defy propriety and follow your heart. And to you, James, for going with her. My only wonder is that you came back so soon. Are you married yet?"

"No," said Blair in a dazed voice.

"Do you still wish to be?"

"Yes!" burst out Helen, which seemed to break her beloved's trance.

"The marriage contract—"

He shrugged. "I don't think we'll have any difficulty about that. Sir William, I am sure, can be made to see reason." Especially if Gareth gave him no choice.

"The guests," said Helen hesitantly.

"Oh yes, I suppose we'll have to tell them. I'll send my mother to the church." Everyone stared at him in disbelief. "If she won't go, I'll have Sophronia step in," he added. "She'd delight in calling off a wedding."

Cleo made a noise suspiciously like a smothered laugh. It made Gareth smile wider. He loved being able to make her laugh.

The runaway lovers exchanged a glance, then Blair stepped forward.

"Wessex," he said humbly. "I must apologize. You would have been well within bounds to call me out over this."

"What good would that do?" he asked, surprised. "You're my right arm, James. You might have told me earlier you had feelings for Helen, but—" he shot Cleo another glance "—in the end your timing was nothing less than perfect. Allow me to wish you great joy." He shook hands with his cousin. Helen hurried to his side, and he raised her hand to his lips. "And of course, since you're to be married," Gareth went on, "I must make you a wedding gift. A manor house, I think, somewhere nearby. You must be able to visit often."

All three of them regarded him in shock. James just nodded, his jaw working as if he couldn't speak. Helen covered her mouth with both hands, her eyes wide with hopeful joy. Gareth clapped James on the shoulder. "I don't believe anyone else knows you've returned," he said meaningfully, "but don't take Jack's carriage this time. There's no reason to drive Hippolyta into the ground when the archbishop himself will be here. I suggest concluding your courtship in more ... comfort."

Blair blinked a few times, then began to grin. "Wessex, I shall be in your debt forever," he said, before grasping Helen's hand and pulling her out of the room. Gareth watched them go and even raised a hand in farewell.

"That was extremely generous," said Cleo in the quiet that followed.

He nodded.

"You want them to be happy together," she said, amazed.

He nodded again.

She bit her lip. "What will you tell the wedding guests?"

He lifted one shoulder. "That I won't be marrying your sister. It's fairly simple."

She studied him. "What will your family say?"

He cocked his head to one side, a slight grin tugging at his mouth. "My mother, I expect, will be delighted. She wants me to be happy, and I would never have been happy married to your sister, as charming and lovely as she is." He started pacing toward her deliberately. "My sisters will be thrilled at the excitement of it all, particularly as they will still have Helen as a cousin. Sophronia may be put out, I grant you, at the absence of scandal and uproar, but she knew the first night that Helen and I were never meant to be."

"What did Mr. Blair's note say?" she asked, even as a soft blush stained her cheeks. "Why didn't you tell my parents when you found it?"

"Good Lord, why would I do that?" He grimaced. "Your father might have tried to do something foolish, like stop them."

"Stop them! But they were already gone—" She stopped abruptly, her eyes widening. "When did you find it?"

"Last night," he said. "About two hours after dinner. I couldn't sleep and went to my study, where James had left it. I daresay they couldn't have got much past Dorchester by then."

"Last night!" she gasped.

Gareth nodded. "I knew they would need as much time as possible to get well away. I had gone to my study to plot how I could persuade your sister to jilt me. You might imagine my relief upon discovering that she had already worked out how to do it. All I needed to do was stay quietly in my study."

She appeared unable to speak. Gently he pulled her into his arms and kissed her, loving the way her body softened against his until they fit together like two halves of a whole.

"If they hadn't run off, I don't know what I would have done," he whispered. "Do you know, I saw my place in hell waiting for me as the wedding day approached. That's what I would have earned, marrying your sister when all I could think of was you. Especially like this," he added, casting a suggestive glance down at her ripped gown.

"When?" she asked softly. "When did you start thinking that?"

Gareth shook his head. "The moment you stepped out of the carriage a fortnight ago." She looked at him suspiciously. He nodded. "Oh yes, lightning struck as you stepped out of the carriage. Toppled one of my oldest oaks to the ground, don't you remember? Split it right down the middle, and the whole thing fell. Much like my heart did when you looked at me."

"You don't believe in love at first sight!" she protested. "You said so the other day!"

"No, I don't, which is why I looked again, and again, and again, until I was quite sure I would go mad from it. I just knew." He nuzzled her neck, his mouth skimming over her collarbone and up the side of her neck. "When did you start?"

The blush that colored her face, all the way down to her neckline, was brilliant. "Almost as soon. But of course I knew it was wrong— you were betrothed to my sister ..."

"But not any longer." He paused. "Are you not pleased she's marrying Blair?"

"Of course I am!"

"Why?"

"Why?" she exclaimed. "Why, because they're in love!" He raised an eyebrow. "And," she hesitated only a moment, "and because if you didn't marry Helen ..." She paused again. "Then you would be free."

"Yes."

"And—" She wet her lips. "—and then it wouldn't be wrong of me to want you."

"Oh, no," he answered at once. "That would never be wrong of you. In fact, I was hoping you might keep on wanting me for the rest of your life."

Later, Cleo told herself she would remember that moment for the rest of her life. The scent of oiled leather and horses, the faint buzz of bees in the shrubbery outside the window, the morning sun slanting across the dusty floor. And Gareth, looking at her as if he had never seen anyone half so wonderful. She couldn't stop a small smile. "Is that a proposition?"

He laughed. "Proposition? My darling, I'm at an end to propositions. I made my last offer of marriage in a letter addressed to your father. May I make this one myself?" And he sank to one knee as he spoke. Cleo thought she must be goggling at him like a fool. "My darling Cleopatra," he began, then paused. "Are you truly named for Cleopatra?"

"Yes," she said dazedly. "And Helen for Helen of Troy. Father has classical fancies."

"Ah." He cocked his head to one side. "I wish I'd remembered that sooner."

"Why?" Cleo still couldn't quite take in that he was on his knees before her. Even Matthew hadn't proposed on bended knee; he'd asked her over his shop counter, which had been romantic enough, but nothing like this.

"It would have made things clearer," he said. "My parents named me Anthony, after all. Anthony never married Helen of Troy."

She cleared her throat. "He never married Cleopatra, either."

"This Anthony will," Gareth declared. "If she'll have him."

Cleo gazed down at him, his brooding dark eyes fixed on her, his thick hair still ruffled from their activities in his study. "Shall I roll myself in a rug and have myself delivered to your rooms?"

"Make certain it's a soft rug," he retorted, "for I would unroll it before the fire and not let you off it for an hour."

Cleo pretended to think. "I may have such a rug, in the shop ..."

His eyes ignited. "That sounds like yes."

This time her smile was wide and unrestrained. "Because it is. A hundred times yes."

# ABOUT THE AUTHOR

Caroline Linden was born a reader, not a writer. She earned a math degree from Harvard University and wrote computer software before turning to writing fiction. Ten years, eleven books, three Red Sox championships, and one dog later, she has never been happier with her decision. Her books have won the NEC Reader's Choice Beanpot Award, the Daphne du Maurier Award, and RWA's RITA Award. Since she never won any prizes in math, she takes this as a sign that her decision was also a smart one. Visit her online at www.CarolineLinden.com.

### ~ALSO BY CAROLINE LINDEN~
IT TAKES A SCANDAL (COMING IN 2014)
LOVE AND OTHER SCANDALS

### ~THE TRUTH ABOUT THE DUKE~
THE WAY TO A DUKE'S HEART
BLAME IT ON BATH
ONE NIGHT IN LONDON
I LOVE THE EARL (NOVELLA)

### ~THE BOW STREET AGENTS~
YOU ONLY LOVE ONCE
FOR YOUR ARMS ONLY
A VIEW TO A KISS

### ~THE REECE FAMILY~
A RAKE'S GUIDE TO SEDUCTION
WHAT A ROGUE DESIRES
WHAT A GENTLEMAN WANTS

WHAT A WOMAN NEEDS

# HOW ANGELA GOT HER ROGUE BACK

Katharine Ashe

# CHAPTER ONE

"*Pride and Prejudice ... and Zombies* ... graphic novel?" Angela Cowdrey muttered and flipped through the slick pages. "What'll they think of next?"

"Dark Avengers! Yesss!" Her friend Cyndi's teenage brother smacked his palm on a comic book to the beat of the musical monstrosity blaring from his earbuds. The book's cover was awash in blood spatters and fangs.

"Dark Avengers, obviously, Ange." Cyndi gave her a sideways grin and ran her rainbow-colored fingertips through the box of buttons on the comic-book store's checkout counter. "Someone's gotta kill all those zombies."

"I thought Elizabeth and Darcy were covering that."

Cyndi plucked out a button proclaiming "School Sucks – WONDER WOMAN SWALLOWS" and held it to the lapel of Angela's peacoat. "What do you think?"

"Is there no honor and decency in the world today?" Angela tucked the zombie novel back on the shelf and pulled out another. "*Shapeshifters IV: Jesus vs. the Brontë Sisters*. Hmm. Guess that answers my question."

"Don't take it so hard." Cyndi shrugged. "It's just trash."

Angela glanced at the clerk slumped on a stool behind the counter. A copy of *The Hitchhiker's Guide to the Galaxy* was open over his knee. He was oblivious.

"I'm not taking it hard," she said. "I'm thinking I should read this stuff."

"In all that extra time you have between TAing, grading, graduate student union organizing, and finishing your dissertation?"

"And the article for the *American Historical Review*."

Cyndi tossed the button back in the box. "I thought you already turned that in."

"Revisions. The editor wants me to include a detail that I haven't figured out yet. But I will." Angela leaned against the bookshelf and squeezed her sore eyes shut. All the coffee in the world couldn't make up for a week without sleep. But she wouldn't get a job after graduation by dreaming away the nights. And her empty bed didn't mind. It never did. Never had.

Lately, though, she hadn't even been sleeping when she did go to bed. The Michigan winter was wind-chill five below but she was sizzling beneath her skin.

Just excitement over the article, probably. "I'm going to nail it, Cyndi. I'm going to discover the clue no scholar ever has. I'm going to finally break open the biggest mystery in the history of British insurance fraud ever."

"Wow, Ange. That's super duper." Cyndi whistled low.

"Come on." Angela laughed. "It's a big deal. I'll be short-listed for every job I apply to and I'll have a subject for my next book."

"Next book? The first one isn't even finished yet. You haven't even graduated."

"I will." Despite her Evil Advisor who'd made her write a chapter that her dissertation didn't even need—thereby forcing her to live in graduate-student poverty for another year. She'd had good interviews at the American Historical Association meeting last week. One of the interview committees had flipped over her discovery of Arnaud Chappelle's memoir. If she could just find in that memoir the clue to why Chappelle had revealed the crimes of a particular Englishman, Sir Richard Howell, she'd be golden.

"And *of course* I've got my second book planned already. It's one of the first questions they ask in interviews," she said, running her fingertips along the bindings of the graphic novels. A little sizzle zinged through her. "Maybe my third book will be on how American authors are rewriting the history of Britain to include zombies and vampires. I really should read these."

Cyndi shook her head. "It's not like you're in American Culture or even Literature. You're a historian, for Chrissake. You don't have to read this crap." She gestured dismissively at the display.

"Yeah, but this—" Angela pulled the zombie graphic novel from the shelf again and flipped through it. "—this is what a lot of my students first think of when I mention Jane Austen. Or the Brontës. Or Byron. Keats. Nelson. Wellington. King George. Queen Victoria.

You know, all of nineteenth-century British history. I need to inform myself."

"You're way too conscientious. If you're going to spend time doing anything other than studying it should be going out, relaxing, dancing, having a drink." Cyndi yanked the novel away and shoved it in the shelf, smashing a thin comic book back behind it.

"Cynd." Angela reached for the ruined comic book in the crevice. "Have a little respect for the printed word."

"There aren't enough words in there to deserve respect." She gave a saccharine smile to the guy behind the counter. He ignored her.

Angela pulled out the smushed comic book. It looked like an accordion. "You're a literature snob."

"You're killing yourself." Cyndi cocked a pierced brow. "Angela, you need a life."

"Okay." Her tingling fingertips worked the bent edges of the paper. For a cheap comic, it was thick, high-quality stock. "I'll get right on that, chief."

"No. I mean it. You work like a sled dog."

"The job market is so tough now, Cynd. It's what's expected."

"It's an excuse."

She flattened the comic book against the side of the shelf and smoothed it with her palm. "Your point?"

"You need a man."

"I can't believe people still say that to single women." The wrinkles wouldn't straighten. The smashing had permanently damaged it. "You're a dismal feminist."

"I'm post-feminist. Maybe I wasn't clear enough. Angela, you need to have sex."

The clerk's scruffy head came up.

Angela blew a drape of hair from in front of her eyes, but it dropped forward again. She tucked it under her wool hat and looked at the clerk. "I'd like to buy this." She placed the ruined comic book on the counter. "And no, she wasn't suggesting you."

"Why not?" Cyndi said. "He's cute. Put a clean shirt on him and you wouldn't even know he works at a comic-book shop."

"*Cynd.*" She pulled money out of the tattered wallet she'd bought in London eight years earlier during her undergraduate study abroad semester—the same day she'd first visited the British National

Archives. The first visit of many. She gave a bill to the clerk. "Sorry about her. She just switched medications."

He dropped change into her palm. "Hey, I'm available if you change your mind." He grinned.

"Good to know. Thanks." She slid the comic book into her satchel and went to the door. "I'm going home, Cyndi." She glanced at her friend's brother still blissfully immersed in his dark, rockin' universe. "Alone," she added in a stage whisper. "Without a man with whom I will have sex. Because I am a post-post-modern feminist who makes choices and is happy with them." Not really the truth. She was ... sizzly. "You, on the other hand, despite your nipple rings, are a relic of the 1950s American suburbs and a pain in my ass. Good night." She pushed the door open and with a jingle of the bell a blast of frigid air swept in.

"Angela, I'm just—"

The door slammed shut. Wind sheered horizontally along State Street, nearly knocking her boots off the icy sidewalk. She secured her satchel on her shoulder, tucked her chin into her collar, and headed up the street.

Cyndi was a nag and totally indiscreet. But she was right.

Angela wasn't satisfied. She was doing well in grad school, and if she kept working her butt off, she'd probably get a job as a horrifyingly overworked junior professor that paid about as much as a hostess at Chuck E. Cheese. On the other hand, she was intellectually fulfilled.

But she wasn't happy. If she needed any proof of that, she could find it in her best friend after five-and-a-half years in Ann Arbor. The university was huge, with an international faculty and graduate students in every discipline under the sun. Yet her closest friend in town was a tattoo artist who moonlighted as a barista at a local café.

Three months ago she'd let Cyndi give her a tattoo of a golden eagle soaring across her right shoulder. When her mom had dragged her out of school midyear to follow a horse wrangler to Colorado, she'd been ten. One day she'd looked up into that endless sky, seen the eagle, and cried, longing to be that free.

Her tattoo looked exactly like the way she remembered that eagle.

No one would ever see it.

Maybe she'd gotten some weird infection from the tattooing, and the zingy sizzling thing was from that.

But it wasn't just that. Something felt wrong. *Missing.* Not stimulating conversation or invigorating debates. Not friendship. And not a man, though she'd like one of those someday, and sex. But she'd gone without sex for twenty-seven years and she was still alive.

Something else.

Honor, maybe. Decency.

"Try to explain it to me," Cyndi had said a few days earlier over cups of tea at the café.

"Okay, take my specialty, the British Empire," she'd said. "There was nothing decent about it."

"Violence, racism, elitism, sexism, colonialism, slavery, war," Cyndi counted off on her fingers. "Bad stuff. So?"

"So it's not like I want to go back to some golden era when people were more honorable and decent than they are now."

"It's a pretty appealing fantasy."

"Sure, but it's historically inaccurate."

"So what do you want?"

"I want ... I don't know." Her fingers had tightened around the cup. "I want that feeling I get when I see some lanky undergrad give old Mr. Grady on the corner a hot meatball sub. You know, that feeling like there's more good in the world than bad, like you get all filled up with emotion and weep because there's just *so much* untapped possibility."

Cyndi shook her head. "Ange, you think too much."

"Maybe I just know too much about how awful people can be. I mean, look at this guy Arnaud Chappelle I'm working on. He was a Class A slime. Hundreds of people, maybe thousands, died because of his greed, yet he ended up a miserable old parolee anyway."

"I don't think the problem's that you know too much. I don't think it's your head at all," Cyndi said. "What did Goethe say? 'All the knowledge I possess everyone else can acquire, but my heart is all my own.'"

*All my own.*

The brick apartment building that was the height of architectural fashion a century ago loomed in the cold before her. She dug her keys out of her pocket, and her gloved fingers fumbled for the building key on the ring. She found it and reached for the lock, then started back.

A man stood just on the other side of the thick glass door. His dark golden hair was tousled. His eyes were like slate. He looked directly at her and flattened his bare palm against the windowpane.

Then he was gone.

Just gone. As if he hadn't been there at all.

Angela blinked. She blinked again.

Still no man.

Her breaths were fogging up the windowpane. She unlocked the door.

The entryway was vastly overheated, and empty. She stood still, listening for footsteps on the stairs, but there were none.

She shook her head. Too much caffeine, obviously. Or maybe too little.

She pushed her gloves into her pockets, unbuttoned her coat, and opened her mailbox.

Water bill. Phone bill. Both of which she couldn't pay. Postcard from her mother in St. Kitts, the make-it-yourself kind with a picture of her on the beach in a bikini, arms around her latest boyfriend, Ron. Or Roy, maybe? It'd been eight months since her mom had last written or called. It could be four boyfriends past Roy by now.

Cyndi teased Angela about being the Oldest Virgin in America. If she knew her mother, she'd understand why she'd adamantly taken the opposite path.

She started up the stairs to the fourth floor.

Her apartment was underfurnished but cozy. She shed her coat, hat, scarf, and boots, threw her satchel onto the couch, and went to the kitchen. She filled the teakettle in the 1920s sink and set it on the gas burner, then opened her tiny fridge and pulled out a box of leftover Thai chicken and stuck it in her minuscule microwave.

She liked her place and it was affordable. But Ann Arbor still didn't feel like home, not even after almost six years of grad school. London had a little bit, but not entirely. Cambridge, Massachusetts, during college definitely hadn't. Neither had Philadelphia or LA or Louisville or any of the other places her mother had dragged her to, following loser guy after loser guy.

She ate standing up at the stove. When the kettle whistled she packed the tea infuser with loose-leaf jasmine, then went to the couch, slung her satchel onto the table, and turned it upside down. The accordionized comic book tumbled out with her laptop and files. She pushed it aside and opened her laptop.

"Okay, Arnaud," she mumbled, flipping open a thick folder and rummaging through photocopies. "Tell me why you spilled the beans on Sir Richard Howell when you kept your mouth shut 'til the day you died about everybody else who did dirty dealings with you. I know you want to, you scoundrel." She transcribed a line from the diary she'd photocopied at a private archive in Dorset six months ago, translating from Arnaud's native French as she typed. She'd already read it through, but she'd missed something. She must have. Her sizzling blood told her she was on the edge of a discovery. "Or should I say, you *coquin?*" She grinned. "Or maybe I should just stop talking out loud to a guy who's been dead for two centuries."

The twining steam from her teacup dissipated. She reached for the cup, and her eyes strayed to the comic book on the edge of the table. The bent cover caught the lamplight. In scrolling script resonant of Parliamentary deeds, the title read *Lady Angela*.

"Well, what do you know?" she mumbled.

There was no author name on the book, only the title. The cover was plain, the calligraphy original. She ran her fingertips over the lettering to feel the subtle texture of the ink. It didn't just look historical; it felt authentic, the sort of fine-quality stock she'd seen plenty of in English archives.

She set down her teacup and opened the book.

The art was rough, the style suggesting sketches swiftly drawn, all done in black ink on off-white matte paper. There were no dialogue bubbles, only captions every few frames. Like Arnaud Chappelle's two-hundred-year-old diary, it seemed to be a memoir narrative.

In the simplest terms, this one recounted the birth, youth, and young manhood of a guy with light hair wearing garments that pointed to the early nineteenth century—a lacy gown at birth, short pants as a boy, then tail coat and cravat and breeches. As comic book protagonists went he was pretty typical: chiseled features, impossibly broad shoulders, narrow hips, long legs with lots of cut muscles to which the breeches inaccurately clung. Nineteenth-century English stockinette could stretch pretty well, but it wasn't Lycra.

He was a sportsman. In one frame he played cricket, in another he was hunting, in another boxing, in another rowing. A whole page was given over to a carriage race that resulted in him sprawled on his back in the road with an awful grimace on his face.

Angela leaned in closer.

His face ... it looked like ...

She clamped her eyes shut. She really needed sleep. Or a whole lot more caffeine.

She stood up and went to the kitchen with her cup to refresh her tea, grabbing up her scarf and wrapping it around her neck as she returned to the couch. Her turn-of-the-century apartment was poetic with its arched windows and theater-tiled bathroom, but the quaint old radiators were useless against the Michigan winter. Then again, she always felt cold these days, as if winter had penetrated her bone marrow but summer wasn't long or hot enough to heat it back up before fall came again.

Except for the sizzle lately. The deep sizzle.

She settled again before her laptop, but her fingers strayed to the comic book. Pretending she wasn't curious, she casually flipped the page.

Drawn in a completely different style with such exquisite grace and delicacy that even in black and white they seemed alive were two images: on the left, a trio of summer flowers identified in the caption as *Oxeye Daisy, Cornflower,* and *Poppy*; and on the right, a majestic bird with lethal talons. A golden eagle.

A little shiver ran across Angela's shoulders, directly through her tattoo.

She turned to the final page. It was a close-up of the man's back. His shoulders brushed either side of the frame and he'd turned his head to look around at the reader. His mouth was rendered as a sensuous curve and his eyes were beautiful: warm and dark and sparkling with confidence.

Then he winked.

*At her.*

Tea leaped in tiny splashes from the cup in her shaking hand. She'd had some pretty weird dreams because of exhaustion, but she'd never before hallucinated.

Her gaze dropped to the caption. It was three words: *ANGELA, COME BACK.*

# CHAPTER TWO

The picture didn't wink at Angela again, though she stared at it until she fell asleep and again the following morning while coffee brewed. Sleep deprivation did scary things to the brain, which of course was why torturers used it.

She packed up her laptop and files and left *Lady Angela* on the kitchen counter.

Cyndi had texted her overnight: "Sorry. U have to b who u r, and I'm ok w that."

Angela typed with her thumb, "Ur a pain but I <3 u" and dropped the phone into her coat pocket.

The sky was frigid blue, with wispy clouds that made the sun look gray: a typical January morning. Her blood was zinging more than usual from all the coffee. She started toward campus, then halted and retraced her steps along the salty-white sidewalk to her car.

In a miraculous event greater even than a comic book hero winking at her, her ancient Toyota started on the first try. She pulled onto State Street and headed north.

It didn't take her many minutes to get to the dam over the Grand River. Leaving her satchel in the car, she walked up the path from the gravel lot toward the river, taking deep breaths of the freezing air. She coughed, and clouds of smoke haloed her.

She reached the dam and headed toward the bench closest to the structure. The path hadn't been well cleared, and black ice crossed it in strips as she picked her way along. But sitting on that bench and listening to the winter birds and watching the river never failed to clear her head.

Today she needed head-clearing in a big way.

It wasn't until she slipped that she realized how close she'd veered toward the bank. The slope from the bench was shallow, but ice had formed in a slick ramp.

She fell, scrabbling at the ground for purchase, her gloves useless as she slid into the water. *It wasn't even dramatic*, the absurd thought occurred to her as she sank, her peacoat and boots like anchors. She'd always figured drowning would be dramatic.

Her lungs gave out.

She'd figured wrong.


"*Treason?*" Trenton Cambridge Ascot, Viscount Everett, swung around to his father.

The Earl of Ware's face was drawn as he stared out the window at the game of cricket on the Duke of Wessex's lawn. "And fraud."

Trent scowled. "What's a little fraud when you're already hanged for treason?"

"At least it will be with a silken rope." The earl turned his attention from the men cavorting about with bats and balls and wickets. "The peerage still enjoys a few privileges."

"Not including immunity from blackmail, apparently." Trent raked his hand through his hair. "Good God, Father, how did this come about?"

"Two years before your mother died, I made some investments," the earl said, thrusting up his square jaw and broadening his stance as though expressing any lingering grief over his beloved wife's death was unmanly. "I wanted to finally restore the estate's fortunes that your grandfather had depleted, for your sake, as your mother always wished. I invested her dowry in a shipping company that supplied our soldiers abroad with munitions—as a silent partner only. Within two years, four ships were taken by French privateers."

"And all along your partner, Sir Richard Howell, was selling the ships' manifests and itineraries to the French, then collecting insurance on the sunken vessels on this end."

The earl nodded, his attention again straying to the lawn where Trent knew he'd rather be now. Damn it, even *he'd* rather be out there playing cricket, and that was certainly a lifetime first.

"But that was years ago. Why did you wait until now to tell me this, Father?"

"Sir Richard will arrive to join the festivities here tomorrow. He expects to finalize plans with me."

"He's bluffing. You refused his offer to partner in opening a mine on our land and he's trying to threaten you into doing it anyway."

The earl shook his head. "He has documents that implicate me. Documents I signed. I've seen them."

"Father, tell me now: were you knowingly guilty of the crimes of which he is threatening to accuse you? I would rather know now than be surprised with the truth later."

"I had no idea of it, Trenton. I only regretted the investments in those ships and cargos and railed at my poor luck. I thought it all of a piece with the disasters of those years."

"Disasters," Trent repeated. The death of his mother in childbirth, a year later the loss of the infant to fever, then two years after that Trent's own accident that left him crippled for months.

"Truth be told," his father said, "a few ships seemed as nothing in comparison to losing my wife and little Edward. Then your accident. To imagine that my son might never walk again ..."

"Father," Trent said, going to him. "Forgive me." His father was a bull-headed son of a bitch, but he'd always taken great pride in his family, and he cared for them in his way.

The earl put a heavy hand on his shoulder. "You are a good man, son. I've always been proud of you. You wouldn't have mixed yourself up in this sort of thing."

He wouldn't have. Trent made certain never to take chances or stir up trouble. Long ago he'd learned that fulfilling his father's expectations in public was the only way to be able to do what he truly wished in private. Only his mother had ever understood.

"What do you intend to do, Father?"

"I will do as he bids me, to save the honor of this family and your inheritance."

"But what about the tenant farmers? Those families have been on our land for centuries."

"They will have to become miners." His father shook his head. "Howell is no fool. There's enough iron ore in the ground to make Ware the richest estate in Devonshire."

"I don't like it." Trent sank down on the edge of a chair and lowered his brow to his hand. "Blackmail. Good God."

"There's more, son."

"What more could there be?"

"He insists that I make the partnership secure by ..." He turned again to the cricket match.

"Father?"

"Sir Richard wants you to marry his daughter."

Trent's head snapped up. "Marry his daughter?" But he understood. "The mine would be established in her name too, as part of the marriage settlement, wouldn't it? Sir Richard wishes to bind himself to it legally."

The earl nodded.

"Will she also attend Wessex's wedding?" Trent's neck cloth was choking him. "Is this to be settled immediately?"

"She arrives tomorrow with her father."

Trent shot to his feet. "I need air." He headed to the library door. The collection at Kingstag included a two-volume set of original drawings depicting the wildflowers of the Americas. But Trent didn't have the heart for that now. He had to get away from his father.

Half of the duke's male guests were at cricket. As Trent exited the house, Frank Newnham shouted at him to join the game. "Crash, old chum! We could use a top batsman like you over here!"

Trent waved and strode into the park. He could go to the stables where the rest of the gentlemen were using the excuse of ogling Jack Willoughby's new carriage to spend time there playing cards and drinking. He could get himself disguised beyond memory. Then he'd be too miserable tomorrow to even care if Sir Richard Howell's daughter was the sort of girl he'd like to be blackmailed into marrying.

But not yet. Now he needed air and space. The outdoors.

The far end of the lake stretched beyond a copse. He made for the trees. He always thought more clearly in nature, and he needed to stop the runaway wreck of his anger.

His father had meant well, but he was an idiot.

Affection, duty, gratitude—Trent felt these toward the earl in quantity. Respect, no. Not for years. The Earl of Ware's entire world consisted of tennis, boxing, cricket, riding to hounds, boating, horse racing, and whatever other sports his cronies preferred. For twenty-nine years he'd made it clear to his eldest son that any other pursuit was womanly and foolish. "A man proves his worth in the saddle, on the pitch, or in the ring, son," he'd said every day of Trent's boyhood. "Now show me what kind of a man you are. Make me proud."

The earl had trusted Richard Howell with his investments simply because in those days Howell was a prize-winning pugilist. He'd signed legal documents without reading them, without even instructing his man of business to read them.

Fists tight, Trent rounded the path at the edge of the lake and stopped short.

There was a body in the deep water. Ten yards out. *Struggling.*

He didn't hesitate; he'd won every swimming competition he'd entered since he was ten. He tore off his coat, grabbed at his boots, and dove.

By the time he reached the spot, the body was entirely submerged, the water around it still. He levered his arms under the form and thrust its head above the surface.

Small, but not a child. A woman? *God almighty*, a heavy woman! He pulled and struggled backwards and got her to the bank. She was too heavy. He pushed her against the embankment, leaped out, and hauled her all the way onto the ground.

Wrapped in thick wool from head to toe, she remained motionless as water pooled around her. Her face was pale and slack, and lovely, like a cool alabaster statue of some ancient goddess and just as lifeless.

He dropped to his knees, knocked the cap off her head and tore at the muffler circling her neck.

"Breathe." Trapped in soaked wool, the coat buttons protested. "*Breathe*, damn it." He yanked. A button popped free. He wrenched the lapels apart, flattened his palms on her chest, and pushed.

She convulsed. He rolled her onto her side, and the coughing and retching began. Hand on her shoulder to steady her, he turned his face away and bowed his head, catching his breath.

After some time her sputtering subsided. She groaned. "Oh ... my God."

With soggy wool gloves, she tried to push herself up to sit. Trent grasped her shoulders and assisted her. She turned her face toward him. Even plastered with dark hair, it was lovely.

"Thanks," she croaked. "That ... was ... bad."

He released her.

"Thought I was done for." She coughed. "You saved me."

Sweet intonation, albeit water-logged. Sharp vowels. An American, perhaps.

"It was my honor. I'm glad I happened along when I did." He glanced at her heavy coat and gloves and her boots sprawled out before her, the hem of her skirt at her knees. "Enjoying a swim on this fine summer day, were you?" He made his voice light.

With a dripping glove, she pushed the long, lank strands from before her eyes—beautiful eyes of a rich dark-brown shade, like the feathers on the wings of a male cappercaillie.

"What—" she said. "It's January."

Addled wits. Common after an accident. He'd been confused for days after the carriage wreck.

"You've had a nasty turn, of course," he said. "Perhaps you shouldn't try to speak for a bit. I'll—"

"I slipped on the ice and fell into the river."

She was delirious. Perhaps her brain had suffered without air. This day could not get worse. First his father's horrible revelation and now an injured drowning victim.

An injured drowning victim with the prettiest eyes he'd ever seen—intelligent eyes, despite their befuddlement, above a pert little nose and full lips whose natural pink was deepening every moment as life returned to her.

"Perhaps you would like to return to the house and ..." How to suggest to a lovely, delirious American with whom he was not acquainted that she must change her clothes? "Get dry." Oh, that was brilliant. Eloquent, really.

"I'd ..." She seemed to catch her breath and blinked a few times. "Hot. Heat." She turned her head and peered at the copse, then the lake, then the park across the lake, then at him again. "Summer?" she said weakly.

Feeble minded. Or mad. Perhaps she'd been this way before she went into the lake. Why else would she have gone in wearing coat, cap, gloves, and men's boots?

"Madam. Allow me to—"

She grabbed his forearm. "Where am I?"

"Dorset, of course." He tried to sound casual, as though he weren't kneeling beside a dripping madwoman, dripping himself and growing doubtful he would be able to return her to the house without a struggle. He tried to draw away, but she held fast.

"Dorset, *England?*" she said.

"The very place. Now, miss, I—"

"No." She clutched his arm tight. "I fell in the water in—" Her gaze snapped to his face and she released him abruptly. "Who are you?"

Apparently Americans did not require an introduction. Brazen, the lot of them.

"Everett at your service." He affected a bow. "Now, do allow me to escort you back to the house, where I've no doubt your maid will put all to rights again."

This time she allowed him to help her to her feet, but then she pulled away and drew off her gloves. He retrieved his coat and boots and came to her side.

"Give me a minute, will you?" she said, unbuttoning her coat and coughing damply.

"Of course."

She removed the coat. Beneath, she wore a wool pelisse of some sort and a narrow skirt that reached only to her calves. The wet skirt clung to her shapely thighs all the way up to her—

He averted his gaze. Terribly bad form to get hard staring at a madwoman's legs.

"Listen," she said slowly, "I'm going to need a little help here."

"As you require, madam."

Angela was having trouble breathing—and not because her lungs were saturated with lake water.

*Lake* water.

She'd fallen into a river. In midwinter. In Michigan.

She'd think someone was playing a joke on her if the gorgeous, wet man standing before her and speaking with a mouthwateringly decadent English accent weren't familiar.

But he was familiar. *In comic-book black and white.*

"I'm dreaming," she said. "I must be dreaming. This is a dream."

He tilted his head, his dark golden hair beginning to dry and catching the sun's glimmer. "You are not dreaming," he said in a voice like melted chocolate, "but perhaps you should rest. You've had quite an ordeal."

"Ordeal." *Understatement.*

Comic-book man. Summer. Dorset.

In the distance, the Duke of Wessex's massive house, Kingstag Castle, rested on the rise beyond the trees. She knew it was Kingstag Castle because she'd visited it during the summer, *seven months ago.* The tour hadn't taken them quite this far into the park, but she'd strolled along the lake at its other end after they'd gone through the public rooms in the house. In fact, recently she'd been planning on writing to request access to the family's archives when she next returned to England. The seventh Earl of Ware, Sir Richard Howell's one-time business partner, had known the duke well; his eldest son and the duke had gone to school together. Although the earl hadn't been involved in Sir Richard's shady dealings with Arnaud Chappelle, you never knew what secrets could be hidden away in family archives. She'd found Arnaud's unpublished memoir in one of those little archives, after all.

Her shallow breaths caught painfully, but not from the lake water.

"Did you say your name is Everett?" *It couldn't be.* "As in, for instance, Mr. Everett Smith?"

He peered at her curiously for a moment. Then the corner of his gorgeous mouth tilted up in quiet chagrin. "I fear my manners are challenged by the Atlantic's vast expanse, madam."

"The Atlantic?"

He tilted his head. "You are an American, are you not?"

She nodded.

"Then forgive my previous arrogance. My given name is Trenton Ascot."

She'd been wrong. Early-nineteenth-century English fabric could cling to muscular thighs like Lycra did, at least when the fabric was soaking wet. For the muscular thighs at which she was staring belonged to Trenton Ascot, Viscount Everett, the Earl of Ware's son.

Which was not possible. Because he'd lived two hundred years ago. So there must be a modern Trenton Ascot, a descendent of the Trenton Ascot who was the son of the Earl of Ware she knew from her studies of Howell.

Then why was he wearing period costume?

A movie. An historical film. Or some sort of reenactment. Yes. That was it. She'd stumbled upon one of those big reenactment events where actors pretended to be real historical people to amuse the tourists.

Then why was sweat dripping down her neck because she was standing in the full midday sun of high summer? In *England.*

"I need to sit down."

He dropped his coat and boots and came to her swiftly and wrapped his arm around her waist. This was good. A gentleman of the Regency era wouldn't put his arm around a strange woman. It just wasn't done.

He took her hand firmly in his. "There is a boathouse not fifteen yards away. Do you think you can walk there?"

She nodded. He guided her along the edge of the lake.

She had to ask. He'd think she was a nut case, but she had to.

"Are you Viscount Everett? The son of Henry Ascot, seventh Earl of Ware?"

He stiffened. "The very one." He was frowning. A lock of hair had fallen over his brow. His eyes were like smoky slate, the same color they'd been through the glass door of her apartment building.

*Which was impossible.*

"Dizzy now." She stumbled. "Very."

He cinched her waist tighter and guided her into the little boathouse. He urged her onto a bench beside the door. Everything inside was neat as a pin, including a punt, a two-seater boat for rowing crew, oars, and some rope. It looked like any old boathouse.

She had *not* traveled two centuries into the past. Or to England. That happened in books and movies. Not in reality.

"Now," he said briskly. "Will you be all right here while I go up to the house to fetch your maid? Or perhaps you would prefer I find your—" He glanced at her left hand. "—family?"

"Family?" This wasn't real. How had she gotten here? "My family isn't here."

The frown of concern on his handsome face deepened. "Your maid, then?"

"I don't have a maid." She should just tell him the truth. But if she didn't believe what she was thinking, he sure as hell wouldn't. Unless he was pulling her leg—this man who looked exactly like the man in the comic book with her name on it.

Maybe she should play his game and see where he took it. Yes. Yes, that sounded like a good idea. Right? "What I mean is, my maid hasn't arrived yet."

His brow rose. "Have you come to the duke's wedding alone?"

"No. No, of course not." *Wedding?* Duke. Wessex? Okay, play the game. Be cool. "It's just that my family sent me ahead, so I wouldn't miss any of the fun. My father's trapped in London on business, you see."

He nodded. "Forgive me once more, madam, if you will," he said with that same slight, self-deprecating smile that was too beautiful for a real person. He had to be an actor. "I'm terribly ignorant of all sorts of matters. Not being acquainted with any Americans, I don't— That is to say, I am not ..." His chocolate voice melted away as his gaze slid down her legs. His smile faded.

*Hot.* He was *so* incredibly hot. And it was at least seventy-five degrees and she was wearing wet wool that was beginning to steam.

"Um ..." She couldn't think. "I ..."

His gaze came up to hers again. "You should change your gown."

Something in the way he said the words made her throat close up. Suddenly he looked adamant.

"I should," she gurgled. Think, Angela. *Think.* "But I'm afraid I don't have a change of clothing. Yet. My luggage is coming with my maid." Oh, great. Why not just tell him you're an orphan waif and you were thrown into the lake by your evil guardian? Sounds kind of authentic, in a Dickensian sort of way.

He crossed his arms. The damp linen clung to his biceps and triceps. The responding heat in Angela's panties was *entirely* authentic.

"You'll catch a chill if you remain in those garments," he said like he was trying to sound casual. His crossed arms tightened. He didn't seem to be used to chatting with soaked women in private.

There was no way in hell that a man this gorgeous from the twenty-first century would not be used to chatting with women in private. No. Way. Either he was a really great actor, or ...

She couldn't think it.

"My sister is about your height," he said. "She will have suitable clothing for you." He went to the door. "I will return shortly. Will you be all right? Alone?"

She nodded.

He paused, scanned her body, and left her sizzling on the little wooden bench.

No one came to the boathouse while he was gone. Angela's head ached, her lungs felt like they'd been through a Cuisinart, and the humidity in the tiny building was oppressive. She removed her sweater, boots, and the thick winter tights she always wore with skirts, then finger-combed her hair and tied it in a knot.

She studied the contents of the boathouse. Not one object had a product name emblazoned on it. There were no life jackets to be seen, and the oars and boats were wooden, not synthetic materials.

When her rescuer returned, he was wearing boots and a coat over the rest of his wet clothing.

"You didn't change your clothes," she said, standing up.

He scanned her anew, his gaze lingering on her bare feet, then rising swiftly to her face. "No," he said a little hoarsely, and set a pile of clothing on the bench. "My sister was absent. I was making a hash of searching her belongings when her maid entered and assisted me. I do hope they suit." He moved to the door.

"The maid gave you a change of your sister's clothes just like that?"

"I told her my sister had fallen into a puddle."

"And she believed you?"

"It was that or the truth." He ran a hand through his hair, tousling the dark gold locks in an incredibly sexy gesture of discomfort. "Secluded boat house. Lone woman in need of clothing ..."

"Oh. Right." Her heartbeats sped. "Good thinking."

"I will await you without."

The gown was of exquisite white muslin with tiny rosebuds embroidered all over the skirt. The silk petticoat and linen chemise were each as light as feathers. He'd also brought a set of simple stays and a pair of pink satin slippers.

Angela closed her eyes.

Stays. He'd brought *stays*. And enough clothes to dress three women in the twenty-first century. Even in England.

It was real. But *it couldn't be.*

She was trembling hard as she slipped the shift over her head. She'd been to every museum exhibit of British imperial culture she could and she'd read dozens of books about the English cloth trade and garment industry and even Regency-era fashion. She had a pretty good idea of how to dress in these clothes. She also knew that the stays were essential for the proper fitting of the gown, but try as she might she couldn't fasten them. The hooks were too small and her hands were too shaky. She was probably in shock. Physical shock. Mental shock. Spatial shock. Temporal shock.

She went to the door and peeked out. "My lord?" The words sounded funny. She'd never spoken with an actual nobleman before. Or an actor pretending to be a nobleman.

He stood with his back to the boathouse. He looked over his shoulder, and Angela's heart turned over. *Just like in the comic book.*

"I need help," she managed to say.

She half expected him to refuse, but he came toward her.

"Do the garments—"

"They're great." She stepped out of hiding behind the doorframe. "It's just that I ..."

His attention dropped to her hands pressing the stays against her ribs, then shifted up to her breasts. They were entirely concealed by the shift, but his gaze made her feel like he could see right though cloth, like Superman.

"I can't fasten the stays on my own," she croaked.

A dark flush rose in his chiseled cheeks. Standing in the thin chemise and unfastened corset beneath his gaze, she felt hotter than her mother on that Caribbean beach, and just as sexy.

*Sexy.*

She hadn't felt sexy in ... *ever.*

It felt good. It felt really good.

She didn't even care if he was an actor.

She turned her back to him and looked over her shoulder like he had in the comic book. Like he had in the comic book when he'd told her to come back.

# CHAPTER THREE

He stepped forward and put his hands on her. Not on *her*, exactly. But close enough. She could hear his uneven breathing at her shoulder, and tension stretched in the warm air surrounding them. By the time his arms dropped to his sides she was quivering again, her mind spinning.

"Thank you," she said.

"My pleas—" He paused. "Pleasure."

"Could you help with the gown, too?"

"As you wish." This time he didn't turn his back. He watched her pull the petticoat over her head and tie the ribbons with trembling hands, then the gown.

"Have you taken a chill after all?" he said, the melty chocolate voice back again but deeper now.

"No. I'm fine." She turned her back to him.

He fastened the gown. He took his time. The caress of his fingertips against her spine couldn't possibly be accidental.

"You're very good at this." She tried to sound relaxed. "I suppose you've had some practice."

"Are all Americans like you?" he said, his voice close.

Like *her*? The Oldest Virgin in America?

"No."

He stepped back. "Pity."

She slipped the shoes onto her feet. "I'm—"

"Trent!" A young woman fell into the doorway. Her cheeks were flushed and her gray eyes were frantic. "I found you! My maid told me you had been to my chamber and I had to chase you all the way down here. Our beast of a brother is positively plaguing my friends! He spread marbles in the bedchamber corridor this morning, and

285

yesterday it was face powder on the tea biscuits. Papa berates him but
it only makes him worse, of course. I beg of you to take him in hand.
My friends and I cannot possibly enjoy all the young bachelors here
if Henry is forever playing pranks on us." Her attention shifted to
Angela and her face broke into a smile. "But whatever are you
doing?"

"Charlotte, may I introduce you to Miss ..." He glanced at her left
hand again.

Angela's tongue stuck. The seventh Earl of Ware's daughter had
been named Charlotte.

"Miss ...?" repeated Lord Everett, who was, in fact, an early-
nineteenth-century man.

"Cowdrey," Angela whispered.

"Miss Cowdrey," he said. "Please allow me to make you known
to my sister, Lady Charlotte Ascot."

"It's such a pleasure to make your acquaintance, Miss Cowdrey.
I'm terribly sorry to bother you with my brother Henry's nastiness,"
Lady Charlotte said, coming into the boathouse and glancing around
before taking in Angela again in a cheerful sweep. "But you do look
pretty in my gown! Doesn't she, Trent?"

He smiled.

"Thank you for the loan of it," Angela said.

"Oh, I have dozens, I daresay." She laughed gaily. "That isn't
even one of my favorites."

"Charlotte," her brother said quietly.

"Oh." Charlotte's fingertips leaped to her lips and she seemed to
finally notice Angela's bedraggled state. "I am an awful peagoose,
Miss Cowdrey. I pray you, don't mind me at all. If you are a friend of
Trenton's, then you are a friend of mine, too."

If they were actors, they were doing a spectacular job of keeping
in character. Obviously his was to be the responsible older brother.
He was good at it; his sister responded to him with affection and
trust, even when he was gently reprimanding her, and even when he
was stealing her clothes for a strange woman in a boathouse.

"But what on earth are these?" Charlotte picked up her tights.
"What marvelous stockings! But why are they wet? Is it a swimming
costume, Miss Cowdrey?" Her other hand snatched up Angela's
white lace bra. "And this? It cannot *possibly* be useful for swimming."
She giggled.

"Charlotte," the viscount said, "would you be so kind as to walk with us to the house? Miss Cowdrey is awaiting the arrival of her family, and I suspect she would be glad for a cup of tea in the meantime."

"How wretched they were to send you along without them." Charlotte linked her arm. "I shan't leave you alone until they claim you. Who are they? I don't know of any Cowdreys attending the duke's wedding."

"Miss Cowdrey is American. Her family may not be known to your friends."

He was suspicious; his eyes were now hesitant. He didn't recognize her. But he *was* the man from the comic book. *And she was here.* She could no longer deny it.

"Oh!" Charlotte exclaimed gaily. "Well, I am so pleased to know you. You are my first American. Is she yours too, Trent?"

His gaze dipped to her mouth. "Yes. My first."

He gestured them out of the boathouse. Angela tucked her tights and bra inside the pile of soggy clothes on the bench and looked up at him. He nodded silently and went out.

He understood her wish to keep her dip in the lake a secret. As she walked arm-in-arm with Charlotte and he followed, she felt him watching her. It was a good thing Charlotte Ascot was a big chatterbox, because Angela couldn't manage a single word.

By the time they neared the house she'd recovered a little. "I'm going to head off this way now," she said, slipping out of Charlotte's hold. "To the ... um ... stables."

The viscount's brow went up. "The stables?"

"Yes. To check on ... my horse."

*He didn't believe her.*

"Thank you so much for the gown, Lady Charlotte," she said. "I'll return it as soon as my luggage arrives. And thank you, my lord, for— Thank you." She tried to curtsy and mucked it up.

She escaped. He didn't follow her. She was equal parts relieved and disappointed.

Set at a distance from the sprawling house was a quadrangle of long, one-story buildings: the carriage house and stables. She tried opening a door. It was locked from the inside. But she could hear voices inside. Lots of male voices, and laughter. Maybe the stable hands were playing craps or something.

On the path between the house and stables, a humungous oak tree looked like it'd been split by lightning and seemed to be in the process of being dismantled. For a while she hid in the shadows of one of its large branches that hadn't yet been chopped up, trying to catch her breath and think and watching a good-looking couple strolling back and forth over the same stretch of pathway again and again. They kept looking at the ground as if they were searching for something. She considered asking them to search for the secret passage back to the twenty-first century while they were at it.

Her rational mind couldn't accept it. The evidence pointed to time and space travel: winter had become summer and Michigan had become Dorset. The other evidence—the gorgeous man in the comic book with her name on it—wasn't in any way interpretable.

She stared at the strolling couple. They just had to be reenactors. Who else but actors would walk up and down the same uninteresting path over and over and look like they were enjoying themselves?

It was all for the tourists. It had to be. Then where were those tourists? Everybody she saw was wearing period costume.

Finally she headed toward the house and went inside. It was spectacular, just as fantastically elegant as it had been when she'd visited last summer. The principal differences were the absence of brass posts and velvet ropes cordoning off the private areas from the public, and also of electric lights. Unlit candles in gold candelabra adorned the tables on either side of the foyer, and oil-lamp sconces ascended the wall of the grand stairway. The air even smelled different, with a hint of flowery herbs, maybe lemon oil, and candle wax.

Passing footmen in livery, who stayed poker straight and proper, she went up the sprawling stairs and wandered through the corridors—also lacking electric lights and switches—until she found an unlocked door to an empty bedchamber. She slipped inside, locked the door behind her, and sat down on the bed.

She'd nearly drowned. She was exhausted and confused and overwhelmed. Leaning her shoulder against the bolster, she rested her head. She'd just sit for a few minutes, think, gather her thoughts. Figure ... things ... out ...

— ⊶∞⊷ —

"Wake up, silly girl! Even I don't sleep in the middle of the day, and if I do it's certainly not in a bed."

Not a day under eighty, small like a bird, with bright red hair piled atop her head, the woman staring down at Angela pursed her lips.

"Dreadful," the woman muttered.

Angela sucked in breath, coughed on a remnant of lake water, and remembered everything—drowning, being rescued, Lord Melting Chocolate, and his hands on her as he fastened her into his sister's gown.

She had to find out why she was here. He didn't recognize her. He couldn't help. She was in a foreign place. She needed allies. No time like the present to start gathering them.

But first she really had to pee.

She sat up on the bed. "I'm so sorry. Is this your room?"

"It is. And who are you, missy?"

"Angela Cowdrey." She slid off the bed and shook out her skirt. It was totally wrinkled and her hair smelled like a lake. "Who are you?"

"Ha! I like the spirit on this one."

Angela looked around the room. No one else was present.

"I'm glad you do," she said to the crazy old lady, "because I have some strange questions to ask and I'd really like straight answers."

"Ha again!" the woman cackled, the feather sticking up out of her impossibly red hair wiggling as she spoke. "Impertinent girl."

"Could you tell me what year it is?"

"Eighteen thirteen." Her eyes narrowed. "You think my mind's gone, don't you? So does Henrietta. And the duchess. Everybody does."

"No. I don't think that at all. I think mine is."

"Ha! You're an American. I can hear it."

"I am. May I ask you another question?"

"Lady Sophronia Cavendish."

"Thank you. But actually that wasn't my question. Is this all an elaborately staged reenactment?"

"Eh?"

"Are you all actors dressed up to look like early-nineteenth-century people, pretending to be living in 1813 and doing a fabulous job of it?" There, she'd asked.

"Sadly, I am not an actress, although I did a turn or two on the boards in my youth," Lady Sophronia said wistfully. Her eyes sharpened again. "Are you, missy?"

"An actress? No. I'm ..." Confused. And as suspicious as Lord Melting Chocolate. And a little frightened, because even if it wasn't 1813, it really was summertime, not January, and she really was at the estate of the Duke of Wessex, not in Ann Arbor. "I'm lost."

"Well, aren't we all, child?" Lady Sophronia exclaimed. She took Angela's arm. "Come now. We'll have a nice chat and become acquainted. My Henrietta is off chasing that delicious rogue, Jack Willoughby—and it's about time!—so we shan't be bothered for a while, I suspect."

Angela went with her into an adjoining room, where they sat down in gilt-edged chairs and a maid in perfect period costume set out a gorgeous high tea with little sandwiches and perfect cakes and cookies.

Angela stood. "I'm so sorry, but could you tell me where the bathroom is?"

Lady Sophronia's skinny brows flew up.

"The loo?" Angela tried. "The WC?"

The old lady cracked a laugh. "The nearest water closet is too far away, so I don't bother with it. I hear Gareth plans all sorts of improvements for his new duchess. Responsible young man. Far too stiff-necked for my tastes, of course. But someday a girl of wit and spirit will knock him off his polished boots. Mark my words!"

Angela fidgeted in discomfort.

Lady Sophronia pointed to a silk screen in the corner. "Make yourself at home. Henrietta says I'm half-deaf, so I won't hear a thing." She laughed again.

Behind the screen was a chair fitted with a porcelain chamber pot set into the seat and a pile of small linen cloths. For wiping?

"Oh ... no," she whispered.

"See? I didn't hear that!" Lady Sophronia shouted and laughed merrily. For the first time in the two hours since she'd been in nineteenth-century England, Angela smiled.

They took tea, and everything Lady Sophronia told her was historically accurate. She spoke about the guests at the Duke of Wessex's wedding celebration in detail. Angela didn't recognize some of the names, but she could tell that this woman wasn't acting. By the time Sophronia mentioned the Earl of Ware's family, her heart was beating hard.

"Trenton was his mother's family name, of course. Elizabeth Trenton. Beautiful woman. Her eldest son got her looks and his father's athletic figure. And good heavens, what a figure!" Lady Sophronia fanned herself with a lace kerchief.

Angela needed a fan too. She hadn't been touched by a man in a long time. The caress of his fingertips on her back lingered.

"Aha!" Lady Sophronia exclaimed. "I see you've encountered Crash Ascot already. I would be blushing too if I were your age. I'm blushing anyway! Devilishly appealing."

"Crash?"

"Dreadful accident. Recovered marvelously, though. Took the fox at Beaufort's Hunt eight months later."

Angela nodded and wished she had her laptop to take notes. Even her phone.

Her phone! It was in her coat pocket. It wasn't waterproof, but if it worked … Why hadn't she thought of it before?

Because she'd been in shock. And apparently she couldn't think straight with Trenton "Crash" Ascot staring at her bare feet.

She needed to find him, get her phone, and have a chat with him about a comic book and his appearance in her apartment building's foyer two hundred years in the future.


Trent didn't consider himself a blindingly brilliant man. But he had a reasonably good mind and he hadn't ever wondered about his sanity. *Before.*

She was thoroughly brazen.

He couldn't stop thinking about her.

At dawn he'd walked out into the park, trying to find peace and sanity in his usual way. It hadn't sufficed. He'd returned to his bedchamber equally bemused.

She had requested his assistance dressing with mild composure and only the lightest dusting of pink upon her cheeks.

He had, in fact, small experience dressing a woman. When his friends were all taking mistresses in town, he'd tried it too. It hadn't suited him. He would certainly welcome a sweet-smelling, willing woman in his bed every night, but not if he had to pay her to be there.

Miss Cowdrey smelled like newly fallen snow—fresh and clean and cool. But when he'd allowed his fingertips to stray from the buttons to her back, she'd been hot.

He studied her garments he'd brought from the boathouse to his bedchamber. He'd never seen anything like them, especially the little lace garment. It could be a garter of some sort, but it was shaped entirely like another part of a woman's anatomy. He certainly hadn't seen anything like these clothes on a lady of quality. Perhaps Miss Cowdrey was not a lady. Perhaps he had invited a common thief into his friend's house, made her acquainted with his innocent sister, and within days all the duke's guests would be missing watches and jewels and purses.

He went to her coat hanging on his clotheshorse, still damp despite a night dripping lake water onto the floor.

Tempting.

*He mustn't.*

He dipped his hand in a pocket. Empty. From the other he withdrew a heavy, flat rectangular box that fit in his palm. Too flat for a snuff box. Perhaps it was for calling cards. He pried at the dark glass lid. It remained fast shut.

He slid it into his pocket. He should find Wessex or the duchess and ask about Miss Cowdrey's family. Then he would be obliged to tell them about the incident at the lake.

He could not do that. His honor must defend her virtue.

But he did need to return her clothing. He was borrowing his father's valet during this visit, and if old Cooper found a lady's garments in his bedchamber, he'd tell the earl. Then their sojourn in the boathouse would be revealed.

That couldn't happen. Unless he wanted his father to stand trial for treason and fraud, he was marrying Sir Richard's daughter. Every feeling rebelled at the notion. But Miss Howell was an innocent party. He would at least begin married life without shaming her from the start.

But then how to return these clothes? He couldn't very well go around asking the footmen and maids the location of Miss Cowdrey's bedchamber.

So he went where any bemused man would when faced with a mysterious woman whom he'd rescued from drowning and then helped to dress, and whose soft brown eyes glimmered with desire when trained upon him. He went to the stables to drink.

Even after all these years, it made his gut ache to look at a vehicle like Jack Willoughby's phaeton. Averting his gaze, he greeted his friends and headed for the whiskey.

A glass later, he wasn't any less confounded. Leaving the stable, he headed for the gardens where nuncheon was set out near a lawn set up for battledore and shuttlecock.

Passing through a covered portico in the Italian style, he saw her. A hundred yards away, she was crossing the lawn toward tents erected by a stately oak. She wore a white gown—his sister's again?—and her stride was purposeful and broad. She barely seemed to notice the game of battledore and shuttlecock as she crossed between the players, her shoulders thrust back and her arms and head bare.

He'd forgotten to borrow a bonnet for her. And a shawl.

He started forward.

"Lord Everett! Do wait for us!" Girlish giggles tripped down the portico toward him, followed by the giggling girls themselves—at least five of them, all dressed in maidenly white, none over the age of seventeen by the looks of it. His sister, her face a portrait of irritation, brought up the rear. Behind her, their fourteen-year-old brother darted around columns, stalking like a cat in pursuit of a herd of mice.

Trent squared his shoulders. He needed a bonnet and shawl, and who knew when he'd find Charlotte again soon? Also, if he were with the girls, Henry wouldn't dare bother them.

He turned to the girls and smiled.

**"I** come from the Cowdreys of Charleston." Angela scooped up another poppy seed cookie and dropped it into her mouth. She was starving. And sore from sleeping on a stiff little sofa in an unused parlor. And desperately in need of a shower.

"Charleston," the woman she'd been chatting with said thoughtfully. "Where is Charleston, Frederick?"

"It's that fine little town we visited near Boston. Isn't it, Miss Cowdrey?"

"Yes, indeed." She didn't have a southern accent, but if someone called her out on being from South Carolina, she could fake it. She'd lived in Atlanta for two years in middle school. It was astounding how little these people knew about America. She could stay here for days faking her origins and her reasons for being at the party.

But she didn't want to keep pretending she was somebody's distant cousin, and she was pretty sure sharp-as-a-tack Sophronia had seen through that lie immediately. She didn't have any idea why the eccentric old lady hadn't told on her to the duke and his mother yet. But maybe that's where she'd gone after breakfast.

She had to find Trenton Ascot again. Earlier she'd discreetly asked a footman where the younger gentlemen at the house party might be. He'd pokered up and said he couldn't say. Fat chance. Servants knew everything that went on in an English great house. But the very fact that she was thinking in these terms meant that she was beginning to believe this carnival was real.

It couldn't be. It couldn't be. *It couldn't be.*

It had to be.

Beyond the badminton game—*correction*, battledore and shuttlecock—a man was walking across the lawn surrounded by half a dozen girls in white dresses.

Trenton Ascot.

He was looking straight at her. Her moment of reckoning was nigh. Her knees felt mushy. Nothing in graduate school had prepared her for this. Nothing in *life* had prepared her for him.

As he paused, disengaged his arm from the girl clinging to it, and bowed to the giggling group, a man at the luncheon buffet near Angela said, "I say, isn't that Sir Richard Howell coming this way?"

"At Wessex's wedding?" the woman beside him said. "Well, he's certainly come up in the world, hasn't he?"

"Come now, m'dear. He's one of Gentleman Jackson's favorites, and he's in Parliament now, don't you know."

His wife sniffed. "He attended Mrs. Portman's ball a fortnight ago and I daresay I could smell the shop on him." She whispered to Angela, "Trade."

Angela pivoted and stared at the man approaching with a young woman on his arm. His jowls hung thick and loose like a bulldog's and his eyes bulged out a little under bushy brows. He had a round belly crossed with a garish gold watch chain that hung from his pocket, and his lapels were extra wide. She'd never seen a picture of Howell, but this was exactly as she'd pictured him. Exactly.

*Sir Richard Howell.*

She couldn't breathe. Blindly, she reached for the edge of the refreshment table.

"Miss Cowdrey," Trenton Ascot's melty voice said at her shoulder. "You appear flushed. Shall we find you a cool place in the shade to rest? Then I might restore to you your bonnet and shawl, which I have retrieved just now from my sister." Brandishing a straw hat and fringy lace shawl, he took her hand, tucked it into the crook of his arm and led her away from the tent.

"I—" Her tongue stalled. "I can't rest right now." She tried to pull away, but he held her fast. "Is that man really Sir Richard Howell?"

"Don't point, Miss Cowdrey." He drew her away from the tents toward a path. "It marks you as a foreigner."

"I am a foreigner." More foreign than he knew.

Oh God oh God oh God.

*It was real.* She couldn't pretend it wasn't anymore. Not in any little way. She was in Regency-era England. She knew this because the subject of the paper about wartime maritime trade that she was currently revising for the *American Historical Review* and that, along with her dissertation, would get her a decent job, was standing thirty feet away, accepting a glass of lemonade from a footman.

She yanked free of the viscount's hold and pivoted. "I have to go speak with him."

He grabbed her hand, trapped it firmly against his side, and dragged her along. "Don't fight me, Miss Cowdrey. I have several pressing questions for you, and at present I am not inclined to patience." Even demanding, his voice was like melted chocolate. And the muscles in his arm were just as good to feel as they'd looked through wet linen. She glanced up. His chiseled jaw was tight.

"I have some questions for you too," she said.

"Then clearly we must both assuage our burning curiosity. What good fortune, then, that I managed to find you." He slanted her a narrow look with his smoky gray eyes.

"Were you looking for me?"

"I suspect that you know I was." He guided her into the shade of a path bordered with trees that led down the long lawn away from the house.

"I didn't."

"Do you not wish your clothing returned to you, then, Miss Cowdrey?" he said and drew her along the gravel walk. "If that is indeed your name."

She pulled away and backed up.

"That is my name," she said. In the dappled sunlight falling between tree branches, he looked less than sanguine and completely gorgeous, especially with a woman's hat and shawl hanging from his hand. He had an athlete's hands: strong, the veins prominent under tanned skin. Good lord, he was really handsome. She'd never known men like him. Her friends and the men she occasionally dated were all skinny, pale intellectual types. She'd only ever come close to masculine beauty once: during the summer between junior and senior year at Harvard, she'd kissed a Spanish exchange student in the Place de la Concorde on a dare from one of her friends. He'd been good looking in a dark, Latin way.

Viscount Everett's gorgeousness was all about golden boy virility. He was a classic jock, as the comic book had narrated and Lady Sophronia's comments the night before had confirmed.

Angela didn't know how to talk to jocks. The only ones she ever spoke with sat at desks in the classes she TA-ed, and there weren't many; early British history tended to attract girls enamored of Tudor England. Anyway, the teacher–student relationship was a whole other power dynamic and she was completely comfortable with it.

She wasn't comfortable now.

"My name really is Angela Cowdrey. I live in the United States, and I'm—" She just had to say it. She had to tell him the truth and hope he'd do the same in return. "I'm not actually supposed to be here," she chickened out.

"I did get that impression. You are not in fact on the duchess's guest list?"

"No, I mean I'm not supposed to be here in England. And I don't know why I am."

"You do not know why you traveled across an ocean to visit another country?"

"No. Yes. I'm doing research on Sir Richard Howell, so I think it must have something to do with him. I really do need to talk with him."

"I'm afraid I cannot allow that, Miss Cowdrey." A muscle in his jaw flexed. "Sir Richard is not a man of good character."

"I know!"

His brow shot up.

"I—I mean," she stammered. "I'd heard that." *Tell him the truth.* He was in the comic book. *He knows you. He just doesn't know he knows you.* He might be able to help. Why else would he have been the one to fish her out of the lake?

"Miss Cowdrey, do you have malicious intentions toward the duke, the duchess, or any of their guests?"

"No!" Fear zigzagged through her. Apparently he did not know her. "No, absolutely not."

"Why were you in that lake yesterday? Why do you lack family, companion, or maid here? Why do you go about without a bonnet or shawl?" He reached into his pocket. "And what is this?"

"My phone!" She darted forward and grabbed it. She pressed the power button. Nothing. But even if the battery was dead, the phone wouldn't pick up a signal in the nineteenth century.

The. Nineteenth. Century.

Why was she here? To discover why Arnaud Chappelle had revealed Sir Richard's crimes? But that was ridiculous. As intriguing a mystery as it was to her fellow scholars of the British Empire, in the real world nobody cared.

"Phone?" His voice was rough. Their fingers had brushed. He flexed his hand.

She looked up and her breaths stuttered. Up close he didn't look threatening or angry or even suspicious. Up close he looked a little befuddled and ... *edible.*

# CHAPTER FOUR

**T**rent watched the color rise in her cheeks and her delectably full lips part and thought perhaps he should step away from her. The path was secluded, sunlight touched her skin and shone in her warm, intelligent eyes, and he was a bit muddle-headed. From the whiskey, no doubt. He was also aroused, which unfortunately he couldn't blame on the whiskey.

"Lady Sophronia said they call you 'Crash,'" she said, not moving away as a modest lady would but staring directly into his eyes. Her breasts lifted on a deep breath. They were barely concealed by the gown; she had more to fill the bodice than his seventeen-year-old sister. He imagined brushing a kiss across the swell of one of Miss Cowdrey's breasts, then the other. "Did you—" she said upon another tantalizing breath, "—crash into—" Another breath. "—a tree? Or something?"

He dragged his attention up. "It was a stone wall, if you must know. And I did not precisely crash of my own will. That blackguard Abernathy locked wheels with me and forced me into the ditch."

"Locked wheels?"

"Curricle race."

"Ah." Her lashes flickered and her gaze retreated into pensive shadow. "Of course," she said quietly.

Trent couldn't seem to draw full breaths. "When you do that ..."

"Do what?"

"When you pause to think for a moment, to consider ..." For God's sake, his own thoughts were slow as tar. "It seems as though you are taking notes. Are you?"

"Taking notes?" She licked her lush lips. "Sort of, I guess."

"Are you a lady journalist hoping to reveal scandals at Wessex's wedding?"

"No. What scandals?"

"Who are you, Miss Cowdrey?"

"I am a historian of England." Her face was clear and fresh, her eyes completely guileless. "I wrote my dissertation on maritime trade during the period of the Napoleonic Wars. If I can manage it, it's going to be published in 2015 with Harvard University Press."

He felt drugged, as though the whiskey had been spiked with laudanum. Her lips were so close, the warmth of the day everywhere, the birds and summer blooms and trees. He was in his favorite place in the world, immersed in nature, and a lovely American woman was spouting nonsense to him. "Harvard University Press?"

She nodded. "It's called *Shipping Lanes: British Enterprise and the Making of Empire from 1778 to 1832.*"

He struggled. "You do not think you are inventing this."

"I'm in fact not inventing this." Her eyes were luminous, begging him to believe her.

"Which means you must be mad."

"I'm not."

"But if you are mad," he said, "or perhaps if you are merely an apparition that I am seeing because in fact I am mad, then why do I want to kiss you so much?"

Her eyes snapped wide. "You want to kiss me?"

"Very much." More than he'd wanted to kiss any woman.

"I'm not insane," she said. "And you're not either, because I am in fact really here, to which about fifty people over at those tents as well as Lady Sophronia can attest."

"The year 1832 has not yet occurred, Miss Cowdrey."

"It has where I come from, Lord Everett."

"You expect me to believe this?"

"I'm a good swimmer, but you dragged me out of a lake in England after I'd fallen into a river in America and was drowning. You have no proof of that river's existence or that I can swim, I realize. But it's high summer here and I was wearing a coat and gloves and boots because at home it's the dead of winter. I don't know anybody at this party. Not a single soul. But I am writing a paper on a slice of history in which one of the guests at this wedding plays a crucial role." Again she watched him as though assessing. But not calculating. *Thinking*. "Logically, you know the pieces don't fit together," she continued. "And they don't—logically—unless you add another variable to the equation. Another time."

*Dear God.* Thoughts in her head *and* a pretty face. Lovely face. Beckoning eyes. Perfect breasts. Her assertions were irrational, but at present that seemed entirely immaterial to Trent.

He couldn't stop himself. "I'm going to kiss you," he said.

Her lashes flickered. "I'm pretty sure I would really like it if you did."

He touched her arm and a shock of energy went through him, like a ray of light straight through his chest. What in God's name was happening to him? "I've never done this before," he uttered helplessly.

Disbelief sparked in her eyes. "You've never kissed a woman?"

"I've never kissed a lady in a garden." Her lips called to him, ripe and full and dusky pink that he must taste.

"Really?" she whispered.

"I am an honorable man, Miss Cowdrey." He wanted those lips beneath his. He had to have them. He bent his head. "A gentleman who respects women doesn't just—"

She went onto her toes and pressed her lips to his for a long, soft moment of innocent pleasure. Trent hadn't kissed a woman in this manner in so long he didn't know what to do. So he simply accepted it and felt desire he'd never even imagined.

"There," she said, drawing away, her eyes sparkling. "You didn't need to do it after all, because I did. You retain your honor, my lord."

"Not for long." He reached up and curved his hand around the back of her neck and drew her mouth up against his.

She showed no virginal hesitation. She opened her lips to him and laid her hands on his chest, and quite swiftly Trent wanted more. Much more. Her mouth was sweet and humid, her lips softly returning the pressure of his, her scent filling his senses, and he couldn't hold himself back. Both hands at the base of her neck, he speared his fingers through her hair and with his mouth urged her lips apart. Her tongue darted into his mouth, then stroked his lower lip. He followed it with his, caressing until her fingertips pressed into his chest. Then he delved.

Oh, God, she was delicious. Hot and wet and eager. He wanted to kiss her like this, deep and wet, for hours. He wanted to know every bit of her mouth and tongue. Her lips. *Her lips.* Her perfect lips kissing him, tasting him, sucking on his tongue. An image of what else those perfect lips might do occurred to him.

He thrust her away.

Her eyes were half-closed, her lips damp and a little swollen from his kiss. "W-Wow," she whispered.

He raked his hand through his hair. He felt completely out of control. "I wanted to do that," he said inanely.

"I still want you to do that."

"Don't tempt me." His voice was gruff, unfamiliar to him.

"Why?" She gave him a little one-sided grin that curved her delicious lips into the temptation he feared. "Are you an only-one-kiss-in-the-garden kind of guy, Trenton Ascot?"

"Yes." It was the hardest word he'd ever uttered. "Adamantly yes."

The pleasure faded from her face. "Was I that disappointing?"

He choked. "Uh ..." He stepped back. "No. *No.*"

"Then—"

"Miss Cowdrey, at the risk of offending you unpardonably—"

"Oh, no." Her face crumpled. "You're married, aren't you?" She laid a hand over her eyes. "I knew it."

"I—"

"This sort of thing always happens to me. Like my first year in grad school when Nathan Farquis vowed he just had to have me, then it turned out he'd been dating Liz Kinkaid in Cultural Anthropology for a year. We'd already gotten half-naked when she just walked in. I felt like a skunk. It was all totally his fault, but somehow he became the martyr to Liz's vengeance, and nobody in Anthro spoke to *me* for the next two years."

Trent tried to still his spinning head. "I am not married," he said. "And Mr. Farquis is clearly a rogue, which I am not." Usually.

Relief washed across her lovely eyes. "Oh, good. Here I was getting ready for Lady Everett to come running around that corner and—" She looked over his shoulder. "Speaking of running."

A shower of rapid footsteps sounded on the path behind him, but he couldn't attend. All he could see was her "gotten half-naked" with a faceless rogue, who in Trent's imagination had a paunch and hairy back, which was something of a comfort. But then Trent replaced the faceless rogue with himself and his vision got spotty.

Her fingers twisted together. "I'm sorry. That was too much information—about Nathan—I realize. I'm nervous and I tend to talk a lot when I'm nervous ... or in front of a lecture hall, actually, too. I'm doing it again. Talking."

"You needn't be ... *nervous.*" It was the biggest lie he'd ever uttered. He himself was currently a blithering mess.

Then the untimely intruders were upon them. The white muslin crew that he had encountered earlier surrounded them, no longer entirely white. Their skirts were spattered with mud.

"Trenton!" Charlotte cried. "Henry is a beast! Look what he has done!"

"Oh, wow," Miss Cowdrey said. "What a mess. We should get you all back to the house and cleaned up before anybody sees you." She took his sister's arm and the arm of one of the other girls, entirely oblivious of the mud smearing her own arms and gown.

"Thank you, Miss Cowdrey." Charlotte leveled a beseeching look at him. "Trent, *please* help us with Henry."

Their brother had gone too far this time. He wouldn't listen to their father's threats and reprimands. Trent would have to see to the problem himself.

On the walk back to the house, Miss Cowdrey made certain conversation was lively and distracting enough that the girls were soon in high spirits again despite the mud. The American with the lush, eager lips and secretly scandalous history spoke with modesty and affection about her family in South Carolina and their "oyster bakes" that were popular among society there. Her stories enthralled the girls.

Other than musing on how the ancients had considered oysters an aphrodisiac—which of course she didn't know—Trent managed to keep his thoughts relatively pure. Then he met her gaze for an instant, her eyes glimmered, and he thought perhaps she knew about the oysters after all. She smiled a seductive little smile, and he was quite certain that she did, and that he was doomed.

**N**ever before in her twenty-seven years had Angela felt sexy.

She felt sexy now. She felt like one of those club bunnies who wore open-heeled stilettos and short-shorts and proudly displayed their deep cleavages. She didn't have a deep cleavage, and she wouldn't put her butt into mini-shorts if someone paid her a million dollars. She was poor, not desperate.

But inside she felt like a bunny. Her blood was sizzling. Not like before. Now it was sizzly all the time.

She refused to attribute this amped-up sizzle to a single passionate kiss with an unbelievably hot man on a garden path. Feminists worldwide would drum her from the league for thoughts like that. Men had been defining—and constraining—female sexuality for centuries. That sort of misadventure was not on Angela's program.

Still, the way he'd looked at her before he kissed her ... And then afterward ... She'd turned him on. When they'd kissed, she'd felt him get hard. Just remembering it made her unbelievably hot.

But the sexiness bubbling in her wasn't even about that. It was about freedom, as if suddenly she'd been released from prison, and she hadn't even known she'd been in prison until now.

And now she was free. Nobody here knew her. Nobody here knew she was a poor workaholic without a life. Nobody knew she was the Oldest Virgin in America. If only for a moment in twisted time, here she could be different. She could be anything she wanted.

She wanted to be sexy.

For the first time in her life, she wanted to tear a page out of her party-girl mother's book and be uncompromisingly feminine and entirely available. *Exclusively* available to one golden-boy jock whose kiss made her want to wrap her legs around his waist and learn what it was like to ride a guy until dawn.

It was, however, difficult to imagine doing this while wearing a virginal white gown covered in tiny rosebuds. That hadn't deterred Trenton Ascot from giving her the best kiss of her life, of course. But if he really were the honorable only-one-kiss sort of guy, she'd need to generate some irresistible encouragement for him to break his rule.

She sought out Lady Sophronia in her suite of chambers.

"My lady, I have two requests."

"Impudent girl! I adore you! Where are your people?"

"My family hasn't arrived yet."

"Then you shall live here in my suite with me and Henrietta until they do. I will have a bed made up for you. A girl like you shouldn't be wandering about the house alone. There are rogues and rascals afoot, Miss Cowdrey." She slapped a wrinkled hand over the knife she always wore at her hip. "We ladies must band together for safety. Until, that is, a particularly handsome rogue or rascal happens by, then it's every woman for herself." She cackled merrily.

"Thank you. I'd really like to stay here with you. That was, in fact, my first question."

Lady Sophronia poked a macaroon between her cherry red lips. "The second?"

"How might a woman go about learning more of a gentleman about whom she is particularly curious?" It wasn't only her need to tempt him into more kisses. Trenton Ascot had a very bad opinion of Sir Richard. It was too big a coincidence, especially since Sir Richard's illegal deeds weren't public until 1814. And, of course, the Earl of Ware had briefly invested in Sir Richard's shipping firm, though Angela thought that'd been years ago.

She had a very strong feeling that Lord Everett wasn't telling her something important. Professional pride was at stake. If she couldn't get to the bottom of an historical mystery while living in the midst of it, she was a failure as an historian. More importantly, it had to be the key to why she was here.

"What gentleman interests you?" Lady Sophronia said. "The deliciously brooding and enigmatic Lord Bruton?" She passed a bottle of smelling salts beneath her nose and her eyes rolled up. Angela started forward in alarm. Sophronia's eyes snapped open. "I do adore a dark and mysterious man. If I were ten years younger ..."

She'd still be fifty years too old for the Earl of Bruton.

"Not Lord Bruton," Angela said. "Lord Everett."

"Aha! I knew it. You've developed a tendre for him, clever girl."

Developing a crush on a man who lived two hundred years in the past didn't seem very clever to Angela. "I need information about him."

"Gossip," Lady Sophronia said with a snap of her bird-claw fingers. "Never fails."

"I've tried that." Angela had skipped the formal meals; she didn't want to bump into the duke or his mother. But at tea yesterday and breakfast and tea today she'd asked people about the viscount. No one had anything intriguing to say. He was a bruising rider, an excellent fencer, a splendid tennis player, a capital boxer, a dead-on shot, and any cricket team's anchor. He was devoted to his brother and sister, a dutiful son, and exceedingly proper with all the ladies, who admired him for his good looks and fine physique. By all accounts he was pretty low key, not a big socializer or an extrovert. If Angela hadn't turned to molten lava when he'd put his tongue in her mouth, and if he hadn't saved her life then kept that secret from everybody despite his suspicions, from the reports of others she'd think he was a total bore.

"You must look in a man's drawers to discover his vital assets, child," Lady Sophronia said.

Angela's mouth fell open.

"Not *those* drawers, Miss American Hussy!" The old lady guffawed, then tapped the end of a cane decorated with silk flowers on her dressing table. "*These* drawers. Men are nincompoops. They hide everything of value in top drawers then wonder why their wives and servants know all their secrets."

Angela laughed. "I'll take that under advisement."

"Well?" Lady Sophronia pointed the flowery cane at her. "What are you waiting for? The gentlemen are all in the stables, or so says my maid who heard it from the second groom. This is your opportunity. Go!"

"Go?"

"Bachelors' wing. Third door on the right. Hurry now!"

"Shouldn't I wait until it's dark out?"

"Caution, Miss Cowdrey?" Lady Sophronia threw her a skeptical look. "I hadn't expected it of you."

"Not so much caution as I don't want to be caught poking around in a Lord of the Realm's drawers."

"Unless he is wearing them, of course."

In one second flat, Angela got hot all over.

The feisty old lady wiggled her brows.

Angela waited until after Sophronia's maid said all the lady guests had retired to bed. Then, candle in hand, she crept through the empty corridors until she reached the bachelors' wing. Counting one door then two, she stopped before the third.

It opened. No lock? Seemed careless for a man possibly hiding secrets about his father's former business partner's fraud and treason.

She started by searching his drawers, as recommended. They were well ordered and sparsely filled. Despite his good looks and athleticism, Lord Everett was not a clothes hound or a slob. That was nice to discover. With the subtle, masculine scent of the cologne he wore wafting from his things, her nervous energy crept a notch higher.

The dressing table produced *nada*.

Guilt pricked at her, then anxiety. But seriously, what could they do to her if they discovered her snooping? Give her the cut direct?

Her amusement didn't last long. What if she never went back home? What if she ruined her reputation then got trapped in this era? There weren't many roles for women in Regency high society: lady, servant, shopkeeper, actress, prostitute.

She couldn't think about it. She was going home, just after she learned the secret of Arnaud's revelation.

Through another door was a sort of big walk-in closet called a dressing chamber. It had plenty of space for the viscount's traveling trunk and a handful of coats of excellent quality. She reached for the clasps on the trunk. No locks here either. He really didn't seem to have anything to hide.

She searched it anyway. Linens: drawers, shirts, and neck cloths, all neatly folded and clean. She dug beneath them and pulled out a large leather portfolio folder with a scrolly "E" embossed in gold in the corner.

Sitting back on her heels, she opened it across her knees.

The drawings were not of sports events or naked women. Instead, with great care, compassion, and whimsical grace, they depicted plants and animals. Not showy or sophisticated plants; there were no cabbage roses or orchids. Instead, in pencil or pen with occasional watercolor accents, there were humble flowers: buttercups, wild violets, honeysuckle. The animals weren't horses or hunting dogs, but woodland creatures and wild birds—a hare, a door mouse, an ugly little blind mole, and an exquisite series of a single fox rendered with aching tenderness.

Each drawing had a caption beneath: *Lily of the Valley*, *Grass Snake*, *Green Woodpecker*. The writing was the same as in the comic book's captions. Exactly the same.

Heart beating hard, she folded the portfolio closed, replaced it in the trunk, and left the dressing room. From the other side of the bedroom door, voices sounded in the corridor.

She halted, the candle wobbling in her hand. The door handle turned. Angela held her breath. The door didn't open. Beyond it, men's voices rumbled. Laughter. The door handle fell back into place.

Without thought, she set down her candle on the bed table and went for the only place of possible concealment—the window. During her long study of the house when she'd been hiding by the fallen oak, she'd noticed that some of the windows featured wide ledges. Slipping through the heavy drapes, she pushed up the pane and climbed out onto the ledge.

It wasn't as wide as it looked from the ground. In the dark, she shimmied down onto her butt and clung to the decorative iron rail that ran along the ledge at about knee height. The night air was cool, stirring a lock of hair that had worked loose from the pins. Her hair was way too straight for Regency styles, but she'd tried hard to fix it the way she saw the other women did. She simply couldn't be discovered as a fraud before she learned how Sir Richard had come to be one.

But this—this window ledge hiding—was really stupid. Even if no one on the ground noticed her, she couldn't very well stay out here all night. She could try to creep out after he went to sleep. But what if he was a light sleeper?

"Pondering the fate of cutpurses and thieves, Miss Cowdrey? Or are you planning on jumping?"

Her hand flew to her mouth. "You startled me."

"Now imagine my surprise." Lord Everett leaned a shoulder against the window frame. He was wearing buff-colored trousers, a dark blue coat that hugged his broad shoulders, a snowy white shirt and elegantly tied cravat.

"I heard you come in and I panicked. I was—"

"Plotting your next crime?"

"I am *not* a criminal." Her emphasis threw her off balance. She grappled for the rail, but he'd already grasped her arm to steady her.

"I think I believe that," he said, not releasing her as he stepped over the windowsill and hunkered down beside her. Drawing up his knees, he set the soles of his boots on the bottom rung of the rail.

307

His hand slid away from her, and he looked out at the park stretching into darkness. Only the corner of the stables was visible, and further away the glimmer of the lake. "Though I'm not quite certain why," he added. "Perhaps it was the manner in which you handled my sister and her friends yesterday."

"A criminal wouldn't have done that?"

The corner of his mouth ticked up. "Not being acquainted with any criminals, I cannot say for certain."

He was acquainted with Sir Richard. But did he know he was a criminal? It had to be the reason she was here. Why else would the river have transported her back two hundred years to this exact time and place? To him?

"Are you sure you don't know any criminals?" she prodded.

His brow lowered. "Miss Cowdrey, what are you doing in my bedchamber?"

"I'm not from Charleston, South Carolina," she said, turning her face to look at him but mostly to catch his scent better. He smelled *so good*, not like pine-fresh soap or minty aftershave but like a real live man—like the way books smelled good, like real things you could touch and hold. In the delirium of kissing him she'd noticed it, and she'd been dying to smell him again. "I live in Michigan," she continued, "and the only family I have is a mother who barely remembers I exist. But that's the single lie I've told you. Aside from saying I had a horse in the stable, which I don't. But that's all. I swear it."

He nodded slowly.

"I need to say something to you," she said. "Tell you something." The sizzling was all mixed up with a strange, fleeting hope.

"Another confession?"

"No. Actually, I need to ask you a question."

He waited in silence.

"Did you draw the comic book?"

He didn't look at her like she was a lunatic. But he didn't speak right away either.

"Comic book," he finally said. "Another study on maritime trade that hasn't yet occurred, but in comedic style?"

"No. A thin book depicting in sketches moments from your life. Your christening. A walk as a young boy along a garden path with a lady I think must have been your mother. Some sports events at college and afterward maybe. That curricle race where you got your nickname."

"I see." He faced the park again. "Why would I have created such a book, do you think?"

"I don't know. But I'm sure you did."

"But I did not. Have you found it in my belongings here?"

"No. I read it before I came to England." There was no going back. She might end up in Bethlehem hospital for the insane, but she didn't think this man would be the one to send her there. "I found it in the future, in the place I came from before I showed up in that lake and you rescued me. So even if you haven't drawn it yet, you might still. In fact, I'm pretty sure you do."

He lifted his brows.

"I've seen your drawings," she said.

Only the briefest pause betrayed him. "My drawings?"

"Your portfolio." She gestured inside the room. "They're supposed to be secret, aren't they?"

"Not at all." He waved a hand in denial. "I store that portfolio in my dressing room in my luggage beneath my shirts and cravats because it is happiest there."

She tilted her head and gave him the you're-full-of-hilarity look Cyndi always used.

He seemed to be resisting a smile. "Privacy is not, I presume, at a premium in America?"

"Not so much anymore. You're amazingly talented. Why do you hide it?"

"It's a distraction," he said loosely. "A pastime. Nothing of note."

"Nothing of note? Baloney! They're fantastic. The series of the fox is breathtaking. Touching. Playful and tender. The sleeping fox was my favorite, and then to be shocked with the last, the dead fox ... Tears sprang to my eyes."

She stood and squeezed past him to climb back into the room. She went to the dressing chamber and dug out the portfolio again. "Just look."

"I've seen them." His voice sounded tight. He was leaning against the dressing chamber doorframe, his arms crossed.

She opened to the final image of the fox. "You haven't done another series of studies like this, have you? If you have, I'd really like to see it."

He didn't respond.

"Why the fox?" she asked.

He didn't want to answer her; his rigid stance made that clear. His arms tightened across his chest.

"I won't tell anyone," she said quietly.

"When I was twenty years old, shortly after the carriage accident, I made a particularly fine showing at the Duke of Beaufort's Hunt. That fox's tail and paws were my prize."

"But you didn't see it as a prize, did you? The study is ultimately tragic. Did you intend it as—"

"My penance." He loosened his arms, came toward her, and took the portfolio from her hands to set aside. "Now, Miss Cowdrey, enough of that." His voice was smooth again. "There are more interesting studies to be pursued in my bedchamber at this time of night."

"I'm sure there are. But I'm not finished talking about your drawings."

"But I am." He grasped her arms gently and moved close.

She looked up. "You put great care and attention into them."

"Yet my attention seems to have strayed." His thighs brushed hers. His scent of subtle cologne and gorgeous man was just too unbelievably good.

"Why are you trying to change the subject?" she said, breathing like she'd just run three miles.

He bent his head and spoke at her cheek. "I prefer action to words."

"It seems you prefer images to words, in fact."

His arms dropped to his sides. "You are tenacious."

"And you are avoiding an uncomfortable subject. Obviously. Why are you hiding your talent in a box?" It must have something to do with the comic book. *She had to know.*

For a moment he said nothing. "I think you should leave."

"I hadn't planned on staying. But you've trapped me against this wall, so unless you expect me to dematerialize right now I'm not going anywhere."

"Dematerialize." His voice smiled. His fingertips beneath her chin tilted her face up and his mouth hovered above hers. He set his hands on the wall to either side of her head. "You do say the damnedest things."

He was all around her, his thighs gently pushing her to the wall, his incredibly hard, muscular chest that she'd touched in the garden so close. She could touch him again if she wanted to. He was inviting her to. And she wanted to a lot.

*No rules.*

"I'd like to dematerialize with you right now," she said, because it definitely felt like living.

"Capital idea," he murmured. He tilted his head so his lips slanted above hers. The briefest brush of his mouth sent a jolt of heat straight through her. He did it again and she heard her own breaths go ragged. He was teasing her. Making her want him more. *Trying to distract her.*

It was working.

She forced out words. "But only if you tell me why you keep your drawings a secret."

He stilled.

"It's time for you to leave, Miss Cowdrey." He backed away from her. Turning his gaze aside, he gestured toward the door.

Angela sagged. Then she straightened, sucked in her gut, and left.

Lord Everett was not going to help her solve the mystery of her presence in the early nineteenth century. He was obviously the key to it. But she couldn't force him to believe her. She was on her own now. Just as she'd always been.

# CHAPTER FIVE

Trent couldn't avoid it any longer. He must finally acquaint himself with Miss Howell. After a struggle with Henry that morning, the earl had exercised his frustrated anger by railing at Trent for playing least-in-sight whenever Sir Richard and his daughter were about. Trent couldn't admit that rather than actively trying to avoid the Howells he'd been spending his time trying to find one astoundingly brazen and intoxicatingly lovely American among the dozens of houseguests across the vast estate.

But he knew his duty. It was time to fulfill it. His father's mistake and Sir Richard's villainy had left him no choice.

A group of ladies were playing the piano and singing in the drawing room. Not one person in society expected him to enjoy such sedate entertainment, and he couldn't very well go searching for Miss Cowdrey in Lady Sophronia's apartments. He had no excuse not to seek out Sir Richard's daughter.

He found her with her father on the terrace overlooking the gardens. It was lit with lanterns and might have been a fine place for a flirtatious assignation with a lady, except that the lady he wished to flirt with was nowhere to be seen and this one was being forced upon him.

"Sir." He bowed to Howell.

"My lord," Sir Richard said with narrowed eyes. "I'm pleased you've finally found time to greet your father's old friend. This is my Jane. Jane, say hello to Lord Everett."

She had a high brow and eyes that protruded a bit—but takingly, in a style common to the old Dutch painters—complemented by a straight nose and pale skin. The combined effect was not unpleasant. Then she opened her mouth.

"Hello, Lord Everett." Squeaky and breathless at once. He nearly cringed.

He must simply become accustomed to it.

"I see you are wearing your blue coat tonight," she said, the squeak pronounced on certain vowels, but now with an affected lisp. "I like the blue one, though your gray coat is quite nice too."

"Are you interested in fashion, Miss Howell?" *Oh, God.*

"Oh yes, my lord. It is my entire life," she said earnestly. "Why, just look at this flounce." She pointed at her hem. "It's called a Paris Champignon and it's ever so popular abroad this year. I had one sewn onto this gown because Cissy Pendleton sewed one onto her pale green muslin gown and I said to myself, 'Jane Howell, if Cissy Pendleton can sew a Paris Champignon onto pale green muslin then you can sew it onto pale yellow silk.' What do you think, my lord?"

Trent's hands were ice cold. "It suits you well, Miss Howell."

"Oh, I *did* hope you would think so." Her protruding eyes bulged a bit more. "But mostly I hoped you would wear your blue coat tonight, or your brown coat, actually, because either *would* look well with this gown, truly. I was awake almost all night worrying over it, imagining you might wear the gray coat and then I should have worn something entirely different tonight. But you have worn the blue coat after all, and the blue coat is superior to the brown coat, so I am vastly happy. Papa, doesn't Lord Everett's coat look well beside my gown?"

Sir Richard patted his daughter's hand. "Of course, dear. Now I'll leave you two young ones to chat while I find Lord Ware and discuss matters of business." He slanted Trent another narrow look. Trent understood the threat. He bowed. Sir Richard nodded and walked away.

"What I really hoped to ask you, my lord," Miss Howell said, "is whether you prefer silk to muslin? Muslin is all the rage in France this year, but I think it horridly common already, don't you? Papa says if a fabric costs less, then it is more eco-eco- ... not as expensive. But I think if I wear a gown that costs less to have made up, then if the lady sitting beside me at a tea table, for instance, has a gown of more expensive fabric, then I will find myself so agitated that I won't be able to eat a bite, even if my gown of muslin is of finer quality than her gown of silk, which a lot of muslin is these days, of course, much finer than silk. Wouldn't you feel the same, my lord?"

Trent's mouth opened and closed then opened again. Her protruding eyes were fraught.

He replied—he didn't know what—and she seemed pleased with his response. But as despair burrowed into him, all he could think was that there would be no more garden kisses or moonlit windowsill conversations with a lovely, brazen American. He would be the dependable son, fulfilling expectations, as always. He would save his family's honor.

**F**rom the edge of the lawn below the terrace, Angela watched Lord Everett approach Sir Richard Howell and his daughter in the lantern light, the brief exchange between the three, and then Sir Richard's departure. The viscount chuckled at something Miss Howell said and she laid a hand on his arm, and Angela felt like someone was stabbing her ribcage.

Which was ridiculous.

She didn't own Trenton Ascot. She barely knew him. Just because he'd called to her in the future and she'd nearly drowned coming to him didn't mean anything.

No. That was a crock. A total lie she had to tell herself so she wouldn't feel insane jealously every time he spoke with another woman. Yesterday she'd wanted to poke out witty Rosanne Lacy's eyes just because of the smile he'd given her when they'd passed on the lawn.

*Of course* it meant something that he was her partner in this mystery. She just didn't know what yet. It could mean he was somehow wrapped up in Sir Richard's dirty dealings with Arnaud Chappelle, and this little journey to the past was her ticket to scholarly fame. Or it could mean that the viscount was in trouble with Sir Richard and she, with answers from the future, was the only person who could help him. Or it could mean that this was her fairy godmother's way of providing her with a really hot fantasy before she had to run home from the ball at midnight. Or it could mean that she and Trenton Ascot were soul mates across time and meant to be together forever. Or it could mean that she was having an elaborate time-traveling schizophrenic episode.

The problem was that Miss Jane Howell was not part of any of the scenarios Angela had come up with to explain her presence in the past.

She needed to speak with Sir Richard. What exactly she would ask him still gave her trouble. She couldn't reveal the future, and she didn't think he'd tell her any truths about his criminal past if she asked. But she should start by getting an introduction to him.

Tearing her attention away from the disturbing tableau of lady and lord enjoying each other's company in the romantic glow of lanterns, Angela walked around the outside of the house in the dark. Sir Richard would either be in the drawing room or on his way to bed. Or he could be in the stables. The men seemed to spend a lot of time there. Apparently one of them had brought a really nice carriage and they were all admiring it.

*Men.*

On the path to the outbuildings she encountered young Henry Ascot.

"Good evening, ma'am."

"Hello, Mr. Ascot. Where are you headed at this time of night?" Not off to shut out the world with his MP3 player, thank God.

He was already taller than her and teen-lanky, but he'd gotten his father's looks—uncompromisingly square brow, dark hair, and brown eyes. Now those eyes glared.

"Have you come from my sister?" he said.

"No. Should I have?"

"I thought you and she were bows."

"I like her and I think she likes me. But I'm pretty much past the age to run around like she and her friends do." She wasn't interested in chasing around all the eligible bachelors at the estate. Only one.

He grunted and crossed his arms exactly like his older brother did when he was uncomfortable.

"Henry—" she said. "May I call you Henry?"

He frowned. "Why?"

"Because I'd like to give you some advice and I think we should be friends before I do that."

He looked wary. "What sort of advice?"

"The sort that's about women. Girls, actually."

His brow got stormy. "I don't care a jot about girls."

315

"Hmm. Well if that's true, you're wasting a hell of a lot of time following your sister's friends all over the place playing pranks. Aren't you?"

A glimmer showed in his glower. She'd bet he'd never heard a lady say "hell." Angela used the same tactics on her students. She learned colloquialisms common to college-aged kids and sprang them on them when they thought she was being esoteric. It worked every time to get their attention. Now it was working on Henry. He was listening.

"You know," she said casually, "if I were a younger lady, I think I'd like to be admired by a good-looking young man, even if he was my friend's brother."

He dug a toe into the pebbled path and screwed up his face.

"I mean, don't get me wrong," she said, "I'd be incredibly irritated if he kept playing pranks on me and my friends. But if he did just the opposite, I might start to think he was all right. Maybe even more than all right." She shrugged and stepped away. "But if you'd rather torment the girl you like ..."

"Who said I like anybody?"

She halted. "Henry, it's better to please than displease. Haven't you ever heard the saying 'You can catch more bees with honey'?"

His frown didn't let up.

"If you want the girls' attention," she said, "why don't you give them something they like rather than dislike?"

His brow cleared. He understood. Then he frowned again. "What do girls like?"

Chiseled jaws. Smoky eyes. Deep kisses in dappled sunlight. Sitting in the dark on a window ledge touching shoulders. Being pressed up against a dressing room wall.

"Flowers," she said. "Jewelry. Pretty gowns."

Henry scowled.

"And kittens," she added on an inspiration.

He perked up. "S'truth?"

"Yes. Definitely." Every single woman graduate student she knew had cats. Even Cyndi had a cat. Angela was the only unattached woman in Ann Arbor who didn't have a cat, and that was because her apartment building didn't allow pets. "You know what? Let's go find some." She moved toward the stables. "There's always a litter of new kittens in a stable, and the duke's stables are so big there may be more than one."

She didn't bother trying the door closest to the house; that, apparently, was where the fancy carriage was. She headed toward the far end, and Henry followed. He caught up with her at the door and tugged it open, then stepped back to allow her to enter before him.

A little bit of pleasure tingled in her chest. Even at fourteen—surly and grouchy—he was a gentleman. She loved this era. No wonder she studied it. She'd lied to Cyndi a little. She'd been looking for honor and decency in the nineteenth century for years. Funny she should finally find it in an adolescent boy.

They discovered kittens, a litter of five soft little wonders of blotched brown and black fur that looked just about old enough to be weaned. In the corner of the empty stall, they tumbled over each other in eagerness to reach Henry's outstretched fingers.

Angela glanced at the boy beside her. He didn't look much like his older brother, but his smile was just as genuine.

He stood straight. "I beg your pardon for being such a noddy back there, Miss Cowdrey."

"Thank you, Henry. I hope these little critters suit your purpose."

"May I escort you up to the house?"

She smiled. "I'd like that."

"Should I wait 'til the morning to bring her down here?" he asked as they walked toward the mansion that sparkled with candlelight from behind dozens of windows. "*Them*, that is."

"That sounds like a good plan. Best to treat her—*them* like ladies."

Ahead on the path, the silhouette of a man against the backdrop of the glowing mansion became the silhouette of Trenton Ascot. Angela tried to ignore the achy sizzle of infatuation inside her. She hadn't been this far gone in years, not since college, and never quite so quickly and acutely with anyone. It felt pathetically unintellectual and devastatingly impractical and *good.* So good. It felt like living.

"Good evening, Miss Cowdrey." He approached. He moved his athlete's body with confident grace, beautiful and utterly masculine. "Henry, I should reprimand you for stealing a march on me with the lady I've been searching out all day. But instead I will congratulate you for winning her company. Well done."

Henry gave his brother a wide grin. "We've been to the stables and are just on our way up to the house."

"The stables?" His attention cut to her. "To look in on your horse again, Miss Cowdrey?" He smiled. Not ironically. *Intimately.*

"'Course not, Trent," his brother said. "We were looking for kittens."

The viscount nodded. "Naturally."

"Come on then." Henry started up the path again. "I'm fagged to death. It's bed for me."

"Henry, I should like to steal this lady back from you," he said in his melty voice. "In fact, I am going to now."

"Suit yourself. Good night, Miss Cowdrey. And thanks!" He headed toward the house.

"Were you planning on asking me if I wished to be stolen back?" Angela tried to sound breezy, but she couldn't stop staring at his face. It seemed so familiar. That was just because of the comic book, of course. But he felt so real to her. So ... *right.*

"No." He stared after his brother for a moment. Then he came to her. He halted too close according to the rules of his society. "Kittens?"

She loved his smoky-slate eyes. She wanted to grab his face with her hands and pull him in to kiss her. She was dying for him to kiss her again.

"I thought he could use some alternatives to mud and marbles."

"And my scapegrace brother took to this idea?"

"He loved it."

His brow lifted.

"I can be very persuasive," she said. "It's my profession, you know: convincing people of my point of view through reasoned argument based on sound evidence." She shrugged. His gaze slipped to her shoulders, then along her arms. Angela got all sorts of hot and needy inside.

Maybe he would kiss her now. If he didn't make it happen, she would.

*No rules.*

Whatever the reason Father Time had for thrusting her back into the past, Angela knew one thing: before she left, she wanted to break every rule she could. And she wanted to break them all with Trenton Ascot.

# CHAPTER SIX

**T**rent allowed his gaze to trace the curve of her bodice hugging her breasts. "New gown, Miss Cowdrey?" He had never before in his entire life asked a woman about her clothing. After Miss Howell's discourse earlier, he thought he never would.

But this woman made him do and say things he'd never imagined, like stand on a path in the dark and stare at a woman's perfect breasts bound in layers of fabric and wish those layers to Hades.

"Lady Sophronia found it for me," she replied, fingering the sleeve. "It doesn't have all those buttons up the back. Easier to put on and take off by myself. Still no maid, you know?" She offered a little grin. "And at the house there aren't usually helpful gentlemen standing around when I need to dress."

"I am relieved to hear that."

"You are?"

He nodded, bemused, dazed, intoxicated. She spoke with the freedom of a girl yet swayed her hips with the allure of a woman. She had the most perfect teeth he'd ever seen and toenails painted the color of the summer sky. With the merest flick of her lashes and the soft, direct light in her eyes she made him dizzy. "Yes." She made him want to do things he shouldn't do. "Would you care to take a stroll through the garden?"

"Now? It's nearly midnight."

This was a mistake. "Now."

"Sure," she said with slight hesitation, but her eyes remained bright. She did not wait for him to extend his arm but started off along the path that led back to the formal garden. He went after her, but he did not touch her. That would be truly foolish.

319

*Katharine Ashe*

"Are you enjoying the party, Miss Cowdrey?" he asked because he wished to hear her voice, a simple pleasure that he had been denied all day.

She slanted him a skeptical glance, then her attention slid to his mouth. She blinked rapidly twice. "I don't really know how to answer that."

"Honestly, perhaps."

Her brow furrowed beneath a loose strand of hair as dark and silky as Russian sable. Trent wanted to reach up and brush it aside and feel her soft skin again. He was so thoroughly drawn to her. When she was not in sight, he could not cease thinking about her. When she was near, he could not cease staring.

"I'm a little perplexed, actually," she said. "I could swear that the Duke of Wessex's wife was named Cleopatra. I love that name, so when I read something about him last year in a book on the parliamentary leaders of George IV's reign, I remembered the duchess."

"Cleopatra is the name of the elder sister of Miss Helen Grey, the duke's betrothed." And there was no George IV ... yet.

"No. I'm pretty sure it's his wife's name." She halted. "Maybe he doesn't marry Miss Grey this week. Maybe he marries her sister instead."

"Cleopatra Barrows is a widow."

"So? Dukes can marry widows."

"Yes. But they don't typically switch one sister for another the week of their weddings."

"Maybe not typically. But not never. After all, women from the twenty-first century don't typically time travel two centuries into the past. At least I don't think they do." A crease formed at the bridge of her nose. "I shouldn't be saying things like this."

"Things about time travel?"

"Things about history that hasn't yet happened. I don't want anything I say to affect events to come. As an historian, that would be astoundingly irresponsible."

"You can trust me not to repeat your revelations."

"Because you think I'm making them up." She spoke without distress.

The path had come to a divide. In one direction lay the terrace and the house and the people who would make it impossible for him to be with her alone, to speak with her privately, to watch her move and think and breathe. In the other direction the hill descended toward the lake.

He should not.

He must not.

He gestured toward the dark path to the lake. "Shall we?"

The anxiety slipped from her face. "To the scene of the crime?" She grinned. "As it were."

"I recall you insisting that you are not a criminal."

"I'm not." She bent her head and seemed to concentrate on her footsteps as she walked beside him along the gently sloping path. "I saw you on the terrace tonight with Sir Richard Howell's daughter. You two seemed ..." She paused. "On good terms."

"As it were?"

Her gaze jerked up, her face serious. "Do you know her well?"

He did not want her to mistake his interest in Miss Howell, but he could not tell her the truth. He shook his head. "No."

She looked away quickly.

The moon was a slim crescent of silver, the lake before them glittering beneath brilliant stars. All was quiet, only the quick high-and-low song of a late nightingale in a nearby tree, an owl's *hoo-oo-oo-ooo* at a distance in the park, and their slow footsteps on the path. Trent breathed in the scents of summer, and the peace. This was what he wanted, every day, every night—not what his father wished of him. For once he wanted to be who he really was.

"I haven't told you something important about that comic book," she said into the warm night.

"Withholding information is a sure sign of subterfuge, Miss Cowdrey."

She turned her gaze up to him again. "You don't believe I'm involved in subterfuge." Her words were certain.

"I don't." He didn't. He never really had. If that made him as much of a fool as his father had been with Sir Richard, then it was only what he deserved for working so hard for so many years to be the sort of man the earl expected him to be.

"On the last page of the comic book," she said, "you drew yourself in a close-up. You're looking out from the page."

"Am I?"

"I know you think I'm inventing this."

321

"Go on, Miss Cowdrey."

"Back home, in the future before I came here, I was looking at that drawing of you, and—" She halted on the path and turned fully to him. "—and you winked."

"I had also drawn myself winking?"

"No. *That* picture winked, like it was animated. Alive. Like you knew I was looking at you at that moment. I know this must sound completely insane."

"Perhaps because it is."

"But that isn't the— the *thing*—" She closed her eyes. "Oh good lord, Angela, just tell him."

Trent's heart was beating uncomfortably hard. "Tell him what?"

She opened her lovely intelligent eyes. "The caption. The captions were in your handwriting, the same as in the drawings in your portfolio that I saw in your room."

"You've already said you believe that I drew this book. The similarity of penmanship would follow, would it not?"

"Yes. But it's not that. It's ... The caption on that last drawing, the one that winked—" Her breasts rose on a tight breath. "—it said *'Angela, Come Back.'*"

Her cheeks had grown dark beneath the starlight. She lifted her palms to them. "I know. It's totally insane."

He nodded. *Totally insane.* As insane as how much he wanted her, a strange woman he had pulled out of a lake, who seemed to have no family and no purpose to be at this house. Except his family. She had helped Charlotte and her friends. And now Henry.

"I don't draw human subjects," he could only think to say.

"But can you?"

He should lie. He should deny it. He should return to the house and surround himself with people so that this temptation would end. "Yes. I can." He wanted to draw her—her eyes that illuminated a lovely face and her lush lips that he could feel in his dreams and her lithe body he ached to touch.

"It's awfully warm for so late at night in England, don't you think?" she said abruptly, breaking the silence. She set off along the path again. They were nearly at the lake. He didn't respond. She was speaking of *the weather.* She was making an attempt to return to normalcy, perhaps to pretend she had not spoken of impossibilities.

She went to the edge of the water, bordered in stone here as it was on the far end and glittering black beneath the stars. Trent could not follow her. He couldn't think when she was near. He didn't want to. But she was offering him a game now, a game of normalcy, and he must play it with her.

"I haven't taken a shower in days," she said and looked over her shoulder at him. "Want to swim?"

He crossed his arms. "And ruin your new gown?"

"I'll take it off." Her eyes were luminescent. She was staring at his arms across his chest. "I'll take it all off," she said. "If you will."

His throat closed. *Not normalcy*, apparently.

"We could be discovered," he barely managed.

"Nobody's anywhere near. If they were, you wouldn't have brought me out here. You're too responsible and honorable."

He wasn't being honorable now. He was being a thorough rogue. He hadn't brought her out here to be responsible. He'd brought her out here to kiss her again.

"Miss Cowdrey, this would be a good moment to save yourself from my baser instincts."

"If your baser instincts are what I think they are, Lord Everett, I like them. And I don't want to play by the rules. I've been playing by rules my entire life, trying to make it work no matter where I was, no matter how hard it was, no matter how likely I was to have it all pulled out from under me at a moment's notice. But *this* isn't my life." She spread her hands out toward the house in the distance. "This is another life altogether—another time and world. So I'm going to break every rule I can get away with. Starting now." She reached around behind her and began unfastening her gown. An impish smile creased her lips. "Want to come?"

Yes. No. And no.

"*Angela*."

The harshness of his voice halted her. The bodice of her gown gaped over her breasts barely confined in the corset. "Trenton?"

"What if—" He couldn't say it aloud. He'd sound like a lunatic. "What if—" He dragged a hand through his hair.

"What?"

"What if when you go back into that water you disappear into the future?"

323

She stared at him for a long, silent moment, the music of crickets all around them.

"You believe me," she whispered.

"I don't know if I believe you."

"You believe me."

"I ..." *Dear God.* "I think I believe you. It makes me a madman, but I think I do."

Without a word, she removed slippers, stockings, petticoat, and corset. Then slowly she drew the chemise up her body, sliding it over her skin that glowed pale in the starlight, revealing graceful, slender legs, softly curved hips and waist, and breasts more perfect than he had even imagined. She tugged the chemise off entirely and let it dangle from her fingers for a moment before dropping it. A tiny scrap of white lace hugged her hips and dipped between her thighs. Like a Siren she stepped out of it with silken ease and tossed it away with her toe.

She reached up and pulled the pins out of her hair. It fell about her shoulders in a satiny, tangled mass he ached to run his fingers through.

"Well," she said, "I'm in." She pivoted and he glimpsed a flash of black markings across her shoulder as she dove.

He held his breath. The water didn't move. He breathed in hard, then again. Panic gathered in him.

He lurched forward.

She broke the surface. "Oh, wow! This is wonderful." She spread her arms and floated onto her back, her breasts poking above the dark water. "I've always wanted to skinny-dip. It feels fantastic."

"Skinny-dip?" he managed hoarsely.

"Take a dip wearing only one's skin." She turned onto her front and took a few long strokes toward the center of the lake, her arms white against the night, the water gleaming on her skin. From a distance, the markings on her shoulder rippled like a bird's wings. "You should try it, my lord."

She liked calling him that. It seemed to amuse her, as though she were playing a game. An innocent game.

"You did not disappear," he said, his breathing ragged.

"I wasn't ready to go."

"Is it in your control? Going and coming?"

She shook her head. She stroked backward. "Now come on." She beckoned with her hand. "If I can do this, you can too. I know you want to."

"Do you?"

"Stop stalling."

Paddling in place, her chin beneath the water, she watched him as he removed his boots, coat, waistcoat, and cravat. He pulled his shirt from his trousers and she stared unabashedly. He'd never imagined that shameless honesty could be so erotic. By the time he'd discarded his trousers his arousal was evident. He dropped his drawers and came to the edge of the bank.

"Lord Everett," she said in a sultry voice, "you are one fine specimen of a man."

"I am to understand that as a compliment, I gather?"

"Oh yeah."

He dove. The water was cool and tasted of sky and earth. He surfaced, shook his head, and swept droplets from his eyes.

She gave him a bright smile. "Want to race?" She pointed in the direction of the opposite bank.

He allowed himself a grin. "I will win."

"What happened to being honorable and gentlemanly?"

He lifted a brow.

She laughed. "I'll race you anyway. Ready? Set. Go!" She started for the far bank.

He caught up with her easily and stretched out his hand to touch her shoulder. She darted forward. For a moment he stared at the lithe line of her back and soft mounds of her behind, then he set off after her again.

He reached her within yards of the bank and grabbed her ankle.

"No!" She came up sputtering and laughing, dashing hair from her face. "That's cheating!"

He released her. "You did not specify the terms of the race."

"Cheating is always against the rules."

"I thought you were enthusiastic about breaking the rules." He moved beside her and brushed strands of hair from her shoulder. She turned her head to watch him.

"What is it?" He stroked his fingertips over the image of the bird, the black lines impressionistic rather than realistic, but evocative nevertheless.

325

"It's a tattoo." She was breathing hard, from her swim or perhaps his touch. "Body art, we call it in my era."

"The twenty-first century."

"It's a golden eagle." Her gaze shadowed as she met his. Her shoulders were smooth and gleaming. He stroked his fingertips along the graceful curve, and her lips parted as her eyelids fluttered down. She was perfect—natural, simple loveliness without need of adornment. Perfect.

He traced the lines of the eagle with the barest caress.

"Have you ever drawn one?" She seemed to hum the words, low and sultry in her throat.

"No."

"Why not?"

"I have never seen one with my own eyes."

"Well, now you have. Sort of." She stretched her arm out and stroked away, moving out into the lake again, slowly now. He wanted to follow her, to take her into his arms and touch her again. Again and again.

He swam the few strokes toward the bank and leaned back against the stone that still held the sun's warmth. His heartbeats were fast, the stars overhead shimmering.

She made an arc of the lake then turned again toward him. Her strokes were even, strong and clean, as though she swam often, as though she was in fact the strong swimmer she claimed to be. Perhaps she was. He knew nothing of her, nothing at all, only that this was the best night of his life.

When she neared, she did not slow. She came right to him, wrapped her hands around his shoulders, and slipped her body against his in the deep water. Her mouth found his.

She was warm and soft—the pressure of her breasts on his chest, her thighs brushing his. He took her waist in his hands and held her tight against him, skin to skin, delving into her eager mouth, following her tongue into hers. She moaned and pressed closer and he slid his hand up and cupped a perfect breast, as he'd wanted to do since the moment she had undressed in that boathouse.

She was soft and wanting and willing in his hands, and so beautiful, her shape and fullness. Sliding his thumb between them, he stroked the peak. Oh, *God*. It wasn't enough. She clung to him and he took both of her breasts in his hands and caressed as she consumed his mouth. Then she spread her thighs and stroked her sex against his.

"*Oh*," she gasped. "Trent." Her mouth sought his neck, and he held her to him and had no idea what to do.

"Angela, you are beautiful," he whispered, because he had much more to say, none of it manly or even particularly cogent.

She brought her lips to his again and he drank from her, hungry for her mouth and her hands on his skin.

"What now?" He could not be ashamed that his voice was unstable.

"I don't know," she said against his lips. "I've never done anything like this before."

"Never?"

"Not even close."

"At the risk of offending you unpardonably—"

"You like that phrase." She nipped at his jaw.

"What is your age, Angela?"

"Twenty-seven. That is, seven-and-twenty."

*Seven-and-twenty.* A widow, perhaps, claiming to be a maiden? She usually showed none of the confident brass of a Bird of Paradise. But this temptress in his arms was no shy spinster.

She twined her fingers into his hair. "And, yes, I'm a virgin."

He couldn't breathe. "You are telling me this only now, after you have rubbed your naked body against mine?"

"I didn't plan this. I'm not a tease."

"I am not entirely believing you." He was going to *die*.

"I understand. And I agree; sex isn't a good idea, for several reasons. But maybe I can make up for it in another way." Her warm hand wrapped around his erection. She pressed her mouth to his ear and flicked her tongue inside it. "But first you'll have to get this—" She squeezed gently. "—out of the water." Another tongue caress, this time slow. "So I can breathe."

He grabbed her shoulders, dragged her off him and looked into her eyes in disbelief. She smiled and gave a quick nod.

He leaped out of the water like it was on fire.

His buttocks were barely on the ledge when she moved between his knees, took his cock in her hand and, looking up at him through lashes glittering with starlight, closed her lips around the head.

She took him in deep.

Her mouth was soft and wet and hot and capable. She used her tongue and her full lips, then her hands too, and Trent dropped his head back and stared blearily at the stars as she worked him.

"I've never done this to such a handsome man." She licked the length of him from base to tip, then the head, and he shuddered. "Or to a man with such a big—"

"*Don't* tell me," he groaned. "I don't want to hear about anyone else."

"Regency-era double standards." She stroked. "You're happy for me to do this, but you don't want me to have ever learned how."

"No."

"As a man in this world, you can be as sexually adventuresome as you wish." Her lips caressed confidently, then her tongue. "But I'm supposed to be a virgin 'til the day I die unless I marry."

"No." He didn't care about that. Not anymore.

"You want to be the ones who set the rules."

"No." He wanted to be the only one. *Her* only one.

The surging rush came swiftly, suddenly. She was sucking on him when he came. A cry of pleasure broke from her in unison with his moan. He swung his head up and saw her hand under the water between her legs.

In a fluid movement of satisfaction, she released him and sank back in the water, her eyes closed, lips parted, her lovely face lifted to the night. Trent stared and couldn't stare enough. He wanted her. Even now he wanted her. More and more.

He fell back and covered his face with his hands.

"That," she said languorously, "I enjoyed."

He could speak no rational words. No man could be this fortunate.

But he wasn't fortunate, in fact. She would leave, inevitably. Unless he could make her stay.

*No.* He could not wish that. Brazen, scandalously sexual, and unwisely adventuresome she might be, but he would never ask her to be his mistress. He would not be that sort of husband. Concerning some matters, at least, his father had taught him well.

She glided through the water to the bank two yards away and rested her arms on the stone and her chin on her hands. Now, at this moment, he could slip into the water with her, take her into his arms, and make her his. Then he would be honor-bound to wed her. Then there would be no saving his father and his family.

*Madness.* He closed his eyes.

"Trent?"

"Angel?"

She was silent. He turned his head to see her smiling softly.

"Yes?" he prodded.

Her smile slipped away. "I need you to know, I'm not a prostitute. I haven't even had that many physical encounters with men. I know that in this era a woman who does what I just did— even a lot less than that—is considered whorish. But in my era it's pretty common."

"I think I want to live in your era."

She laughed. Then her smile turned wistful, which was insane and adorable and breathtaking. He looked up at the heavens and laid his palm over his face again.

"Please don't regret this," she said.

"I am far from regretting this," he said.

A gentle splash mingled with cricket song. The nightingale with insomnia had finally gone to bed. He would return tomorrow evening and look for it. He didn't yet have a nightingale for his catalogue.

*The Flora and Fauna of Great Britain,* he would title it. He would take it to the publisher he'd long since researched and see it reproduced for naturalists everywhere. In his dreams.

He drew a deep breath and sat up. Halfway across the lake already, she was headed toward the opposite shore.

He climbed to his feet. "Where are you going?"

"To find Sir Richard and talk with him," she called over her shoulder.

*What?* "At this time of night?"

"He's probably in the stables. All the men are. I'm surprised you weren't tonight."

He wasn't because he'd been busy being interviewed by his future bride about his wardrobe. His gut was sick.

"You mustn't speak with him."

"I have to." She was nearly to the far bank. "It's the only way."

"The only way for—*Blast.*" He dove into the water and cut it with quick strokes. By the time he reached the other side, she had already donned her undergarment and was fastening the stays about her ribs. He grabbed up his clothing. "The only way for what?"

"The only way to find out why I'm here." She avoided looking at him. "I told you, back home I was researching him. I'm sure I'm here because of him." She'd used her petticoat as a drying cloth and now donned the gown without it, fastening it swiftly.

Trent tugged his drawers on. *Blast it,* everything was wet and sticking. "You cannot speak with him." He struggled with the linen.

"Why not?"

Because Sir Richard was reprehensible and Trent was going to marry his daughter. He didn't know which information he wanted to protect her from the most. "You expect he will have answers for you? That he will believe your story?"

"I won't tell him." She grabbed her slippers and stockings from the ground and started up the path barefoot. "I'll just ask a few questions and see where that gets me."

His shirt clung to his damp skin impossibly; he couldn't tuck it into his trousers. *Damn it.* "Angela!"

She halted and finally looked at him. "Trent, I need to know."

He could tell her nothing. "Don't. I pray you."

She screwed up her brow. Then she shook her head and continued up the path.

*Blasted* obstinate, brazen, strong-willed female.

Lovely, forthright, honest, tempting female. Tempting beyond endurance. Her gown caressed her soft behind as she walked with a graceful confidence like no lady he'd ever seen. Oh, God. He wanted her.

Half-dressed, his skin drying in the warm night air, he watched her disappear up the rise into darkness. When she was gone, a patch of white drew his attention to the ground. Her petticoat.

She left garments behind without concern, like cotton grass that released its white seed down to be carried away on the breeze. Like she'd just left him behind to go find Sir Richard Howell. With her face flushed and eyes hazy. Dressed like she'd just been rolled in the hay.

Trousers, shirt, waistcoat, and coat barely on, boots in hand, Trent bolted toward the house.

# CHAPTER SEVEN

She hadn't been to the stables. The handful of gentlemen that greeted Trent when he burst through the door were so far gone they didn't even notice his state of undress. But at the house anyone still awake would notice. He slipped in through the servants' entrance and went to his father's chamber.

The earl's face was drawn. "What in God's name happened to you?"

"I had a bathe in the lake. Did you speak with Sir Richard tonight?"

"In the lake? Good God, Trenton—"

"Did you, Father?"

"I did." He removed a cigar from a case.

"And? Is it finished? Is the contract signed?"

"Not yet."

Trent's lungs began to function again.

His father took up a candle from the table, lit the cheroot, and took a pull. "Sir Richard requires that you offer for the girl formally. He wants it all done in the usual fashion so that it cannot be undone for any reason." He gestured dismissively with the cigar. "Tradesmen know nothing of honor, of course."

Trent bit down on his retort. "When you finished speaking, did he retire for the night?"

"How should I know that? I didn't follow the weasel to his lair," he snapped. Then his brow loosened. "Son—"

Trent closed the door behind him with every ounce of self-control he possessed.

He had rarely ventured belowstairs in any house since he was a boy. Wessex's servants snapped to attention.

"My lord!" the housekeeper said in surprise. "May I be of service?"

They located Sir Richard's valet. The fellow said his master had retired to bed two hours earlier. Trent made a thin excuse then and, chewing his anxiety, went to his bedchamber. He didn't put it entirely past Angela to visit Sir Richard in his private quarters. If she had, and Howell misused her, he'd kill the villain without a second thought.

After a brief, fitful sleep he arose early and lingered in the breakfast parlor overlong. Every guest in the house came through, it seemed, except Miss Angela Cowdrey. By mid-morning he was frantic. He could not go to Lady Sophronia's suite in search of her; he would not cast dishonor on her like that.

He could not dishonor the woman he'd bathed naked with in a lake. The woman who claimed she was from the future.

Oh, God. He'd actually gone insane.

But a few mornings earlier, when he'd been sitting against the base of an old willow sketching a pair of red-legged partridges in the grass nearby, he'd seen his old schoolmate Gareth Cavendish and Cleopatra Barrows strolling at a distance. With his attention supposedly on the birds but his thoughts entirely on Angela, he hadn't marked it then. But they'd been walking close and Wessex had bent his head to Mrs. Barrows for a moment that became a minute ...

No. It couldn't be. Wessex was far too responsible and honorable a fellow to dally with his betrothed's sister the very week of his wedding. Or ever.

And Trent was far too responsible and honorable a fellow to bathe naked with a maiden in a lake at midnight within sight of the altar himself.

He needed clarity, sanity—if only for a moment. Crossing the lawn in search of Angela and coming upon his friends engaged in yet another interminable cricket match, he did the unthinkable: he threw himself into the sport.

An hour later, wretchedly hot and even more out of sorts than before, he sought out the coolest, quietest place in the house, and true sanity.

High as a hang glider from her midnight escapade with Trent, Angela couldn't sleep. Instead, she paced the little bedchamber she occupied in Lady Sophronia's suite and bit her nails.

Trent wasn't telling her everything. She couldn't believe he was in league with the bad guy. But she'd been wrong about men before—tragically wrong—just like her mother, over and over again.

Finally leaving her room, she spent the morning tracking Sir Richard but never catching up with him. The house and estate were huge, and being a woman in early nineteenth-century England was incredibly inconvenient. She couldn't ask outright where he was or people would wonder why. Even though she didn't know anybody, she kept getting trapped by ladies who wanted to chat, including the duchess. Her Grace thanked her for her help with the girls after the mud incident the other day without once broaching the delicate subject of her uninvited presence in her house. Maybe Sophronia had made some kind of excuse for her.

After that nerve-wrecking interview, Charlotte and her friends dragged Angela to a bedchamber where kittens romped about.

Finally leaving the girls and kittens behind, Angela paused in a deserted corridor, leaned against the wall, and closed her eyes. She had to be honest with herself: she didn't really have the heart to find Sir Richard. An awful certainty was crawling around her head that as soon as she talked with Sir Richard, her purpose for being in the past would be fulfilled and she'd have to leave.

She wasn't ready to leave yet. She wasn't ready to leave Trenton Ascot yet.

All morning she'd figured she'd bump into him. It was like he'd vanished. Not surprising, given her previous day-after experiences. She'd thought he was different, though. Decent. Honorable. The kind of guy who wouldn't ditch her after a one-night stand.

Every time her mother had promised they'd settle down and stay in one place for a whole year—that *this* boyfriend was different—Angela hadn't believed it. Why was she kidding herself now? If anything, men of the European historical past were even less likely to treat a woman well than modern men.

But grumpy pessimism wasn't going to get her any further in 1813 than it did in 2013. She pushed away from the wall, started up the hallway, and ran smack into Viscount Everett coming around a corner.

He stepped back instantly. Her face went flaming hot.

"Hi!" she chirped like a bird, then made it worse by adding, "I mean ... hiii." Oh yeah. No wonder guys flocked to her in droves. She would bang her head against the wall now if he weren't standing in front of her looking unbelievably sexy. Concealing the gorgeous body she'd seen *and felt* close up last night were trousers, a shirt, and a waistcoat. He held his coat in his hand and his hair looked damp and dark around his neck and brow.

He bowed. "Good day, Miss Cowdrey."

"I'm pretty sure we're on a first-name basis now," she said. "Don't you think?"

The corner of his mouth tilted up in that delicious half-smile that made her want to jump him. "I daresay."

"Um ..." She refused to let this be awkward. This wasn't just some guy she'd met in a café. "What've you been doing today?" Oh, *lame.*

"Playing cricket." He gestured with his coat over his arm. "But I have retreated inside in search of—" Just above his cravat, his Adam's apple did an awkward bob. "—shade," he finished.

Angela's own throat was thick. He hadn't been about to say in search of *her.* He didn't look hopeful, or even horny. He looked ... guilty.

"Oh," she mumbled.

A really awful moment passed during which neither of them said anything and Angela's heart did a medieval Dance of Death in her chest cavity.

Then they spoke at the same moment.

"I am on my way to—"

"I was looking for—"

"—the library."

"—Sir Richard."

He frowned.

"But I'd rather see the library," she said with total honesty.

He offered her a tentative smile. "I suppose you must be familiar with libraries, given your studies."

She couldn't tell if he was teasing her or sincere. "I am," she said. "I'd love to see the library here. I visited Kingstag last summer as a tourist and ... I mean ..." How much could she say?

"Go on."

At moments, like now, he was so calm, so composed, so lordly, despite everything. Undoubtedly that's what made the moments when he was not composed or lordly especially exciting, like twelve hours ago, just about the time he'd told her she was beautiful.

She took a wobbly breath. Her heart was beating way too fast and she was way too hot for midday standing in a hallway.

"I'd like to see it," she said. "Do you know where it is?"

He gestured to the door right behind her.

She went in before him. The room was empty of people and completely spectacular. Double tiers of wall-to-wall bookcases framed a huge fireplace of white Italian marble and broad windows. A balustrade ran along a narrow gallery, giving access to the second tier of shelves by an elaborately carved wooden staircase that wound upward like a corkscrew. The floors were carpeted in thick Persian wool of rich, dark patterns, and a table with straight-backed chairs plus a few overstuffed easy chairs were arranged for perfect reading contentment. A pair of globes graced a corner of the room—one of the earth, the other of the heavens.

"Oh, wow," she sighed.

"That's what you said about skinny-dipping," he said at her shoulder in his chocolate voice.

She turned her head to look up at him. "I am a woman of many pleasures."

She'd really said it! Aloud! And he was giving her that one-sided smile.

With more confidence than she'd felt all day, she moved toward a shelf. "What brings you to this particular shady spot, my lord?" Then she saw it and knew. On a side table rested two oversized, leather-bound books she recognized immediately. They'd been on display in the British Library for months during her junior year abroad in London. She went to them and touched the gilt titles embossed into the cover reverently. "Oh, seriously, wow," she whispered, and opened the cover with great care to reveal the hand-inked title page. This was no printer's copy. This was one of only ten original editions.

"Such reverence, Miss Cowdrey?" he said from where he remained at the doorway.

"Indeedy-o, Lord Everett." She turned to the first gloriously hand-colored plate: an American cardinal perched on the branch of a white pine. "And you're not going to fool me that you weren't coming here for these." She fingered the binding of the second volume sitting beside the first. "Père Jean-Pierre Fableau's *Les Merveilleuses des Amériques* was unrivaled among the works of French naturalists in the eighteenth century. Those French Jesuits knew the New World's wilderness like nobody else, including Spanish and English explorers." She cast him a quick grin. "If you'll excuse me for saying so."

"Why should I not excuse you for speaking the truth?"

"So if you'll so easily admit to coming here to look at these books, which I've no doubt you've already done at least once, which is why they're sitting on this table," she said, turning another page, "why did you look so uncomfortable before you told me this was your destination?"

"Habit." He moved into the room and came to her side. "You are unique in knowing my shameful secret. No one else, you see, has gone searching in my drawers."

His voice was easy, teasing now, but a note of uncomfortable truth played in its depth.

She looked up at him. "Why is it shameful that you draw?"

"How do you know of the importance of Fableau's work?" he asked instead of answering.

"I took a summer seminar at the Newberry Library in Chicago on a fellowship from the National Endowment for the Humanities."

"I am not familiar with that library."

"It hasn't been founded yet." *Neither has Chicago.* "The seminar was about Old World explorers in the New World. My professor was particularly interested in the work of naturalists," she explained, because she could only tell him the truth now. "Since early naturalists didn't often have the funds to hire ships of their own, they sailed with merchants and sometimes even on naval vessels."

"Thus your interest in them."

Butterflies jumped around her stomach. "You've been paying attention."

"To every word, however fantastical." He traced the line of her lips with his dark gaze. "What else have you studied, Mistress Scholar?" he asked in a low voice.

"Oh, this and that. British India. The French Revolution. The slave trade. You know, relevant subjects."

"Relevant subjects," he repeated then drew a long, slow breath, still looking at her lips.

"Before you say anything," she said quickly, "or kiss me—though I'd really like you to do the latter, and I'm always happy when you do the former—I wish you'd tell me why you're not allowed to be an artist."

His gaze rolled up toward the gallery. "Angela—"

"No, Trent. There are plenty of famous male artists now, and plenty before now. For God's sake, Leonardo DaVinci was a master at drawing long before he painted. Art was the sole realm of men for centuries. Millennia, actually. It was entirely a man's world."

"That may be," he said, his jaw tight, "but the world of art, even the humble sort that I enjoy, is anathema to my father."

Her lovely eyes went wide. Trent's neck cloth pulled at his throat mercilessly.

"Your father?" she only said.

"My father reveres the pitch above all."

"The pitch?"

"The playing field," he pushed on, the words coming gruffly, as though they were forcing him to voice them aloud. "Art, music, even reading are not of value in the Earl of Ware's household. The last time a member of my family cut the pages of a book was so long ago I don't recall it. My father's set and the boys he encouraged me to associate with prefer vigorous activity—sport, war—to anything resembling the contemplative arts, simple stillness or ..."

"Or what?"

"Or natural beauty." That very quality stood before Trent now, yet instead of taking her in his arms, he was blathering. But he could not seem to halt the words. "In my world, art is feminine. Weak. Less than British."

"It sounds like in ancient Rome, how solid, masculine *gravitas* was required of the male elite."

"Precisely, although how you know of *gravitas* I cannot fathom."

"My undergraduate major." She waved it off. "But Trent, there are men of your class who are indisputably masculine and artists both. Look at Lord Byron—"

"Whom my father loudly declares England well rid of. But at least he writes poetry, a noble art."

"Drawing isn't noble?"

"It is positively ignoble, suitable only for craftsmen, commoners, and females. Never for a man of honor."

"That just isn't true. I could list dozens of—"

"*Enough*, Angela."

Her mouth snapped shut and her honest gaze retreated. Trent nearly groaned in frustration. But his hands were cold and damp and his pulse was quick. Since his mother's death twelve years ago, he'd not spoken of this to anyone.

"All right," she said, her sweet voice clipped now. "If we can't talk about that, why don't you explain instead why you don't want me to speak with Sir Richard Howell?"

*Hell.* He'd never felt more like he was imprisoned in the fiery inferno, peering through the confining bars at heaven just out of arm's reach.

"I cannot," he uttered.

She nodded. "Fine." She closed Fableau's masterpiece and went to the door.

"Angela—"

"Trent, I know he is a very bad man. I know this for a fact. That you won't tell me what you know about him worries me. It worries me a lot." Her rich eyes entreated. "But the thing is, I don't have a bad feeling about you. Rather the opposite." Her voice seemed to catch. She cleared her throat. "I'm really honored that you've confided in me, even if I forced you to it."

"You attribute to me more honor than I deserve."

"I don't think so." She stood still as the statue he had first imagined her, as lovely and distant as a beauty carved of alabaster, as though she were waiting for him to speak. He did not; he had nothing he could honorably say. Finally, she nodded once then left the room.

—◦◦◦—

No pleasure was to be had now in the library, nor solace. He wanted her every moment, yet he could not have her. She was thoughtful and clever and wise and honest and insane and she was like no other woman he'd known. In order to save his father, he was shortly to be betrothed to the unappealing daughter of a man he loathed.

There was nothing to be done for it. He went to the stables and started to drink.

He was on his third brandy, leaning against the wall, continually replaying the vision of Angela's sweet curves in his mind and the sensation of her mouth on him, when he heard her name spoken.

"—the American," one of the men at the card table was saying. "Miss Cowdrey."

"No," Jack Willoughby said. "She's not Lady Sophronia's companion. That's Henrietta Black."

"Miss Cowdrey's been spending time with the old eccentric. Two peas in a pod, I say. Though one's much prettier than the other, of course." The fellow guffawed as though he'd said something clever. In his cups. Trent ignored him.

"Lady Grey insists that Miss Cowdrey has no connections," another man said. "Says she's an upstart colonial with no family to speak of and should be cut."

"Cut one of Wessex's guests? I say, that would be terribly bad ton, old chap."

"Goes about the estate alone, without any companion," the other added. "Never a good idea for a girl that pretty."

"Americans are a brazen lot," the first said with a chuckle.

Trent couldn't resist agreeing in silence, and thanking God for it. Otherwise he wouldn't have had the best night of his life, and he would still be the only person alive who knew his true passion. *Both of them.*

"Immodest females like Miss Cowdrey," Sir Richard's voice rose above the others, "lacking in decorum and modesty, have clearly not felt the backside of their lord and master's hand often enough."

Trent's entire body went cold. He'd been so lost in his thoughts he hadn't seen the villain enter. He stood and faced the card table.

Sir Richard's cravat was perfectly starched, his coat was of expensive fabric and cut, and the pin in his neck cloth was fashioned of gold and diamond. But he still looked like refuse.

"Sir," Trent said in a voice deepened by nine fingers of brandy. "The lady in question is a close friend of an American cousin of my family," he blatantly lied for perhaps the third or fourth time in his life, this time without a mote of discomfort.

The two gentlemen who'd been discussing Angela tugged at cravats and looked away uncomfortably.

Sir Richard's eyes scanned him slyly. "Unsavory connections can be so plaguing, can't they, Lord Everett?"

Trent saw red. This upstart popinjay manipulating his family's fate was the truly brazen one. He must be chastised.

"Sir," he said, "you will now retract your ungentlemanly remarks about the lady, or I will have satisfaction for it."

Sir Richard's gaze darted about at the faces then back to Trent. "Come now, my lord," he said, laying his cards on the table and spreading his palms up. "I meant no particular insult to the girl. Her situation is merely indefensible."

"Crash, old friend." The Earl of Bruton laid a hand on his shoulder. "A duel is no way to settle anything. Don't rise to it."

But Trent had already set aside reason and sanity. He wanted blood. He shrugged off Bruton's hand. "Name your seconds, Howell."

Sir Richard's cheeks paled. "Come now, son. Is this necessary? It's not as though the chit is your responsibility."

But she was, in every way that mattered.

"Hallo!" Jack Willoughby exclaimed. "I say we bring this down a notch, gents. How about a round of whist instead of a duel, then? Much less troublesome."

"Excellent idea, Willoughby," Bruton grumbled.

"Everett doesn't play cards," someone else called out with a laugh. "Crash, challenge him to a boxing match. See if the old man has any tone left to him."

Trent stared at Sir Richard. "Will you fight me, sir?"

Sir Richard shook his head with a chuckle. "Now, that wouldn't be good sportsmanship, would it, son? I've at least two stone on you and a decade of prize-winning fights under my belt."

"Will you deny me the opportunity to defend the lady's honor? That's hardly gentlemanly of you, is it?"

Murmurs of approval all around.

Sir Richard's jowls colored again. Then his eyes narrowed. "I have just the solution, my lord. Tomorrow should be a fair day. Why not have a friendly little ... carriage race?"

Silence descended.

Trent's heart pounded. He held Sir Richard's gaze and spoke to the room at large. "Can anybody lend me a carriage?"

# CHAPTER EIGHT

Gentlemen's laughter and the enthusiastic clinking of glasses echoed throughout the stable.

"To Everett!" someone called out. "A lady's honor is always safe with him!" More laughing, this time ribald. Trent accepted it with the appearance of manly good humor he'd perfected for years. He usually felt it, but never more so than now.

Sir Richard had barely been able to offer his hand to shake at the end of the race. The blackguard was well trounced, and Trent felt on top of the world. He'd climbed onto the miniscule seat and taken the ribbons of Willoughby's phaeton with sheer terror freezing his veins. But the carriage had handled smoothly, and the horses' mouths were marvelously soft. Within minutes Trent remembered that he enjoyed driving. He'd always enjoyed it.

It was the racing he hated.

Then he thrashed Sir Richard, with several carriage lengths to spare.

"I say, Crash, that was a fine show," someone called out. "We'll have to come up with a new name for you, won't we, gentlemen?"

"Huzzah!" the cry went up.

"To Hippolyta!" someone else shouted.

"Huzzah! Huzzah!"

Trent grinned, but he was eager to be about his next task. Sir Richard had disappeared, no doubt to lick his wounds. But Trent didn't need him now. Now he needed a particular lady. He left the stable and went searching.

He finally found Miss Howell in the garden. She was sitting in the shade of an enormous oak, arranging and rearranging her skirt to either side of her on the iron bench.

"Good day, Miss Howell." He bowed.

"Good day, my lord." She stood and curtsied. "Perhaps you saw me just now. I have been practicing methods of displaying my skirt on a bench when I sit. I do believe I have come upon the method that is to my gown's greatest advantage, though of course it would not suffice for taffeta."

"Miss Howell, I should like to speak with you about a delicate matter."

"I heard that you bested Papa in a race this morning, and now I see it must be true that you were racing. Your boots and breeches are dusty. But I suppose you might have got that dust on a walk. Leather and buckskin do attract dust in the country wretchedly, don't they? I always tell Papa to avoid wearing buckskin in the country because it attracts dust, although of course we spend very little time in the country, as we live in town, which of course I prefer as all the most interesting people are in town and what is there to do in the country anyway? But if we were to be obliged to spend time in the country, I would tell Papa every day to avoid stepping on roads that are dusty. No one likes dusty boots, do they, my lord?" She raised her eyes in question.

"Miss Howell." He drew a steadying breath, but he'd never been more certain of anything, except swimming in a lake with a lovely American. "Do you understand your father's plans for you? For us?"

"That we are to marry and I will become a viscountess?" she said. "Yes. Papa said you would ask his permission before you asked me. But he has not yet informed me of that. Are you here to request the honor of my hand?"

"No. I am not." He folded his hands behind his back and spoke gently. "Miss Howell, I mean you no disrespect. You seem a perfectly unexceptionable lady and any man should be honored to have you as his bride. But I am not able to be that man for you."

Her round eyes stared up at him. "Then you do not intend to ask for my hand?"

"I do not. I do not believe we would suit."

"Oh." She blinked twice. "In truth, this news comes as a relief to me."

The air shot out of his lungs. "It does?"

343

She nodded. "Given my complexion, I would prefer to marry a man with dark hair. Your hair is quite handsome, but it isn't dark at all, and I'm afraid I would be perpetually out of sorts with you for it."

"Because of the color of my hair?"

"Yes. You look very fine in knee breeches, much better than Sir Kennett," she said thoughtfully. "But Sir Kennett has black hair, you see. And while he is only a baronet, we appear to great advantage beside each other, so I cannot begrudge him his less elevated title. Can I?"

"That is generous of you."

"Sir Kennett is madly in love with me and has already asked for my hand, but Papa said I mustn't accept because he wished me to wed you. But if you will not wed me, I will wed Sir Kennett instead, and I am sure I shall be the happiest married lady in England."

Trent smiled. "I hope you are. I wish you all the best."

"Thank you, my lord." She curtsied. He bowed. He started off, then paused and returned to her.

"Miss Howell."

"My lord?"

"If your father is displeased over this turn of events, and if he should express his displeasure in a manner that you cannot like, I hope you will appeal to me for assistance."

"Oh, you are kind, my lord. But he will be quite happy with Sir Kennett as a son-in-law. He owns two sugar plantations in the West Indies."

Trent's step was lighter, his heartbeat quick as he reentered the house and asked the butler for his father's whereabouts.

"His lordship has gone shooting with Lord Warnford, my lord. I do not expect them back until the ball this evening."

Trent ground his molars, gathered his sketchbook and pencil, and went into the park.

Angela awoke with a start to a shadowy room. She dragged her head off the bed where she was sprawled and shuffled to the mirror. After another sleepless night, she'd gone to the stables to finally confront Sir Richard, only to be told by a stable hand that all the men were off at a carriage race. Frustrated and crabby, she'd returned to her bedchamber and promptly fell asleep.

"Ugh." Lines from the bedspread crisscrossed her cheek, her eyes were bloodshot, and her dress was all wrinkles. She couldn't join the party tonight looking like this, but she had to finally talk to Sir Richard. And she wanted to see Trent more than she'd ever wanted anything. Despite their fight—or maybe because of it—the sizzling zing had morphed into all-out fever. She needed to know if he was angry with her for lecturing him, and if it really had been just a one-night stand for him.

She went into Lady Sophronia's chambers.

"Miss Cowdrey, you look a state!" She waved away the maid laying out dinner. "I don't know where Henrietta has gotten to, but sit, sit. Then we will dress you properly for the ball."

"Ball?"

"Dancing and champagne! Hate the stuff myself—dancing, that is—adore champagne, of course—but Her Grace is fond of elaborate festivities. Now eat. Then we will make you stunning."

Angela doubted it. She'd never been a stunner. That was her mother.

But when the maid brought out a beautiful gown of blue watered silk embroidered with beads and sequins that sparkled all across the low-cut bodice and down the skirt like rainfall, she didn't object. When they'd finished dressing her and arranging her hair with bejeweled combs, she barely recognized the woman staring back at her in the mirror.

Lady Sophronia clapped her bony hands and beamed. "Yes, yes! This will do. It surely will."

Angela really felt like a fairy princess going to a ball as she descended the main stairs and found her way to the ballroom. Music lilted along the corridor. She passed the footmen to either side of the door and paused on the threshold.

Everybody was there, gorgeously gowned and coiffed and primped and elegant. Nobody was dancing yet, though the orchestra was playing.

Then all at once, half of the duke's houseguests turned in her direction. Fans flicked open and people whispered in their neighbors' ears while staring at her.

So much for the famously stiff reserve of the English.

Somebody must have seen her and Trent in the lake. If the duchess kicked her out of her house now, how would she talk to Sir Richard? And ... *Trent*.

Oh *no*. What had she been thinking to break the rules like that? It couldn't end this way. She'd never see him again because she'd acted like a stupid party girl, like her mother, ignoring the consequences to herself and anybody else, when she'd never been anything other than the nerdy girl who sat in the corner reading while the party raged around her. She should've known she wouldn't get away with it. She should've used the damn brain she'd been depending on for twenty-seven years.

She didn't see him anywhere in the clusters of guests. Maybe he was hiding from everybody's censure? But no. Not a viscount. He could do anything he wanted. Women in this society suffered for breaking rules, not men. He was probably just trying to avoid her because that's what guys did after one-night stands followed by uncomfortable conversations in which they were badgered about their life choices.

*What kind of an idiot was she?*

Failure stared her in the face, in addition to at least thirty of the duchess's guests, and the sharp ache of inevitable heartbreak. He hadn't tried to find her since their argument, or even before it. He'd bumped into her by accident near the library. He could've found her at any time before or since then.

But she'd only said what she felt. She'd been honest with him. If he didn't like it, then he wasn't the man she hoped he was anyway.

She sucked in a fortifying breath and looked for Sir Richard in the crowd. She wouldn't let herself fail. She'd take the hits when they came, and before this was all over, she'd discover why she'd been thrust into the past.

A firm little hand wrapped around hers.

"Angela!" Charlotte whispered in her ear. "You are finally here! I've been dying to speak with you all day."

She dragged her to a corner. Necks craned to follow their progress as the orchestra launched into a jaunty tune. Charlotte halted abruptly behind a group of older men.

"Where have you been?" she demanded in a whisper loud enough to be heard in Times Square at midnight on a Saturday. An elderly man turned and his bushy brows bent in disapproval.

"I was asleep most of the day," Angela answered quietly.

"Then you haven't heard?" Charlotte didn't look like she was about to chew her out for skinny-dipping with her brother.

"Heard what?" Images of mewling kittens hidden in the girls' underwear drawers came to her. "Oh no. Did Henry do something awful?"

"No! It is my elder brother who has done something grand." Charlotte gripped Angela's hand. "Late last night Trenton challenged Sir Richard Howell to a duel!"

Angela's stomach fell. What horrible thing was he hiding from her that he'd fight a duel over it?

"A duel?" she said weakly.

"Yes! Apparently they were nearly at swords drawn when Trenton's friends insisted he mustn't, so they had a carriage race instead. Trenton beat that mushroom, of course. But, Angela, a carriage race!"

Angela shook her head. She felt ill and gigantically relieved at once. *No duel.* No danger. No Trent bleeding to death while she cried. "I thought gentlemen had carriage races all the time."

"Some do. But my brother was nearly crippled after an accident he incurred in a carriage race. He hasn't driven in nine years."

"Oh." *Oh.* "Charlotte, why did he challenge Sir Richard?"

"That is the wonderful part." Charlotte's eyes were bright. "He did it in defense of a lady's honor."

The hits just kept coming. She couldn't breathe. It had to be Miss Howell. Why else would he challenge Sir Richard, of all people? "What lady's honor?"

"Yours, of course!" She beamed.

Angela's cheeks went piping hot. They did know about the lake. Oh, no. No. Please God, no. But Trent had defended her. "What did Sir Richard say about me?"

Charlotte stared blankly at her. "That you are American." She may as well have added, "Duh."

Angela abruptly felt weak all over. "Nothing else?"

"Not that Bridget Cavendish who told Alexandra Cavendish who told Kate Lacy who told me said."

"I don't believe it," she whispered.

"You should. It really doesn't require a lot for gentlemen to do foolish things like race carriages." Charlotte shrugged. "At least gentlemen like Sir Richard. But not my brother! Isn't it wonderful? I can see that you like him, and now it is clear that he likes you too. Oh, I will be so happy to have you as a sister."

"Charlotte, I'm afraid you're getting ahead of yourself." Way ahead. There had to be another explanation.

Charlotte's pretty young face fell. "Don't you like him?"

More than she could stand it. She liked the way he spoke and the things he said and how he looked at her and his incredible drawings and the way he tasted and kissed and the way she felt all wobbly and sexy and smart and adventuresome and strong when he was around.

He'd challenged a man to a *duel* for her?

"It's more complicated than that," she could barely say.

Charlotte frowned. "I don't see why it must be. In fact, I'm certain it is not. Why, just look at him now over there. He's been watching you since the moment you walked in the room."

Angela's heart did a tsunami across her chest.

Trent stood at the opposite side of the candlelit ballroom nearly in shadow, gorgeous in formal wear, and he was, in fact, watching her. He offered her the slightest bow, and the corner of his mouth tilted up. It wasn't an "I'm trying to blow you off but, damn, you just caught me" smile. It was an "I'm glad to see you" smile, simple and pleased.

"Go over there," Charlotte whispered.

"I ..." She couldn't speak with him now. Not yet. Not unprepared. Not so confused. Not so *in love*.

She was totally in love with him. A man from another century that she'd met five days ago.

No. She couldn't be in love. Love didn't happen that quickly. It was just star-struck infatuation. Infatuation for a man who had defended her honor in a carriage race despite his mortal fear of carriages, and despite their argument.

"You must," Charlotte urged. "You have not yet thanked him." She pressed the small of Angela's back. Whoever said Regency-era ladies were physically reserved didn't know Charlotte Ascot.

She went, wending her way through the little groups of guests while others started to line up, gentlemen on one side, ladies on the other, for the first set. Trent watched her come, scanning her body only once then fixing on her face until she stood right in front of him.

She couldn't make small talk. Not now. "I heard what you did today."

"Did you?"

"Congratulations."

He nodded.

"What did Sir Richard say about me?"

He looked steadily into her eyes. "Nothing he could not have said about any other lady at this party."

"Is that true?"

"Mostly. You are the only American present." His smile was gorgeous.

"But ..." She twisted her fingers together. "*Why?*"

A woman nearby lifted her lorgnette and peered curiously at them.

Trent grasped Angela's elbow and led her into an adjoining room where guests were enjoying refreshments that were laid out on a table, then into yet another room. Much smaller than the others, it was lit only with firelight and a few candles on a far table, and empty. He drew her away from the doorway, then released her. But he stood close.

"Why?" he repeated her question quietly.

Angela shook her head. "You defended my honor. *Mine.*"

His gaze slipped down to her lips. "Of course."

"Despite our argument yesterday? And ... and the other night?"

He moved a half-step closer and stroked a fingertip along her cheek. "Rather, because of yesterday and the other night," he said in that melting chocolate voice that made her joints liquid.

She fought against the delirium of unwise happiness. She loved his touch. She loved his honor and decency. And she loved it that he still wanted to touch her. "That doesn't make sense."

"Possibly not." His strong hand cupped her jaw. "But there it is. Nothing about you makes sense, Miss Angela Cowdrey."

"Thank you, Trent."

His hooded gaze traced her features. "I think I like it better when you call me 'my lord.'"

"Why? Because it puts me in my place?"

"Because there is not a hint of deference in your tone when you use my title." His smile was slow now.

"You like a woman who isn't afraid to speak to you as an equal?"

349

"I like you." His mouth hovered above hers. "So I suppose that explanation suits."

"Charlotte told me you haven't driven a carriage in nine years, not since the accident."

"Charlotte speaks when she should not."

"Apparently it's common gossip."

"Hmm." Both of his hands curved around her face and turned it up. "That won't do, will it?"

"I, uh ..." Less than forty-eight hours earlier, she'd been naked in a lake doing things with this man that she couldn't say aloud, yet now she felt like a sixteen-year-old in a dark corner at the prom, never been kissed and dying for the star quarterback to be her first. "Um, no?"

His gaze was on her mouth. "Let's offer them something more interesting to gossip about, shall we?"

"Here? But—"

He didn't give her time to protest. With the door open and a hundred people right beyond it, he covered her mouth with his.

The floor opened up beneath her. He kissed her like he wanted to kiss her forever, like he was perfectly happy just kissing her and then like he intended to do a lot more than kiss. Her entire body wanted him. When he nibbled her lower lip she moaned, and he caught the sound in his mouth.

"Hush," he murmured against her lips. "You will make the violinist jealous." He traced the tender inner edge of her lip with the tip of his tongue.

She'd never felt anything as bone-meltingly hot as Trenton Ascot's mouth on hers. "The violinist?" she sighed.

"He's Italian. I heard him earlier saying that he intended to relocate to America," he whispered, dipping to her neck and feathering kisses over her skin that made her shiver with wanting him. "Thinks American girls are much more suited to the temperament of an artist like him than Englishwomen."

She slipped her hands into his coat to feel the body she'd felt with her breasts and belly in the lake. "You're making that up."

"Not at all." He lingered on the hollow beneath her ear and she caught her breath. "And I rather agree with him."

"Did you invent what Sir Richard said about me being American?"

He pulled back to look into her eyes. His were hazy with desire. *For her.* He wanted *her.* In the ballroom, the violin vaulted into a vibrant solo.

"He said little, though enough," Trent said soberly now. "But I had an additional reason for wishing him ill."

Her hands dropped from his chest, her heart thumping hard. "What reason?"

"Sir Richard is attempting to blackmail my father."

"*Blackmail?* What about?"

"During the war, my father made unwise investments controlled by Sir Richard, who then committed treason and fraud and now wishes my father to pay for the crimes."

"But ..." Her mind was spinning. *Treason and fraud?* It couldn't be coincidence. The cello joined the violin, their counterpoint harmony dancing in a bright ascent. "How? Why now? The war is still raging in Europe."

"Sir Richard wishes my father to mine iron ore on his lands, from which he will take a large share of the profits. If my father does not comply, he will accuse him of his own crimes. My father is innocent, of course. But Howell has documents to prove otherwise."

"Trent—" She swallowed over the excitement gathering in her.

"So you see I enjoyed giving that scoundrel a thrashing—"

"Trent."

"—even if it was only to eat the dust churned up by my carriage wheels. Somewhat puerile, but that's most men for you."

"Trent!" She grabbed his lapels. "I know why I'm here."

# CHAPTER NINE

The violin spun into a glorious romp. The cello joined it, their voices merging in a delirious tangle of joy.

Trent's brow creased. In the golden candlelight, he really did look like Adonis. Albeit a confused, wary Adonis. "Do you?"

"It's my research! I know how to prove your father's innocence," she whispered.

"What are you telling me?"

"That I can help. I just need to do one thing to prove Sir Richard is lying about your father. But I can't tell you more. I can't risk altering history." But she would. Except that actually she wouldn't. In sole possession of Arnaud Chappelle's memoir, only she could know now, at this moment, finally, who had convinced Arnaud to turn informer on Sir Richard.

"Angela—" Trent was obviously struggling. "You mustn't—"

"No. I can help. You've got to believe me." She put her hands on his chest again and slid them beneath his coat, the sizzling zing threatening to burst out of her. "But more urgently, right now you've got to kiss me."

His hands came around her shoulders. "You truly wish to help my family?"

"I don't just wish to. I'm going to."

He was looking at her so oddly, his eyes glittering. "I have told you what no one else knows. My family would be ruined if this became public."

"You can trust me. You already trust me. I think you know that."

"I think you may be a madwoman. I don't know why I trust you."

"You do know why." *I love you.* "Trent, I—"

He cut off her words with his mouth.

First he kissed her deeply, deliciously. Then his hands found her waist and he pulled her against him until she could feel through the flimsy stuff of her gown and his coat every hard contour of his athlete's body. Then his palms slid to her butt and pulled her against his erection.

She nearly climbed up him. He helped her, his hand beneath her thigh and mouth on her neck as she struggled against her narrow skirts to get closer—much closer, feeling him, aching for more contact—oh, sweet heaven—closer ...

He dragged her off him to arm's length.

"Good God," he whispered on hard breaths. "There are over a hundred people within yards."

"Not having nearly as good a time as we are, I'm guessing," she panted.

He released her and backed away a step. "Miss Cowdrey." His chest rose and fell jerkily. "I regret that I must at this time bid you good night."

"*Good night?* Hasn't the ball just started?"

He raked a hand through his hair. "Angela, I must go."

"Where?"

"A cold lake might do the trick. But I'm not even certain of that," he added on a mumble, "given my new appreciation of lakes."

"Trent."

"Angela—"

"You don't need to do this. I'm not a lady. We don't have them in twenty-first-century America. You don't need to protect my virtue or reputation. I'm just an ordinary woman."

"And I am just a gentleman. Or I usually am when an intoxicating American isn't tempting me to be a rogue."

"So this is my fault?"

"*No.* Never." He stepped forward, grasped her arms, and kissed her hard on the mouth very swiftly. "Allow me to treat you with the respect you deserve, I beg of you."

How could she fight that? She'd been longing for honor and decency, and now she was getting it at the most inconvenient moment possible.

"Won't you even stay for one dance?" she tried again.

"I'm afraid I am in no condition for dancing at present."

She didn't bother looking down; she'd already felt what he meant.

She nodded. He released her and with a single great breath turned and exited through the opposite door.

Angela couldn't go back to the ball. Her hair was a mess from his hands in it, and her lips were tender. Everybody had probably seen them go anyway. While they were kissing, twenty people could've been taking turns peeking in the door for all she knew. But it wouldn't matter if her reputation was ruined. Tomorrow she'd head to Southampton, where at this moment Arnaud Chappelle was living in miserable semi-squalor in a rented flat near the docks. After that ...

She couldn't think about it. If finally solving this historical riddle and saving Trent's family meant returning home, that had to be. Just because she was infatuated with a man here didn't mean she wasn't going back.

Climbing the stairs to Lady Sophronia's suite, she repeated that thought in her head over and over again.

She crept in the back door and to her borrowed bedchamber. Lying down on the bed, she closed her eyes and imagined waltzing with Trent. Then she imagined him taking a cold shower. She imagined that shower turning hot and steamy, and her walking into the room dressed only in a towel. Then she imagined dropping her towel and stepping into the shower with him, and his hands circling her waist ... and the shower walls got so steamy she couldn't see anything else.

She bolted upright in bed.

It took almost fifteen minutes stealthily creeping through the dark corridors of the giant house, pausing to hide when servants passed by, to reach the bachelors' wing. Hands shaking, she knocked on Trent's door.

Nothing happened. *Oh, no.* What if a valet opened the door? Worse, what if Trent was in there with some other woman?

No. Not possible. Not remotely possible.

He opened the door himself. She tried to breathe. He'd removed his coat, waistcoat, and cravat and his shirt was open at the neck, revealing a delicious triangle of collarbone and breathtaking pecs. His hair was tousled, as though he'd scraped his hand through it a few times. He frowned. His smoky eyes looked thunderous.

"I—" A tennis ball was apparently stuck in her throat. "I—" she tried again, but he wasn't moving. Or speaking. *Oh, my God, Angela, this time you've gone far too far.* "I—"

He pulled her into the room and dragged her into his arms.

There was very little of her that remained untouched by his strong and talented hands as they stood there making out at the closed door. First he stroked her arms with slow, sensual caresses and threaded their fingers together intimately. Then he pinned them above her head against the door and brought his body against hers as he took her mouth in an absolutely carnal kiss. One hand holding her wrists above her, with the other he explored her body with great thoroughness.

He began with her face, the curve of her jaw and her lips. She took his finger into her mouth and sucked and he moaned and kissed her deep. Then he touched her throat, her neck, following with his mouth, making her writhe, and then the swell of her breasts above her bodice. His tongue stole beneath the fabric and played with a tight nipple and she nearly exploded.

His hand cupping her breast was all she needed to begin begging him to release her wrists so she could touch him too. He silenced her with his mouth, caressing her tongue while his hand caressed her nipple through the fabric until she spread her thighs in silent, desperate invitation.

Finally he gave her what she wanted, his arousal against hers. With their bodies in complete contact through layers of clothing, they rocked against the door like horny teenagers, her hands trapped above her, his palm tight on her butt forcing her to ride him.

She came so fast she choked on her moan. "Oh-h, *yes.*"

Releasing her wrists he pulled down her tiny puff sleeves and freed her breasts from the gown and corset demi-cups. The cool air touched them as his hand dipped between her legs, massaging her through her skirts, so good, perfect, his body, his touch. He bent and stroked his tongue across an aching nipple and her orgasm convulsed again.

"*Oh.*" She couldn't breathe. It was almost too much. "Stop. Oh, please."

"You needn't fear for your virtue." His voice was deeply husky, and breathless like hers. "I will not dishonor you. I only want to touch you. I need to touch you, Angel."

"I—*ohh!*" He caressed and inside she was wild. *Not possible.* She'd never had three orgasms in a row, and fully clothed at that. But she was so primed for him. She wanted her skirts up and him inside her. "I want you to dishonor me. I mean, I want to be with you. All the way." She ran her hand down his waist and grasped his erection. "Whatever happens tomorrow, now I want you." She stroked him through the fabric of his trousers.

He groaned. "Angela, I—"

"It's not the same in my century. A lot of women aren't virgins when they get married. They don't have to be. And I may never get married anyway, so it doesn't matter. Please believe me." Her voice dropped to barely a whisper. "Don't make me beg. And please don't make me wait."

He swept her up into his arms and carried her to his bed.

There were way too many clothes between them. But he was clearly as impatient as she. Together they pushed up her skirts, unbuttoned his trousers and dragged off his shirt. Then they were skin to skin like they'd been in the water, but this time he was on top of her, between her thighs, his chest and shoulders all smooth, taut muscle, and she was dizzy.

"Angela, my God, you feel good." He pressed hungry kisses to her throat, his hand running over her hip beneath her gown. "I want to do this right for you." His voice was rough, a lock of dark golden hair falling over his brow. "Allow me to do this slowly. Allow me to undress you and love you as you deserve to be loved."

She *deserved to be loved?* This couldn't be real.

The need to have him was just too powerful. "I don't think I can wait that long." The rhythm of his hips against hers was making her insane. If she didn't fight it, she'd come like this again, too quickly. "I want you inside me. Now."

His smile turned raffish. "That suits me as well." He bent to her lips and kissed her like he was drinking from her, making her feel him and want him everywhere inside her. His hand moved between them and she felt the head of his penis stroke her entrance.

"*Trent.* I'm—"

"My angel." He held her gaze as he fit himself inside her.

"Oh, wow," she whispered, overwhelmed. "This feels incredible."

"Agreed," he said with tight restraint. "No pain?"

She clasped her thighs around his hips. "No pain."

"It's about to feel even more incredible, Miss Cowdrey."

He made good on his word. With each slow, sensuous thrust he went deeper into her, deeper and hotter and wetter until they were locked together and she was dying of pleasure. If only she'd known ... If only she'd really understood what this was like ...

She still would've saved herself for Trenton Ascot.

She gripped his arms, the delicious spiral of anticipation mounting inside her slowly now, languorously, as if her body wasn't in a hurry this time. "Can you make it last?" she whispered.

"As it happens—" He thrust harder, grabbing her hips and pulling her to him. "—not this time," he growled, thrusting again. "I've been wanting this since the moment you took your mouth off of me in that lake. You're mine now, Angel. Mine."

It went fast then, hard and sweaty and spectacularly urgent. She gripped the bedpost behind her and held herself steady. He was touching something deep inside her, so deep, with each thrust it was unbearably good. If this was the G-spot everyone raved about, she finally understood. She couldn't get enough. She never wanted him to stop. "Oh, God! *Oh.*"

He lifted her hips from the bed. "So tight." His muscles went rock hard. "Angela. *Angela.*"

She felt him come inside her. She'd never imagined a woman could feel it, and it was amazing.

Finally he went still, and she gulped in breaths and ran her hands down his arms that were slick with sweat. He dipped his brow to rest on her shoulder.

"I am appalled that I just took your virginity half-clothed and sideways on top of this bed," he mumbled roughly against her neck. "Without even removing my shoes."

"They didn't get in the way." Her fingers played in the damp hair at the nape of his neck and she slid her other hand around to his back. He was all muscle and masculine beauty and quiet humor and natural goodness and decency and honor and she never wanted to let him go.

"They won't have the opportunity the next time." He kissed her neck, then her shoulder, then lingered on the curve of her breast, his mouth a warm pleasure on her. "No matter how insane your soft skin and sultry eyes and seductive smile drive me."

Sultry eyes? Seductive smile? *Her?* "Next time?"

"As soon as I catch my breath I will send these skirts and whatnot of yours to perdition." He nuzzled her neck. "Then I vow I will make it last."

"I am dreaming." The words slipped out of her mouth. "This can't be real. I really must be dreaming."

He lifted his head and his cupped his palm gently around her cheek. "Yet I am finally wide awake," he said quietly. "So either your dream is of my reality, or my reality is only within your dream."

"That's what I'm afraid of. The latter. I'm afraid I'll wake up tomorrow morning alone in my apartment in Ann Arbor."

"Tomorrow morning," he said and placed a tenderly sexy kiss on her lips, "you will awaken in this bed in my arms. And then we will see about what must be done to ensure that you awaken every morning in that manner."

She wanted to cry and laugh and die all at once. So the only real option was to kiss him.

Then the foreplay of "next time" began, the tantalizing removal of one piece of clothing at a time and the exploration of his every muscle and sinew with her hands and mouth. When he decided it was his turn to reciprocate, he didn't give her a choice. Laughing, she reminded him that he'd said he'd make it last this time. Soon, however, she couldn't laugh because she was too busy moaning and begging him again not to make her wait.

He made good on his word. Again. Much better than good.


Angela didn't wake up the following morning in her apartment. As tiny threads of dawn seeped through the cracks between the curtains, she drew out of Trent's embrace and crept around the room finding her clothes. On the bed, sprawled in the tangled sheets so she could appreciate every contour of his breathtaking chest and shoulders and arms in the pearly gray light, Viscount Everett breathed deeply and evenly. He didn't even flicker an eyelash.

For him to sleep like that, his conscience had to be clear about what they'd done. That made him either an actual rogue, or ... *no.* She couldn't let herself read anything into what he'd said the first time they'd done it, or afterward about waking up in his arms every morning. Men of his status had mistresses. He'd be typical of his class in expecting her to become his.

But after the second time, when they were lying side-by-side and he was stroking her hair and they'd talked of her studies and his art, they'd talked like friends, like they'd known each other for much longer than a week. Just like in the library. Like they understood each other.

She knew men of his world talked to their mistresses like that—intimately, meaningfully. Their private correspondences proved it. But she would never know if Trenton Ascot did. She would never get the chance to find out what he wanted of her.

She dressed, then went to the writing table and pried the cap off the inkbottle with a quiet *pop*. She made a mess of writing, splashing blobs of ink all over the paper, but when she was finished she carried the note to the bed and set it on the mattress beside him.

She drank in her final sight of him, aching to touch him, to run her fingertips over his chiseled jaw one last time and kiss his gorgeous mouth. Mostly, she wanted to tell him she thought she was falling in love with him, that she'd never felt like this before—appreciated and desired and alive and just *so right* with him.

On silent feet, she went to the door and opened it carefully, then turned and took a long last look at him before slipping out into the dark corridor.

It took her a harrowing ten minutes to get back to her room in Lady Sophronia's suite without bumping into any servants. The old eccentric was sitting in a cushiony chair dressed in her nightgown and bathrobe with a scarlet nightcap laced in fluttery purple ribbons perched atop her bad dye job.

Her eyes snapped open wide.

Angela smiled. "Good morning, my lady. Do you by any chance have a carriage?"

The drive to Southampton port wasn't long, the road wasn't as bumpy as she'd expected, and the coachman was downright chipper. In the end, she'd decided to bribe the Earl of Ware's coachman with the ruby broach Lady Sophronia gave her for the purpose. He'd agreed pretty readily after she explained her errand was for the good of Lord Everett, Lady Charlotte, and Master Henry, and that they'd be back within the day. But he'd refused the broach and only asked for the price of a pint at the posting inn in Southampton.

Still, she was as nervous as all get out by the time they pulled up before the dilapidated boarding house where Arnaud Chappelle had hired a room for the past two years while he wrote his memoir.

She could see the words on the first folio of that memoir like she had the document in front of her now: not only the address of his residence while he lived under an assumed name and secretly wrote a treatise about the despicable deeds of his past, but also his abject apology for those deeds, calling on the mercy of God and the souls of the innocent people he'd harmed.

It was an apology that only she had ever read, and it was the key now to saving Trent's family.

It was one thing knowing all about a man from the past, but quite another to be knocking on his door. By the time it finally opened, she was a nervous wreck.

The man who stood before her was anorexically thin, dressed soberly and neat as a pin in a black coat and black breeches, and had a French look about the mouth.

"Good day, ma'am," he said in slightly inflected English and bowed. "If you have come concerning the grocer's bill, I deeply regret that I am as yet unable to pay. I shall endeavor to do so at your husband's earliest convenience, however, or else he may call the authorities if he so desires." He spoke wearily, and his eyes were giant pools of defeat.

"I'm not the grocer's wife, Monsieur Chappelle."

The pools of defeat widened. Then he dropped his chin to his chest and shook his head. "I am discovered. *Le jour du Jugement dernier* has at long last arrived. But I knew it would someday arrive, *non*?" He shrugged. "The law, it will always pursue those who flout it." A sad smile creased the drooping skin of a face that must've once been round. He wasn't above fifty, but he looked much older. In two short years he'd gone from fat prosperity to emaciated dejection.

"I'm not the law," she said. "But I know about what you've done and I need your help. May I come in?"

"If it is wicked deeds you wish me to perform, madam, I must tell you now that I am well out of that business."

"I know," she said. "I know that you go to confession every day repenting of those wicked deeds, even though it takes you an hour to walk to the hermitage. I know that you eat only day-old bread and watered prunes and once a week allow yourself boiled chicken. I know that you suffer every minute—awake and in your dreams— over the loss of your son to brigands at sea two years ago. And I know that inside this flat there's a memoir written in your hand that describes every wicked deed you've ever done." Her heart pounded. "But I don't care about that."

His face was ashen. "How do you know of my memoir? I have told no one of it. Are you an angel sent from heaven to exhort me to cleanse my soul in the fires of earthly judgment?"

Angela shook her head. "No, but I do know things. Monsieur Chappelle, I need your help. Sir Richard Howell is going to use lies about the business transactions he did with you to ruin the Earl of Ware and his family—his two sons and his daughter. His younger son, monsieur, is only fourteen."

A bony hand went to his chest and clutched at his waistcoat. "The age of my Henri when God saw fit to take him from me in payment for my sins."

She nodded. "This boy's name is Henry too." She let that sit for a moment. "Please, monsieur, may I come in?"

Tears stood in his eyes. During her research she'd never felt a jot of anything but disgust for this man who in his greed had destroyed the lives of countless families. But he was just a man, after all, able to feel pain and grief like everybody else. She wished that felt satisfying to her. It didn't. That evil caused pain and suffering for everybody, even the evildoer, wasn't any kind of consolation. Looking at his misery, she just felt empty. And abruptly, for Angela doing history was no longer about crossing every "t", dotting every "i", and solving mysteries, or even about getting a great job. It was about mending broken hearts. This man's would never be mended. But she would at least give him a chance to mend the wounds he'd inflicted on others.

Head bowed low, Arnaud Chappelle gestured her into his flat.

361

# CHAPTER TEN

**W**ith eyes bleary from lack of sleep, Trent read Angela's note three times before he understood it. But only one detail of the splotched message truly mattered to him: she had gone.

Where? She did not specify.

Why? To save his family.

How? He'd bloody well discover as soon as he was dressed.

He did not await the assistance of his father's valet. In his haste, he cut himself thrice while shaving, then donned mismatched boots.

Neither Lady Sophronia nor her companion, Miss Black, could be found anywhere in the house. They could not be interrogated.

Since Angela had no horse or carriage, she must have departed Kingstag on foot and could be easily overtaken by a man on horseback. Grabbing his hat and duster, he ran to the stables. There he learned from one of the hands about the curious departure of his father's traveling chaise and Fields, the family coachman, several hours earlier, with only one passenger: the American lady.

Half-mounted, paralyzed and rendered mute, Trent finally understood her plea in the note. *Promise me that if this trouble gets cleared up, you'll tell your father the truth. I may not be around to hear your promise, but I swear I'll know if you've made it.*

Swinging into the saddle, silently he promised. He vowed. He prayed. Then he spurred his horse down the drive, certain on only two accounts, that she did not intend to return and that he must— *would*—convince her otherwise.

**T**he Earl of Ware's traveling chaise and team had not been seen that day at any inn or posting house along the London road within many miles of Kingstag Castle. As the sun touched the horizon, Trent turned his horse about and retraced his route.

She had gone, absconded with his family's carriage and horses and servant, an unlikely scenario for a thief. But a thief she most certainly was not; Trent had known that for days already. So Fields must have taken her willingly.

He searched the surrounding roads, learning only as darkness fell that the carriage had taken the route to Southampton. Perhaps she intended to sail soon. But it had already become too dark to travel further. He returned to the duke's house and gave the order in the stable that his horse should be prepared for departure at first light.

Charlotte met him in the great hall.

"Where have you been?" she exclaimed, and looked over his shoulder. "And where is Miss Cowdrey?"

"I don't know."

"You don't *know*? Papa thought you had gone off to avoid having to marry Miss Howell. I've no idea why you should have meant to do something so stupid as marrying Jane Howell. She is the greatest ninny I've ever met. So I knew he couldn't be telling the truth. Still, I didn't tell him what I thought. But perhaps I was wrong." She looked around him to the door again.

"Wrong about what?"

"That you and Angela had eloped to Gretna Green, of course!"

"Charlotte, Gretna Green is a sennight's journey away. And what sort of man do you imagine me to be that I would elope with a lady instead of wedding her publicly and honorably?"

Charlotte's eyes popped wide. "Then you *do* wish to marry her!" She grabbed his hands and her face was all smiles. "Oh, I am transported! I hoped you admired her because I am quite certain she admires you, and I like her ever so much."

Trent's heart was beating hard and rather unevenly. "You were justified in your hope." While his sister spoke of admiration, he feared that what he felt for the brazen American that had swept in and out of his life like a migrating monarch butterfly—unique and vibrant and lovely—was considerably stronger.

"But then where is she?" Charlotte demanded.

"She departed this morning in Father's chaise, and I have been—"

"But Fields returned with the carriage this afternoon."

He grasped her arm. "She was not with him?"

"No. Only a very strange Frenchman who insists on speaking with you. The duchess invited him to take tea in the drawing room, but my maid heard it from the third footman that he spent the afternoon on his knees in the library with a Bible before him. Catholics are alarmingly pious, aren't they?"

Trent bolted up the stairs. "Where is he now?" he called back to her.

"Still in the library. But what about Angela? Where has she gone?"

In the library, Trent asked the same of the lanky Frenchman who introduced himself as Arnaud Chappelle.

"I will tell you of her odd departure, monseigneur," Chappelle said, "but first you must allow me to unburden my soul upon a matter of grave sin."

"I am no priest, sir," Trent said, barely restraining his impatience. "Tell me only where you last spoke with Miss Cowdrey. Then you may confess your sins to a man of the cloth, if you will."

"But you see, monseigneur, it is your family that my sins have harmed. Allow me this confession. Allow me this last hope of salvation." In his eyes was the same defeat Trent had felt when his father told him the news of the blackmail.

He nodded.

The tale was wonderful. The documents the Frenchman produced from a leather satchel were more wonderful yet: proof of Sir Richard's crimes, including letters in which Sir Richard boasted how he had pulled the wool over the Earl of Ware's eyes, making him sign documents without his knowledge of their true content. He'd hoped to benefit from it in the future, far beyond the immediate gains he and Chappelle would make in collecting insurance on the sunken ships and the payment from Chappelle's former revolutionary confreres for the information. Howell had been planning his blackmail for over a decade. But now Trent had in his hands all the proof he needed to see his father exonerated and Sir Richard hanged.

"Thank you, monsieur. In revealing this, you know you will be tried as a criminal of war, do you not?"

"I wish only to pay for my sins, monseigneur. When Mademoiselle Cowdrey came to me this morning and asked me to aid your family, I knew my period of penance had finally begun."

"Where is she now?" Trent's throat was thick. "Where did she go?"

Chappelle offered a serene smile. "Where all angels go when their tasks are complete. She returned to heaven, monseigneur."

Trent grabbed Chappelle's cravat and yanked him forward until they were nose-to-nose. "Where is she, God damn it? If you have harmed her, I will tear you apart. The judges will have nothing to hang when I'm through with you."

"But, monseigneur," he gasped, his hands stretching out to his sides in a helpless shrug. "It is true. She disappeared."

"Do you mean to say she eluded you?"

"No. She disappeared before my eyes. *Et voila!* It is like that with the angels, no?"

Trent loosed his grip. "You're insane."

"I did believe so at first, monseigneur," Chappelle said with a shake of his head. "But, you see, your coachman saw it too."

Trent ran to the carriage house faster than he'd run any footrace in his life, with Chappelle at his heels. He found Fields polishing the panels on the traveling chaise. The sensible Englishman, who had been with the Ascot family for thirty years, told the same story as the delusional Frenchman.

"Gone like that, milord!" He snapped his fingers. "Didn't trust my own eyes 'til Mr. Chapel here said he'd seen it too. The boy holding the team nearly swooned dead away, milord."

Trent's lungs flattened. "When?" *It could not be.* "Where?"

"Well, she was climbing into the carriage. I lowered the step, offered my hand, and she smiled at me—she's a taking young lady, milord, if you don't mind me saying—"

"*Fields.*"

"Then she disappeared."

Chappelle was nodding.

"Never seen an angel before, milord. Didn't know they still visited us mortal folks," Fields said a bit queerly. "Didn't know that

I'd really given it a thought as to whether I believed in them. But I'll say, I do now, or else I've gone as loony as this bloke here."

**T**rent walked as a man half asleep to the house and his bedchamber, where the night before he'd made love to a woman who had turned his world upside down. He opened his traveling trunk and stared at the garments she had worn when he rescued her from the lake. Atop them was the petticoat she'd left behind after they swam.

He could not now return them to her. She was gone. But before she'd gone, she had altered the course of his future.

He found his father in his bedchamber, dressing for dinner.

"Trenton." The earl perused his person. "Why are you not dressed?"

"Father, a Frenchman is here, a man by the name of Chappelle, who worked alongside Sir Richard to make profit from the ships in which you invested. He bears proof that Sir Richard tricked you into signing those documents, and other evidence as well: lading bills, communications from his former Jacobin confreres, and the like. He has gone now to Wessex to make a full confession. I suspect Gareth will have the fellow locked up for the night so as not to disturb the festivities. But no doubt you would like to speak with him as soon as possible."

His father stared as though Trent were speaking in a language he did not understand. "How did you—"

"Miss Cowdrey found him. I don't know how, exactly." *Because two centuries in the future, she knew everything about Sir Richard Howell?* "She wished to help."

"You told a stranger of our family's troubles?" His brow darkened. "Has she designs upon you, son?"

"She hasn't." *Or she would not have gone.* "But as Sir Richard's attempted blackmail is now moot, I shouldn't think that matters."

"Of course it does. She is nobody."

He fisted his hands at his sides. "She saved our family's honor, sir. And your life. You ought to be thanking her rather than disparaging her."

The earl frowned. "I will do so when I have spoken with this Frenchman and seen the proof for myself." He adjusted his cravat and slipped a silver cigar case into his coat pocket. "Until then, you will continue to consider yourself bound by honor to Sir Richard's daughter."

Trent's anger gathered at the apex of his ribs. "That won't be necessary. Yesterday Miss Howell and I came to the mutual conclusion that we would not suit."

"Before this Frenchman arrived?"

"Well before. I cannot wed where I am not inclined."

His father squared his shoulders and broadened his stance. "You will wed to suit me and the title you will someday bear."

Trent shook his head. "Even now, when matters are entirely out of your control—for both the ill and the good—you're like a cock in the ring. Father, your business with Sir Richard is finished, and so am I. Consider this font of obedience dry. Whatever demands or expectations you have of me in the future, I will not oblige."

He turned to depart. But he had made a vow, after all—a vow she would never know he had fulfilled. Matters of honor, however, required no validation.

He faced his father again. "And furthermore," he said evenly, "I despise hunting. I've hated it since I can remember. Shooting birds too. And fencing and boxing. And while I'm at it, cricket and tennis as well, although not quite as vehemently as the others, I'll admit." He felt a tight tug in his chest. "I do enjoy swimming." He looked the earl directly in the eye. "And I love to draw. Nature. Birds, animals, plants. I am simply mad about it. And I am very, very good."

For a moment his father looked stunned. Then he gripped Trent's shoulder. "Your mother always said you would someday stand up to me," he said solemnly. "How does it feel to finally be a real man, son?"

"Oh, good God." Trent pulled out from under the heavy hand and went to the door. "If you need me, I'll be at the lake until the wedding. With my sketch book."

The Emergency Room folks at U of M Hospital had done an amazing job of preserving the gown that Lady Sophronia lent Angela. Since she'd only been in the water a few minutes and in the car for only a few more until she made it to the ER, she'd just gotten a mild case of hypothermia. She hadn't even lost a single toe, the nurses informed her cheerily. Thank goodness those joggers had come along when they did and fished her out of the river.

Yeah. Thank goodness.

Angela stared blankly out the second-floor window of Tisch Hall at the snow flurries circling the graduate library in swirling gusts, and she doodled the outline of the empire-waist gown on her notes. She gave only half an ear to the president of the Graduate Student Union Organizing Committee droning on. And on. And on. She'd heard it all before: everyone was in an uproar because the university administration wouldn't pay a living wage to teaching assistants, not when it was subsidizing their tuition too.

Nothing they ever discussed in these meetings got them anywhere. Nothing they ever did mattered.

Except that something she'd done *had* mattered.

At least, she hoped it had. She wouldn't know for sure until after graduation. Then she would be able to return to England and do the most difficult thing she'd ever done: visit the estate of the Earl of Ware and get admittance to the family archives.

She already suspected what she'd find there. The minute she'd gotten home from the hospital, she'd checked all the books and articles that mentioned Sir Richard. They hadn't changed. Arnaud Chappelle had handed over to the British government every piece of information he had on Sir Richard Howell's illegal dealings during the war, then spent the rest of his life languishing in an English jail.

She hadn't changed history. She'd made it. Ironic, since the only detail of history she really cared about anymore was out of her reach. Until May.

Unless the call she'd made to a friend at Oxford got her an answer first.

She squeezed her eyes shut. She was chasing windmills. It hadn't been a dream. But it was over. She was here. He was there. Rather, he wasn't even there anymore. No telephone call was going to change that. She had accomplished what she'd gone back in time to do.

It was over.

Her chest hurt. Everything hurt. Nothing she did made the hurting stop—tea, countless laps across the indoor pool, attempts at sleep, reading the comic book again and again, hearing his voice in her memory, feeling his touch, and leaving big droplets of tears on his sketches. At night in bed, with her hand on the last page, she couldn't breathe.

"—a petition is the only way!" The GSUOC president was now shouting and gesticulating violently. "If we can get two thousand graduate students from all departments and all schools on campus to sign—"

Angela cracked open her eyes. The gown in the margin of her page looked miserable too. She was a lousy artist, unlike the man she'd left forever with nothing more than a note on the pillow like in some bad soap opera.

She should have told him she loved him. She should have at least had the courage to do that.

No. Not the courage. The *heart*. The heart that for years she'd held in the vise grip of her intellect.

Not anymore. Now her heart was finally free, and full, and hurt like hell had run over it with a tractor-trailer. Now it was starving for passion and play and companionship and—yes—a man. One man in particular. One man who had rescued her from drowning, kissed her even though he knew he shouldn't, and made love to her like he never wanted it to end.

It just couldn't end. It *couldn't*.

Heartbeats swollen and quick, she fished her phone out of her satchel, scrolled down her contact list to her mom's number, and texted, "I love you, Mom. I hope you're happy. Love, Angela."

Dropping her phone back in the satchel, she grabbed her coat and went to the door.

"Where are you going, Angela?" someone whispered beneath the president's shouting.

"To go jump in a lake."

It took her eleven minutes to run to her car, drive to the river, pull the comic book out of her satchel, and run up the path to the dam. Stripping off coat, gloves, hat, scarf, and boots, she made it to the bank just as a biker zoomed around the corner of the path.

"Hey!" he shouted. "Hey, what are you doing? Don't do that! Wait!"

She took a huge lungful of frozen air and, clutching Trent's drawings in her fist, dove.

The pencil rested motionless on the sketch book nestled in the grass before Trent. Not two feet away, a spectacular specimen of a grizzled skipper larva was methodically spinning the edges of a wild strawberry leaf together in preparation for a meal. Trent watched it and made no move to take up the instruments of his craft. Despite the solitude, the peace, and the glory of nature surrounding him, he could not.

He wanted to draw only one thing. But if he did, he may as well walk himself to Bedlam.

And yet ... No one would ever know if he drew it except him. *Unless she did.*

He leapt up, hand raking through his hair, and paced through the long grass. The twittering song of goldfinches and the leafy wings of brimstones and the buzzing of honeybees and the scents of wild honeysuckle filled him.

As swiftly as he'd arisen, he halted before his tools, seized them, and pressed the sketch book to the trunk of a young oak.

He worked swiftly, without nuance or precision, the sketches mere outlines in coal. In minutes, he'd covered half-a-dozen pages with images—his baptism at St. Anne's in Wareford, walking with his mother in the garden, taking a trophy in rowing for the first time, the curricle debacle nine years earlier—before he halted, sucked in a shaky breath, and sank to his knees in the grass.

"I have gone mad," he said to the caterpillar. "I have gone mad," he repeated, because it seemed the sort of thing a madman would do.

The caterpillar ignored him.

His gaze caught a cluster of oxeyes nearby. He reversed the page he'd last used and carefully outlined the white daisy petals and its textured yellow center, his breaths coming more slowly now, evenly, as he sank into the familiar task. Then he drew a cornflower beside the daisy because the gown that he had removed from her the night they'd made love was cornflower blue. Then, because the daisy and cornflower looked forlorn as a mere duo, he added a half-bloomed poppy, rather more crimson than her lips, but certainly descriptive of her character. Vibrant. Alive. Passionate. Brazen.

On the next page, he drew a golden eagle. He drew it in flight like the eagle across her shoulder.

Then, because he was a madman, he turned the page over and drew the image she had last described to him. His hands shook as he carefully spelled out the caption, then folded the pages together and set them on the summer grass at his side.

He waited until the sun cast long shadows of every tree and each blade of grass.

She did not come.

As dusk gathered, he collected his pencil, coal, paper, and the foolish sketches, and walked to the lake. It was empty of all but a few decorative lily pads, the water still as glass. Of course.

She would not come. She had not been an angel or anything of the sort. He'd no idea what she had wanted of him, but he would inevitably discover it soon enough. Perhaps his initial notion that she was a lady journalist seeking scandalbroth with which to make her name had been on the mark. Or she was an opportunist hoping to bear a nobleman's bastard child and be set up for life afterward.

But he couldn't believe it. He didn't believe it. He did not know her identity, but he knew *her*.

As he walked along the bank of the lake, he dropped the pages into the water and watched them sink. Then he turned toward the path to the house and—regrettably—sanity.

Angela sputtered, shivered, and popped to the surface of the frigid Grand River.

"No." Her teeth chattered as she recognized the dam and the Michigan riverbank. "*No*. No!"

She struggled to dive under again.

She bobbed right back up.

She couldn't sink. Her body simply wouldn't let her. As her skin prickled with ice and her lips and fingers went numb and her lungs compressed, she floated.

The biker was shouting at her from the shore. She couldn't make out what he was saying. The pain in her feet was turning to numbness too. If she didn't swim to the bank and get out now, she really would lose toes this time.

With lethargic strokes and tears heating her cheeks for an instant before they crystallized to frost, she dragged herself to the bank.

Heart shattering like frozen glass, she grabbed hold of the biker's hands and he hauled her ashore.

# CHAPTER ELEVEN

"There you are!" Charlotte clutched Trent's elbow and dragged him up the aisle of the church filled with wedding guests. "Where have you been? I simply must tell you the most extraordinary news. I am bursting with it!"

"Henry again?" Poor fellow. In love with a girl who didn't care a jot about him. At least he wouldn't have to wait until he was nine-and-twenty to learn that lesson.

"No! It's Lady Sophronia." Charlotte whispered, pulling him down on the pew beside their brother and father, just behind Lady Sophronia and her companion, Miss Black.

"Well, get on with it, child," Lady Sophronia whispered over her shoulder. "I haven't got all day for you to tell him. The ceremony is about to begin." She gestured to the Archbishop of Canterbury standing at the side of the chancel while his clerk adjusted his gold-embroidered mitre and stole.

Charlotte grinned. "Brother, you will not believe it, but guess who Lady Sophronia intends to adopt as her ward? Oh you *must* guess."

His attention shifted to Miss Black for a moment, then he offered his sister a tolerant eye.

Her grin broke into a full smile. "No!" She leaned close to his ear. "Henrietta has accepted Lord Willoughby's proposal of marriage and is no longer in Lady Sophronia's employ."

Willoughby stood at the head of the church, awaiting his role as best man to the duke. At this moment, the least likely man in the place to settle down to married life—or any other single pursuit—was gazing at Miss Black with a broad, besotted grin on his face.

Trent's gut felt heavy. "Charlotte—"

"Now guess. Who else needs a respectable and wealthy patroness to establish herself in society?" She was nearly bouncing in her seat. "Guess!"

"I cannot presume to."

"Then I will tell you." Charlotte gripped his arm. "Miss Cowdrey!"

Trent's heart stumbled. "Is she here?" Despite himself, he turned and scanned the pews full of people.

"No." Charlotte's lower lip protruded. "I thought you might know if she is coming."

He swallowed back the ache—like a man—like his father would—and shook his head.

"Oh." His sister's eyes dimmed. She leaned forward and spoke at Lady Sophronia's shoulder. "Your solicitor will find her, won't he?"

Lady Sophronia cast him a scathing glance. "He will indeed."

Trent turned his face away. He didn't want to know who Angela truly was and why she had gone. Finally, one lesson his father had taught him would be useful: stoic strength in the face of pain.

A hush washed over the guests from the rear of the church to the front as the Duchess of Wessex glided up the aisle. Just before the chancel she halted and faced the congregation.

"I'm afraid there will be no wedding today," she said. "Miss Grey and my son have decided, quite mutually, that they do not suit after all and no longer wish to be married. I'm dreadfully sorry for such late notice, but I do hope you will understand."

Everyone was talking—some whispering, some chattering at full volume. Some stood while others remained seated, as though disbelieving and still waiting for a ceremony. Of course they didn't believe it. A duke didn't cancel his wedding at the last moment.

Unless ...

Trent's blood rushed in his ears. *Unless the duke intended to marry his bride's widowed sister instead.*

The duchess's serene voice rose above the hubbub again. "You must all join me in wishing Miss Grey very happy with Mr. James Blair. Mr. Blair is our cousin, and we are delighted that he has secured Miss Grey's affections." Her smile was at once pleasant and commanding. "I invite you all to extend your stay at Kingstag Castle a few more days for another ball, in honor of Miss Grey's marriage to

Mr. Blair and to celebrate my son Wessex's recent betrothal to Mrs. Cleopatra Barrows. I couldn't be happier for both couples."

A moment of silence gripped the guests. Then everybody was talking again at once.

"Paper," Trent heard himself utter. "Pen. Ink."

Charlotte wrinkled up her nose. "What did you say?"

"I need paper." He stood and moved into the aisle. "And a pen." The archbishop's clerk hovered in the corner of the chancel. Trent dashed up onto the dais in two strides.

"Have you paper and pen? Perhaps the marriage license? Or a spare page from that book?" He pointed desperately. "Anything?"

The clerk's nose pinched. "My lord, you cannot tear a page out of the *Book of Common Prayer*. It is simply not done."

"Give him the marriage license," the archbishop said with a roll of his eyes. "Wessex won't be using it, after all."

"Good heavens, Your Grace." With a sniff, the clerk produced the license.

"Pen and ink?" Trent insisted.

They were found in the sacristy. Trent flipped the document to its blank side, dipped the pen in the bottle, and drew.

*Arnaud Chappelle's memoir offers no hints as to the reason he chose to publicly reveal Sir Richard Howell's crimes while maintaining silence on all others,* Angela typed into her laptop. The quiet, early-morning mumbling of café patrons and the grinding of the espresso machine surrounded her in a cocoon of scholarly concentration. *We might presume he was motivated by an outside source, an anonymous character who at present eludes history's probe.* The keyboard clicked softly beneath her fingertips. *But until further documentary evidence presents itself, this historian must remain mute on the subject. And so, although the mystery of his public repentance may never be discovered, Arnaud Chappelle's story here comes to a close.*

She clicked Save, backed up the article, opened her email, and typed a cover letter to the editor of the *American Historical Review*. She attached the article to the email and clicked Send.

Leaning her elbows on the tiny café table, she rested her chin on her palm. The *AHR* might reject her revisions, but she couldn't lie, and she sure as heck couldn't tell the truth.

Even without an *AHR* article, she might get a decent job. Both Dartmouth and UNC had invited her to on-campus interviews. Her classmates were impressed. Her Evil Advisor was pleased. She should be elated.

No emotion was further away. She no longer felt like she was missing something, because now she knew what that something was. Now she just felt empty.

Behind the counter, Cyndi whipped off her apron, picked up two steaming mugs, and came to Angela. She plunked one mug down on the tiny café table next to Angela's laptop. "Triple shot caramel latte. Just what the doctor ordered."

"The doctor ordered sleep and Zoloft because she thinks I'm crazy for swimming in two-degree water. *Twice*," Angela said.

Cyndi dropped into the chair across from her and snapped Angela's laptop shut. "I know something that'll cheer you up."

"I don't need cheering up." She needed Trenton Ascot.

"Bull." Cyndi took a swig of her latte. "You know that comic book you bought the other day? The one you said you loved? Well, yesterday the comic-book-store guy found this in the back room." She pulled a folded page out of her back pocket and dropped it onto Angela's laptop. "It obviously went with the one you bought, maybe pages that had fallen out? He didn't know where to find you, so he brought it to me at the tattoo parlor. It's a totally transparent excuse to see you again. He asked me to give you his number." Pointing to the upper corner of the page where ten digits were carelessly scrawled, she waggled her pierced brows. "I think he's hoping you'll take him up on my offer."

Angela couldn't move. She recognized the paper. It was similar stock to the book Trent had drawn, but this time with writing across it. A legal document. A *marriage license?*

"So, are you going to call him?" Cyndi said. "Though he's probably not awake at this hour, being a scruffy comic-book-store guy and all."

*Call him ...*

Angela reached for the paper. It was in fact the marriage license of the Duke of Wessex and Helen Grey. With shaky hands, she unfolded it to the inside.

The sketches were in the same style as the others. The image in the top panel showed a man and a woman standing before the altar of a church filled with people. The couple faced each other and he held her left hand in both of his. The man was Trenton Ascot. The woman was her.

Below, in the bottom frame, he stood alone in the middle of the aisle, looking out of the page at her and extending his hand. The caption read: *DON'T MAKE ME WAIT.*

"Ange?" Cyndi's voice came to her through a fog. "Ange ... is that *you*?"

Her throat was too clogged with tears to speak. She nodded.

On the table beside the latte, her iPhone buzzed. The display showed a number in England. Through the cloud of tears she fumbled for the phone.

"Hello? Angela Cowdrey here."

"Miss Cowdrey," the voice on the other end sounded distant but clear. "This is John Wright, vicar at Saint Anne's Church in Wareford. Mary Raj at Oriel College rang me up yesterday with your query. I managed to unearth the parish register from the period of your interest. Would you care to hear what I've found?"

She clutched the phone to her ear. "Yes. Please, Reverend Wright."

"You asked after the seventh Earl of Ware's eldest son, who became the eighth earl."

"Yes."

"Putting together a family tree, are you?" he asked pleasantly.

"*What?*" she whispered.

"Oh. I'd imagined you'd been named after your— But here now, perhaps it will be best if I simply read the entry to you: 'Trenton Cambridge Ascot, Viscount Everett, married June the 24th, Year of Our Lord 1813, to Angela Merriweather Cowdrey in the—'"

"Stop! Please stop!"

"But wouldn't you like to hear—"

"No!" She'd already heard the only thing she needed to know. "Thank you! Thank you so much, Reverend. You've been so helpful."

"Glad to be of assistance. If you should need anything more, do ring."

She set down the phone with a trembling hand. "Cynd." Her heart flew.

"Ange?" Cyndi leaned forward. "Angela, you have a really weird look on your face."

She couldn't quite breathe. "Cyndi, you know how you said I needed to get a life?"

Cyndi nodded.

"Well, I think I did. But not quite what you expected. Or what I expected. Not quite what anyone would believe. But I did." She swallowed hard and gripped her friend's hand. "Thank you."

"What do you mean no one would believe it?" Cyndi frowned, then looked down at the drawing again. "Ange?"

"I can't really explain it. But ... I've got to go."

June 24? The day of the duke's wedding? What did that mean? And the river hadn't worked. How was she supposed to get there this time? She stared at the image of Trent with his hand outstretched. It looked so real, it seemed that as she stared they shared the same smile, the same breaths.

She reached out and touched the page.

Sketch in hand, Trent stood in the aisle of a church full of milling people, staring at the door to the narthex like a fool—an insanely hopeful fool whose heart pounded so hard he could hear it over the murmurs and bustle of the duke's erstwhile wedding guests.

Heaving in a huge gulp of air, he extended his hand.

"Trent?" Charlotte said. "What on earth are you doing?"

A commotion sounded beyond the nave doors. Trent's pounding heart jerked into his throat.

The doors burst open. Beauty appeared in the aperture.

Trent dropped the sketch and walked to her.

She was weeping; his vibrant, brilliant, brazen angel's cheeks glistened with tears. Reaching her, he took her face in his hands and captured her mouth beneath his. She wrapped her arms around his waist, pressed her body to him, and he claimed her as his own before two hundred people.

Finally he allowed her air. She buried her face in the crook of his neck, and her slight body shook with sobs in his arms.

"Why do you weep, Angel?"

"I'm—" Her voice was muffled against his cravat. "I'm a little overwhelmed, you know."

"Only a little?" Gently he tilted her chin up. "Leap through time often, then, do you?"

"Once a week so far." Tears spilled from her eyes afresh. "I've had enough already, though. I'm calling it quits starting now." Her smile trembled. "How did you know how to bring me back?"

"I drew the book you had described, but you did not come. So I drew another." He stroked the moisture from her cheeks. "I would have continued drawing until you returned to me."

"But that's insa—"

"Angela Cowdrey, because of you I have dived into a lake fully clothed, stolen women's garments, kissed a lady to within an inch of her virtue in a garden, climbed out a third-story window in the dark, and 'skinny dipped' at midnight. And for the first time in my adult life, I have admitted to my secret passion. My only passion—except you. You have changed me and I will never be the same. Marry me."

"*This* is insane. My head is spinning. I don't know how this can be. We've only known each other a *week*."

"The Powers That Be do not seem to consider that insufficient time."

"Time," she whispered. "You called to me across time."

"And you came to me. You had already decided to marry me."

"I've never been proposed to in a comic book before." Her mouth curved into a radiant smile. "I couldn't resist."

He pressed his lips to her brow and held her tight. "Angel, do you think you could love me?"

"I'm pretty sure I already do." She lifted her lips to his.

"Angela!" Charlotte exclaimed. "You are finally here and kissing my brother, so you will marry him after all. Splendid!"

It was only then that Trent noticed the people around them, some gaping, some whispering, the crowd of watchers spreading outward until the attention of all but the stone statues of saints were upon them. He took Angela's hand and addressed the crowd.

"I am pleased to announce that Miss Cowdrey has accepted my suit."

"With the way the two of you are carrying on there," Lady Sophronia cackled, "the wedding better be soon!"

A matron gasped. A cluster of girls giggled. Several gentlemen cleared their throats. Charlotte sighed. The duchess appeared beside them and with a regal smile said, "Why not today?"

"Ha!" Lady Sophronia crowed. "Saving face splendidly. You outdo yourself, Alice."

"Do I?" The Duchess of Wessex lifted a single brow, her smile lingering. "But a man must follow his heart. Why delay?"

"Oh, yes!" Charlotte clapped. "Everybody we know is already here anyway."

Trent looked down into his lady's eyes. "Will you, Miss Cowdrey?"

"I will, Lord Everett." She squeezed his hand. "But don't we have to wait until the banns are read? Three weeks or something like that?"

"Not if a special license can be procured," Trent heard his father say from the crowd. He met the earl's benign gaze and bowed, acknowledging the only thanks he would ever receive for saving their family from ruin. It was more than enough.

The earl gestured to the Archbishop. "Your Grace, will you do the honors?"

The Archbishop rolled his eyes anew and extended his palm to his clerk. "Paper, pen, and ink. Again."

"But, Angela," Charlotte pouted, "You simply cannot get married in *that.*" She pointed down. "What is it, anyway? A kerchief?"

More feminine giggles and several strangled male utterances.

Trent ran his gaze up the entire length of Angela's stockinged legs to the tops of her shapely thighs. Her boots were enormous, but her skirt was no more than a suggestion. His blood heated. "No," he barely managed. "She cannot."

Angela laughed, her cheeks pink. She leaned in to his shoulder and whispered, "Wouldn't you know, I've never worn this skirt before today."

"Is that what you call it?"

"It's your fault. I've been feeling unusually sexy these past few days. I wonder why?"

Then, because she had changed him, he bent and pressed his lips to hers to feel her laughter.

"I will see to the special license while you dress," he said huskily against her cheek. "But don't become too comfortable in your wedding finery. It won't be on you for long."

"Promise?" she murmured.

"Oh yeah."

She smiled brilliantly.

Not taking his eyes from her, he said over his shoulder: "Charlotte? If you will?"

His sister grabbed his bride's hand and half a dozen girls scampered down the aisle, dragging with them the woman he had come to love in a heartbeat that stretched across two centuries.


Angela got married wearing a delicate pink gown with a white tulle overskirt and tiny beads on the bodice. When the ceremony was over and they recessed out of the church, Trent whispered that she was lovelier than a dog rose. It was the most beautiful thing anyone had ever said to her.

An hour later at the party, he laced his fingers with hers and in his melting chocolate voice informed her that he was taking her upstairs. Moments later in the privacy of their bedchamber he removed the gown that made her look like a wildflower, making good on his word yet again. As he trailed kisses along her shoulder, then lower, then lower still, she came to appreciate Trenton Ascot's dedication to honor more than she'd ever imagined possible.

# EPILOGUE

January 26, 2013

www.AnnArborPost.com

*A student matriculating at the Rackham Graduate School of the University of Michigan, Angela M. Cowdrey, allegedly disappeared in Merçi Café on Tuesday at approximately 8:24 AM. Police are examining the testimony of the fourteen witnesses. Scientists at the university's Neural Biology Laboratory suggest that a possible contamination of the air in the café due to a gas leak may have precipitated a mass hallucination. Ann Arbor Gas Co. denies any wrongdoing.*

*Cowdrey's friend, Cyndi Jefferson, who was present in the café at the time and claims to have seen Cowdrey disappear, commented, "I'm devastated, but I'm not. She definitely got a life."*

Kingstag Castle

25 June 1813

**B**ridget Cavendish walked toward the lake, kicking pebbles off the path as she went. Now that the wedding day was past, all the guests would soon depart. She was happy for the married couples, of course, even if Lieutenant Newnham was now the only attractive unmarried man left in all of England, it seemed. But after a fortnight's excitement of switched brides and sudden marriages and betrothals, Kingstag would be unbearably dull. Her friends Kate and Charlotte were packing at this moment, with her sisters Alexandra and Serena helping. They were all making plans for London next year, when Serena and Kate would be making their debuts and dancing with any number of handsome gentlemen in regimentals, while she would be chained to her mother's side like a child.

She'd been permitted to attend all the wedding festivities this past fortnight. She would die if she had to be deprived of all the fun next year.

If only something exciting would happen. Perhaps she should visit Great-great-great-aunt Sophronia. Sophronia always listened to her and even encouraged her to try her ideas. And now that Henrietta would be leaving—no doubt to spend her time racing about the countryside in Lord Willoughby's magnificent phaeton—and Angela, too—which was a terrible pity because she had such brilliant opinions about what girls ought to be allowed to do—Sophronia was sure to be just as bored as Bridget. Yes, together they would surely come up with something ...

Her toe bumped a large rock. She scowled down at it, then her eyes widened.

Bending, she picked it up and wiped the dust from it on her white muslin skirt that was already smeared with marmalade anyway. Who was to notice a little dust?

Heavy, flat, and shiny, the metal-and-glass rectangle rested comfortably in the palm of her hand. Bridget turned it over curiously but couldn't see a catch to release. Did it open?

"What've you got there?"

Hiding it behind her back, she pivoted to the boy sitting against a tree in shadow. "What's it to you, Henry Ascot?"

He stood, dropping the flower from which he'd been plucking petals like the moonstruck loony he was. Lud, but her sister Alexandra's pretty face drew them like flies. This one was worse than most. She clutched her treasure behind her as he approached.

"Curiosity, is all," he said and stopped just before her. She had to bend her neck to look up at him and it struck her that he was a great deal taller than she'd thought. He was six months younger than her and it was absolutely not fair that a pipsqueak like Henry Ascot got to be so big and tall while she was trapped far below.

"Don't think I've ever seen you stand still for a minute 'til now," he said. "Must be something worth seeing."

She narrowed her eyes. "You can't have it, Henry Ascot."

"I didn't say I wanted it, Bridget Cavendish."

"*Lady* Bridget Cavendish," she corrected him.

He seemed to consider that for a bit, which was imbecilic. Who needed to think to come up with an insult?

"I'll call you Lady if you show me what you've found," he finally said.

She blinked. He blinked back.

She pulled the object out from behind her. They stared at it.

"What's that?" He pointed to the indentation at one end, a circle with a pale white square atop it.

"How should I know?"

"It looks like a secret button," he said perfectly sensibly, actually.

"If it's a secret button, then ..."

Their eyes met. Henry frowned. Bridget grinned.

She pressed it.

They gaped.

"Lady Bridget Cavendish," Henry Ascot said in a hushed voice, "you're a genius."

# AUTHOR'S NOTE

Abundant thanks for assistance with this story go from my heart to my sister authoresses Caroline Linden, Maya Rodale and Miranda Neville, who made fiction-writing into a whole new sort of fabulous fun with this project. I offer special thanks also to Anne Brophy, Laurent Dubois, Marie-Claude Dubois, and Nita Eyster.

For my wonderful readers, who greeted the news of a time-travel story from the pen of this author with gleeful enthusiasm, I am honored and deeply grateful.

# ABOUT THE AUTHOR

Award-winning Katharine Ashe is the author of *How To Be a Proper Lady*, one of Amazon's 10 Best Books of 2012 in Romance, and eight more intensely lush romances set in the era of the British Empire and laced with adventure. Upon her debut in 2010 Katharine was honored with a spot among the American Library Association's "New Stars of Historical Romance," in 2011 she won the coveted Reviewers' Choice Award for Best Historical Romantic Adventure, and she has been nominated for the 2013 Library of Virginia Literary Award in Fiction.

Katharine lives in the wonderfully warm Southeast with her beloved husband, son, dog and a garden she likes to call romantic rather than unkempt. A professor of European History, she has made her home in California, Italy, France, and the northern United States. For more about her books and to read excerpts, please visit her at www.KatharineAshe.com.

## ~ALSO BY KATHARINE ASHE~

### ~THE PRINCE CATCHERS~
I MARRIED THE DUKE

### ~THE FALCON CLUB~
HOW A LADY WEDS A ROGUE
HOW TO BE A PROPER LADY
WHEN A SCOT LOVES A LADY

### ~ROGUES OF THE SEA~
IN THE ARMS OF A MARQUESS
CAPTURED BY A ROGUE LORD
SWEPT AWAY BY A KISS

CAPTIVE BRIDE (A REGENCY GHOST NOVEL)

If you enjoyed *At the Duke's Wedding*, please consider posting a review of it online.

The Lady Authors invite you to visit them online at www.AtTheDukesWedding.com for behind-the-scenes glimpses into the making of this anthology and more about their other books.

CPSIA information can be obtained at www.ICGtesting.com
Printed in the USA
LVOW10s0554101214

418100LV00037B/1092/P

9 780986 053900